Uprising

Scott G. Mariani

W F HOWES LTD

This large print edition published in 2011 by
W F Howes Ltd
Unit 4, Rearsby Business Park, Gaddesby Lane,
Rearsby, Leicester LE7 4YH

1 3 5 7 9 10 8 6 4 2

First published in the United Kingdom in 2010
by Avon

A CIP catalogue record for this book is available
from the British Library

ISBN 978 1 40748 363 4

Typeset by Palimpsest Book Production Limited,
Falkirk, Stirlingshire
Printed and bound in Great Britain
by MPG Books Ltd, Bodmin, Cornwall

MIX
Paper from
responsible sources
FSC
www.fsc.org   FSC® C018575

As ever, many sincere thanks to Keshini Naidoo and Sammia Rafique at Avon for all that they do; to Inspector T.B for helping the author maintain a semblance of realism in all matters police procedural; and to all the other usual suspects involved in this story's long, slow evolution from a mad spark of an idea into the book that is now in your hands.

for Lisa

SINCE THE DAWN of civilisation, vampires preyed on human beings, drank their blood and regarded them contemptuously as an inferior species, a mere disposable resource.
For aeons, the vampires ruled.

But things have changed. With the birth of the modern age and the explosion in human telecommunications and surveillance technology, many vampires realised that they could no longer carry on the old ways. Something needed to be done if the ancient culture was to survive.

In the last quarter of the twentieth century, the World Vampire Federation was founded to control and oversee the activities of the vampire community. No longer would vampires prey unrestricted on human beings and turn them into creatures like themselves. New biotechnologies enabled the Undead to walk in daylight, living among us, in our cities, our streets. Strict laws were imposed to control vampire activity

and allow their community to carry on.
Quietly. Unnoticed. Undisturbed.

These laws were enforced by the Federation's
Vampire Intelligence Agency, or VIA, with a
licence granted by the Ruling Council to hunt
and destroy transgressors.

**But not all the vampires were willing
to obey . . .**

PROLOGUE

The Scottish Highlands
November 1992

Outside the cottage, the storm had reached its peak. Rain was lashing out of the starless sky, the wind was screaming, the branches of the forest whipped and scraped violently at the windows.

The lights had gone out, and the old place was filled with shadows from flickering candles. The twelve-year-old boy had been cowering at the top of the creaky stairs, listening to the argument between his parents and his grandfather and wishing they'd stop. Wanting to run downstairs and yell at them to quit fighting. Especially as he knew they were fighting about him—

. . . When the thing had come. A creature that looked like a man – but could not have been a man.

The boy had seen it all take place. Watched in speechless horror, peering through the banister rails as the intruder crashed in the door and strode through the hallway. The argument had stopped

3

suddenly. His parents and his grandfather turned and stared. Then the sound of his mother's scream had torn through the roar of the storm.

The creature never even slowed down. It caught his father and his mother by the arms, whipping them off their feet as though they weighed nothing. Like dead leaves. It dashed their heads together with a sound that the boy would never forget. Candles hissed, snuffed out by the blood spray.

Then the thing had dropped the bodies and stepped over them where they lay. Smiling now. Taking its time. And approached his grandfather.

The old man backed away, quaking in fear. Spoke words that the boy could not understand.

The thing laughed. Then it bit. Its teeth closed on the old man's throat and the boy could hear the terrible gurgle as it gorged on his blood.

It was just like the stories. The stories his parents hadn't wanted his grandfather to tell him. The boy shrank away and closed his eyes and wept silently and trembled and prayed.

And then it was over. When he opened his eyes, the killer had gone. The boy ran down the stairs. He gaped at the twisted bodies of his mother and father, then heard the groan from across the room.

The old man was lying on his back, his arms outflung. The boy ran to him, kneeled by his side. Saw the wound in his grandfather's neck. There was no blood. All gone.

Claimed by the creature.

'I'm dying,' his grandfather gasped.

'No!' the boy shouted.

'I'll turn.' The old man's face was deathly pale and he gripped the boy's arms so tightly it hurt. 'You know what to do.'

'No—'

'It has to be done,' the old man whispered. He pointed weakly at the sabre that hung over the fireplace. 'Do it. Do it now, before it's too late.'

The boy was convulsed with tears as he staggered over to the fireplace. His fingers closed on the scabbard of the sabre, and he unhooked the weapon from its mounting. The blade gave a soft zing as he drew it out.

'Hurry,' his grandfather croaked.

The boy pushed the sword back into the scabbard. 'I can't,' he sobbed. 'Please, Granddad. I don't want to.'

His grandfather looked up at him. 'You must, Joel. And when it's done, you have to remember the things I told you.' His life energy was fading fast, and he was struggling to talk. 'You have to find it. Find the cross. It's the only thing they truly fear.'

The cross of Ardaich. The boy remembered. Tears flooded down his face. He closed his eyes.

Then opened them. And saw that his grandfather was dead.

The storm was still raging outside. The boy stood over his grandfather's body and wept.

And then his grandfather's eyes snapped open and looked deep into his. He sat upright. Slowly, his lips rolled back and he snarled.

For a second the boy stood as if mesmerised. Then he started back in alarm as his grandfather began to climb to his feet. Except it wasn't his grandfather any more. The boy knew what he'd become.

Candlelight flashed on the blade as he drew the sabre. He raised it high and sliced with all his strength – the way the old man had taught him. Felt the horrible impact all the way to the hilt as it chopped through his grandfather's neck and took the head clean off.

When it was done, the boy staggered out into the storm. He began to walk through the hammering rain. He walked for miles, numb with shock.

And when the villagers found him the next morning, he couldn't even speak.

CHAPTER 1

Eighteen years later
October 27

Pockets of thick autumnal mist drifted over the waters of the Thames as the big cargo ship cut upriver from the estuary, heading for the wharfs of the Port of London. Smaller vessels seemed to shy out of its way. With its lights poking beams through the gloom, the ship carved its way westwards into the heart of the city.

On the approach to the docks, the beat of a helicopter thudded through the chill evening air.

Eight sailors of mixed Romanian and Czech origin were assembled around the helipad on the forward deck, craning their necks skywards at the approaching aircraft. At their feet lay a row of five steel-reinforced crates, seven feet long, all identical, unmarked, that had been wheeled up from the hold. Most of the crew preferred to keep their distance from them. The strong downdraught from the chopper's rotors tore at the men's clothing and hair as its pilot brought it down to land on the pad.

'Okay, boys, let's get these bastard things off our ship,' the senior crewman yelled over the noise as the chopper's cargo hatch slid open.

'I'd love to know what the hell's inside them,' said one of the Romanians.

'I don't fucking want to know,' someone else replied. 'All I can say is I'm glad to be shot of them.'

There wasn't a man aboard who hadn't felt the sense of unease that had been hanging like a pall over the vessel since they'd left the Romanian port of Constantza. It hadn't been a happy voyage. Five of the hands were sick below decks, suffering from some kind of fever that the ship's medic couldn't identify. The radio kept talking about the major flu pandemic that had much of Europe in its grip – maybe that was it. But some of the guys were sceptical. Flu didn't wake you up in the middle of the night screaming in terror.

The crewmen heaved each crate onto the chopper and then stepped back from the blast as the cargo was strapped into place. The hatch slammed shut, the rotors accelerated to a deafening roar, and the chopper took off.

A handful of the ship's crew remained on deck and watched the aircraft's twinkling lights disappear into the mist that overhung the city skyline. One quickly made the sign of the cross over his chest, and muttered a prayer under his breath. He was a devout Catholic, and his faith was normally the butt of many jokes on board.

Today, though, nobody laughed.

Crowmoor Hall
Near Henley-on-Thames, Oxfordshire

Forty miles away, the gnarled figure of Seymour Finch stepped out of the grand entrance of the manor house. He raised his bald head and peered up at the sky. The stars were out, seeming dead and flat through the ragged holes in the mist that curled around the mansion's gables and clung to the lawns.

Finch couldn't stop grinning to himself, though his big hands were quaking in fear as he nervously, impatiently awaited the arrival of the helicopter. He glanced at his watch.

Soon. Soon.

Eventually he heard the distant beat of approaching rotor blades. He rubbed his hands together. Took out a small radio handset and spoke into it.

'He's coming. He's here.'

CHAPTER 2

*The Carpathian Mountains, Northern Romania
October 31*

It was getting dark when Alex Bishop emerged from the path that cut through the woods and spotted the old tumbledown house across the clearing. She just hoped that her informant had been right. Lives were on the line.

She quickly checked the equipment she was carrying on her belt and unsnapped the retaining strap on the holster. The steps on the porch were rotten and she stepped over them, treading carefully. The peeling front door swung open with a creak and she could smell the stench of rot and fungus.

Inside, the house was all in shadow. Alex stepped in, peering into the darkness. The door creaked shut behind her. The red-orange glow of the sinking sun was receding fast across the cobwebbed window panes.

Her sharp ears caught something. Was that a thump from somewhere below her feet? She stiffened. Something was moving around down there.

She followed the sound through the front hall towards a doorway. A rat, startled by her approach, darted into the deepening shadows.

A muffled yell from behind the door. Then another. Shrill, scared, all hell breaking loose.

Someone had got here before her.

She kicked the door open with a brittle cracking and splintering, and found herself at the top of a flight of stone steps leading down to the cellar. She wasn't alone.

From her hidden vantage point at the top of the stairs, Alex took in the situation at a glance. Three young guys in their twenties. One lay writhing in a spreading, dark pool of blood. Two were still on their feet, one clutching a wooden cross, the other holding a mallet in one hand and a stake in the other. Both howling in panic, wild, demented, as the cellar's other occupant rose up from their friend's body and took a step towards them. His mouth opened to show the extended fangs.

Vampire.

The guy holding the cross rushed forward with a yell and thrust it in the vampire's face. It was a brave thing to do – textbook horror movie heroics – but foolish. If he'd been expecting the vampire to cover its face and hiss and shrink away, he was in for a shock.

The vampire didn't blink an eye. Alex had known he wouldn't. Instead, he reached out and jerked his attacker brutally off his feet. Pulled him in and bit deep into his shoulder. The young guy fell twitching to the ground, blood jetting from his ripped throat.

There was nowhere for the remaining guy to run as the vampire turned his attention to him and backed him towards the corner of the cellar. The young man had dropped his mallet and stake and cowered against the rough wall, pleading for his life.

The vampire stepped closer to him. Then stopped and turned as Alex walked calmly down the cellar steps. He stared at her, and his blood-stained mouth fell open. Recognition in his eyes.

'Surprise,' she said. She reached down and drew the Desert Eagle from its holster.

The vampire snarled. 'Federation scum. Your time is over.'

'Not before yours,' she said.

And fired. The explosion was deafening in the room. Even in Alex's strong grip, the large-calibre pistol recoiled hard.

The vampire screamed. Not because of the bullet that had ripped a fist-sized hole in his chest, but because of the instant devastating effect of the Nosferol on his system – the lethal anti-vampire poison developed by the Federation's chemists and issued under strict control to VIA field agents like Alex Bishop.

The vampire collapsed to the cellar floor, writhing in agony, staring at his hands as the blood vessels began to bulge out of the skin. His face swelled grotesquely, eyes popping out of their sockets. Then blood burst out of his mouth, and his hideously distended veins exploded in a violent spatter of red that coated the floor and the stone wall behind him. Alex turned away from the spray. The vampire continued to twitch for a second, his body peeled apart, turned almost inside out, blood still spurting out from everywhere; then he lay still.

Alex holstered the gun and walked over to the young guy in the corner, grabbed his arm and hauled him to his feet.

He gaped at her. 'How did you—'

She could see that he had wet himself with fear. These amateurs had no idea what they were into.

'It takes a vampire to destroy a vampire properly,' she said as she unzipped the pouch on her belt. Before he could react to the meaning of her words, she'd taken out the syringe of Vambloc and jabbed it into the vein under his ear. He let out a wheezing gasp and then lost consciousness. By the time he came around, his short-term memory of what had just happened would be completely erased.

Alex replaced the Vambloc syringe and took out the one that was loaded with Nosferol. Leaving the young guy where he lay, she stepped over to his two dead friends and injected each of them with ten millilitres of the clear liquid. Standard procedure, to ensure they stayed dead. She carefully recapped the needle with a cork and put the syringe back into its pouch.

13

Two minutes later she was heading back out into the evening with the unconscious body over her shoulder. As she strode out of the house she tossed a miniature incendiary device into the doorway behind her. She was halfway to the trees before the whole place went up in a roar of flame, bathing the murky woods in an orange glow.

Hiding the traces of another day's work.

'Rest in peace,' she muttered. She took out her phone, keyed in Rumble's number at the London HQ.

'Harry. You were right. It's happening.'

CHAPTER 3

The Oxfordshire countryside, five miles from
Henley-on-Thames
The same night, 12.05 a.m.

'Come back here, Kate!'

But she was already out of the car and trudging over the rough grass towards the road.

'Piss off,' she fired back over her shoulder as she stamped away. Dec thumped the steering wheel and swore loudly.

Kate was fuming as she reached the road and kept walking. No way she was getting back in that car. She'd walk all the way back home to Wallingford if she had to.

If she was angry with Dec Maddon, she was even angrier with herself for having accepted the boy next door's invitation to go out for a drive. She liked him, she really did. But when he'd suddenly produced the little white pills and offered her one, she'd got scared. Scared of getting into trouble. Scared that he was trying to get her into a state where she'd have sex with him.

And scared that she'd give in. He was a few months older than her, not far off his eighteenth birthday. Better looking than any of the boys at school, and he drove a Golf GTI. He was exciting and wild. Maybe a little too wild. Kate drew the line at taking drugs.

She walked on as fast as her wobbly heels would let her. Shivering now, feeling the dampness of the mist and wishing she'd put on something heavier than the flimsy cotton top – but refusing to regret that she'd got out of the car.

It was a couple of minutes later when she saw the headlights coming up behind her. She turned and put out her thumb. The car sounded its horn at her and drove on. She did the V's at the disappearing taillights. 'Wanker!'

She kept walking. The dark empty road was spooky, but she didn't care. So what if it was Hallowe'en? She wasn't a kid any more. She was more concerned about the cold. Really getting to her now.

Then, a little further up the road, she saw another car approaching. She was about to put her thumb out again when it signalled and pulled up. She trotted over to it. Big square headlights, the luxuriant purr of a very expensive car. She noticed the Rolls-Royce radiator grille as she walked up close. The driver's window whirred down.

Kate peered inside. 'Thanks for stopping,' she said.

Dec Maddon sat there muttering angrily to himself and slapping his forehead with his palm. What an eejit, blowing it like that. His dad was gonna kill him if this got back. The ecstasy pills were a new thing – in fact he'd never even touched the stuff in his life before deciding it would be a cool thing to try tonight with Kate – but of course nobody would believe him. He was in the deepest shit imaginable. Kate probably wouldn't want to talk to him again, and her stuck-up bitch of a mother would have a field day.

He'd been crazy about Kate Hawthorne ever since his family had bought the house next door. She was beautiful, with china-blue eyes, tumbling red curls that looked like something out of an old painting and a smile that made his day – and up until now he'd been pretty sure the signals she'd been putting out meant she kind of liked him too. Trust him to go and fuck it all up.

He sat there fulminating for a few minutes before he decided to follow her. He'd explain. She'd understand . . . he hoped.

He started the car and bumped over the verge onto the country road, turning right to head back towards home. The mist drifted in his headlights. He was certain he'd spot her pretty quickly.

And he did. But she wasn't alone. She was just getting into a black Rolls that was pulled over at the side of the road. She shut the door behind her, and the big car moved off.

Dec followed it for a few miles. The mist was rapidly thickening, and he was so focused on tailing the Rolls that he began to lose all sense of direction. They were deep into the winding country lanes now, way off his normal routes. After a while, the Rolls indicated left and glided through a tall gateway. Automatic gates closed behind it, blocking him out.

He parked the Golf at the side of the road. His breath was misting in the cool night air as he walked up to the gates and ran his hand down the cold wrought iron bars. He looked up.

Two giant birds were peering down at him out of the drifting fog. He stared up at their curved beaks and great wings, and it was a moment before he realised he was looking at stone statues perched on the gateposts. The way their eyes seemed to bore into him made him strangely uneasy. He looked away from them, and that was when he noticed the tarnished bronze plaque on the craggy wall. He had to pull away some of the moss sprouting over the stonework to read it.

CROWMOOR HALL.

What was this place? Some kind of stately home, he thought. Some rich guy's place. What was Kate doing here?

Face it, Dec. You're just not her class. She's a solicitor's daughter and you're just a mechanic like your dad.

He was about to walk away, but then felt a powerful urge to go in there and have it out with her. He couldn't let things end like this.

He started climbing the high wall.

CHAPTER 4

Jericho, North Oxford

Joel Solomon awoke with a gasp and jerked bolt upright in his bed. For a moment the night terror still gripped him, before he remembered where he was. This wasn't eighteen years ago. This was here and now, and he was home in his ground-floor flat in the peaceful street on the edge of the city. Everything was all right.

The luminous hands of his bedside clock told him it was 12.34 a.m. He rubbed his face, blinking to clear away the remnants of his nightmare. When his heart eventually stopped thudding, he sank his head back into the pillow and closed his eyes, inviting sleep to return.

But it wouldn't. He knew it couldn't, not now.

I'll turn. His grandfather's voice still rang inside his head.

He'd never wanted to relive those memories again. Since the age of fifteen, after three years of counselling, psychotherapy, hypnosis, he'd thought he was free of them for good. Suddenly, the nightmare was back. Twice now, within the space of just a few days.

His fingers clenched into fists under the bedcovers as the images returned once again. The years hadn't dulled their awful vividness. Seeing the sabre blade come whooshing down and sideways. Feeling that awful crunch as the sharpened steel went slicing through cartilage and bone.

He took a deep breath. It didn't happen, he willed himself to believe. You imagined it. You were in shock. The brain plays strange tricks. Imagining all kinds of things that aren't real.

That was what the doctors had persuaded him to believe – that there weren't monsters out there, lurking and watching in the dark. That the only evil in this world was human. Like the psychopathic murderer who'd broken into the remote cottage that night and done those terrible things. That the only time Joel had ever touched the sabre was when the old man had let him play with it.

And that the rest was just the figment of a deeply traumatised child's imagination.

It had taken a long time, but he'd eventually learned to trust the words of logic and reason repeatedly drummed into his head like a mantra by the men and women in the white coats.

At this moment, though, he wasn't so sure. He swung his legs out of bed and looked out of the window at the mist in the streetlights outside. So much for grabbing a decent night's sleep before his early morning start. He knew what he had to do to clear his mind.

He walked to the bathroom, took a quick shower, and then pulled on his motorcycle leathers and left the flat. Out in the misty street, he swung his leg astride the Suzuki Hayabusa sportsbike, thumbed the starter and rode off.

CHAPTER 5

What a place, Dec thought as he crept through the manor house grounds and the turrets and towers loomed up through the mist. The cars outside were all Aston Martins and Bentleys and Rollers. He made his way to the brightly lit windows where the music was coming from, and peered through.

What he saw inside was a huge, glittering ballroom. There had to be a couple of hundred people in there, dancing, drinking, partying. The women were all in long dresses, and the men wore tuxedos and strange black cloaks. Every face in the room was hidden by a mask.

He skirted the outside wall and peeped around the corner. The front entrance was at the top of a flight of steps and the door stood open. He trotted inside, just in time to avoid being spotted by an old guy in a butler's uniform. Finding himself in a huge hallway, he ducked down a corridor. A door was ajar, and through it was the biggest washroom he'd ever seen. On a chair by the door was someone's discarded cloak and a black mask; Dec grabbed them and darted away.

With the cloak over his shoulders and the mask over his face, he wandered through the ballroom and scanned the crowd for Kate. He felt desperately out of place and hoped he didn't too obviously look it. A string quartet were playing, and dancing couples spun across the polished floor. Waiters sifted through the crowd with champagne glasses on silver trays.

Then, through a gap between the dancers at the far end of the ballroom, he caught a glimpse of Kate's unmistakable red hair. She had her back to him, but it was definitely her. She was walking with a man towards a curtained exit. His hand was pressed to the small of her back, as though guiding her gently but firmly. Was he the guy in the Rolls, Dec wondered. He looked like the moneyed type. Expensive suit, fancy haircut. Dec couldn't see his face, but there was something vaguely familiar about the guy. Nothing especially distinctive – he wasn't fat, wasn't thin, not short, not tall. But Dec was sure he knew him from somewhere. He thought he could see a certain nervousness in the man's step as he escorted Kate through the room.

Dec suddenly realised that Kate and Rolls-Royce man were part of a larger group all heading in the same direction. Six of them in all, three men and three women, including Kate. He couldn't help but notice how hot the other

24

two women looked, both dressed in revealing outfits and high heels. The blonde was like something out of a magazine and the other one with wild, tousled raven hair, was just stunning even with her mask on. Her slinky crimson dress showed off the toned muscles of her shoulders and arms. Gold bracelets on honey skin. She and Rolls-Royce man seemed to know each other. When she turned to smile at him he seemed to shrink away a little from her, as though wary of her, and she gave a seductive giggle.

The two other guys in the group were eye-catching for different reasons. One looked like a tree. He was black and massive, six foot six of solid muscle under a tuxedo that looked ready to split if he moved too brusquely. The other guy's head barely came up to his chest. Wiry, stoat-like, with eyes that darted behind his black mask.

Dec watched as they all filed through the curtained doorway. None of the other partygoers seemed to pay them any attention as they left the ballroom.

Dec pushed his way through the crowd to the doorway. He discreetly pulled the curtain aside and followed. Keeping well back, he followed the strange group through corridors and hall-ways. Every so often he could see Kate, still being ushered along by Rolls-Royce man. What was wrong with her? She seemed to be walking strangely, as if dazed, or in a trance of some kind.

The group of six passed through another doorway. Dec waited a moment, then crept to the door and inched it open to see a flight of stone steps spiralling downwards into shadow. He swallowed hard, and followed, hanging back to stay out of sight.

He could hear the people's steps echoing up towards him.

Then nothing. He trotted faster down the steps and found himself on a landing that branched out in several directions, leading to more stairs. Which way had they gone?

He kept going, wandering through the maze. It was dark down here, and he was beginning to get disorientated. He bumped up against a rough wooden door and his fingers felt the cold iron ring handle. He turned it and the door creaked open.

He was in what looked like a vault or crypt beneath the manor house. It seemed to run the whole length of the building, stretching far ahead into darkness, lit only by flaming torches that cast flickering shadows across the stone floor and the forest of pillars that held up the ceiling.

Dec felt suddenly chilled.

He heard the sound of voices, and turned to see the group he'd been following. They were assembled in a circle about forty yards away, surrounded by lit candlesticks. Kate was no longer with them. Instead they'd been joined by another man, dark, elegant and stately in his tuxedo. He wore no mask and Dec could make out his slender, chiselled features in the candle-light. He exuded an air of quiet authority and even from a distance it was clear that everyone deferred to him. Almost as though they were afraid of him; especially Rolls-Royce man, who now looked even more nervous than before, a sheen of sweat on his brow. He appeared on the edge of panic, but then the man who seemed to be the leader put a hand on his shoulder and said something to him in a low, mellifluous voice. Dec didn't catch the words.

With a noise that echoed through the vault, a trapdoor in the ceiling fell open above the group's heads and something emerged from it. Dec strained to see, then nearly bit his tongue off when he saw that the strange object being lowered from the trapdoor was a girl. Naked. Hanging upside down from a chain, steel manacles around her ankles. She was struggling in terror, her screams muffled by a gag.

Dec crept closer. Pressed himself against a pillar, hardly daring to look. His mouth was dry, his heart hammering. Now he could see the girl more clearly. She had short brown hair and marks on her neck that looked like a spider on a web.

Dec could sense the group's excitement as she

swung overhead, sobbing, too weak to struggle. Only Rolls-Royce man looked agitated. He began trying to back away, but the two women took his arms and gently restrained him, smiling and kissing him.

The black-haired beauty had something attached to her belt, slung low at her left hip. It was a sword in a scabbard. She drew it out with a slithering whisper of metal on metal and a clinking of gold bracelets. The long, curved blade glinted in the torchlight.

The leader nodded to her.

As Dec watched in horror, the woman lashed out with the sword and cut the throat of the hanging girl. A torrent of blood splashed down over the group. They stood with upturned faces, in a frenzy of pleasure as the blood spattered down over them and trickled over their lips. The women moaned and smeared it over their faces, their bare shoulders, their breasts. The leader stood back and watched with apparent indifference as the giant black guy and the little weaselly one began greedily licking and slurping the blood from their flesh.

Rolls-Royce man was quivering – Dec couldn't tell if it was with wild excitement or with terror. The black-haired woman sheathed her sabre and beamed at the man through the blood on her mouth. She reached out and laced her bloody fingers behind his head, drew his face towards her. Buried it in her cleavage like a mother offering milk to a baby, and threw back her head with pleasure. Rolls-Royce man's face came away sticky with blood as she released him and he staggered back a step. He looked ready to collapse with fear and excitement.

Only the leader stood aloof, quietly licking his lips as the last squirts of blood rained down from the dying girl. She let out a gurgle, then hung limp.

Dec was barely able to focus his thoughts. Then it hit him.

Where's Kate?

A second trapdoor fell open and then he saw her. Naked and chained, just like the other girl. Her pale body gleamed in the firelight, her hair hanging down in a mass of curls.

The black-haired woman wiped the blood from her mouth, leaving a glistening red streak of it across her face. Cruelty flashed in her eyes as she drew the sword a second time and poised herself for the strike, like a beautiful, lethal cobra. The blonde was watching in anticipation, open-mouthed.

Dec wanted to scream out but his throat was paralysed with terror. Just as the blade was about to slash Kate's neck wide open, the leader raised his hand.

'Stop, Lillith. Anastasia, back away. I want this one for myself.' His voice echoed in the crypt. The woman called Lillith lowered the weapon and stared at him. The blonde froze, like a dog being given a command.

29

'That's not playing fair, brother,' Lillith said archly.

'Release her.'

Lillith snarled.

And Dec almost collapsed.

Not because he'd never seen a human snarl before.

But because of the teeth. They hadn't been there before – he was certain of that. But now, suddenly, horrifically, her canine teeth looked like an animal's. They were long and curved and sharp, protruding whitely from her bloody lips.

The leader took a brisk step towards Lillith and slapped her hard across the face. She was hurled off her feet with a scream of pain and rage. He pointed a warning finger at her. Then turned to Kate and reached out to stroke her skin.

'She's mine,' he said.

Dec had seen enough. He had to get out of this place. Call the police, somebody, anybody. Get help. He turned away, barely breathing, desperately trying to control his racing pulse as he tiptoed back through the crypt as fast as he could.

Making it to the stairs, he began to run like a maniac, swallowing back the bile that kept rising up in his throat.

For a few terrible minutes he was lost inside the enormous house, stumbling through the plush corridors. Ripping open a door, he found himself inside an old-fashioned library. French windows looked out across the dark grounds. He ran over to them. They were locked. He had to get out. Looking around him in panic, he spotted a large quartz paperweight on a desk. Grabbed it and lobbed it against one of the windows, which shattered with a tinkling of breaking glass. He clambered out of the jagged hole and staggered out into the night.

He never looked back at the house. He sprinted to the wall, scrambled over it and dashed to his car. His hands were shaking so badly that he could hardly get the key into the ignition, but then the engine fired up and he took off down the country lane.

As he drove wildly away, he tore his phone out of his pocket and went to dial 999.

The battery was dead. He tossed down the phone and drove faster through the misty night. There had to be somewhere he could stop and make a call, but all he saw around him was countryside. He pressed his foot down harder on the accelerator and kept it there for five straight minutes. Was there nothing here? Where was he?

Miles passed, and then he noticed a light through the trees. A house, maybe a country pub.

Dec stared at the light for half a second too long. By the time he looked back at the road, it was already too late. The tight bend rushed up faster than he could react. The Golf ploughed into the verge, left the road and smacked straight into a tree, and the expanding airbag punched him in the face as he went flying into the wheel.

He had no idea how much time went by before he woke up in the wrecked car. He tried to move, and cried out at the excruciating pain in his left wrist. His head whirled with nausea. He felt the blackness rising.

No. No. Got to get help. Got to help Kate. Got to get—

That was his last thought before he woke up again to the glare of flashing blue lights and there were two police officers looking down at him.

CHAPTER 6

VIA Headquarters, central London
Next morning, 6.28 a.m.

Alex pushed through the steel and glass doors of Schuessler & Schuessler Ltd and crossed the broad foyer to the reception desk. Fresh off the plane from Bucharest, she was wearing a long dark grey Ralph Lauren cashmere coat over a merino wool polo-neck and jeans. The heels of her Giuseppe Zanotti knee-high studded boots clicked on the shiny tiles.

Kindly old Albert, the night watchman, was coming to the end of his shift, and she gave him a sweet smile as she signed in.

'Early start this morning, Miss Bishop,' he said.

'Well, you know me, Albert.'

'We haven't seen you for a couple of days.'

'I had some overseas business to take care of.'

'Busy busy.'

She grinned. 'Always.'

She skirted the plush reception area, past the leather armchairs and the tinkling fountain,

33

headed for the lift and rode it all the way to the top.

Schuessler & Schuessler were a large legal firm and occupied the lower three floors of the building. The legal people had no idea what really went on behind the doors of the company that occupied the upper two floors.

The lift opened onto a small, bare landing and Alex stepped over to the only door leading off it. It bore the words 'KEILLER VYSE INVEST-MENTS' in gold lettering. She took a strip card from her handbag and ran it down the slot, hearing the clunk as the lock opened for her. On the other side of the door was a long windowless corridor, walls and floor tiled in gleaming white. She passed through another door at its far end and entered a second reception.

At a desk sat an austere-looking woman in a dark suit, her hair scraped back into a bun. Alex knew there was a pistol under the desk, loaded with Nosferol-tipped rounds and aimed right at her as she walked over to the fingerprint and retinal scanner and ID'd herself to the voice recognition system. Steel doors whooshed open and Alex stepped through into a square ante-room. Inlaid into the centre of the polished granite floor was a large circular emblem bearing the VIA insignia.

This was the nerve-centre of one of the world's most secretive organisations, operating under the auspices of a worldwide Federation whose existence was known only to a very select few.

Alex nodded greetings to familiar faces as she cut a path through the airy open-plan office space where VIA operatives talked on phones, typed at computer terminals and watched the latest developments on the giant screens that monitored the agency's global activities.

At the far end of the upper floor was Rumble's private office. She walked in without knocking.

Harry Rumble, medium build, slim and greying elegantly round the temples, was dressed in a charcoal pinstripe suit. He could have passed for a City businessman; he was anything but. He was the chief of the Vampire Intelligence Agency, the Vampire Federation's security wing, set up to police its hundred thousand or more members across the world.

The Federation, embodiment of the modern age of vampirism. VIA's role within its global empire, working under the watchful eye of the Federation Ruling Council, was to control the registration of new members and enforce the three laws that were engraved on the crystal plaque above Harry's desk.

1. A vampire must never harm a human

2. A vampire must never turn a human

3. A vampire must never love a human

The enforcement part was Alex's job – as a lot of renegade vampires had found out the hard way.

When they stepped out of line, she moved into action.

Rumble peered up at her over his half-moon glasses as she walked in. She knew he didn't need them but just wore them because he thought they made him look sophisticated. Vampires could see like a cat.

Xavier Garrett, Rumble's assistant, stood across the other side of Rumble's desk. He was tall and vulturine with a high brow and oiled black hair, wearing the same sombre, crumpled suit he always wore. He flicked a look up and down Alex's body, and one corner of his mouth twisted up into the best rendition of a smile he could do.

'Cool as a body on ice, hotter than a chilli pepper,' he said. 'Looking good this morning, Agent Bishop.'

Alex and Garrett's relationship was a simple enough one of mutual distaste. He regarded her as insubordinate and a maverick, and hated that she had Rumble's ear. She regarded him as something that made slimeballs look good. Neither of them made any secret of their feelings.

'Hey, Garrett. The undertaker called earlier. He wants his suit back.'

Garrett's smirk twisted into a sneer.

'Did you get my report, Harry?' she asked Rumble. She was the only VIA field agent to call the boss by his first name and not 'sir'.

That drove Garrett crazy with envy, and she enjoyed it.

Rumble nodded. He tapped a key on the laptop in front of him and the screen's reflection lit up in his lenses.

'You did a good job out there,' he said. His brow was creased with worry. And that was an unusual expression for Harry Rumble. He turned to Garrett. 'Xavier, you didn't check those shipment dates with Slade yet, did you?'

'I was—'

'*Now* would be a good time.'

Garrett curled his lip, getting the message, and left the office.

When they were alone, Alex said, 'What, so private even your assistant doesn't get to hear?'

Rumble peeled off his glasses and sat back in his chair chewing at one of the stems. 'Franklin hasn't reported back from Budapest.'

Franklin was Alex's senior field agent counterpart stationed at VIA's Munich operation. After rumours of vampire attacks had started appearing on blogs in Hungary, Rumble had sent him in to investigate.

'He arrived there Saturday. No word from him since Tuesday. I don't like it.'

'You think something's happened to him?' she asked.

'It's not like him to go silent on us,' Rumble sighed. 'But that's not all. Look at my screen.'

Alex moved round the edge of the desk so she could peer at Rumble's laptop. 'Whoa.'

'My feelings exactly.'

The screen showed a map of the world. Capital cities marked in white. VIA stations marked in blue. Little red flags marked the locations of recent illegal vampire activity. Once in a while, a vampire would defy the regulations and go rogue, feeding uncontrolled on humans in their area, failing to use their Fed-issued Vambloc supply with the result that victims frequently remembered details of the attacks, their wounds didn't heal quickly, and they got sick. In extreme cases, where the vampire returned to the same victim for several feeds over a period of a few days, they died and were turned.

It didn't take much for localised panic to spread and rumours to circulate like wildfire through the blogosphere. When that happened, VIA field agents were deployed to deal with it.

Which wasn't a frequent occurrence. The Federation generally had things tightened down pretty well, and Rumble's operations map normally didn't feature more than one or two red flags at any given time.

But what Alex was looking at right now was a mass of them, clustered across Europe, spreading east to west.

'That's definitely unusual,' she said.

'More than unusual. It's unprecedented.'

'You told me we were getting a rise in rogue activity. You didn't tell me it was this bad.'

'I was hoping it'd level out,' Rumble said tersely. 'But that isn't happening. Reports are just flying in. Dexter in Copenhagen, an hour ago. Carbone in Barcelona late last night. I don't even want to think about what'll happen if the human media get a hold of it.' He paused, anxiously chewing his lip. 'The strangest thing is—'

'What?'

He swivelled his seat away from the desk and looked at her. 'These attacks are happening at night. All of them. It's as if they were avoiding the daylight. Why aren't they using the Solazal the Federation provides them with?'

'I've had a feeling for a long time this might happen,' Alex said. 'A Trad uprising.'

'A what?'

'It was only a question of time before the Traditionalists started a backlash against us, Harry. Our glorious Federation may have done its best to stamp out the old ways, but I've always wondered how many of the die-hards were still out there, waiting for their chance to get back at us.'

Rumble looked pointedly at her. 'Come on. Even if you're right, there's no way a few scattered malcontents could organise themselves into a significant threat. Not on this kind of scale, and so fast. It's not feasible.'

'We were there when the Federation took over, remember? Not all vampires were happy about it, if I recall. All they needed was a leader. Maybe they've found one. The Trads and the Feds, fighting it out.'

'The Trads and the Feds? Give me a break.'

She shrugged. 'Maybe the time's come, Harry.'

CHAPTER 7

The mighty Thames river snaked through much of England, yet in places it was little more than a muddy stream crowded by banks of reeds.

Dawn wasn't far away, and the riverbank creatures were beginning to wake. A solitary swan glided over the misty surface of the water; then swam for the refuge of the vegetation as a small rowing boat appeared.

Seymour Finch's gnarled fists were tight on the oars, propelling the boat along through the murk with powerful strokes. The quiet, dark places were where he most loved to be, far from prying eyes. And he had a job to do, now that Mr Stone and his inner circle had retired to their rest.

Finch manoeuvred the rowing boat into the bank, so that it nestled among the rushes. He shipped the oars then reached down for the bundle that lay between his feet. He smiled as he thought about what was inside, wrapped in plastic and sacking cloth.

Mr Stone had let him do what he wanted, once the others had finished. Finch's intense terror of his employer was matched only by his deep devotion. He was honoured to have been set the tasks he had. He would carry them out to the letter. He would have his reward.

Finch's strong fingers closed on the folds of the sacking cloth. He hauled the bundle upright against the inside of the boat, then drew out the sheath knife from his belt and cut the rope so that the contents spilled out overboard and splashed into the water.

Finch watched the ripples, then reached for the oars. He was about to start turning the boat around to head for home, when he saw the swan a few yards away.

He stared at it. The first rays of the dawn were beginning to melt through the mist, and shone like gold on the majestic bird's white plumage as it glided like a galleon across the water.

He wanted to tear its head off and eat its flesh.

CHAPTER 8

You could cover a lot of distance very quickly on a bike like the Hayabusa, and Joel had been riding around for most of the night. His route had taken him all around Oxfordshire, and, as the fog had lifted in the hours before dawn, he'd sought out fastest, twistiest sections of country A-road where he knew the speed cameras were few and far between. His advanced police motorcycle course had made him a very quick and very safe rider. He knew exactly how far he could push the machine before he reached the very limit of his concentration and reflexes – and the faster he sliced through the countryside bends, the further from his mind he could drive the haunting remnants of the nightmare's memory.

The first light was creeping over the horizon when he pulled up in a layby on the edge of a sleepy village. He killed the engine and sat back in the saddle, taking a few moments to soak up the tranquil silence. Feeling much better now, restful, clear headed and ready for another day, he peeled back the sleeve of his leather jacket to check his watch.

It was time to go to work. He fired the Suzuki back up and pointed it towards Oxford and Thames Valley Police Station.

As Joel walked in off St Aldates and into the station foyer, the blonde station duty officer gazed admiringly at the Detective Inspector's lean six-foot frame. But he was too deep in thought to notice the look she was giving him. He waved distractedly as he walked past the front desk and headed for the staff canteen.

The place was nearly empty, just a few uniformed coppers coming off their late shifts and a handful of early-bird civilian personnel sitting at the plastic tables over tea and pastries. The police were always run ragged by the party mayhem and endless alcohol-related violence of Hallowe'en night. It got worse with each passing year, and today most of the officers looked pale and tired and ready for their beds.

Joel knew the feeling. He ignored the trays of doughnuts and Danish pastries, grabbed a coffee and went over to a corner table. The coffee was the same old thin, insipid brew that only came to life after the fourth sugar. He sat sipping it, gazing out of the window at the rising sun.

At a table a few yards away, three constables, two male and one female, were relaxing over a pot of tea. Joel knew them all well. The balding skinny guy was Nesbitt, the woman was Gascoigne, and the one doing all the talking was Macleod. Big

Bob Macleod, two years from retirement, a pork pie of a man, a wheezing, red-faced heart attack waiting to happen. He was coming to the end of some anecdote or other that had the other two grinning broadly. Far away in his thoughts, Joel hadn't caught a word of it.

'Give me a break, eh?' Macleod chuckled in his gravelly voice. 'I mean, like we didn't have enough bollocks to deal with in this job.' He flipped his fat wrist over and winced at his watch. 'Look at the time. I'm off home for some kip.' He heaved himself up from the table, grabbed his hat and started off towards the exit.

'Hey, Bob,' Nesbitt called after him. 'Watch the Count doesn't get you.'

'Better start eating garlic,' Gascoigne said.

Macleod's face twisted in disgust over his shoulder. 'Bugger that.' He reached the exit, then turned suddenly and did a comic snarl at them, showing yellowed teeth. 'Yaarrghhh!' There was no mistaking the Christopher Lee Dracula impression. The other two constables fell about laughing as Macleod left the canteen.

Joel turned to them. 'What was that all about?'

Gascoigne stared for a moment, as though surprised that the DI was taking an interest in their jokes.

'Nothing much, sir. Bob was just talking about the suspected drug driving incident out near Henley last night. Teenager wrapped his car around a tree, sprained his wrist. Seemed to be

45

off his face when we found him. There were pills in the glove compartment. Looked like ecstasy to me, we don't know yet.'

The police procedure in a case like this was pretty straightforward. The pills would be tested, along with a sample of the suspect's blood. When the lab results came through after a week, maybe two, they'd know whether they could press forward with possession and drug driving charges. But that wasn't Joel's interest.

'I don't get it. What's with the Dracula thing?'

Gascoigne snorted. 'Oh, just daft. When we brought him in, he kept rambling on about ghouls and vampires. Wouldn't stop talking about them.'

'Vampires?'

Gascoigne looked perplexed. 'You really want to know?'

Joel nodded.

'Well, apparently, the reason he crashed his car was because he was running away from a vampire lair that he and his girlfriend stumbled on. She was taken by them, needless to say.'

Joel frowned. 'Not reported missing, though.'

Gascoigne shook her head. 'Course not, sir. Tucked up safely in bed at home in Wallingford. I talked to the parents myself.'

Joel nodded thoughtfully. Hallowe'en and ecstasy pills. A lethal combo for an overactive imagination. The drug was well known for its ability to produce all manner of wild hallucinations. But still, the mention of vampires had pricked up his ears.

And sent a tingle down his back, too. It was ridiculous, but he couldn't fight back his curiosity. 'Do we have him in custody?'

'I wouldn't waste my time on it, sir. He's spent the night in the JR.' JR was what Oxford locals called the John Radcliffe hospital. 'Probably be out sometime today, if he gets the all-clear. Then all he has to worry about is whether we're going to book the silly sod for drug driving or just for possession.'

'What's his name?'

'Declan Maddon. But like I said, sir, I wouldn't waste time on it.'

CHAPTER 9

VIA HQ, London

The sun was slowly rising over the city as Alex and Harry Rumble finished her debriefing. She stood up and walked over to the window. Watching the orange glow of the sunrise creeping across the skyline made her think of her Solazal. She quickly reached into the back pocket of her jeans and slipped out the tube. Popped a tablet in her mouth and felt it sizzle sweetly on her tongue.

Rumble leaned back in his chair, took another worried glance at his screen and then shuffled some notes on his desk.

'Anyway, whatever the hell's happening, VIA business goes on as usual. Another job's come in for you.'

She turned away from the window, chewing the Solazal tablet. 'I just got back from Romania, Harry.'

'This is just routine. Shouldn't take long. Are you carrying?'

'Just my backup.' She flipped back her coat to

reveal the stainless steel, short-barrelled .44 Magnum Smith & Wesson riding behind her right hip.

'You call that thing a backup piece?' Rumble handed her a sheet of official VIA notepaper from his desk. She snatched it from his hand, scanning the words with quick green eyes. The name on the sheet was Baxter Burnett.

'The movie star?'

Rumble nodded.

'I didn't even know he was one of ours,' Alex said.

'He was turned back in the late sixties, but it wasn't until the nineties that he got bored and tried his hand at acting. It turned out the big moron had talent.'

'I should have guessed. I've been watching his movies for years and he's never aged a day.'

'Yes, well, that's exactly the problem,' Rumble said. 'We can't allow him to go on drawing attention to himself. I want you and Greg to go and have a word. Nothing too strong. Just refresh his understanding of the situation.'

Alex blinked. 'Excuse me? And who is Greg?'

'I should have mentioned it,' Rumble said with a sly grin. 'Greg Shriver. That's *Lieutenant* Greg Shriver, formerly US Marines, just flown in. Your new partner.'

She groaned. 'Don't do this to me. I work alone, for fuck's sake.'

Rumble gave her a stern look. 'Hey. Don't give

49

me that "I work alone" crap. There isn't an agent on this team I cut more slack to, but even you shouldn't push it.'

'Jesus Christ, Harry.'

'He's a fresh recruit, so he's going to be a little raw. Show him the ropes, train him up. I know he'll learn fast, and he'll be learning from the best. I'm counting on you, all right?' Rumble slid a file across the desk at her. 'Read it. He's good material for us.'

Alex flipped through it. Like all vampires, she could read ten times faster than a human. 'And when do I get to meet wonder boy?'

'Right now.' Rumble stabbed a button on his phone and talked to the speaker. 'Jen, show him in, will you?'

A few seconds later Rumble's secretary, Jen Minto, ushered the new recruit into the office. Greg Shriver was about thirty-five, lean, dark and extremely nervous-looking as he walked in.

Alex stuck out her hand as her boss introduced them.

'Special Agent Alex Bishop.'

When they shook hands, she noticed that his palm felt a little damp with sweat. Some very fresh vampires retained those kinds of human attributes for a while.

'They tell me you and I are going to be working together,' Greg said.

'Yup. Lucky me.'

'Baxter's taken the Trafalgar Suite at the Ritz

50

while he's in town promoting the new *Berserker* movie,' Rumble said. 'He's expecting you, but you'd best get going.'

'Is that *Berserker 6*?' Alex said. 'I saw the fifth one. Complete piece of shit.'

'Did you see him in *Raptus*, though?' Rumble said. 'Now *that* was a pretty damn good movie.'

'We're going to see Baxter Burnett?' Greg asked, wide-eyed.

'Let's move, new blood,' Alex said.

Back down in the car park behind the S&S building, Alex bleeped the locks of her black Jag XKR. She slipped into the driver's seat and Greg got in beside her. He moved like an overgrown puppy, clumsy and too full of energy, and slammed the door so hard it made the glass shake.

She threw him a hard look. 'Break my car, I'll slice your head off.'

'Sorry,' he muttered. 'I keep forgetting how strong I am now. Like the night-vision thing, too. I feel pretty weird, still kind of dazed.'

'That's hardly surprising,' Alex said, allowing him a smile. 'One minute you're getting on fine with your human life, the next thing some vampire's sticking their teeth in you. Kind of changes things.' She started the car and pulled away aggressively, the acceleration pressing them back in the leather seats.

'That how it was for you?' he asked.

'Etiquette lesson one. You never ask anyone how

they turned. Unless it's *me*, your superior, asking *you*.'

He mumbled an apology.

'What's that accent? Tennessee?'

'Raised in Memphis. You're good.'

'I've done a lot of moving around in the last century or so,' she said. 'But never mind my story.' She glanced sideways at him. His shirt was open three buttons, and she could see the slim chain around his neck and the pressed tin tags nestling against his chest. 'Love the dog tags.'

He reached up and touched them. 'Keepsake, I guess.'

'So you were in the Marines. What happened?' As she talked, she was speeding the Jaguar through the London traffic, darting through tiny gaps between buses and black cabs.

Greg took a breath. 'Yeah, I was doing okay. Made lieutenant younger than my father did, things were looking good. There was this guy on my squad, his name was Tadd. Always screwing around with weapons, kind of obsessive about them. Anyway, one day we're out on manoeuvres with an armoured vehicle division and Tadd is playing around with the Browning .30 cal on one of the Hummers. I was standing talking to my captain when, bang, Tadd lets off an accidental shot. Caught me right between the shoulder blades.'

'Hero's death. Nice.'

'You said it, after I was decorated in Iraq and

all. Anyway, I'm lying there in the military hospital and the pastor's just read me the last rites. I haven't got long to go. Then, when nobody's looking, this doctor that's been hanging around me giving me the eye comes over and whispers in my ear, "*Psst!* Wanna live a little longer?"'

Alex gave a short laugh.

Greg went on. 'First I thought it was the morphine, fucking with my head. But now I see it's for real, the guy's telling me how he's going to bite me and turn me into a vampire. Said something about recruiting me. I figured, why not, I'd nothing to lose. Only a jackass would turn down an offer of eternal life. Anyway, then I woke up and I was at the Federation rehab centre with my gunshot wound healed up like I'd never taken a bullet. That was two weeks ago. And here I am.'

'I'll bet the Feds had their eye on you the moment you were brought into the hospital,' Alex said. 'Good army record, no wife or kids, they'd have had you down as an ideal VIA recruit. That vampire doctor was there to pick out the right candidates. When the opportunity comes up to grab someone who looks like they'll be an asset, they haul them on board. You know about the probation period, don't you?'

'A year, right?'

She nodded. 'To see how you shape up. Then the Federation Board decides whether you can stay.'

'And if I can't?'

'You don't want to know.'

He sighed. 'The only thing that really bugs me is that I'm never allowed to see my folks again, my sister, my friends.'

'Yeah, well, think about it. One minute they're weeping over their dear departed's coffin, the next you show up on the doorstep. That's why you were posted here to London, to keep you far out of temptation's way. That's how the Federation works. We can live among humans, that's fine. But we can't get too close to them, can't get emotionally involved in any way. It's too big a security risk, in case someone spills the beans. Strictly forbidden.'

'So let me get this right,' Greg said. 'Since the Federation was formed in, what?'

'Nineteen eighty-four.'

'Since then, it's been illegal for vampires to actually turn anyone else into a vampire, correct?'

'Unless it's an official recruitment, sanctioned by the Federation authorities. That's to keep out what you might call undesirable elements. The kind of vampires that give vampires a bad name, draw the wrong kind of attention to us. The twentieth century changed everything. Internet, communications, surveillance. The world's a pretty small place now. That's why the Federation was created, to maintain a low profile for the community.'

'And to protect humans?'

She glanced at him. '*Protect* humans? That's our

54

food resource you're talking about. We're not doing this because we love humans. This isn't some politically correct thing. We're doing this to survive.'

'What happens to vampires that don't play by the rules?' Greg asked.

'That's where VIA comes in. Basically we go after them and kick their arses into line.'

'We kill them?'

'Destroy them. Already dead, remember.'

Greg made a face. 'Right.'

'Only if we absolutely have to, the ones that won't listen to sense. Mostly they end up cooling their heels in the Federation Detention Centre for a while. But if they've done something really bad, or really stupid, sometimes the Ruling Council will vote for a termination. There was one last year. Rock star. Found out that this guy was a vampire, offered him five million quid to make him into one too. The vampire went for it. Two days later the rock star rose up as one of the Undead and the vampire walked off with the five mill.'

'Oh, boy.'

'Everyone's happy, until the day after that, the rock star forgets what he's become, walks out onto his balcony at sunrise and – whoosh. He went off like a magnesium flare. Some journo got the shot of him burning up. There was a whole thing in the press about human spontaneous combustion.'

'Yeah, yeah, I remember that. That was Bobby Dazzler, the lead guitarist of Wild Boys.'

'He certainly dazzled everyone that day. Of course, Bobby's name wasn't on the Federation register and we soon tracked down the guy who had turned him, who was now suddenly spending like a sailor and renting a yacht down in St Tropez. The Council didn't waste time on him. He got zapped. Lethal injection of Nosferol. That's one of the special drugs that the Federation produces. We have our own fabrication plant in Italy.'

'I know about the drugs,' Greg said. 'Got the whole lecture already. Like this stuff here, for instance.' He dug a plastic bottle out of his pocket and gave it a shake. The thick green liquid inside clung to the glass.

Alex glanced at it. 'That's that shitty blood substitute they give out to newbies like you who aren't able to juice for themselves yet.'

'Tastes pretty bad, but it seems to keep me going. What is it, anyway?'

'Synthetic crap, kind of vampire baby food. But you can't stay on it forever. You're going to have to learn to feed naturally.'

He pulled a face. 'I'm not looking forward to that part.'

'Don't worry, it's easy. When you get hungry enough, it'll come naturally. What about your Solazal? You got your supply of that too? I don't need to be worrying about you?'

He looked blank. 'My what? Oh, right. Those little white pills.'

'Shit. When was the last time you took one?'

'Uh, sometime yesterday, I think.'

Alex slammed her foot on the brake and the Jag skidded to a halt in the traffic to an angry chorus of horns.

'You *think*? Have you any idea what's going to happen when the effect wears off and you're still out in daylight? Fizz, it's over, just like Bobby Dazzler. And on my champagne leather seats?' She reached into the glove box and handed him a packet of pills. 'Get one down you right now.'

She took off again as he sucked on the pill. 'Get this in your head. Solazal is a photosensitivity neutraliser, and it's the centre of your life from now on. You take one every twelve hours without fail, or you'll fry.'

'Kind of a departure from tradition, isn't it?' he said sheepishly.

'Modern age, babe. Got to keep up with the times.'

CHAPTER 10

Kate Hawthorne was awoken by the sound of her mother coming into her room.

'Come on, young lady. Can't lie there all day. It's nearly ten past eight and you're going to be late for school.'

Kate groaned and crawled in deeper under the duvet. 'Leave me alone.'

'That's what you get for all this late night cavorting about,' her mother snapped. She ripped open the curtains and then marched over to the bed to yank back the edge of the duvet. Kate flinched as the pale autumn sunlight hit her in the face. It was hardly bearable. She tried to grab the duvet back from her mother but fell back, half blinded and gasping.

'Look at you. What on earth's the matter with you?'

'Please, Mum. I've got a terrible headache.'

'You've been drinking, haven't you?'

'I haven't been drinking.' But the truth was, Kate realised, she could hardly remember a thing about the night before. She vaguely recalled being with Dec, then the argument. Storming off down the road; the big posh Rolls stopping for her.

And that was it. The rest was a big, yawning blank. How had she got home? Had the man brought her back? Who was he? And where had she seen his face before?

Kate squinted up at her mother. The expression of tight-lipped disapproval made it perfectly clear that her daughter had *not* been driven home to 16 Lavender Close in a Rolls-Royce. That would have been cause for celebration for Mrs Gillian Hawthorne.

'You don't have to look so sour.' *You old cow*, she wanted to add. She kept it back, but it must have shown in her eyes, because the disapproving look on her mother's face deepened a couple of tints.

'The police called here earlier about your boyfriend.'

'He's not my boyfriend,' Kate protested.

'That'll be why your neck is covered in lovebites. Little tart.'

Kate put her fingers to her neck and winced. *Did Dec do that?* 'What about the police?' she murmured.

'He crashed his car last night. Drunk, no doubt.'

Kate tried to sit up in bed, and the ache thudded through her head. 'What? Is he all right?'

'He'll survive. That's what cockroaches do, isn't it? *Why* couldn't you go out with Giles Huntley?'

'I hate Giles Huntley. He's a creep and he has bad breath.'

'At least he has a good education and a future

59

ahead of him when he goes to Cambridge. He's not going to spend his life poking around in filthy grease under a car bonnet. Have you *seen* the state of Declan Maddon's fingernails?'

Please make her shut up, Kate thought. The pain felt like a blunt chisel blade being hammered into her skull and then twisted from side to side. Her vision was exploding with it.

And still her mother went on. 'You know what's going to happen if you keep this up, my girl, don't you? Pregnant. That's what happened to Chardonnay Watson, isn't it? Going around with lowlifes. Next thing, a bun in the oven. What a disaster. Mind you, with a name like Chardonnay it was to be expected and it's probably all she was good for anyway . . .'

Kate watched her mother ranting on. The words faded out in her ears. For a brief instant she felt a rush of emotions surging up inside her, momentarily blanking out the pain in her head. Feelings she'd never had before, and a sense of power that was almost overwhelming.

Before she knew what was happening, she had her mother by the throat. Shaking her like a terrier with a rat. Screaming, 'Shut your fucking mouth!' Her mother's tongue hanging out, her face turning blue as she throttled the life out of her.

But then she was back on her bed and her mother was still standing there, going on at her.

What was happening? Was she going crazy?

'—should have done a long time ago. St Hildegard's

60

will be a far better environment for a young lady. You'll make proper friends, with the right type of people.'

'Boarding school?' Kate burst out.

'Didn't you hear a word I said? Starting after the Christmas holidays. And in the meantime, you won't be going anywhere near that family of pikeys next door, I can tell you.'

Kate buried her face in the pillow as her mother went on and on. The migraine was making her want to cry, and she felt sick to her stomach. And weak, so terribly weak, as though the energy had just been sucked out of her.

But somehow, deep inside, she knew something was different about her. Something had happened. Everything felt somehow sharper. More defined. Smells, colours, the floral pattern on the wallpaper her mother had insisted on for the bedroom.

Kate knew she had changed. How and why, she didn't yet know.

But for some reason she couldn't understand . . .
She wasn't afraid.

CHAPTER 11

The Ritz Hotel, London

Alex walked into the grand entrance lobby and crossed the red carpet to the desk, with Greg trailing along behind her.

'We've come to see Mr Burnett in the Trafalgar Suite. He's expecting us.'

Two minutes later Alex rapped on the door of the suite. It opened and a woman in her late fifties, with a thin face and short hair, stood in the doorway giving them an icy stare.

'Where's Baxter?' Alex said.

'He's busy at the moment. I'm his agent. You can talk to me.'

Alex's nose twitched at the woman's human scent.

'I don't think so. Out of the way.' She shouldered past her and through the door. Greg followed, looking around him in awe at the decor. The agent tried to squeeze in after them; Alex shoved her hard out into the corridor and slammed the door in her face.

Baxter Burnett wasn't that busy. He was settled

back confidently on a plush sofa in the suite's living room, his feet up on a table and his arms behind his head. He looked like he'd been working on his tan, and his hair was immaculately groomed. The sleeves of his white shirt were turned up just enough to show off the toned muscles of his forearms and the chunky gold watch on his wrist. He smiled a glittering Hollywood smile as Alex and Greg walked into the suite.

'You certainly have a way with people, Miss—?'

'Special Agent Alex Bishop. What we have to discuss with you isn't for human ears.'

Baxter just kept on grinning his million-dollar grin. Alex motioned to Greg. 'This is my colleague, Agent Shriver.'

'Have a seat,' Baxter said graciously. He turned and snapped his fingers. 'Charlie!' A heavyset assistant came out of the next room. His unsmiling gaze landed on the two VIA agents.

'Charlie, get this lovely young lady and her friend a drink,' Baxter said. Charlie stared a second longer, then went away.

'It's okay,' Baxter said easily. 'Charlie's one of us.'

'I can see that,' Alex said. She and Greg sat on armchairs facing Baxter, and a few seconds later Charlie returned carrying a tray with three cut-crystal tumblers brimming with red liquid. He laid it down on a coffee table before leaving the room. Alex took a glass and sipped it. Greg sniffed uncertainly at his, pulled a face and set it back down on the coffee table.

Baxter was giving Alex admiring looks. 'Anyone ever tell you, Agent Bishop, you have beautiful eyes?'

'Plenty of times. Let's get down to business. Your first big movie break was *Down and Dirty*, am I right?'

Baxter smiled. 'That was a good movie. You a film fan, Agent Bishop?'

'As a matter of fact, I am.'

'But you didn't come here to talk movies, I imagine.' Baxter looked at his watch, like saying he was a busy man and didn't have all day.

'Of course we did,' Alex said. 'We take a great interest in your work. But here's the problem. We couldn't help but notice, Baxter – *Down and Dirty* was twelve years ago.'

'Yeah, so?'

'Our sources tell us that a week ago, you read for the part of Jake Gyllenhaal's younger brother in the new Universal production, *Firestorm*. Is that true?'

Baxter reddened slightly. 'Sure it's true. It's a great role for me. What's the big deal?'

'Baxter, you're so fucking stupid,' Alex said. 'Don't you think people will think it's a bit peculiar, you never ageing? You think you can go on playing thirty-year-old guys for evermore?'

Baxter's composure was slipping fast. 'So I have boyish good looks. So did Mickey Rooney. So does DiCaprio. I work out. What the fuck is it VIA's fucking business what I do, anyway?' He stood up, spilling his drink over himself; a red arc across white cotton. 'This is what you assholes came here for, to hassle me about the roles I take? Get the fuck out of here. Charlie! Show these two dipshits the door!'

Alex leapt to her feet. She was on him in two steps, grabbing him by the throat and throwing him violently back down on the sofa. Her hand snaked inside her coat and came out with the stainless steel .44 Smith & Wesson revolver. She shoved the three-inch barrel of the magnum point blank in his face.

'What ya gonna do, shoot me?' Baxter snorted. 'You can't hurt me with that thing.'

'Let me tell you something, Baxter. I am a senior special agent of Vampire Intelligence. That means I'm authorised to use Nosferol-tipped bullets. I have six of them right here. You *do* know what Nosferol is, don't you?'

Baxter's cocky grin left him and his face fell.

'Of course you do,' Alex said. 'Do not fuck with us, because if I want to terminate you right now, I have the authority to do that and nobody will ask questions.' She lifted his chin with the barrel of the magnum and thumbed back the hammer. Baxter went pale as he felt the hard *click-click* resonate through his jawbone.

Alex went on. 'This is a matter of Federation security, Baxter. You're in the public eye and the Federation wants vampires to keep a low profile. You go on like this, you're a risk to everyone. That makes you expendable.'

Charlie came into the room, a threatening look on his face. Keeping the gun and her eyes on Baxter, Alex called out to him, 'Stay right there, Charlie. One more step, I blow his head off and yours next.'

Charlie wavered, his eyes wide, and backed off.

'Okay, okay. What do you want from me?' Baxter couldn't take his eyes off the gun, putting his palms up, hands shaky.

Alex stepped away from Baxter, uncocking and lowering the gun. 'Do what Irene DeBurgo did, and Jeff Caplan. You're worth, what, eighty million? Get yourself a Pacific island hideaway. Retire, become a recluse. And if you can't do that, get yourself a good makeup artist and start acting your age. Either way, I don't give a shit. You know I'm a movie fan, Baxter. I see you playing Jake Gyllenhaal's little brother, I'll come after you and I will fucking destroy you. That's a promise.'

CHAPTER 12

'You wouldn't really have shot Baxter, would you?' Greg asked as they got back in the Jag.

Alex twisted the ignition and the car roared as she pulled out of the Ritz car park onto the street. Apart from a few gulps of Baxter's Bloody Mary made with real blood, she hadn't had a proper feed since before the Romania trip and she was feeling drained.

'For being a lousy actor, I might have. But I hardly think the guy's going to bring down the Federation single-handed, whatever Harry might say. I just wanted to put the point across.'

'I think he got it. His face when you told him about the Nosferol bullets.'

'Only thing we fear,' she said. 'Apart from decapitation.'

'So it's true that all the stuff about garlic is a myth?'

'Sometime we'll have lunch at Rudi Bertolino's place. He makes the most amazing ragu sauce. Loaded with garlic. And you've probably noticed you can still see yourself in the mirror, too. As if the laws of physics don't apply to us, just because we're not human.'

'And what about crosses?'

Alex popped open a button on her blouse as she drove and fished out the little gold chain she wore around her neck to show him the tiny crucifix dangling from it. 'Frightened? On a scale of one to ten.'

'Uh, I'd say that's a one,' he said, peering at it.

'There you go. We can walk into churches, drink the damn holy water if we feel like it.'

'So, basically, what you're saying is all these old legends are bullshit.'

She shifted in her seat and didn't reply.

'What?' he said, noticing her expression.

All but one, she was thinking. 'Nothing. Don't worry about it.' She drove on, and the tingle of apprehension soon passed.

'What's the key for?' he asked. She glanced at him, and saw he was looking through the open neck of her blouse at the little black antique key she wore on a thong around her neck beside the crucifix.

'You ask too many questions. And keep your eyes out of my blouse.'

'Sorry.'

There was silence between them for a while. Greg broke it by asking sheepishly, 'So where to now?'

'I'm dropping you back at HQ. You've got paper-work.'

He looked at her. 'Vampires do paperwork?'

'Every piece of fieldwork has to be written up for the official record. Harry wants me to show you the ropes; that means from now on you get to take care of the boring stuff. I have better things to do.'

After she'd offloaded Greg at the office, she headed into Soho. It was mid-morning, and the hunger was pressing. She needed someone's blood. Now.

She knew the backstreets and alleys as well as anyone would who'd been stalking them on and off for a hundred years.

'You,' she muttered to herself when she spotted the guy coming out of the café. She could smell the red juice in his veins as he walked up a narrow street. There was nobody else about. Nothing but piles of rubbish bags and a scuffed yellow builder's skip at the kerbside. She followed, gaining on her target.

She gave a little cough as she got close behind him. He turned, and his eyebrows rose as he took in the sight of the tall, attractive, elegantly dressed woman approaching him with an alluring smile.

'You dropped this back there,' she said, holding out a twenty-pound note.

He looked at it with a puzzled expression. 'Did I?'

'It fell out of your pocket.'

'Really? Wow. I didn't even know I had—' He shrugged, took the money and thanked her.

The fish had taken the bait. She stood there, smiling, one eyebrow raised suggestively. He hesitated. The hand with the wedding ring slipped unconsciously into his pocket: sure sign he was interested. Alex sidled up to him, letting him feel her breasts crush up against his chest. He seemed to be up for it. She moved up as though to kiss him. In her mouth, the long curved fangs were extending into place, ready. His neck was exposed, a fat blue vein pulsing enticingly. She moved in and he didn't back off.

It was in the bag. The blood rushed to her eyes and her predatory vampire instinct took over as she went in for the bite.

And then the phone went off in her pocket, distracting her, and the guy came to his senses and walked off, flushed and bemused and still holding her banknote.

She answered the phone.

'Damn it, Harry,' she said irritably. 'You just cost me a feed and twenty quid.'

'How fast can you get over to Oxford?'

'Pretty fast. What's in Oxford?'

'There was a car accident late last night. Single driver, a teenage kid. The police took him to the John Radcliffe hospital. I've got a report from one of our people inside that the kid was ranting and raving. Something about a ritual blood sacrifice taking place.'

'The V-word get mentioned?'

'Said he found a whole nest. Apparently he

was running away from it when he crashed his car.'

Alex frowned. 'More rogue activity?'

'It's a possibility.'

'Or it could be just the usual Hallowe'en hysteria. We get this every year, Harry. I'll bet you anything this kid was on drugs.'

'He was. But I think you should check it out nonetheless. We can't afford to take chances here.'

'Why does it have to be me? Can't you send Gibson?'

'Gibson's in Athens.'

Alex sighed. 'Fine. I'm on my way.'

CHAPTER 13

Ever since the conversation he'd overheard in the canteen, Joel hadn't been able to shut the story of Declan Maddon out of his head. Maybe he was going crazy. Maybe he'd been working too hard and his brain was going into meltdown.

But he'd just *had* to go and talk to this kid. After a fraught and unproductive morning of pushing paper around, he'd seen a ninety-minute window open up in his schedule and grabbed it. The John Radcliffe hospital was on the edge of the city, off the Oxford ring road. Joel rode fast. Just before midday and the sun was shining brightly now – it was turning into one of those beautiful autumnal days that seemed to be getting rarer with each passing year.

The staff nurse looked as perplexed at Joel's request as she was by his appearance in bike leathers and boots.

'Again? The police were here last night talking to him.'

'I have just a few more questions,' Joel said.

Dec Maddon was on the second floor, sharing

a near empty ward with a frail old guy who looked like he was dying. The kid was propped up in his narrow bed with his left arm in a sling. His face was pale and his eyes were rimmed with red, with dark circles around them. He stared up in sullen indignation as Joel approached his bed and flashed his police ID.

'Hello, Declan,' Joel said cordially.

'I told them I didn't take the fucking pills,' the kid said sourly. 'And my name's Dec. Not Declan. Nobody calls me Declan.'

Joel scraped a chair across the tiles and sat down next to the bed.

'How about we start again? Hello, Dec. I see you've been in the wars.' He glanced over at the old man at the other end of the ward, but he didn't seem to be in a fit state to overhear much. 'I hope you don't mind me asking you a few more questions?'

'Haven't we done this already?'

'Tell me what you thought you saw last night,' Joel said, as quietly and patiently as he could.

'I don't *think*,' Dec said. 'I *know*.' His dark-ringed eyes were fixed on an invisible point somewhere above the foot of his bed. There was a grim set to his jaw. 'I know what I saw, and there's only one word to describe it.' He sank back into the pillow and his voice trailed away to a mumble. 'You wouldn't believe me anyway. I tried to tell the others, but nobody wanted to listen.'

'Try me,' Joel said.

Dec turned to look at him. 'I saw vampires,' he said slowly, solemnly.

Joel met his gaze, searching his face for any signs of irrationality. He could see none.

'It's fucking crazy,' Dec breathed.

'But you believe it, don't you?'

'Yes. I do believe it. I'm telling you the truth. And it's not the pills. Not what the cops think. Because I swear I didn't take any. I wish I'd never gone anywhere near those fucking pills.'

'You told the officers you saw these people murder your girlfriend.'

Dec's brow creased up into a deep frown. He looked away. Shook his head, and Joel could see the dismay in his eyes.

'I didn't see . . . I ran,' he muttered. 'I couldn't take any more.' He gritted his teeth, looked back at Joel. 'But she was there. She was . . . she was hanging there, and they were all standing round her.'

'Kate's safe at home, Dec. It's all been checked out. She's fine. Nothing wrong with her.'

The kid let out a long, whistling sigh. 'Yeah, I know. They told me this morning.' He bit his lip in agitation. 'But you don't understand. These people are vampires. If they bit her or something—'

Joel let out a long breath. 'They turned her, you mean. She's going to become one of them. She's sitting in school right now with the rest of her classmates, and when she gets home tonight she'll be watching TV with her parents or up in her

74

room chatting to her friends on Facebook, but really she's one of the Undead. That's a heck of a story. But you know, this isn't the movies.'

Dec's eyes were crazed. 'You're just like the others. You think I'm making this up. You think I just imagined those fuckers standing there covered in blood, and the bitch with the sword—'

'Kate wasn't hurt. Whose blood are you talking about?'

'Jesus *Christ*, I've been through this a hundred times,' Dec moaned impatiently. 'The other girl. That's whose blood. The one they fucking killed. Like a sacrifice. That bitch just slashed her head half off and all the blood came pouring down and they were just gulping it back and I saw their fucking *teeth*. Get it? Big long teeth on the bastards.' He flopped back into the pillow and shut his eyes with a moan. 'Ah, fuck it, what's the use?'

Joel was quiet for a long time, watching him. He could see the teenager was close to despair. He'd been there himself. He suddenly felt a pang of shame.

'I'm not like the other coppers, Dec.'

Dec opened his eyes. 'Meaning what? You believe me?'

'I didn't say that.'

'Huh. Of course.'

'But I want you to tell me everything. Starting at the beginning. I want to know where this happened. Why you and Kate were there in the first place. Every detail.'

75

'It was foggy. I was lost. I don't know—'

'Okay. Tell me the rest.'

And Dec did. As he told the story, his voice became increasingly strained and his face grew pale and moist. Joel watched and listened carefully, trying to gauge the look in his eyes. He seemed completely lucid – but then, that was the power of hallucination. Joel had seen it before. You could never really tell.

Then why was his flesh crawling this way?

Visions of the past flashed up in his mind. For an instant he could see himself sitting there in Dec's place on the bed, aged twelve, desperately trying to persuade the authorities of what he'd witnessed. And nobody believing a word. Rationalising, always rationalising.

It's all in your mind. How many times had he heard that?

He swallowed hard. 'Can you describe the alleged victim?'

'Ha. There you go again. *Alleged.*'

'All right. Tell me about the girl they killed. How's that?'

'She was younger than me and Kate,' Dec muttered. 'Fifteen, maybe. Short brown hair. She had a spider on her neck.'

'How do you mean, a spider?'

'You know, a tattoo.'

Spider tattoo, Joel scribbled on his pad. 'Now, what about the other people in the crypt? Would you recognise them again?'

76

Dec nodded. 'There was the big massive black dude, and the little bastard that looked like a rat or something. And there was the woman with the blade. Sure, I'd know them again.' He shuddered.

'Tell me more about the other man. The one you think picked Kate up in his car.'

'He seemed scared,' Dec muttered. 'Like he wanted to be there, you know? But shitting himself at the same time.' He paused, chewing his lip. 'Thing is, I could have sworn I'd seen that fucker before.'

'That's important. Any idea where?'

Dec shook his head. 'Like I said, I didn't see his face. It was just a feeling.'

'The Rolls. You didn't get the registration number, I take it?'

Dec looked sharply at him. 'I didn't exactly know I was following Kate into a fucking vampires' nest, did I? Is this all you can do, fuck about with car registrations?'

'I'm only trying to—'

'You still don't get it, do you? There are vampires out there. They're going to kill everyone, like they killed that girl.' Tears of emotion spilled out of Dec's eyes. His voice was cracking with the strain. 'I've had enough of answering questions. This isn't some shit you can deal with the normal way, like you can line these fuckers up in some ID parade and stick them in jail. Don't you understand? They drank her fucking *blood*! They're *vampires*! That's what I'm telling you, because that's what I fucking

77

saw!' His voice had risen up to a tortured scream that filled the ward.

At that moment, the staff nurse Joel had spoken to earlier came running in.

'I'm sorry, Inspector, but I can't have you upsetting the patient like this.' She glanced worriedly at Dec, who had collapsed back on the bed and was shaking and weeping hysterically. 'I'll fetch the doctor,' she said, and rushed out.

Joel stood and watched the kid. He was sorry he'd caused this. The fact was, he just didn't know what to think.

'Quite a tale, isn't it?' said a voice behind him. Joel hadn't sensed anyone else come into the ward. He swung round. Standing a few feet away was a woman. She was smiling at him.

CHAPTER 14

The woman's sudden appearance, like a ghost coming out of nowhere, startled Joel. For what seemed like an endlessly drawn-out moment, he stood there speechless. There was something mesmerising about her, and it wasn't just her stunning beauty – the thick auburn curls that tumbled about her shoulders and bounced when she moved, the willowy figure and perfect, pale skin, like porcelain. It was the wry, knowing look and the enigmatic little smile on her lips, as if somehow she could read his thoughts. That look . . . it just seemed to hold him there.

He forced himself to snap out of his reverie and was about to say something when the staff nurse returned in a hurry, followed by a tired-looking male doctor in a green smock. The nurse shot Joel a pointed stare as she curtained off Dec's bed and she and the doctor attended to the agitated, sobbing teenager.

Joel turned back towards the strange woman, but she was already gone.

He trotted out of the ward and spotted her a

little way down the corridor. She was hanging around as though waiting for him. As he approached, he felt his heartbeat quicken and cursed himself for it.

'Are you a relative of his?' he asked her. He was pretty sure he already knew the answer.

She shook her head. The smile was still there, teasing him.

'So what were you doing in there?'

'Listening,' she replied coolly. 'Interesting, don't you think?'

'This is a police enquiry,' he said. 'I was taking a statement from a witness, and I'd like to know what you were doing there eavesdropping.'

'My name's Alex. Alex Bishop.' She dipped a hand in the pocket of the long, elegant coat she was wearing and handed him a business card. The momentary brush of her fingers against his was like a million volts of current jolting through his body.

'DI Joel Solomon,' he said. Doing his best to look composed, he glanced at the card. 'So you're a journalist.' He noticed the landline number at the bottom and added, 'London got too dull? A teenager crashing his car out in the Oxfordshire sticks isn't exactly what I'd call a scoop for a hotshot city reporter.'

'Except it's not just about a teenager crashing his car, is it?' she said.

He made no reply.

'Are you interested in vampires, officer?'

'What did you say?'

'You believed him, didn't you?'

Joel blinked. 'What makes you so sure of that?'

'I saw the look on your face,' she said. 'Have you got time for a drink? I'd like to talk to you.'

'I can't discuss police business with you.'

'Like vampires are official police business now?'

He looked at his watch. 'Fact is, I'm in a rush.'

'Shame.' She smiled. 'Maybe I could have helped you.'

Before he could reply, she'd turned and was already walking away. He watched her all the way to the lifts; then she was gone, without looking back.

CHAPTER 15

The hamlet of Sonning Eye,
near the Oxfordshire/Berkshire border
12.17 p.m.

Sandra Roberts threw the stick and watched as Bertie went hurtling after it down the leafy riverside path. It hit the ground and bounced, and the golden retriever jumped in the air to catch it in his jaws.

'Bring it to Mummy,' she called to him brightly. 'Come on, Bertie. Good boy.'

Bertie trotted back to her, the stick in his mouth, and dropped it proudly at her feet, looking up at her with keen anticipation, tail wagging. She patted his head, picked up the stick and threw it again. This time her throw wasn't quite as straight, and it landed in the reeds at the side of the water. Bertie went charging after it.

'No, Bertie! Not in the water!' Last time he'd gone for an impromptu swim, he'd been impossible to recall, had got absolutely filthy and completely saturated the back seat of the Volvo.

Christopher had not been at all pleased. But then again, not much pleased Christopher.

'Bertie, you bloody dog! Get back here now!'

It was too late. Bertie completely ignored his mistress's shouts as he went ploughing straight through the reeds, sending up a spray of mud and water. She huffed in exasperation as he hunted around in the shallows, rustling the long reeds as he sniffed excitedly here and there. Then he seemed to freeze, as if he'd found the stick. *Oh, good.*

'Good boy, Bertie! Fetch now; bring it to Mummy!'

And, thank God, he was responding. She could see the yellow of his fur through the reeds as he scrabbled back onto the bank. Now she was going to get the damn animal on the lead, so he couldn't run off again. She was sure she'd stuffed the lead into her pocket, but it wasn't there. She tried the other pocket. *There it was.*

She looked back at the riverbank. Bertie was up on dry land now, still half hidden in the grass. She called him again, but he didn't respond. She sighed in irritation, went striding over the grass to grab his collar and snap the lead on.

Bertie looked up at her as she approached. He was standing over something, his soggy tail flicking back and forth as if to say, 'Look what *I* found!'

Whatever it was he'd fished out of the river, it wasn't the stick.

Sandra took a step closer, and peered down at the thing. It was grey and bloated and horrible.

It was a couple of seconds before she realised what she was looking at. She recoiled, tasting the vomit that instantly shot up her throat.

The young girl's face stared up at her from the grass. She had no body. All that remained attached to the head was part of the left shoulder and a section of upper trunk. The throat was slashed wide open, black with congealed blood.

Sandra began to scream.

CHAPTER 16

The ham and cheese baguette sat untouched on Joel's desk. He'd peeled half the cellophane wrapping off it ten minutes ago, before realising that the hollow, gnawing feeling at the pit of his stomach wasn't hunger. He couldn't eat a bite.

He'd been sitting staring blankly at his lunch ever since; but what he was seeing in front of him wasn't an uneaten sandwich. It was the pale face and dark-ringed eyes of a badly frightened young guy in a hospital ward, locked in a mental battle against himself. His brain tearing itself in two, striving yet dreading to believe the impossible. The only thing more terrifying than the fear that you were going crazy was the fear that the nightmare was for real.

Joel knew that. He'd been through it before, and he was fighting desperately not to start feeling that way again now. It was as if he were suddenly viewing the world through a distorting lens.

Reality had shifted gears, sidestepped into a parallel dimension where the normal parameters of logic and rationality had been blown away. He was standing on the brink of the abyss, looking down.

He shoved the sandwich out of the way and snatched up his phone. Dan Cleland was Joel's closest contact at the forensic lab. Joel asked him if there was any way they could speed up the tests on the Maddon samples.

'That depends on what you mean by speed up.'

'Today?'

'Hmmm. Pushing it.'

'It's pretty important, Dan.'

Cleland sighed. 'Okay, because it's you. Leave it with me, and I'll get back to you by the end of the afternoon.'

Joel felt better after the call. If Dec Maddon's pills turned out to be ecstasy and the blood sample tested positive for the drug, then maybe he could breathe again. Maybe the world would return to normal. Maybe the vampires inside his head would go slinking back into the world of the imagination where they belonged, and bad dreams would remain just dreams.

Maybe.

Joel lobbed the ham and cheese baguette into his waste bin and reached for his coffee. It was cold.

The Jag was blasting down the outside lane of the motorway at just a shade under ninety, heading in towards London, as Alex talked to Harry Rumble on her phone. He listened quietly as she ran through the account of her morning. There was just one thing she left out.

'What I don't get,' Rumble said after she'd finished, 'is why a detective inspector, someone high up, a guy up to his eyeballs day to day in serious crime, even in a hick town like Oxford, would go out of his way like that to talk to some kid on a petty drugs charge who's raving on about stuff no humans would take seriously.'

'That's because he believes the story, Harry.'

'What makes you so sure?'

'I could smell his fear. I saw the look in his eyes. I don't think he wants to admit it to himself yet. He's holding back. But trust me. He believes.'

Rumble thought for a moment. 'He believes, even though he has nothing to go on but the testimony of a kid who might very well have dreamed the whole thing up on drugs? Then he's either highly impressionable—'

'Which he isn't,' Alex cut in. 'He's young, around thirty. If he's made DI by then, it means he's ambitious and determined and he's no idiot. Guys like him don't *do* impressionable. There's another reason.'

'Like what?'

'I don't know yet,' she said.

When the call was over, she gripped the steering wheel and pressed a little harder on the gas, felt the surge of the Jaguar's engine as the needle

87

flirted with the hundred mark. Her acute senses could make out every minute detail of the rushing tarmac, computing speed and distance to a degree of accuracy that a fighter pilot could only dream of. She was completely in control, completely zoned in. Of course she was: she was a vampire.

So why was her heart fluttering like this?

That was the part she hadn't told Harry.

As she drove, all she could think about was Joel Solomon. And she knew the reason why.

CHAPTER 17

Joel was on his way over to the machine to get himself a fresh cup of warm coffee when he spotted Carter steaming the other way down the corridor with a phalanx of uniformed officers in his wake. He was built like a bear and when he was moving fast, like he was now, the world simply parted to make way for him or it got knocked flat on its back.

Superintendent Sam Carter was thirteen years older than Joel, and they'd been friends for ten of those years, ever since Joel had joined up with Thames Valley. Joel knew him pretty well – well enough to know that behind the gruff exterior was a guy who burst into tears at the mere sound of Dolly Parton's voice, especially when he was drunk, which wasn't unusual for him. And well enough to know that when he had the grim look on his face that he was wearing now, something extremely serious was up.

'What's happening?' Joel asked as Carter swept past. It was like trying to catch a ride on a moving train.

'You want to know? Come with me.'

Carter filled Joel in as the squad car sped out of Oxford and headed south towards Sonning Eye.

'Member of the public found her half an hour ago. Or a piece of her, at any rate. Hell of a mess. The divers are still fishing bits out of the river.'

'Do we know who she is?'

'Not a clue.' Carter looked at him. 'You look like shit, Solomon.'

'I didn't get a lot of sleep last night.' And Joel was beginning to feel it.

The scene was already milling with personnel and vehicles by the time they got there. A quarter-mile stretch of river had been cordoned off with police barrier tape. Extra officers were being drafted in from across the county to keep back the crowd of locals that was quickly growing as word spread of the grisly find. Inflatable launches burbled up and down the river carrying frogmen and recovery equipment. As Joel followed Carter across the grassy bank towards the riverside, he could see a lot of very sick expressions on the officers' faces. Away in the trees, where he thought nobody could see him, a young rookie constable was heaving his guts out.

The police pathologist at the scene was Jack Brier. Mutilated corpses were his stock in trade, but even he looked a little greyer than Joel had ever seen him before. He was crouched over a bodybag in the grass, pulling off a pair of surgical gloves as Joel crossed the inner cordon and walked over to him. A couple of police photographers had just finished up and were packing away their equipment.

'Hell of a thing,' Brier muttered to Joel and Carter. 'Have you had lunch? Then don't look.'

Joel stared down at the thing in the bodybag.

Brier chuckled at the expression on his face. 'Told you. She's seen better days, that's for sure. We've recovered the head, most of the trunk, the left arm and what's left of the right leg. The rest could have floated down into Berkshire by now.'

'What did this?' Carter asked, wiping his mouth with the back of his hand.

Brier shrugged. 'Hard to tell, until we get her on the slab and have a poke around inside. If this was Alaska, I'd say a grizzly had taken a bite out of her.' He gave a dark grin. 'But this isn't Alaska.'

'Jesus,' Carter mumbled. He'd seen enough. He looked away, watching the divers and visibly trying to control his emotions.

'The strangest thing is,' Brier went on. 'I mean, I can't be sure just yet, but look how little lividity there is. And she's still fresh, too. Not been in the water more than six, seven hours tops. Cut a long story short, it looks to me like this young lady has been completely exsanguinated, even before she was dissected.'

'In English,' Carter said.

Joel answered for Brier. 'He's saying something drained her blood.'

91

'Drained her blood,' Carter repeated flatly.

Brier nodded. 'Every last drop of it.'

Joel was still staring at the pieces of the girl's body as Brier got to his feet and went off with Carter to confer with some of the others. Just then, his phone started to vibrate in his pocket. He fished it out and saw that the call was from Dan Cleland.

'And for my next miracle,' Cleland said.

'You got the results already?'

'Just in. Specially for my favourite CID officer.'

Joel tensed. Dan was one of those guys who liked to string things out for effect. 'Well?'

'The arresting officer was right about the pills. Not top stuff, but definitely ecstasy.'

'And the blood test, Dan?'

'Goodness, we are in a tizzy today.'

'If you were standing here looking at a dead girl's head in a bag, so would you be.'

'All right, all right. Well, if your man's dealing, he doesn't use from his own stash. Blood test was clean.'

'What about alcohol?'

'Zilch. Soberer than a Sons of Temperance convention.'

'You're sure about that? Quite certain?'

'When have I ever been wrong?'

'Never. Thanks, Dan.'

'You owe me now, Solomon.'

'Right.' Joel ended the call and was about to flip the phone shut. Then he stopped. Glanced around him. Brier was deep in conversation with his colleagues and Carter was getting belligerent with someone on the police radio. Nobody was watching him.

He quickly turned on the camera function on his phone, crouched down in the grass and took two snaps of the victim. One of her face, the glassy eyes staring right into the lens.

And the other of the spider tattoo on what was left of her neck.

CHAPTER 18

Villa Oriana, forty miles from Florence
1.50 p.m. local time

The butler in the crisp white jacket emerged into the sun carrying the tray with the chilled lemon vodka, prepared exactly the way his employer liked it. He climbed the steps to the balustraded terrace and set the drink down on the marble-topped table at the man's side.

Jeremy Lonsdale ignored him, didn't even glance at the drink until the butler had disappeared back inside the villa. Only then, he reached for the glass and winced as the iced vodka burned away the aftertaste of the lobster he'd eaten for lunch.

He closed his eyes, leaned back in his chair and felt the sun on his face. Soaking into him, its glow burning orange through his closed eyelids. Even in early November, it was still easily warm enough to have breakfast and lunch outside. That was one of the things Lonsdale loved most about his Tuscan bachelor hideaway. The gloom and drizzle of that piteous little island called Britain depressed him. He had no affection for the place and

94

certainly no allegiance. He was just one of the ones lucky enough to ride the wave and enrich themselves before the remains of the dying empire imploded into the Third World country it was waiting to become. Whenever he could, he'd jump on his private jet and come out here to soak up the sun. There'd come a day when he wouldn't return. That had always been his plan.

Lonsdale had been a multi-millionaire for twenty-seven years, which at forty-nine was well over half his life. He could have retired a long time ago, if it hadn't been for his love of his political career. He was passionate about that whole world of lies and deceit. He loved the way he looked in the public eye when he took up some worthless cause to champion the innocent victims of . . . whatever. He loved the flash of the cameras and the simper of the media as he kissed babies in Manchester or Liverpool, while the arms companies that earned him millions a year in investments were churning out products to kill other people's babies in some faraway country nobody gave a shit about, as long as they were kept sated with their television and sport and beer and infantile gadgets. It was all a big game. To win, you just needed the right attitude.

And he'd always thought he was the master of the game, until that day in February. That day had changed everything.

Lonsdale had snatched a week out of his schedule to take a skiing holiday in Lichtenstein.

On the third night, as he lounged in the bar of his luxury hotel with a martini cocktail and some nameless floozy at his elbow, he'd spotted the tall figure across the crowded room. Men of wealth and taste were ten a penny in Lonsdale's world, but this one was different. A man so effortlessly self-possessed, radiating an air of such supreme indifference that he made Lonsdale feel like a schoolboy. He seemed to draw the most beautiful women to him with mesmeric, almost uncanny ease and then dismissed them as though they were nothing. Here was a man who understood power, lived and breathed it. Was he a prince? Unable to recall his face from the society pages, Lonsdale had been desperate to talk to him, but the chance had escaped him when some paunchy dullard of an oil billionaire had appeared to pin him down in gratingly boring conversation. By the time he'd been able to wriggle away from the guy, the fascinating man had disappeared along with his female entourage.

All the next day on the ski slopes, Lonsdale had looked out for him – but no sign, nor the next night.

Finally, on the last evening of the holiday, Lonsdale caught sight of the man again. And this time, nothing was going to stop him from going up and introducing himself.

The man's name was Gabriel Stone. They'd talked until late in the night and, when Stone had invited Lonsdale to be his guest at his mountain home in Romania, Lonsdale had been straight on the phone the next morning to advise his staff in London that he'd been struck down by a virus and wouldn't be back in the country for another week.

Two days later, Stone's helicopter had flown in to land at his home, with Jeremy Lonsdale on board, flanked by the two burly bodyguards his host had provided for his security. Snowy mountains stretched as far as the eye could see. The chopper banked over the towers and ramparts of the old castle, and Lonsdale had been blown away by the power and majesty of the place.

For the rest of the day, he'd been attended to by a tall, bald and cadaverously gaunt man who introduced himself as Seymour Finch, personal assistant to Mr Stone. Lonsdale found Finch's presence uncomfortable. There was something strange and unsettling about him.

It was only after dark that Lonsdale's host appeared, apologising that his business affairs tended to occupy his entire day. The two men had dined together in the great hall, drunk fine cognac and smoked cigars. Stone had been not only a charming and affable host, but a man of culture and intellect. Lonsdale had never met anyone able to quote so extensively from classical literature, the Bible, the Greek philosophers. He knew history as though he'd virtually lived it.

That night, Lonsdale had been woken in his luxurious bedroom by the sound of strange music.

He climbed out of bed, opened his door. The music seemed to be drifting up from somewhere below. He pulled on a satin robe and followed the sound, treading quietly through the castle's cold, dark halls and passageways. The music was like none he'd ever heard before and it seemed to lure him, as though it had some hypnotic quality that whispered in his mind.

He came to the door of what looked like a wine cellar. It creaked open to reveal steps leading down. At the bottom of the steps, another door lay half open. The music was coming from inside.

Lonsdale couldn't help himself. He had to see what was in there. Peeking through the gap, instead of a cellar he saw a decadently opulent room richly decorated with tapestries and exotic rugs and gold-threaded cushions scattered across the floor. On a huge bed was the naked figure of Gabriel Stone, his physique lithe and muscular and perfect, surrounded by three beautiful women who were making love to him.

As Lonsdale watched from the shadows, a hand had touched his shoulder and he'd nearly screamed in terror. He'd turned to see a woman even more beautiful than the ones on Stone's bed. She smiled and put her finger to her lips. Beckoned him away from the door. 'Come,' she whispered. The look in her dark eyes meant just one thing.

Lonsdale had followed her back through the passageways. She was bewitching. Her raven hair was tangled and wild like a gypsy's, and when she glanced back at him with that smile, her lips were red and glistening. The way she moved drove him wild. Every nerve in his body tingled with lust for her as she led him back to his room. Inside, she shut the door with a smile. He was almost panting by now.

'W-who are you?' he stammered.

'I'm Lillith. Gabriel's sister.' She walked him to the bed and shrugged the gown from her shoulders. She was naked under it.

Lonsdale tore at his robe. 'You're beaut—'

'Shh. Quiet.' Then she kissed him, and pulled him down onto the bed.

It had been a memorable night.

When Lonsdale had awoken next morning, Lillith was gone. He'd searched the castle obsessively for her. Returning to the room below, he'd found the door heavily padlocked. He'd spent the whole day thinking about her. She was like a drug, and he wanted more.

Lillith had come back to him for the next two nights. Two more nights of wild, dizzy passion. She was incredible. She did things to him that he'd never imagined possible.

Then, on the third night, just when he thought he was completely spent, Lillith opened up a whole new world for him. The candlelight gleamed on her skin as she knelt there on the bed – and flickered across the blade of the dagger she'd drawn from under the pillow. He'd watched, speechless with excitement, as she held its sharp tip to her chest and slashed herself. A rivulet of blood tricked down her breast. Her lips had opened a little wider, and Lonsdale had seen the white fangs, long and curved. She'd cupped her hands behind his head and pulled him in closer. 'Drink me!' She threw back her head and gasped in anticipation as he lowered his face to her breast and put out his tongue to lick up the flowing blood. Every nerve in his body had been aflame.

In that moment of enthralling wonder, Gabriel Stone had walked into the room, interrupting them. He'd shouted harshly at Lillith, and she'd retreated in fear, covering herself up with a sheet.

Then Stone had turned to Lonsdale. 'You're not so afraid of us, are you, Jeremy? That's interesting.'

'Who are you?' Lonsdale breathed. '*What* are you?'

Stone smiled. 'Do you not know? We are the ones with the power. The power to change your life forever. And I do mean *forever*. You can become one of us. Become everything that a human isn't. You like that idea, don't you, Jeremy?'

'What do I have to do?'

Stone gave another smile. 'You will be contacted.'

Then he was gone, and when Lonsdale looked around, he saw that Lillith had disappeared with him.

He hadn't seen them again for a long time.

The following day, Lonsdale had reluctantly

returned to London. Life had gone on – but it held little appeal. He'd tasted something infinitely more rewarding, and it preyed on his mind until he thought he was going to go insane with frustration.

For three long months, he'd heard nothing. Then one day in early June, the strange man called Seymour Finch had paid an unexpected visit to his London office. Inside the slim briefcase he carried with him was the agreement drawn up by his employer Mr Stone.

As contracts went, it was extremely simple. The price would be twenty million euros, to be wired to a Zurich bank account. Within hours, Lonsdale had arranged the transfer and was choking with anticipation to hear from Stone's people again.

Nothing. As the summer turned to autumn, Lonsdale was beginning to think he'd been the victim of an elaborate con trick. He'd become so agitated that he'd been virtually unable to conduct his daily affairs.

Nothing, until late September, when the man called Finch had returned. Mr Stone's end of the deal would soon be honoured, he said. There was to be a ceremony.

'What kind of ceremony?' Lonsdale asked nervously.

'An initiation,' Finch had replied. 'The first stage in your induction. But first, Mr Stone requires a service from you. A ship will be arriving in London within the next few weeks. You are to use your influence to ensure that its cargo arrives safely, unexamined, unquestioned.'

And Lonsdale, helpless, hooked and counting the days to the ceremony, had seen to it.

But now, as he sat here in the warm Italian sunlight, sipping the last of his iced lemon vodka, he was beginning to have second thoughts.

The initiation had been horrible. It hadn't only been because of what they'd done to the poor young girl they'd slaughtered. It had been the look on Lillith's face, like a wild animal that hadn't fed for days. He kept seeing it in his mind, and it brought a taste of revulsion into the back of his throat.

Was that really the kind of creature he wanted to become?

Sitting here gazing out at the Tuscan hills, he couldn't stop thinking about how all this was going to change when Stone finally took him over the edge. Turned him. The turning point from which there was no return. He'd never again be able to sit outside and enjoy the golden autumnal colours of the trees. The glow of the sunshine on his face would become a distant memory. Not just for a lifetime, but for a whole eternity of darkness. Was that what he really, truly wanted? He'd have to renounce his whole career. Spend the rest of time lurking, hiding, in the shadows. Like a criminal.

Power. Limitless power. But at what cost?

Worst of all, he might never be able to visit Toby

again. Lonsdale closed his eyes. Saw the boy's bright, smiling face in his mind, heard the sound of his laughter.

When he opened his eyes, they were moist.

How could I have been so stupid?

It wasn't too late. Stone hadn't even told him when the next stage would take place. He could still back out. It would mean having to confront Gabriel Stone face to face at his home in Henley. The idea chilled Lonsdale utterly. But it was the only way, and he was suddenly gripped by a pressing sense of urgency.

He tinkled the little silver bell on the table in front of him, and seconds later the butler came running out of the house.

'Roberto, have my jet prepared. I have to return to Britain as soon as possible.'

CHAPTER 19

The John Radcliffe Hospital
4.25 p.m.

'Y ou again,' the staff nurse sneered at Joel. 'Visiting hours are over.'
'Don't give me that,' he said and marched by her.

Dec Maddon was sitting up in bed reading a comic book as Joel walked into his ward.

'What happened to the old guy next to you?' Joel asked, pointing at the empty, neatly made bed.

Dec shut the comic with a surly look. 'Died.'

'How's the wrist?'

'Getting better, so it is. What are *you* doing here? More questions?'

'Good news first,' Joel said, sitting in the chair next to the bed. 'Your blood tests came through negative. Which means there'll be no drug driving charge. You're not supposed to know that yet, so keep it to yourself, okay?'

'Told you, didn't I?' Dec raised an eyebrow. 'So what's the bad news?'

'The bad news is I need you to look at something for me. And again, this isn't something you should be seeing. It's strictly between you and me. Understood?' Joel took out his phone.

'What is it?'

'Something not nice, Dec. You're going to have to be brave.'

'I saw a girl get her throat slashed and a bunch of vampires taking a shower in her blood,' Dec muttered. 'I think I can handle whatever you have to show me.'

Joel scrolled up the photo he'd taken at the recovery scene. Without another word he handed the phone to Dec. The young guy's face drained of colour as he stared at the image on the screen.

'Scroll down. There's another.'

Dec thumbed the button and his face grew even whiter. He dropped the phone in his lap, then sank his head into his hands. 'Shit. That *is* bad.'

Joel took the phone back from him. 'You okay?'

'Yeah, I'm okay. Don't think I'll be wanting dinner, though.'

'Well?'

'It's her,' Dec mumbled through his fingers. 'The girl from the party. The one they killed.'

'Dec, we need to be completely sure.'

The young guy looked up sharply. 'You don't forget something like that. I'm sure.'

Joel nodded. He was silent for a few moments as he got his thoughts together. Confiding in Dec

Maddon was going a long way out on a limb –
but Dec was all he had right now.

He took a deep breath. 'This isn't a regular
murder investigation, is it, Dec? This is something
different.'

Dec looked at him. 'Does that mean you believe
me?'

Joel paused a long time before he replied. 'We
need to keep all this between us. I'm taking a big
chance on you. Don't let me down.'

Dec nodded solemnly. 'I won't let you down.'

'You're going to be discharged from here
tomorrow morning, and you and I are going for
a drive. I want you to help me find the house. You
need to think hard.'

'Things are coming back slowly,' Dec said.
'Details.'

'Like?'

'Like those weird birds.'

'What weird birds?'

'On the gateposts. Like sculptures, you know?
Stone birds. Ravens or something. I can remember
their claws and beaks. Ugly fuckers.'

Joel patted him on the shoulder as he rose to
leave.

'Keep it coming. Write down everything you
remember. I'll see you in the morning.'

CHAPTER 20

Evening was falling by the time Joel rode into Lavender Close on the edge of the market town of Wallingford. He cruised slowly past the gate entrances looking for number sixteen, but couldn't find it until he realised that the Hawthornes' place was the only house in the street with a name instead of a number. The fancy slate sign on the wall read 'The Willows'.

He rolled the big Suzuki up onto the kerb by the gate and killed the engine. Unstrapping his helmet, he looked around him. The houses looked like they could have been made of Lego, all sitting in neat ranks in the amber glow of the street-lamps, each with its crisp little garden. Two of them even had gnomes. The house next door to the Hawthornes' place was the only property that lacked the compulsory manicured lawn and perfect hedge, and instead of a Rover or a Volvo in the drive, there was a builder's van and a couple of go-faster hatchbacks. That would be the Maddon place, then.

He walked in the gate of The Willows, brushed his fingers through his hair at the door, and knocked. A few seconds later a light came on in the hallway, then the door opened and a sour-faced woman appeared on the front step. She eyed the bike and his leather jacket with obvious distaste, and crossed her arms.

'If it's the Maddons you're looking for, it's the next door along.'

'I'm not. Are you Mrs Hawthorne?'

'I'm Gillian Hawthorne,' she said uncertainly. Her eyes opened wide as he showed her his police ID. 'You're a Detective Inspector?' She made no attempt to mask the scepticism in her voice.

'Incredible though it may seem,' he felt like saying. Instead he adopted his most polite tone and said, 'It's your daughter Kate I've come to see. Is she in?'

'If this is about Declan Maddon, shouldn't you be talking to *them*?' She jerked her thumb dismissively at the house next door, keeping her eyes averted from the place as though it would turn her stomach to look at it directly. 'The police have already been here once today. Is Kate in trouble?'

'None whatsoever. I just want to ask her a couple of questions.'

'Oh, very well.' She ushered him inside the hall and made a big show of getting him to leave his helmet by the door. The house smelled of new carpets and air freshener. Gillian Hawthorne called up the stairs, 'Ka-ate!'

No reply.

'She's been in bed.'

'Is she not well?'

'She's just a little off-colour. Do you *really* need to talk to her now?'

'It's quite important,' he replied.

'I suppose you'd better come up, then.'

Gillian Hawthorne led the way up the stairs and stopped at a door.

'Kate, dear?' She turned the handle and Joel followed her inside. The room was dark. Gillian turned on a side light, and there was a groan from the bed. Joel could see the girl's red hair sticking out from under the duvet. He looked around. The bedroom was just like any teenage girl's room. Posters on the walls, TV, computer, a desk covered in magazines, hairbrush, iPod, makeup, mobile. The only odd detail he noticed was the way the floor-length curtains at the far end of the room had been tightly closed together with safety pins. He crossed the room and peered behind them. A French window led out onto a little balcony over-looking the back garden.

'Kate, this gentleman is from the police and he's come to talk to you about *Declan*.' She spat that last word out with disgust.

Joel pulled up a chair. He smiled at the girl as she sat up in bed with a resentful scowl. Her hair was tousled. Her face was pallid, almost white.

'Detective Inspector Solomon. Actually, Kate, it's you I wanted to talk about.'

'What for?'

'I've been speaking to Dec Maddon about

reported incidents last night at a party that he says you and he both attended. I was wondering what you could tell me about it.'

'He's a bloody liar,' Gillian Hawthorne cut in irritably. 'We've already been over and over this with you people. I mean, is there nobody in Thames Valley Police who can understand plain English?'

'Please, Mrs Hawthorne.' Joel turned back to Kate and spoke softly. 'I'd appreciate it if we could go through it again. Just one more time, okay?'

Kate grimaced. 'I don't know what Dec was on about. I came straight home. I didn't go to any party.' She said it very carefully, as if she was reciting prepared lines.

'You're sure?'

She nodded.

'How did you get home?'

'I took a taxi.'

'What time?'

'I don't remember,' she groaned. 'It was late.'

'Where did you take the taxi from?'

'Somewhere. I was walking.'

'So you called the cab company on your phone?'

'Yes. No.'

'Which is it?'

'My head's hurting.'

'Why are you asking her all this?' Gillian said.

'I'm just trying to understand what happened,' Joel replied, keeping his tone gentle.

Gillian gave a snort. 'What happened is that nothing happened.'

'I called them,' Kate said. 'I remember now.'

'That's good. I can make enquiries and find out the name of the taxi firm,' he said, watching her face. 'That way I can find out where they picked you up from.'

She flushed at his words. 'Oh . . . hang on. No. I thumbed a lift.'

The bluff had worked. 'So you didn't take a taxi after all.'

'No.'

'Who gave you a lift?'

'I don't know. A man.'

'What happened to your neck?' he asked. 'Did someone hurt you?'

Kate immediately covered her neck with the collar of her pyjama top. Something flashed in her eyes. Not a look of embarrassment, the way a self-conscious teenager might have reacted. It was a flash of hard white anger, animal rage.

'I fell,' she said in a strange voice.

'It looks like a bite.'

'I'm *telling* you that I fell. Against a barbed wire fence.' The tone in her voice was suddenly harsh.

'Maybe you should let a doctor see that. It looks nasty.'

'I don't need a doctor,' she shot back.

'If there's anything you'd like to tell me about what happened at the party,' Joel said, 'remember you won't be in any trouble.'

'Nothing happened at the party.'

'So you *were* at the party. Dec was telling the truth.'

'No!'

'But you just said you were. I need to know where the party was, Kate. Exactly what happened, and who else was there. It's very important.'

'You're confusing me! I don't understand what these questions are about!'

'Why are you making up stories, Kate? Are you trying to protect someone?'

Kate glared at him. The rage in her eyes burned intensely. For a second it was like being face to face with a snarling dog, and Joel almost backed away.

'Go fuck yourself,' she spat. Then burst into tears. She fell down onto the pillow, shaking and sobbing. Her mother rallied to her side, glaring indignantly at Joel.

'You're upsetting my daughter, Inspector. I'd also like to know what these questions are in aid of. Is this an official police line of enquiry? Because if it's not, I think you should be aware that my husband is a very senior solicitor and that we know our rights.'

Joel stood up. 'I'm sorry if I upset you,' he said to Kate. 'I'll leave you in peace now. Thanks for talking to me.'

Gillian Hawthorne couldn't see him out the front door fast enough. Outside, it was getting colder and the night fog was settling in again, wisping like smoke around the streetlamps.

Joel stopped on the doorstep. 'Out of interest,

112

Mrs Hawthorne, did you put the safety pins on her curtains?'

'If it's any of your business, she did it herself. She says the light hurts her.'

'We had the lights on in her room.'

'Not those,' she said impatiently. 'Just the sunlight.'

'Since when?'

'Just this morning. She'll be fine. She probably has a touch of that new type of flu that's going round.'

'I'm sure you're right, Mrs Hawthorne. I hope she gets well soon.' He turned to go, conscious of her glare following him. He already knew what his next move was going to be. What it could only be. He stopped and turned back. She was still glowering at him.

'One last question, Mrs Hawthorne. Do you own a dog?'

'A dog?' She frowned. 'Of course I don't bloody own a dog. Why would you ask me that?'

'Thanks for your help,' he smiled, and started walking back to the bike.

CHAPTER 21

After his hurried trip back from Italy to the UK, Jeremy Lonsdale had called Seymour Finch with great trepidation. The appointment to see Mr Stone had been set for eight thirty that same evening.

It was only now, as he sat hunched in one of the leather armchairs in Stone's library watching the logs crackle in the fire, that the real fear was beginning to take him. His hands wouldn't stop shaking, and a twitch in his left leg was making his knee bounce up and down uncontrollably. He needed a drink, but Finch had ushered him in with barely a word and had offered him nothing. Did they somehow know what was in his mind? That was a terrifying thought.

'You wanted to see me.' Stone's voice came from behind him, calm and soft.

Lonsdale started and whipped round. The vampire was standing there in a long silk robe over black trousers. The robe was open enough at the chest to show his toned pectoral muscles.

'What a surprise, Jeremy, to see you back so

soon from Italy. To what do I owe the pleasure of this unexpected visit?'

'There's something we have to discuss,' Lonsdale blurted out.

Stone walked slowly across the room and leaned on the mantelpiece. A smile crept over his lips, and the twinkle in his eye was more than just the reflection of the firelight. 'You sound nervous, Jeremy. Is something wrong?'

'I've been reconsidering my options,' Lonsdale said.

Stone raised an eyebrow. 'What options would you be referring to, my friend?'

Lonsdale let out a deep sigh, and came straight out with it. 'The deal's off. I want my money back.'

Stone was quiet for a moment. 'So you no longer wish to join our circle.'

'No. Frankly, on reflection, the idea horrifies me.' Lonsdale cleared his throat and tried desperately to hide the quaver in his voice. 'Now, if you will be good enough to wire the funds back into my private account, minus a ten per cent administration fee which I'm more than happy to pay you, that will be that and we'll say no more about it. I've been pleased to be able to help you by using my contacts and influence. I hope we can remain on cordial terms, and perhaps do business together in the future.'

He stood up and put out his hand.

Stone looked at the hand. He didn't move.

'Now, I should be on my way,' Lonsdale said

briskly. 'There are people expecting me back in London. They know I'm here,' he added.

Stone chuckled. 'That's your way of telling me no harm must come to you. Really. What do you take me for, a monster?'

'I didn't say that.'

Stone walked over to his desk and pressed a button. 'Please sit down, Jeremy. I'd hate for you to leave without a farewell drink.'

Lonsdale hesitated, bit his lip, made a show of glancing at his watch. 'Just a quick one. I think I have time.'

Finch entered the library carrying a tray with two glasses and a bottle of Krug. He laid the tray down, solemnly filled the glasses and left. Stone handed Lonsdale a glass.

'To the future,' he said, raising his own.

'To the future,' Lonsdale echoed uncertainly. He slugged down his champagne and went to stand up again. 'That was lovely. Now—'

'Why such a hurry?' Stone said smoothly. 'Have another. It's a very good vintage, don't you think?' He paused as he refilled Lonsdale's glass. 'You see, Jeremy, I knew what it was you wanted to tell me tonight. That's why I arranged an entertainment for us.' He slipped a little remote from the pocket of his robe. He aimed it at the bookcases to the right of the fireplace and the carved wood shelves suddenly parted and slid open, revealing a giant screen. 'You and I are going to watch a little film.'

'I don't have time for a film.'

'I think you'll like this one,' Stone replied, with a flare in his eyes that forced Lonsdale helplessly back in his chair.

'I trust the scene looks familiar to you,' Stone said as the screen lit up. The warning look had melted from his face and now he looked almost jovial.

Lonsdale gaped. It was himself he was seeing on the screen, on Hallowe'en night, the occasion of his initiation ceremony. He watched in horror as the nightmarish images unravelled. The girl hanging from the chains. The blade slashing through her neck like something on a butcher's slab. The blood cascading down, soaking his hair, sticking his shirt to his body. And all through the orgiastic frenzy, the camera was right on him.

'Stop it,' Lonsdale wheezed. His heart was hammering dangerously now. 'Stop it.'

Stone raised the remote and the image onscreen froze into a close-up of Lonsdale's blood-slicked face and his white, rolling eyes behind the mask.

'You see, Jeremy, the fact is, as you now see, that you *have* no options. The deal must be honoured. Like it or not, you're already part of our family.'

'That could be anyone in a mask,' Lonsdale exploded in outrage. 'Nobody could prove it was me.'

'Jeremy, Jeremy, do you take us for complete idiots? What I am showing you is merely an excerpt. The best bits, if you will. We filmed you coming into the house. Walking in from the car with the delectable Kate Hawthorne. Putting on your mask. Oh, I think people would have little trouble believing it was you. Then there's the footage of your bedroom escapades with Lillith. No mask there, if my memory serves me well.'

Lonsdale gulped back rising bile. 'You could never use this. You'd be incriminating yourself, and your whole bunch.'

Stone laughed. 'That is of little consequence. None of us exist. Nobody can touch any of us, Jeremy. We are free to vanish. You, on the other hand . . .' He shrugged. 'If I may be permitted to use the vernacular: you're fucked.'

Lonsdale opened his mouth to protest, but there was nothing to say. He'd been set up. The initiation ceremony, the whole thing, had been concocted just to entrap him. Stone had never intended to make good on his promise of eternal life and unlimited power. He was trapped, and there was no going back. He slumped in the armchair, defeated.

'Humans are utterly repugnant to me,' Stone said softly, watching him. 'But the creature whose verminous ways offend me most deeply of all is a politician. I'm disappointed in you, Jeremy. I had hopes that you might have been different.'

'Keep the money,' Lonsdale breathed. 'Keep every penny. I don't care. Just let me go on with my life. Please. I beg you.'

'Your life?' Stone smiled. 'That belongs to me

now. When I want you, you'll be ready for me. You are at my bidding, and will provide me with anything I require, at any time, without question or hesitation. Fail me in any way, and every television station and newspaper in Europe will receive a copy of the film. Let the serfs who voted for you know the truth about their future leader.' He snapped his fingers. 'Now get out of my sight.'

Jeremy Lonsdale staggered from the library and found his way to the marbled hallway. Outside, he drew in huge gulps of the cold night air. It wasn't until he was sitting at the wheel of the Rolls, fumbling with the key, half blinded with sweat, that his guts heaved all the way over and the vomit burst down his front.

CHAPTER 22

Canary Wharf, London
9.29 p.m.

'Thanks, Rudi. See you later.' Alex snapped her phone shut. The night breeze ruffled her hair as she leaned on the rail of her apartment balcony. A human would have been shivering in the November chill, but she loved the freshness of the air. She lingered for a moment, watching the city lights dance on the river. The sadness that had been hovering over her all day was descending now. She turned from the balcony and walked barefoot in through the sliding glass door of her living room. Philip Glass piano music was playing softly on her stereo system. She padded across the plush carpet of the modern, open-plan living room, then went up the spiral staircase to her bedroom.

As she passed the bed, her sadness sharpened. At the foot of the bed was an oak chest. She stopped, kneeled. While everything else in her apartment was ultra-modern, the chest was pitted with age, splits in the wood patched here and there with metal plates. She and that old chest went back a long way. It had been a while since she'd last opened it.

She reached for the little key she wore around her neck and unclipped it from its leather thong. It was made of the same pitted black metal as the lock of the chest. It slid smoothly into the lock and sprung the mechanism with a tiny click. She carefully lifted the lid until it rested against the foot of the bed.

Inside were her memories.

The diamond and sapphire engagement ring was still as bright and sparkling as the day William had given it to her. She smiled sadly at it, then closed the scuffed, battered little box and replaced it at the bottom of the chest. There was the bundle of letters, still tied with the same yellow ribbon. The lock of his golden hair. The one photograph she had of him, long ago faded to a dull sepia tone.

She gazed at it. Such a long time ago, but she could still remember every moment they'd had together. She could recall the touch of his skin against hers, the softness of his voice, the infectiousness of his laugh.

I'll come back to you one day, my love.

Those had been his last words to her. A day she didn't like to remember, but whose memory she couldn't chase. Not in a hundred and thirteen years.

I'll come back.

But she was still waiting.

Or was she? As she caressed the faded image with her thumb, she thought about Joel Solomon. It was uncanny. They could have been brothers, twins.

Alexandra Bishop, born 1869, turned 1897, would never have believed in such a thing as reincarnation, as William had. But then, back in those days, she'd never have believed in vampires, either.

She gazed at the picture a while longer, then laid it back inside the chest and shut the lid.

The far wall of the bedroom was one huge solid expanse of mirror. She walked towards it, snatching a remote control off a table as she went. She didn't slow her pace and, just as she was about to walk straight into the glass, she pressed the button on the remote and the partition instantly slid aside to reveal the hidden room beyond. She stepped inside, aimed the remote behind her and slid the wall shut again.

She was in her weapons room.

The place was as utilitarian as it could be. On a steel wall rack were a pair of assault rifles, a cut-down shotgun and two ex-MOD submachine guns. Beside those, another rack holding four identical .50-calibre Desert Eagle pistols. The opposite wall was covered in industrial shelving, and in between was the workbench where she handloaded her own ammunition. She'd never trusted the stuff that VIA issued the agents. Bolted to the bench was a reloading press with a rotating platform that housed half-a-dozen empty glittering brass cartridge cases at a time. Mounted on top, a clear plastic hopper was filled with peppery gunpowder. It was Alex's little personal production line.

She sat at the bench and worked the lever on the press. *Ker-chunk*. One pull to fill up each case with powder. Another pull to ram home the fat half-inch hollowpoint bullets and seat them firmly in the mouths of the cases. After five minutes, she had a batch of thirty .50 Action Express rounds ready – or they would have been, for use on a normal target. For Alex's purposes, there was one more stage to perform.

She sat the cartridges upright in a row on the bench. Pulled on thick rubber gloves and a surgical mask, then took a plastic flask from one of the shelves. The label was marked 'Nosferol'. Beside the name was a little skull and crossbones. If you looked closely, the skull had tiny fangs. Some joker at the Federation pharma plant's idea of humour.

She carefully unscrewed the top. One whiff of the fumes would be enough to destroy her. She hated working with the stuff, but it was her job sometimes to do things she hated.

The level in her flask was getting low. She made a mental note to put in an order for some more. Then, using a squeezy disposable pipette, she dripped five drops into the hollow tip of each bullet, working her way along the line until all thirty were charged with the poison. Still wearing the gloves and mask, she lit a church candle and delicately sealed over the end of each bullet with molten wax. That was the most critical part of the operation. If the Nosferol wasn't completely sealed in, even a tiny leakage could be disastrous to her.

She waited a few minutes for the wax to set, then loaded the cartridges into a batch of spare magazines, ready for use. Job done. She closed up the weapons room, taking the mags and the most worn and comfortable of the Desert Eagles with her.

She was finishing getting changed to go out when she heard the doorbell. The security monitor in the hallway showed Greg standing outside, shifting nervously from foot to foot. She smiled to herself, then put on a stern face and answered the door.

'Right on time,' Greg said.

'Amazing. Let's go.'

CHAPTER 23

'So where is it we're going?' Greg asked as she wove the Jag at top speed through the night traffic. 'Jesus, do you always drive like this?'

'To see Rudi Bertolino,' she said. 'He called me to say he's got some information.'

'The ragu sauce guy. I remember.'

'Rudi's a little more than that. He owns the famous Last Bite Bar and Grill on St James's. Wait till you see it. He's also one of my prime informers.'

'He's . . .'

'You're so coy. Why don't you just say it? Yes, he's one of us, he's a vampire. You'll like him, too. Everyone does. A lot of us hang out there. It's kind of a vampire restaurant.'

'Right. So vampires can actually eat, like, *real* food?' he asked, looking hopeful. The back of a bus was looming up alarmingly fast. 'Watch—'

She twisted the wheel smartly and missed the bus by an inch. 'Sure, we can eat. It's a social occasion, and human food tastes pretty good. Especially if it comes out of Rudi Bertolino's kitchen. Thing is, though, you could pig out on it every day and still starve. There's no nutrition in it, not for us.'

'Shit. For a minute there, I was kind of hoping—'

'We're vampires, Greg. It's what we do. Get used to it.' She sighed reproachfully. 'Not feeding yet, then?'

'Don't bring that up again. Makes me sick even to think of it.'

'Of course it does. That's normal enough. But that feeling doesn't last. Trust me.'

'Wonderful. Looking forward to it.'

'Taken your Solazal today?'

'What are you, my mother?'

'When I see a helpless little vampire baby, I get these irrepressible maternal urges. Plus I don't want you frazzling up too close to me.'

'Thank you so much,' he muttered. 'Helpless little baby. So what information does this Rudi guy have for us?'

'That's what we're going to find out.'

The Last Bite Bar and Grill, open dusk till dawn, was one of central London's most in and super-trendy hangouts for vampires, movie stars, rock musicians, other assorted celebrities and those wannabes that could afford to eat, drink and party there. Rudi Bertolino, its owner-manager, was a vampire with his ear to the ground. For a yacht-owning, Porsche-driving multi-millionaire restaurateur he moved in some pretty low places – maybe that was just him keeping in touch with his past selling fish in the street markets of old Napoli, back when he'd been human. In return for the information he passed Alex from time to time, she turned a blind eye to the fact that he occasionally violated Federation rules by knocking off a human and putting their blood in the food to appeal to the real vampires among his clientele.

'On a strictly assholes-only basis,' he always insisted in his gravelly bass rumble. 'Who's gonna lament the demise of a few pushers, pimps and paedos?' And that was pretty much good enough for Alex.

Rudi's establishment sprawled across three floors between a yacht broker's and a private members' club on St James's. His gold 911 Turbo was parked outside, glinting in the lights from the windows. The music was thumping out into the street. Alex and Greg bypassed the chattering throngs of hopefuls gathered on the pavement and steps outside, who were waiting to get tables. Two doormen dressed in cloaks and fake fangs spotted Alex and ushered her and Greg inside, bowing stiffly as they walked in up the red carpet into the lights and noise.

The place was decked out like a gaudy gothic cathedral, lit by huge candelabras and chandeliers that looked like torture implements suspended on chains from the vaulted ceiling. Marble pillars gleamed in the swirling spotlights from the bar. Sumptuous red satin drapes billowed down from archways thirty feet high.

The joint was packed. About a hundred people were crowding the bar, yelling to get their drink orders in. Waitresses in leather basques with pointy teeth and heavy eyeshadow roller-skated round the tables, and the waiters had slicked-back hair and long black capes. Mock-Transylvanian tapestries and giant framed prints from vampire movies adorned the walls: Christopher Lee, Klaus Kinski and Bela Lugosi as Dracula through the ages; Wesley Snipes in *Blade*; Tom Cruise as Lestat; a larger-than-life cutout of Peter Cushing coming out at you from behind a curtain, wielding stake and mallet.

'This place is incredible,' Greg shouted over the hard rock beat. He pointed up at a black and white print that hung over the bar. 'Hey, I saw that one. The old *Nosferatu* movie – scary guy with the ears and the fingernails. What was his name?'

'Max Schreck,' Alex told him.

'Right.' Greg froze. 'Shit. Over there. At that table. That's—'

'Yes, it is. And no, she's not one of us. She just likes people to think she is. And stop pointing or I'll break your finger off. You're embarrassing me.'

'Alex! Baby! Great ta see ya!' said a booming voice.

Rudi Bertolino stood no more than five feet tall. He was almost perfectly spherical in shape, balding on top with a ponytail that dangled down the back of his Hawaiian shirt, jinking with gold chains and medallions as he came stomping out of the crowd with a huge grin and slipped a chubby arm around her waist. 'Great! Great! Hungry?'

'Only for what you've got to tell me,' she said.

Rudi grinned even wider. 'Shame. You gotta taste the Brasato al Barolo tonight.' He smacked his lips.

'Maybe later.'

'Hey, no problemo. Let's step into my office.' As he led them away through the noisy crowd he jerked his chin back at Greg. 'Who's the guy?' he rasped out of the corner of his mouth. 'New boyfriend?'

'New partner, Rudi. I mean *professional* partner.'

'Since when did you ever—'

'Don't ask.'

'He looks like a dork,' Rudi muttered.

'Leave him alone, okay?'

Rudi led them along a passage and through a door that said 'manager', into an enormous room done out in purple velvet and leopardskin upholstery. 'Come in, come in. Take a seat.' He motioned at a couple of armchairs.

'I see you've been doing some filing,' Alex said. The chairs were covered in heaps of documents. Rudi strutted over and swiped them away, creating a blizzard of paper. 'Fuckin' bills. Fuck 'em anyway.' He threw himself onto a giant red sofa shaped like a pair of lips and put his silver toe-capped boots up on the coffee table in front of him. 'Jeez, it's good ta see you again, Alex. What'll ya have?'

'Something with a bit of body to it,' she said, settling into one of the leopardskin armchairs. Greg did the same.

'How 'bout you, soldier boy?'

Greg looked stunned. 'That obvious?'

'Like anyone would actually want their hair cut like a fuckin' shoe brush.' Rudi laughed as he reached behind him and jabbed an intercom on the wall. 'Daisy, three Red Juice Specials, right now.'

'Red Juice Specials?' Greg asked uneasily.

'Speciality of the maison,' Rudi said. He winked at Alex. 'From the guy's neck to your sweet lips, darlin'.'

Daisy came wobbling into the office in fishnet stockings and high heels, carrying a tray with three tall glasses of thick frothy red juice, iced, with cocktail umbrellas in. Greg stared at them and turned pale.

'Fucksamatter with him?' Rudi said.

'Greg's new to our ways,' Alex said.

Rudi beamed. 'Knew it. Not juicin' yet, huh, boy? Whaddaya, squeamish?'

'Shooting the enemy from a distance, even using a knife in close quarter battle, isn't quite the same as sinking your teeth in and drinking their blood,' Greg muttered, still gazing uneasily at the drinks.

'Relax, you ain't gonna kill anyone, tough guy,' Rudi rasped. 'You get yourself a juicy piece of ass – 'scuse my French, Alex – you bite her right here in the neck, you use the Vambloc after. Kills the

130

infection, she don't remember a thing and the holes heal up so fast, by the time she wakes up you can't even see 'em.' He roared with laughter. 'You're gonna love it, being a vampire. Man, once you get the taste for it, the buzz, the feel of the juice, still warm, flowin' down your throat . . . ain't a fuckin' feeling in the world like it.'

Alex sipped her Red Juice Special. The blood was fresh. 'Anyway, Rudi, we didn't come here to discuss the ethics of vampire nutrition. You said you had something for me.'

Rudi nodded. 'Yeah, well, there's something goin' on, sure as shit. I been hearing stuff. You remember Paulie Lomax, big guy, looks like a turkey?'

'Four-finger Paulie.'

'That's the guy. Know the rathouse pub down at the docks where he likes to drink?'

Alex nodded. 'Makes the Slaughtered Lamb look like Maxim's.'

'Well, Paulie Lomax told me that he and this buddy of his called Vinnie were down there one night last week when they got talking to these sailors. Guys couldn't speak hardly a word of English, but Paulie and Vinnie get the feeling they're seriously fuckin' freaked out about something. After a while they get it out of them that they were on a ship that came in from Eastern Europe someplace. Hardly any cargo on board, just these crates. You wanna know the weirdest? No paperwork. Customs let 'em right through.

131

Could have been fuckin' cocaine, guns, pluto-
nium. But it wasn't. Whatever it was, it put the
shits up 'em. Half the crew got sick.'

'Sick how?'

'Some kinda fever. But this was no ordinary
fever. Guys were getting nightmares, talking about
getting visited in the night in their bunks. And
getting sicker every night. Had these puncture
wounds on their necks. Right here. Ship's doc said
it was mosquito bites. I mean, mosquitoes in
fuckin' fur coats?'

'Go on,' Alex said, frowning.

'From what Paulie and Vinnie could make out,
a chopper came and took the cargo away before
they even got to port. Now the ship's still in the
docks. Captain wants to head home, but two of
the crew are missing and the rest won't get back
on board 'cause they say the ship's cursed.'

'Missing?' Greg said.

'Gone. And you know which crew members it
was? The ones who were sickest from the bites.
One minute they're lying raving in bed, next
they've upped and walked. Sounds like you know
what.'

Alex said, 'I think I need to talk to these sailors.'

Rudi smiled. 'Beat you to it. Paulie told Vinnie
to tell 'em that there's this woman who deals with
this kind of shit, a real expert. They wanna meet
you, tonight, at the dock. Said they found something.'

'Found what?'

Rudi shrugged. 'Whatever it is, sounds like a heavy deal.' He plucked a slip of paper out of his shirt and handed it to her. 'RV's all set up. Details are on here.'

Alex studied the paper. There was just the ship's name, the number of the dock, and the time. 'Midnight tonight,' she read out loud.

'I think it's gonna be worth your while,' Rudi said. 'Now let's go eat. My Brasato al Barolo don't wait for nobody.'

CHAPTER 24

Lavender Close, Wallingford

Joel's grandfather had always told him that even though vampires could theoretically come out of their lairs any time after dark, they preferred to wait until later in the evening when the humans were quiet and restful. And when they didn't kill their victims outright, they always returned for more.

'You must have totally lost it, Solomon,' Joel muttered to himself. For an instant it hit him how completely mad this was. Here he was, lurking behind the garden shed in the back of a nice middle-class suburban property at half past ten at night. Spaced out from lack of sleep, pins and needles crippling his legs after almost an hour of crouching there, and his nose beginning to run from the chill, damp air.

Thinking about vampires.

Suddenly, the whole thing seemed so absurd to him that he wanted to leave. What if somebody caught him here? A Detective Inspector, hanging about like a pervert in the dark, peering up at a seventeen-year-old girl's bedroom window. Not the best PR for the Thames Valley force, and certainly not an ideal career prospect for him.

But still he lingered there, fighting back the doubts, willing himself to endure the cramps and the cold.

He wished his grandfather were here with him. Joel had been thinking about him a lot recently. And here he was, following in his footsteps after all these years. Or trying to. The old man might have known what to do. Joel wasn't sure he had the first idea.

By quarter to eleven, the downstairs lights in the neighbouring houses were beginning to go off, and the upstairs lights were coming on. Curtains were being drawn, blurred figures were moving about behind the frosted glass of bathroom windows. Showers showering, teeth being brushed, the respectable middle-class inhabitants of Lavender Close pulling on their cosy pyjamas and perfume-scented nighties and getting into their warm beds, blissfully unaware of the night creeper in their midst.

And perhaps unaware of other things too. Things too strange and terrible to contemplate in this nice, safe, cosseted middle-class world.

By five past eleven, Joel was feeling desperately uncomfortable. This was plain ridiculous.

No it's not, said the voice in his mind. She has bites on her neck. She can't stand the sunlight. She's lying about the party. Something's happened to her.

She's theirs.
And they'll be back for her.

The houses became dark. Joel had to blow into his hands and rub them together to keep them from going numb with cold. He settled into a position that was as close to comfortable as he could make it, sitting in the dirt with his legs wedged up against the shed wall and his back to the fence. More time passed. His mind wandered. His eyelids were heavy. He felt them close, jerked them open. Felt them falling inexorably shut again . . . and then he was drifting through the void of sleep.

CHAPTER 25

'You can trust Rudi Bertolino,' Alex was saying to Rumble on her phone. She was standing on the kerbside a few yards from The Last Bite, watching the St James's Street traffic roar by. 'He's always come through for me, you know that.'

'It's not that I don't trust your informant,' Rumble said. 'I just don't like mysteries. And with all the rogue activity that's been going on I don't want you going in there alone with a rookie agent.'

'I'm on the clock here, Harry. Who've you got in the area?'

A pause, and she could hear Rumble clicking laptop keys in his quiet office. 'Okay. I'm sending Mundhra and Becker. They'll meet you at the RV point.'

'Copy that. You're a star, Harry.' Alex flipped her phone shut. 'Rumble's sending the troops in,' she said to Greg. 'Let's get back to the car.'

The Jaguar was parked up a sidestreet, less than two minutes' walk away. They headed up past Davidoff cigars and the Beretta boutique, a quiet stretch of street between the crowds around Rudi's

137

place and the hustle of Piccadilly. What seemed to be a pile of rags was lying on a doorstep. As they walked by, Alex saw it was a young homeless woman. The coat draped over her sleeping form was full of holes, and all her possessions were stuffed into a Tesco shopping bag next to her. Her hands and face looked emaciated, already prematurely aged from the life on the streets. Alex halted and gazed down at her.

'You're not going to . . .' Greg said.

'Feed from her?' Alex shook her head. 'They're easy, but most of them are too messed up with alcohol and drugs. Bad blood.' She sighed. 'No, I was just thinking how I almost feel sad for humans sometimes. Look at her.'

They walked on, and turned into the sidestreet where the Jag was parked. They were within twenty yards of it when three youths stepped out of a shadowy doorway and came right up to them, blocking the pavement.

Alex sized them up. They weren't asking for directions. The leader was the gangly white kid in the middle. He was grinning at her through a straggly moustache, and the matted dreadlocks plastered over his ears made him look like a spaniel. He reached into the pocket of his hoodie. Alex followed the movement and saw the cheap kitchen knife flash in his hand.

'Evening, folks. Let's have your money.' He ran his eye appreciatively up and down Alex's figure. His gaze settled on the Tag Heuer watch on her wrist. His grin widened. 'That's a grand's worth of watch the rich bitch is wearing,' he said to his cronies.

Alex turned to Greg. 'Now these specimens, on the other hand, I don't have too much sympathy for.'

'Shut the fuck up and give me your fucking *money*!'

Alex looked at him levelly. 'I don't think so, Dog Boy.'

'What did you call me?'

'You're going to look really funny with that knife sticking out of your arse.'

Dog Boy wagged the knife in Alex's face. 'I'll fucking kill you, bitch.'

'Too late,' she said, looking impassively at the blade. 'I'm already dead.'

'Wha—'

Before he could say any more, Alex had whipped the knife out of his hand and sent him flying over the bonnet of a parked Range Rover. As he scrambled desperately to his feet, his two friends turned and took to their heels.

'Not so fast, Dog Boy.' Alex grabbed him by his dreadlocks, picked him clear off the ground with one hand and held him there so that his feet flailed in mid-air. Ignoring his frantic struggles, she turned to Greg. 'Here's your opportunity.'

'What do you mean?'

'What do you *think* I mean? It's time.'

Greg looked pained. 'What, here?'

'This is how it works, Greg. We've been doing it this way for thousands of years. Just watch me, okay?' She could feel her fangs fully extended, pressing against her lips as she moved in close to the mugger's neck. He smelled unwashed, but all her senses were tuned into the blood pulsing just under his skin, in the canals of his veins. Throbbing. Luscious. Life-giving.

He squirmed and squealed like a trapped rat as her bite punctured his flesh. A few moments of delicious, gasping, teasing anticipation, more than erotic in its intensity, before the blood began to flow. Then she sucked and the warm juice was running over her tongue, trickling down her throat. She held him tight and sucked harder. It had been a long time since her last proper feed. Already she could feel her strength returning as she drank in the human's life energy.

She drank until she felt the mugger's body going limp in her grip, then pulled away with an effort. She wiped the blood off her lips, shoved him into Greg's hands. 'Now it's your turn.'

'I can't.'

'You have to. Do what I did. It's easy.'

'It's pretty horrible.'

'It's as natural as swimming is to a shark, Greg. You need to learn, or you're not going to make it.'

'I know. But some other time, okay?'

Alex sighed. 'Fine. Prop him up against the wall there.' She dropped down on her haunches, took the syringe of Vambloc from its case and jabbed it into the human's neck. He twitched, then slumped sideways and his head hit the pavement.

'Now we're good to go,' she said.

The Jag was just up the street.

'I've let you down, haven't I?' Greg muttered as they climbed into the car.

'Forget it.' Alex took off, pulled out into St James's and left snakes of rubber on the road heading up the hill towards Piccadilly.

CHAPTER 26

When Joel opened his eyes again, he realised with a start that he'd been sleeping. His clothes felt clammy and his body was suddenly racked with violent shivering. It was beginning to rain. He groaned at the time on his watch. How could he have been—?

At that moment, he saw something move on Kate's balcony.

He froze. His heart stopped, then began to pound rapidly.

The figure was barely visible in the darkness. He watched it creep to the edge of the balcony. Heard the tiny snick of the latch as it closed the French window of the girl's room behind it. It paused for a second at the balcony rail, then in one fluid movement, almost faster than Joel's eye could follow, it leapt effortlessly over the rail and dropped down into the garden with barely a sound.

Joel was rooted to the spot, terrified to move or even breathe. In that instant, all his childhood fears came flooding back. For seconds that seemed like hours, he was paralysed. It took a supreme effort to force himself to crawl to the edge of the shed so that he could watch the figure make its way across the dark garden.

Through the mist he could see it was a tall man, dressed in black, walking calmly, purposefully, towards the back gate and the little passageway that wound between the rear gardens of the houses.

Joel scrambled to his feet. He staggered out from behind the shed, heart thumping so loudly he was sure the man would hear it from twenty-five yards away. The rain was steadily becoming heavier as he stepped out into the passageway in time to see the shadowy figure disappear round the corner, already fifty yards ahead, walking fast. Joel broke into a jog. Rounding the corner he spotted the man again.

His innards squirmed.

Was this even a man he was following?

He swallowed back his terror and broke into a run. Maybe it was the most insane thing he'd done in his life, but there was no stopping now.

'Armed police officer!' The words burst out of his lungs, and there was no masking the shrill note of fear in his voice. 'Stop where you are. You're surrounded.'

The figure halted in the shadows, then turned slowly around to look at him.

The rain was pouring now. Joel couldn't make out the man's face, but he could feel the gaze on him, penetrating him to the core, making him feel utterly naked and vulnerable.

And somehow he knew what it was thinking.

You're all alone, human.

It stepped towards him. The face still in shadow, but Joel thought he saw a smile appear on its lips. It took another step.

Joel blinked the rain out of his eyes. Swallowed hard. His mind scrambled desperately. Searching back twenty years. What would his grandfather have done in this moment?

'The cross,' he shouted. 'I have it. The cross . . .' Joel felt his blood icing up as he struggled to remember. He almost bit off his own tongue as it came to him. '. . . of Ardaich!'

The figure stiffened. The head cocked imperceptibly to one side.

'I have it,' Joel said again, mustering up all the strength he could put into his voice. 'It's here. I have the cross, vampire.'

And the thing suddenly turned and ran, its light footsteps echoing in the passage. Joel stood there for a moment, rooted, then sprinted after it. Now he knew what he was chasing, and it was more than he could bear – but he closed his mind and ran on, harder. The passage twisted left, then right, then opened up into the street. The figure moved like an Olympic champion. It vaulted over a wall, crossing a children's play area in three bounding strides. Joel could see an exotic sports car parked up ahead under the dim streetlights. The futuristic gull-wing doors opened, and the figure clambered inside. The engine fired up with an aggressive rasp, and the car took off, wheels spinning on the wet road.

Joel recognised it. A McLaren F1. Just about the fastest production car ever built, a machine he'd never seen before in real life. It made a sound like a Formula One racing car as it screamed away, slaloming at high speed through the vehicles parked in the narrow street. Snatching a glimpse of the registration number, Joel committed it to memory.

The car was almost out of sight when he spotted a single motorcycle headlight coming the other way. The McLaren bore down on it, forcing the rider to swerve. The bike mounted the kerb, hit a patch of grass and skidded sideways. The rider tumbled into the gutter and the machine slid across the pavement with a grinding of metal. Joel broke into a run. The rider was struggling to his feet by the time he reached him, flipping up his rain-spotted visor.

'You all right?'

'The bastard ran me off the road!'

'I saw. Listen, police emergency. I need your bike.' Before the rider could stutter a reply, Joel had bent down and grasped the bars of the fallen bike. It was a sports model, a Yamaha R1. Fast. Not nearly as fast as a thoroughbred race car, but he still had a chance.

The Yamaha's engine was still ticking over. Joel heaved the machine upright with a grunt of effort. Threw his leg over and hammered it into gear, opened the throttle wide and dumped the clutch. The front end lifted off the ground and he hung on tight as the bike accelerated manically away up the street after the disappearing McLaren. With no helmet, the wind roar was deafening. The raindrops were like bullets of ice. It felt as if they could tear his face off. But the pain didn't matter. All that mattered were the McLaren's taillights. Joel screamed after them, head down behind the machine's skimpy Perspex screen, nailing the throttle wide open and his speedometer reading a hundred and forty miles an hour as he blasted out of Wallingford into the dark country roads.

Within a minute, Joel was riding faster than he'd ever done in his life. It was all he could do to keep the Yamaha between the hedges – and still the McLaren was losing him.

Voices resonated in Joel's head.

This is madness. You're going to kill yourself.

And if you catch him. Then what? This is no ordinary criminal. This is a . . .

Vampire. Joel couldn't bring himself to say it, not even in his thoughts.

The McLaren hurtled onwards, steadily increasing the distance between itself and the speeding motorbike. A series of bends came swooping up, almost faster than Joel could react. He threw his weight across the saddle, dragging the machine down into a crazy leaning angle as he sliced into the first left-hander; then, just as he'd made it through that one, he had to hurl the bike over to the right, the road flashing by just inches from his body. Out of the bends and straight on with the gas. Wheelspin at over a hundred miles an hour into the blinding rain.

Joel knew he couldn't keep this level of concentration up much longer. He was going to crash.

Village signs flashed by faster than he could read them. At a hundred and sixty miles an hour the narrow little street was an amber-lit tunnel. The McLaren was moving even faster. Suddenly, a van pulled out of a sidestreet and started turning in the narrow road. The sports car braked hard, swerved to avoid it and spun wildly. It smashed through a garden fence, sending up a shower of torn planking and jagged splinters, then went careening across a lawn before it rejoined the road.

Joel saw he'd gained precious seconds on his quarry – but in the same instant he was almost on the van as it kept turning out across his path. There was no time to brake. He aimed the bike at the rapidly narrowing gap between the van's front wing and the wall of the house opposite. For a terrifying fraction of a second he thought he was going to hit it, go smashing right through the brickwork like a missile and end up as a pile of dead meat in someone's living room. He tucked in his knees and elbows, ducked in low behind the dials, and then somehow he was safely through the gap and roaring onwards up the street after the frenziedly accelerating McLaren.

They were heading towards the outer limits of the village now. A roadsign whipped by, almost too fast for Joel to register that there was a level crossing coming up ahead. Warning beacons were flashing, a bell was ringing. The barriers were down, blocking the road. Beyond the barriers was the clattering rumble of a train streaking by.

The McLaren's brake lights blazed red as it screeched to a halt. The vampire was trapped. The only sidestreet was blocked by a sprawl of building works that stretched from the roadside to the edge of the tracks: Portacabins, tall heaped piles of sand and gravel, cement mixers.

Joel suddenly found himself gaining fast on the car. His heart began to flutter. The chase might be over but the danger was only just beginning. As he shut the throttle and let the bike decelerate, he was imagining the car door opening. The driver getting out. Immortal. Unstoppable.

And no fool. It would know just from the look on his face that he'd been bluffing, he didn't have some mythical cross on him. Then what? He didn't want to imagine what would happen next.

But the car door didn't open. The McLaren seemed to hesitate for just an instant, then its engine rasped and it slewed round in a tight circle and came right for him.

Joel hit the front brake – too hard. The wheel lost traction on the wet road, and with a sickening lurch he felt the front end go out from underneath him. The crash seemed to happen in slow motion. He felt himself sailing through the air. A grunt exploded from his lungs as he hit the ground. The bike slid on its side, sparks showering up from the tarmac. The blinding car headlights sped towards him.

Joel put out his hand just as the car seemed about to run him over.

It didn't happen. Fifteen yards from where he lay sprawled on the wet road, the McLaren skidded into a handbrake turn. Fire crackled in its exhaust muzzles and smoke poured from the wheel arches as it accelerated frenetically back in the direction of the moving train.

Joel held his breath in anticipation of the devastating impact. But just a few yards short of the level crossing barrier the McLaren veered off course. It aimed at the building works near the tracks and hit the tall sand pile at more than eighty miles an hour. Its engine revs screamed as it took off like an aircraft, and with a huge cloud of sand in its wake it sailed straight over the top of the barriers and cleared the roof of the train by inches. He heard the *crump* and the squeal and bounce of tyres as it hit the road on the other side. Then it was gone.

Seconds later, the train had passed by and Joel could see the car's taillights disappearing up the dark country road into the distance.

He struggled to his feet, wiping the grit from his grazed, bloodied hands.

The level crossing barriers were beginning to

rise. With all his remaining strength, Joel wrenched the fallen Yamaha upright – then saw the left handlebar hanging uselessly from its shattered yoke, the broken clutch lever, the hydraulic fluid leaking all over the road. He yelled in rage and let the damaged bike topple over with a crash.

It was three minutes to midnight. He started limping back up the road the way he'd come.

CHAPTER 27

Two minutes to midnight, and claws of mist were groping in from the river as Alex and Greg walked along the deserted quays of the London docks. To their left stood rows of storage units in varying states of repair, and the dark water gurgled against the quayside on their right. The hulls of vast ships bobbed slowly on the swell and cast heavy shadows on the concrete. A dog barked somewhere in the distance. Across the water, the lights of new docklands residential developments were haloed in the mist.

'You're pissed off with me, aren't you?'

Alex said nothing.

'I can tell. Because of what happened earlier.'

'I'm not pissed off with you. I'm worried about you. You can't keep holding out like this, living on vampire baby food. Rudi's right. You're going to have to cross the bridge. Otherwise—'

'I'll die?'

'No, you won't die. You can't die. What'll happen to you is a lot worse than death. You'll wither. You'll become trapped in a twilight world that you'll never be able to escape from. A wraith is what you'll be.'

He looked down at his feet as they walked. 'Is it normal? I mean, do other people, I mean, vampires, do they—'

'Have trouble adapting to it?' She nodded. 'Some. It happens.'

'What was it like for you? The first time?'

'It was easy,' she said.

'I shouldn't have asked. Sorry.'

'It's okay. I don't mind talking about it. It was easy for me because I wanted revenge.'

'Revenge?'

She paused, took a breath. 'When I was twenty-nine, I was engaged to someone. His name was William. The only man I ever loved. He was an artist.' She sighed. 'One night he was walking across Hampstead Heath when three men robbed him and knifed him. He managed to stagger home, but by the time I was called it was too late. He died in my arms. Nothing I could do except hold him until he was gone.'

'I'm sorry.'

'I used to walk out across the Heath at night afterwards. I'd go to the spot where it happened, sit there for hours. I didn't even care if I got murdered. As it turned out, someone did get me. But it wasn't a murderer. And I wanted it to happen. Because that was the only way I could get back at the men who'd killed William. It didn't take me long to find them. And they paid. *That* was my first time. 1897.'

'You still miss William?' Greg asked after a beat.

'Yeah, I do miss him.'

'A hundred and thirteen years is a long time to grieve.'

She nodded. 'Yes, it's a very long time,' she said quietly. 'A lot has changed. I was Alexandra then.'

'That's a nice name.'

'She was a nice person. I miss her too, sometimes.' Alex was going to say more, then stopped.

They walked on a few yards in silence.

'So . . . you aren't seeing anyone right now?' Greg asked.

Alex looked at him curiously.

'I mean, do you live alone, or what?'

She wrinkled her nose. 'Are you by any chance hitting on me, Agent Shriver?'

'You have a really great smile.'

'I'm not smiling.'

'Yes, you are. You were just then. See, there you go again.'

'Definitely not smiling.'

They'd walked a long way from the car. The angular shape of a cargo ship loomed up over them, hardly moving on the swell, just a slight sway of its towering superstructure as the water lapped and splashed against its long, rusted hull. The white stencilled lettering on the vessel's bows spelt out *Anica*.

'That's our ship,' Alex said. Her watch read after midnight. 'But no sailors.'

A sound from the shadows of the storage units

made her turn suddenly. Her face tightened, then she recognised the VIA agents as they approached. 'Becker. Mundhra.'

'It's been a while,' Mundhra said.

Alex nodded. 'This is Agent Shriver,' she said, motioning at Greg. 'Looks like we've been stood up. They were supposed to meet us here four minutes ago.'

'Rumble's gonna be pissed off,' Becker said.

'Maybe they went on board,' Mundhra suggested.

'They were too scared to,' Greg replied. 'That's what we were told, anyway.'

Becker grinned. 'Scared of what? Anyone tell them they were RVing with four vampires out here?'

'Fuck it, I'm not standing here waiting all night,' Alex said. 'Let's check out the vessel. Whatever these guys wanted to show us, we can find ourselves.'

They boarded the *Anica* via a creaky gangway. Most of the ship's length was empty deck, as long and broad as a football field, littered with stacks of oil drums and debris and coils of thick rope, battered steel shipping containers scattered here and there. The superstructure rose up like a dark tower block. Not a single window was lit up. The vessel was like a ghost ship. Alex led the team up clattering steps to a wire mesh walkway high above the water. Through an open hatch, and they found themselves wandering through dark, narrow passages that twisted left and right through the bowels of the ship.

'You would think there'd be someone on board,' Greg said. 'Everything's been left open.' Alex didn't reply, but she'd been thinking the same thing. After a few more turns and a few more open hatchways, they came to a deserted canteen with plastic chairs and tables.

'Someone was here,' Mundhra said, pointing at the half-eaten food on plates on one of the tables. A chair was overturned. 'And left in a hurry,' he added.

'We'll keep looking,' Alex said.

On the next level down, they could hear the echoey creaking of the ship's hull. It seemed almost alive, breathing, like being inside the belly of a giant whale. Pipes and ducts snaked along the grimy metal walls and low ceilings.

'I can smell something,' Alex murmured. She followed her nose a little way further. Put her left hand out and gently pushed open a hatch marked 'STORAGE' as she silently drew her pistol with her right.

Then Greg could smell it too, and experience told him what it was. If he'd still been a human, he'd have been puking out his guts.

They'd found the ship's crew. And until someone found another for hire, the *Anica* wasn't leaving the Port of London in a hurry.

Dim light streamed into the room through a single porthole. The ship's crew had been using the place as a dump for scrap – a burnt-out winch motor, bits of old chain and cable, piles of rusty bolts, lengths of scaffold pipe.

But it wasn't the heaped junk that Alex was looking at. The storage room looked as if it had been hosed down in blood. Gallons of blood. The walls were caked with dried purple-brown swirls of it. Pools had collected in the hollows of the floor, some of the larger ones still wet and congealing. The floor was scattered with body parts so torn and mutilated that it was hard to tell what some of them were. Those that were still recognisable as human arms and legs, heads and pieces of torso, were pale and shrivelled, almost mummified.

'They were drained,' Alex said. 'Probably while they were still alive. Then whoever did this tore them apart.' She stepped over a half-eaten ribcage. 'There are five, maybe six men here. I'm guessing these are the guys we thought we were here to meet.'

Greg was about to say something when the claustrophobic space around them was filled with blasting noise.

Becker had been standing at his shoulder, surveying the scene inside the room. Suddenly he was flying forward, pitching over on his face, screaming in agony, his legs kicking out.

For an eighth of a second, Alex stared down at him. Watched the grotesque swelling of his flesh, his face distorting, the veins standing out from the skin. Reaching burst-point and then erupting in a spray of gore. Even before Becker had spattered like a ripe tomato in a vice, she knew what she was seeing.

The effects of a Nosferol bullet.

CHAPTER 28

Out of the shadows of the passageway came six fleeting, running shapes; and suddenly the darkness was filled with bursts of white-yellow flame as their attackers opened up with automatic gunfire. Alex threw herself flat on the floor and saw the others do the same. Bullets whipped past and slammed into the walls behind them. She caught glimpses of the attackers by the strobe lights of the muzzle flashes.

The leader was female. Her long hair was jet black and wild. The red leather jumpsuit she was wearing could have been painted onto her slim, curvaceous figure. She was cradling a Heckler & Koch submachine gun, and a sword in a scabbard dangled from the gunbelt around her narrow waist.

Behind her was one of the biggest men Alex had ever seen. He was more than six and a half feet tall, and the combat vest he was wearing stretched tightly over his muscular chest and shoulders. His bulk contrasted sharply with the ferret-like, darting shape of the guy next to him. Behind him, another woman, blonde, studded white leather biker jacket, gripping a stubby pistol like she knew how to use it. The rear was brought up by an Oriental male and a Teutonic-looking, sharp-featured female with cropped brown hair, who was clutching a grenade launcher.

They'd walked into a trap. But these six were no vampire hunters. Alex could recognise her own species with split-second intuition. These were vampires. Hunting their own kind. She could worry about the reason why later.

As Greg and Mundhra scrambled for cover, Alex lashed out with her foot. Her heel connected hard with the hatch door and it slammed shut with a juddering clang before the attackers could reach it. She leapt to her feet and jumped over Becker's ruined body to grab a length of scaffold pole from the bloody floor. She wedged it between the hatch door and the opposite wall just in time. Something rammed against the door with the force of a battering ram. The door quivered, but held. Muted gunfire came from outside. Bullets raked the steel and punched a wild pattern of dents in it that jutted proud like rivet heads.

Alex and Greg looked at each other. 'You thinking what I'm thinking?' she said.

'Grenade launcher.'

And if the grenade was primed with Nosferol, in a few seconds the room would be no place for vampires to be hanging about. Alex snatched up

Becker's fallen 9mm Walther and leapt across the butcher's yard in the middle of the room, using the muzzle of the gun to punch out the glass in the porthole. She sprang up into the deep, round recess in the wall and scrambled through. Outside, the cold wind whipped her hair over her face. She dropped ten feet down the side of the hull and landed softly on a walkway. Looking up, she saw Greg emerge and drop down to land beside her, then Mundhra. They sprinted away along the clattering walkway, heading towards the deck.

Less than two seconds later a deafening blast and a shriek of ripping metal shook the ship. The attackers had breached the hatch. Alex glanced back to see the black-haired female leap from the smoking porthole and land like a gymnast on the walkway behind them. The huge black guy came thudding down in her wake, then the others. The woman opened fire with the submachine gun and bullets screamed off the metal wall by Alex's head.

Then it was sixty seconds of frantic sprinting, zigzagging, staying low while bullets zipped all around them, ricochets howling off the walkway rail and the steel floor. Alex leapt down a further fifteen feet to the deck and hit the ground running. Greg was close behind, followed by Mundhra. They retreated up the deck as the attackers kept coming, using the stacks of drums and other ship debris as cover while they

160

returned fire. Greg dropped into a crouch, took careful aim and let off a string of rapid shots that took down the sharp-faced female with the grenade launcher before she could fire another round and blow them all to pieces. Before she'd even hit the deck, she was bursting open like a sausage on a hot grill and her blood was spattering in a wide circle. A voice screamed out *'Petra!'*

With Becker's Walther in one hand and her own Desert Eagle in the other, Alex chased the Oriental vampire in her sights as he leapt behind a stack of crates and old rope. She squeezed off four rounds from each so fast it sounded like one continuous explosion. The strangled shriek and the blood burst from behind the crates told her that now it was three against four. Maybe the odds were evening up. Maybe.

Mundhra gave her the thumbs-up as he aimed his pistol over an oil drum. In the split second that he took his eyes off the enemy, the black-haired female rattled off a string of rounds at him. Mundhra ducked, but not before one of her bullets had sent his gun spinning out of his hand. He yelled in pain and rage as the weapon clattered across the deck. He took a chance and went rolling out to retrieve it.

Too big a chance. The woman chased him with another sustained burst of automatic fire and his body went into spasm as bullets punched a ragged line of holes through his chest. His tortured eyes

161

met Alex's as he went down – then he was spattering across the deck in a shiny slick of blood and meat.

Now it was just Alex and Greg against four, and they were being steadily beaten back towards the ship's great square prow. Alex fired Becker's gun until it was empty, tossed it, then blasted off shots from her Desert Eagle until that was empty too. She did a lightning reload and realised with a shock that she was down to her last magazine.

Greg called across to her. 'I'm out.'

Bullets were whipping and pinging all over the place. They both fell back, pinned with nowhere to go, rolling and scrambling over heaps of debris and coils of rope and chain. Risking a glance over the edge of the hull, Alex could see the mooring cables like silvery spider thread in the moonlight, stretching between the hull and the quay, gently flexing with the movement of the ship. She tossed her Desert Eagle to Greg.

'Make them count.'

As Greg kept their enemies' heads down with steady, well-aimed covering fire, Alex whipped off her belt and looped it over the cable. She thumped his shoulder.

'Hold on to me,' she yelled. He rattled off the last three shots, stuck the gun in his belt and grabbed hold of her waist as she launched herself over the edge, one end of the belt in each hand. The wind tore at their clothes and bullets whipped by them as they abseiled wildly down the cable. The concrete quayside came up fast and they hit the ground running. Alex pointed at the dark clusters of storage units, twenty yards away across the dock.

'That way.'

Glancing back at the ship, she saw what she'd known she would see – their attackers were already swarming over the side and coming after them. The female leader used her gun to ride the mooring cable. Ten feet from the quayside she launched herself into the air, twisted like a cat and landed square on her feet, her eyes shining in the dim moonlight, weapon ready.

Unarmed, Alex and Greg could do nothing but run. They ducked into the shadows, but the woman had spotted them. Furious gunfire raked the walls of the buildings, dust and stone fragments flying, windows exploding into shards.

A door on the left was heavily padlocked and bore a sign that read 'THAMES RIB TOURS'. Alex booted it open with a splintering of wood and they burst inside. It was a storage depot with a flight of concrete steps that led down to a gated boathouse. Five large speedboats were tethered up, drifting gently on the water.

'RIBs,' Greg said. 'Rigid inflatables. Navy SEALs use them.'

Alex leapt into the nearest of the boats. It had been heavily adapted for taking sightseers up and down the Thames tourist trail, but it was the massive Yamaha inboard engines that mattered.

She grabbed the steel cable that secured the boat to the wall and yanked it out with a big chunk of brickwork.

'Make it go.'

Greg jumped in. His jaw was set as he urgently examined the control panel at the helm. He found the ignition switch, hammered the starter. The twin diesels churned into life with an eager roar and white foam boiled up around the props.

And the door of the storage unit came crashing off its hinges. Their pursuers burst inside the building, shooting wildly. Rounds thunked into the fibreglass of the boat and shattered the windscreen. Alex was thrown back into the boat as Greg nailed the throttle wide open and aimed the RIB at the chained wooden gates of the boat-house. They went smashing through, planks and splinters flying, the nose of the speedboat rising high out of the water under hard acceleration. Then they were roaring down the Thames, bouncing on the water, ducking down behind the shattered windscreen. Greg's temple had been gashed from a flying splinter and there was blood on his face.

'Who *are* those people?' he yelled over the noise.

'Vampires,' she yelled back.

'Why? What's happening?'

She glanced back at the docks, now far away beyond the tail of their foaming white wake. The *Anica* was a hulking shadow against the gloomy quayside. No sign of anyone coming after them. But she knew they would. Vampires didn't give up as easily as humans.

'Make it go faster,' she shouted.

He pointed at a gauge on the control panel. 'I'm going as fast as I can, but something's taken a hit and we're losing oil pressure.'

Within three minutes, Alex could see the lights of a second speedboat coming up behind them. It was a long way back, but gaining rapidly.

'Let's lose some weight.' She grabbed hold of one of the RIB's dozen passenger seats and ripped it from its mounting, tossed it tumbling into their wake. Then another.

'Pressure still dropping,' Greg yelled over his shoulder.

Two more minutes, and now their pursuers were just a couple of hundred yards back. Alex tensed, waiting for the first shot. Across the dark water, the London nightscape was alive with light and movement. The Houses of Parliament and Big Ben were lit gold in the distance. Their ears filled with the booming echo of the engine roar as they passed under the arches of Westminster Bridge; then they flashed out the other side and Alex could see the illuminated glass pods of the London Eye suspended high in the sky, and the tiny figures milling about inside them.

'She's going to die on us,' Greg shouted.

Alex felt the whip of a bullet pass close to her, and looked back to see the second RIB drawing dangerously close. There were spits of fire as muzzles flashed. Another Nosferol-tipped round shattered the glass of the instrument panel six inches from Greg's body.

Almost instantly, the engines began to chatter and then stall. A final cough, and then nothing. The boat began to drift.

'Here we go,' Greg said. 'Trip's over.'

CHAPTER 29

Bullets churned up the water as they floated towards the Millennium Pier. Ten feet, five, and Alex sprang up onto the prow of the dead speedboat.

'Come on!'

Without hesitation she leapt through the air and clambered up the side of the pier. She reached out an arm to haul Greg up behind her, and then they were running towards the lights and the crowds of people milling about the foot of the gigantic wheel of the London Eye. A party was going on; it looked to Alex like some kind of corporate event – women in expensive dresses, men in dark suits and ties. Inside the slow-moving pods people were sipping champagne, nibbling canapés, laughing, chattering animatedly. She and Greg attracted a few stares as they pressed through the throng. A fat woman stumbled and dropped her glass with an outraged 'Excuse *me*!' as Alex shoved her out of the way.

The other four vampires weren't far behind. Alex saw their leader heading fast towards them, scanning the crowd. The sword slapped her thigh as she ran.

These idiot humans would think it was fancy dress.

Alex and Greg joined a press of people funnelling inside one of the pods as it passed slowly by on the end of its gigantic steel lattice-work arm. Alex dabbed the blood from Greg's face with a handkerchief as they boarded. 'Whatever happens, stay close to me.'

'I can take care of myself,' he muttered.

'These aren't Taliban insurgents, Greg. You're in my world now.'

As they were about to enter the pod, a stocky guy in a plain suit stepped up to them. The earpiece and mike he was wearing told Alex he was a security official. He ran a cold eye over them. 'Excuse me, folks. You're aware this is a private party, yeah? Can I see your invitations?'

Alex raised a hand. 'Back off, pal. Leave us alone, or I'm going to rip your spine out through your mouth.' She said it with enough sincerity that the guy frowned, paled, then swallowed hard and took a step back. 'Wise choice,' she said as he disappeared back into the crowd.

They stepped onboard and soon the pod was rising slowly into the air. A panoramic view across London opened up below. Alex peered down and saw the black-haired woman shoving through the crowd. The same security guy who'd approached them a moment ago walked up to her and Alex could tell he was demanding to see her invite. Just then, the other three vampires appeared at the woman's side and the security guy began to look nervous all over again. But whatever it was he was trying to stammer out, he didn't finish. The woman stared at him contemptuously for a second, pulled out a pistol and shot him between the eyes, in the middle of the crowd.

'Wasn't his day, was it?' Alex said. She turned to Greg. 'We're going to have company.'

Down below, the party was erupting into mayhem. The crowd dispersed like a shoal of minnows at the approach of a great white shark. The animated buzz of conversation and laughter instantly gave way to screams of panic. The woman stood calmly over the fallen body of the security official. There was blood on her face where his brains had splattered at point-blank range. She wiped a finger through the red on her cheek and sucked it clean. Her cold gaze ran upwards and her eyes locked on Alex's. She pointed and said something to the big man. He grinned. Then all four of them raised their weapons and opened fire.

The glass panels of the pod blew apart, fragments raining down from the ceiling. The pod's other occupants began to scream in terror. A man clutched his arm, blood pumping through his fingers. Another woman was screaming as she clamped her hand over a torn earlobe.

'We need to go higher,' Alex said. She shoved past the petrified humans and launched herself up through the shattered roof.

'I think you're right,' Greg said as he quickly

followed her. A second volley of shots punched through the pod. The humans huddled on the floor, moaning and shrieking.

Standing on the roof of the pod, Alex and Greg were surrounded by the white steel latticework of tubular struts that held the arms of the enormous wheel on its axis. The metal was slick with moisture from the drifting mist, slippery to the touch. If Alex had a plan, it was simply to keep putting distance between them and the enemy until the four vampires ran out of ammunition. Just a scratch from a Nosferol bullet, and it was game over.

The wind crackled in their ears as they hauled and swung themselves from one strut to another. Two tiny spiders on a gigantic steel web three hundred feet across. Alex looked down; they were already a long way above the pod. Greg was making his own way up, ten feet below her and a little way to the right. The river was a black mirror shimmering with coloured lights. The spangled cityscape sprawled all around as far as the eye could see. It was a dizzy drop down, but that was the last thing on Alex's mind.

She knew she'd made a bad mistake. The four vampires had split up. She couldn't see the other three, but the black-haired female had boarded a pod. As it steadily rose into the air, the motion of the wheel was bringing her and Greg downwards in relation to it. In minutes they'd be level with one another. Alex climbed on, using all her vampire strength to keep moving faster – but the laws of physics were an opponent nobody could defeat.

The dark female punched out the glass side of her pod. She stepped out onto the arm with a smile and walked nonchalantly towards Alex. Leaning on a vertical strut, she crossed her arms. 'Going somewhere?' she purred.

'Oh, I come up here all the time,' Alex said.

'You're Alex Bishop, aren't you? Heard all about you, but you don't know me. My name's Lillith. Thought you'd like to know who destroyed you.' She shrugged, then pulled the gun from her belt and aimed at Alex's face. Taking her time, drawing it out.

A gust of wind caught her unawares. Her foot slipped on the shiny, wet steel piping and she lost balance. Grabbing for a strut, she knocked the gun from her grip and it went clanging and tumbling down through the lattice to the water far below.

'Clever,' Alex said.

Lillith flushed, but quickly regained her composure. 'Who needs a gun? More fun this way.' She grabbed the hilt of the sword at her hip, drew out the blade with a ringing of steel and lunged at Alex.

If Alex had stayed where she was, the whooshing sword would have taken her head off. Instead she ducked, moving in towards Lillith's body, and threw a right hook that connected hard with her face. The punch would have knocked a human out cold. Vampires were a little tougher than that. Lillith went sprawling on her back on the pipe, but sprang instantly back on her feet and came on again with the sword poised. Another humming sideways slice, so fast a human wouldn't even have seen death coming.

It takes a vampire to destroy a vampire properly. Alex recalled the words she'd spoken in Romania just days ago. In a quarter of a second the blade was going to chop through her windpipe, carve through her neck and separate the spinal vertebrae on its way out. Her head would hit the water just before her body.

Quarter of a second was enough. Alex stepped back out of the swing of the blade and let herself drop down twenty feet, landing on a broad strut below. She'd lost sight of Greg in the forest of white steel. Where was he?

Lillith peered down at her for an instant, then launched herself into space and landed ten feet away.

The motion of the wheel had brought another pod level with them – and Alex saw that the massive black vampire was in it, accompanied by his weaselly little friend and the blonde in the white leather jacket. The big guy crashed through the glass as though it was nothing and walked out towards them, a 9mm pistol like a toy in his fist.

'Leave her to me, Zachary,' Lillith yelled. But before she could finish, the weaselly one had produced a gun and let off a shot. The bullet sang off a thick pipe inches from Alex's head. At the same instant, Lillith let out a shriek and dropped the sword, clutching her wrist. She'd been hit by the bullet's ricochet. For an instant there was wild terror in her eyes as she anticipated the first bite of the Nosferol's effects; then she peeled back the sleeve of her red jumpsuit, and Alex saw the dented gold bracelet on her wrist that had saved her.

'Anton, you fucking *moron!*' Lillith hissed furiously at the weaselly guy.

He frowned apologetically, letting the gun waver, then tightened his grip and started to bring it back up to aim. His second shot was going to find its mark. But Alex wasn't hanging around for it.

Instead, she threw herself off the wheel.

The white pipework flashed by as she went hurtling down in freefall, and the ground rushed up to meet her. Vampires could take a lot of damage, but she'd never pushed her luck as far as leaping two hundred feet down onto concrete. She was about to find out whether it was survivable.

The impact knocked the breath out of her. She knew to flex her knees to prevent her thigh bones spearing up through her shoulder blades, and to roll like a parachutist. Stunned, she lay there for a moment or two while she tried to ascertain whether her body was still intact or whether she was going to spend the rest of eternity as a pile of mincemeat. Someone screamed in horror. Voices around her.

'Jesus Christ. Did you see that?'

'She fell.'

'Fuck no, she jumped.'

'Ambulance must be on its way.'

'Is she dead?'

'I think she is, yeah.'

'Course she's bloody dead.'

'Oh my God . . .'

Alex stirred, then picked herself up off the concrete and dusted her hands. She seemed to be okay. The crowd that had gathered round her backed off sharply. People were gasping, pointing. Another scream, if anything more shocked than before. Apparently, the only thing scarier than witnessing a suicide was when the body upped and walked away.

Partygoers were milling around at the foot of the Eye in the wake of the shooting. Most were pale and silent, huddled in corners like disaster survivors as they waited in shock for the emergency services to arrive. Women wept in their men's arms. Someone had laid a coat over the dead body of the security guy. The howl of sirens was getting close. It sounded like half the police force and a hundred ambulances were carving through the London traffic towards them.

Alex peered up at the towering wheel. No sign of Greg anywhere. Maybe the fight had given him the chance to escape – but she hadn't seen him come down. Had he managed to board another pod? She narrowed her eyes.

Greg, where are you?

Lillith was a tiny figure perched high above. Not even she was crazy enough to attempt a leap like that.

Alex knew what she was thinking. *We'll meet again.*

And it was something Alex was looking forward to as well.

She let her gaze linger just a moment longer. Then, as the ambulances and police cars came screaming into sight and the place was suddenly swirling with blue lights, she slipped away.

CHAPTER 30

Oxford
12.50 a.m.

T he rain was turning heavy as Mickey Thompson walked through the empty city centre, but he didn't care about getting wet. The atmosphere of the party he'd just left was still with him, making him smile. But the thing that was really putting the spring in his step as he walked past Carfax Tower and headed down the slick High Street pavement towards his digs was the memory of Sally Baker.

He'd worshipped her from afar ever since he'd first bumped into her in the mathematics section at the college library. Three whole terms had gone by, and he'd never been able to pluck up the courage to ask her out. But tonight he'd done it. And she'd said yes.

Mickey made a fist as he walked. *Yes!* So it was dinner, tomorrow night. Then he remembered how late it was. Not tomorrow, today. Even better. He began to worry about where to take her. He couldn't afford much on his postgrad allowance, but he really needed to make an impression here. How about that nice little French brasserie on Little Clarendon Street? Or maybe Chinese? Or was that too obvious? Mexican? Too spicy, maybe.

Those were the happy concerns that filled his mind as he wandered all the way down the High Street, humming a little tune to himself, until he reached the cobbled lane that wound past the Radcliffe Camera.

Mickey Thompson suddenly froze. Stopped, and very slowly turned.

No, he must have imagined it. But he could have sworn someone was there behind him.

He shrugged and kept walking through the rain. *Must have been the wine.*

He walked on under the looming shadow of the circular Radcliffe Camera building.

Hold on. There *was* someone there.

He could hear padding footsteps a few yards behind him. He turned again, and this time he saw the figure.

It stood on the edge of a sodium streetlamp's diffuse amber haze. A tall man, dressed all in black, his body seeming to melt into the shadows. But Mickey could see the long, lean face, and he could see that the man was looking at him. There was a strange glint in his eye. Was that a smile on his thin lips?

Mickey walked faster now, his steps becoming jerky with tension. He glanced over his shoulder through the wet mist. The man was still there, keeping pace with him. Should he turn and confront him? If this was a mugging, could he avoid trouble by offering the guy some money to go away? But something about the man told Mickey he was no mugger. He wanted something else. But what?

Mickey couldn't stand it any longer – he broke into a run. His heart was in his mouth and the sound of his footsteps echoed off the college buildings as he rounded the corner and headed down New College Lane. Up ahead of him, the gothic archway of the Bridge of Sighs hung darkly over the narrow street, the streetlights glinting off its rain-streaked leaded windows. Just a hundred yards further and Mickey would be at the door of the flat he shared with two other postgrad mathematicians. He fumbled for his keys as he ran – and dropped them.

As he groped cursing in the shadowy gutter to retrieve the keys, he realised the man was gone. He let out a wheezing gasp of relief.

'You stupid bugger,' he muttered to himself. 'What's got into you?'

That was when the chill feeling of dread came over him. It started at his toes and spread quickly through his body, and it wasn't because his clothes were damp. It was that horrible feeling that he was being watched. As if by a predator.

He looked up, afraid of what he was going to see.

It was the man in black. He stood framed in the

ornate centre window of the bridge, ten feet above his head.

Mickey backed away. His jaw dropped open.

With a crashing of breaking glass, the man leapt from the window and landed on his feet like a cat on the pavement in front of Mickey.

And before Mickey Thompson could turn and run, let out a scream or wet his pants in terror, the man was on him and he felt the teeth savaging his throat.

London

Alex flipped open her phone and speed-dialled Rumble as she pressed the Jag through the night traffic. It was just after one a.m.

'Jesus, Harry, I've been trying to call you.'

'I was feeding. What's happened?'

'It was a trap. We walked right into it. Becker and Mundhra are down. Greg and I got separated and I can't find him. I've tried his phone about a hundred times. I think they might have taken him.'

Rumble was quiet for a long moment as the news sank in. 'But who—'

'They're vampires. They're better funded than us, they're better organised than us, and they're not fucking about. They have Nosferol, Harry.'

A sharp hiss as Rumble drew a breath on the end of the line. 'Where are they getting it from?'

'There's only one way. Someone on the inside.'

179

'Who?'

'You tell me. All I know is, we're under attack.'

Rumble fell silent once more for a few seconds. When he spoke again, she could feel the urgency in his voice. 'I need to make some calls. Are you coming in?'

'No, I have a visit to make.'

CHAPTER 31

Greg felt an enormous hand press into his back and shove him forward. He could see enough through the black hood over his head to know that he was in a dark place, like some kind of tunnel or cellar. His captors had shoved and prodded him a long way through corridors and down steps after they'd hauled him out of the car. If they were inside a house, it was a big one.

From the echo of the footsteps ringing off stone walls, he figured there were two of them marching him along, one big and heavy, the other light on his feet, like a fox. The two male vampires from the London Eye.

'Move your ass faster,' the big one said in his impossibly deep bass.

'We should have just finished this bastard back in London.' His companion sounded agitated with fury. 'He's the one who did for Petra.'

'Uh-uh. Gabriel wants him.'

'What for?'

'You know Gabriel. Didn't say.'

For an instant Greg thought about lashing out

181

behind him with his foot. He might get lucky. If he could get the element of surprise, if he could somehow shake off the hood, he still could have a chance of getting out of it.

But he knew there were too many ifs in that sentence. He kept walking, his mind working furiously. Why were vampires fighting vampires? And who was Gabriel?

A huge hand grabbed his arm and jerked him to a halt. A moment's pause, then he heard the creak of a heavy door. Down more steps, and the echoes intensified. He could see patches of light through the material of the hood.

'Take it off him,' the deep voice said, and the hood was ripped away.

Greg blinked. They were standing at the bottom of a murky passage facing an ancient studded door. Burning torches flanked the arched stone entrance.

He glanced at his captors in the firelight and saw his guess had been right about the big guy. The giant had to keep his head bowed as he stepped forward and turned the iron handle. The door swung open and Greg was shoved through.

He looked around him at the shadowy, sumptuous room in which he found himself. The air was rich with the tang of candles, and their glow shone across gilt furnishings and red velvet. Snarling ebony tigers loomed out of the shadows from the ornate carved fireplace. The walls were covered with age-worn tapestries depicting battle scenes from a period of history that he could only guess was beyond ancient.

'Second-century Carpathia,' said a voice. Its tone was smooth, almost musical. Greg turned to see a man standing in the shadows behind the flickering candelabras. 'Magnificent, aren't they?' the man said.

'Who are you?'

The man stepped forward into the candlelight. He was tall, but not brutish like his men. He exuded an air of aristocratic grace, regal, utterly relaxed and self-assured.

'My name is Stone. Gabriel Stone. Welcome to my little retreat.' The smile on his lips was warm. 'Do you like it? Speaking as one vampire to another.'

Greg didn't reply. Glancing around him, he could see the items his captors had taken from him earlier laid out on a table a few feet away. His weapon, stripped and unloaded of its Nosferol rounds. His VIA ID, his phone. The pouch containing his Solazal pills and his blood surrogate food supply lay unzipped, its contents spilled across the table's leather top.

Following Greg's gaze, Stone walked over to the table. He picked up the VIA ID wallet and flipped it open, running his eye over the laminated card printed with Greg's name, his turn date and the bold red letter 'P' that denoted his probationary status.

'Just a baby,' Stone chuckled. 'So fresh I can

183

still smell human on you.' He flipped the wallet shut and tossed it down on the table. 'I almost feel sympathy for you, Agent Shriver.'

Greg stared at him. 'Why am I here?'

Stone smiled. 'Have a seat, Greg. May I call you Greg?'

'I prefer to stand.'

'As you wish.' Stone settled elegantly into a plush armchair before reaching for a decanter and pouring a measure of sparkling red juice into a crystal tumbler. 'Care for a drink? Oh, I'm sorry. You're still on the surrogate stuff they give you.' He took a sip of the blood, then reclined in the armchair and looked long and hard at Greg. 'You really have no idea of the kind of organisation you've joined, do you? All you know is what you've been told by your colleague, Agent Bishop.'

'You know her?' Greg said, surprised.

'I know all about her,' Stone replied. 'She's made quite a reputation for herself. Shame, because she'll be destroyed. Every one of them will, and soon.'

'Why do you hate the Federation so much, Stone?'

'The Federation,' Stone echoed with a shake of the head. 'Even after all these years, it's astounding to me that this obscene gang of despots had the temerity to call themselves a vampire *federation*, as though it truly had the collective interests of all our race at heart – as though it had been created by unanimous consensus. The truth is, your precious Federation is no more than a crude dictatorship that simply stormed in and took what it wanted by force. It never tried to win the hearts and minds of the vampire race. It doesn't have our blessing. And it will be obliterated.'

'By you?'

Stone gave a thin smile. 'I've been a vampire for a very long time, Greg. I remember the way it once was. A time when humans lived in fear of us, a time when we truly ruled. Look at the vampire race now. A hunted minority, lurking in shadows like rats in holes. The price of four thousand years of apathy and complacency, during which time we allowed the tables slowly to turn on us. Before we knew it, the humans were out of control. They were too many, too powerful and too organised. It's time for a change.'

'The Federation is that change,' Greg said.

'The Federation is a craven betrayal of everything our race once stood for,' Stone said angrily. 'It imposes heresy under the guise of order. It wilfully denies vampires their heritage. It perverts tradition. Don't be fooled by them, Greg. They are the cancer, not the cure. They are evil.' He smiled, his anger fading as quickly as it had risen up. 'You know, there are still options open to you. Your friends haven't completely brainwashed you. Not yet.'

'I get it. This is a recruitment drive. I should be honoured.'

'You should certainly have a think about it. It's

very generous of me to be willing to overlook the fact that you and your associates murdered two of my brethren this evening. And I don't open my door to just anyone.'

'You want people inside VIA.'

'I already have people inside VIA, and a host of operatives working across the globe to further our plans. But I could always use more.'

'I wouldn't come over to you, Stone. Not in a thousand years. Stick it up your ass.'

'A thousand years is a long time,' Stone said. 'I ought to know.' He shrugged. 'Fine. Have it your way. You're going to deliver a message for me.'

'I think you're getting old, Stone. Your hearing is gone. Didn't I just say you could stick your offer up your ass?'

'I heard you fine,' Stone said. 'Then it's *adieu*, Agent Shriver.'

'A-what?'

'*Adieu*. It's French for "see you in hell".'

'I'll be seeing *you* there, all right.'

Stone laughed. 'You'll be waiting a long time.'

Before Greg could say another word, he felt a presence coming up behind him and half-turned to see the big vampire stepping up fast. The fist lashed out of nowhere, and everything went dark.

CHAPTER 32

The Last Bite Bar and Grill
1.41 a.m.

The party was in full swing, music thumping loudly as Alex walked up to the bar.

'Is Rudi about?' she shouted over the noise to one of the barmen.

'Rudi's got company right now.' The barman raised his eyebrows suggestively. 'They're upstairs.' He jerked his thumb at the ceiling. Rudi's private suite of luxurious rooms occupied the top floor of the building.

'A woman?'

The barman nodded with a sly chuckle. 'We get some hot stuff in here, but this one . . . *hoo hoo*. And if I know Rudi, there's a red leather jumpsuit lying on the floor up there as we speak. So I'd leave it a while before disturbing them.'

'How long ago?'

''Bout an hour. Hey. I said—'

Alex was through the STAFF ONLY door before the barman could stop her and running up the backstairs. A spiral staircase wound up from the second floor to the opulence of Rudi's private domain.

Alex emerged onto a landing that was on the gaudy end of opulent – white satin on the walls and an oversized sparkling chandelier. A gilt-framed oil hung near the double doors of the apartment, depicting Rudi dressed as Napoleon Bonaparte; his chin was raised proudly and his hand was slipped inside his jacket as an epic battle raged in the background, complete with cavalry charges and artillery. But Alex wasn't here to appreciate Rudi's taste in art. She kicked in the door and stormed inside the huge marble-floored entrance hall. A Tom Jones CD was playing from hidden speakers.

She would never have taken Rudi for a traitor. That made her as furious with herself as she was with him. She drew the Desert Eagle.

Apart from the empty Krug bottle and the two crystal glasses, one with a smear of red lipstick, there was no sign of Rudi and his female companion in the mock Louis XV salon. She booted open one of the doors that radiated off the room, and found herself in a gigantic mirrored bathroom with steps leading down to a sunken Jacuzzi. She slammed the door shut, tried another and stepped into Rudi's bedroom.

Rudi was alone on the super-kingsize leopard-skin four-poster, dwarfed by the bed's size. He lay propped up against satin pillows wearing a black bathrobe that had 'R.B.' in large gold letters over his heart. He gazed idly at Alex as she strode up to the foot of the bed and pointed the gun at him.

She was almost speechless with hurt. 'Why?' she asked simply.

Rudi said nothing.

She clicked off the Desert Eagle's safety. 'Answers. Now. I want to know why you betrayed me and who put you up to it.'

Still no reply. No movement.

Alex lowered the gun. 'Rudi?'

He was staring past her, towards the door, as if in some kind of trance. She walked round the side of the bed. Not a flicker of reaction. Reaching a hand out to him, she shook his shoulder.

'Rudi?' she said again.

Only then did she spot the thin red line that ran across his throat and around his neck, oozing a tiny trickle of dark vampire blood.

She nudged him. Rudi's head toppled slowly off his shoulders, bounced off the satin pillow and landed on the bedside rug with a hollow clunk, like a coconut. It rolled over the rug and came to a halt face-up, his sightless eyes staring up at her.

The decapitation had been executed with a razor-sharp blade, leaving his neck stump as smooth as a mirror. Barely any blood. One clean swing, administered by someone very strong and very expert.

Lillith.

It must have happened just minutes ago. Soon,

Rudi's body would start to decompose at a vastly accelerated rate as death, cheated first time round, finally caught up with him.

The other side of the large bedroom, a cool breeze fluttered the curtains. Alex ran over to the open window and peered out over the ledge at the backstreet below. A long way down, but no problem for a vampire.

The slayer was already far away.

CHAPTER 33

*Terzi Pharmaceuticals Fabrication Complex,
the Italian Alps
3.12 a.m. local time*

Achill wind was blowing down off the distant mountains. The sky was clear and the stars were out in their countless millions over the still landscape. Nestling in the foothills, the large modern steel and glass building was the hub of the two-acre site of the fabrication complex. Terzi was one of Europe's smaller pharmaceutical companies, its manufacturing output almost entirely focused on one specialised type of diuretic drug for the medical industry. It had plants in three other locations across Europe, each chosen for its cleanliness of environment. But this particular facility was different from the others, for a very special reason that very few people knew about.

Enrico, the night security guard posted at the front gates, was numb with cold, and his mind had been drifting from tiredness until he'd spotted the faraway headlights winding their way

191

towards the plant. Looked like two medium-sized trucks. As they came closer, lighting up the steel mesh fence and the concrete compound beyond, Enrico stepped out of his hut and walked towards the vehicles with a hand raised. The company took security pretty seriously, and the Heckler & Koch 9mm machine pistol slung across his body slapped against his side as he walked. It was loaded and he'd been trained to use it.

Not that there was anything necessarily unusual or sinister about the appearance of two trucks in the middle of the night. Enrico had been working at Terzi long enough to know two things: one, that even though there was usually a smattering of late-shift personnel about the fabrication plant and labs, the upper east wing in particular *never* went to sleep at night; and that two, you didn't ask too many questions about went on in that part of the building. He'd often seen the labcoats walking about in the third-floor windows. Some of the girls were pretty hot too. But, just like everyone who worked there, they kept themselves to themselves. Word among the maintenance staff and the drivers was that they were involved in some kind of experimental research programme that Terzi was keeping under wraps pending patent. That seemed to explain the strange hours, and the secretive way that unmarked trucks would often turn up to collect unmarked crates of stuff from the delivery bay in the rear.

192

But Enrico still had to make sure the paper-work was all in order, secrecy or no secrecy. As the lead van pulled up at the gate and its window whirred down, he put out his hand and asked to be shown the documentation authorising him to open up.

'Cold night,' the driver said, and Enrico grunted in reply as he scanned the papers.

Wait, this was wrong.

'This isn't—' he started.

But didn't finish.

Enrico was a young man, fit and strong and at the peak of his physical shape. But he was still just a man, and none of his human senses were honed enough to have picked up the silent approach of the figure that had slipped out from behind the van and moved towards him through the shadows. Less than a second later, Enrico's neck was broken.

The van driver watched impassively as the dead guard was dragged into the hut. His killer let the body slump to the floor, then turned to the computer console. A few clicks of the keys, and the gate was automatically unlatched and began to open. A few more clicks, and the security cameras throughout the facility were simultaneously deactivated.

The vans growled slowly through the gates and into the dark compound. Their back doors opened, and eight figures in black tactical clothing spilled out. They stole swiftly and silently into the facility, breaking up into pairs and working their way methodically from room to room, floor to floor. First clear the rest of the building, then move on to the east wing. Those were their instructions, and so far the operation was going perfectly according to plan.

Marta Tucci was sitting at her desk in her ground-floor office, the glare of the laptop shining off her glasses and the front of her labcoat. The screen was covered in technical data, but this late at night she couldn't deal with it. Two years out of university and she already felt jaded with her biochemistry career. She hated working shifts. She should be at home, close to Franco and baby Renata. Sometimes she just wanted to—

That was when the door of her office crashed in and the two men in black burst inside, waving guns at her. She screamed. One of them strode up to her and grabbed her by her long blond hair. He yanked her brutally out of her seat and sent her tumbling to the floor. He fell on her like an animal. Her screaming became a tortured wail as his teeth crunched into her throat. Blood welled up in thick spurts, soaking the carpet as he sucked and gorged on her torn flesh. With an effort he stepped away from her, wiping his bloody mouth with his sleeve and letting his colleague drink from the dying woman.

Between them, the two intruder vampires drank Marta Tucci dry until her body was a pallid husk. They moved on to rejoin the team.

Eight more chemists and two more security men died the same way, bloodily and in terror, as the team swept the Terzi building. Each member had his fill. It was part of their reward for the night's work.

In under five minutes, the figures in black had regrouped outside the security doorway leading into the east wing. The leader stepped up to a wall console and punched in a twelve-digit number. The code was changed daily, but their information was good. The steel doors whooshed open. The team slipped through into the corridor that lay beyond.

The east wing was staffed that night by a group of five white-coated chemists, three males and two females. The team of armed intruders came bursting into the complex of glass-walled rooms that comprised the secret Federation laboratory and brought mayhem. As one of the females ran for cover, a swathe of gunfire punched into the back of her white coat. She fell sprawling on her face, screaming, clawing, dying in agony and bursting apart.

The others stared in horror.

Not just because their colleague had just been gunned down. But because normally, vampires didn't just fall down dead when you shot them. And the chemists working in the upper east wing were all vampires – vampires who knew all about the effects of Nosferol-tipped ammunition, because the production of the poison was one of their key jobs. Suddenly nobody was trying to escape or resist.

Only one of them, a portly male with a blond ponytail, seemed less scared than his colleagues. Nobody noticed, though – they had other things to worry about.

The tactical team worked fast. With the chemists held at gunpoint, the rest of them swept through the lab and found what they'd been sent to find. At the far end of the wing was a vast storage room with steel shelves from floor to ceiling, stacked with hundreds of crates containing litre-sized Perspex jars. Separated into sections, the crates were labelled 'Solazal', 'Vambloc' and 'Nosferol'. It was the latter that the team leader was interested in. He pointed a gloved finger.

'Load those up,' he commanded. 'The rest stays.'

While half the team started grabbing the Nosferol crates and carrying them to the lift in the corridor, others began attaching blocks of C-4 plastic explosive from their tactical vests to the shelving. In minutes, the whole storage room was rigged for destruction.

'You bastards,' one of the male vampire chemists spat at them.

The team leader grinned behind his mask. 'Wait till you see what we've got in the van.' And soon

196

afterwards, when the lift returned from taking down the first batch of crates, two of his team brought in a massive holdall that even vampires struggled to carry. Inside was enough explosive to take out the whole building.

When the lab had been emptied of every drop of Nosferol, the leader signalled to his men to start evacuating the place. It was at that point that the chemist with the ponytail stepped forward, as if he thought he was going with them. The leader hit him hard across the face with the butt of his gun. The blond vampire went sprawling to the floor.

'I gave you what you wanted,' he whined in protest. 'You told me you'd spare me.'

'You piece of shit, Vernon,' his surviving female colleague yelled at him, horrified. 'What the *fuck* have you done? You gave them *Nosferol*?'

'Shut up,' the team leader said, and shot her.

'Now it's your turn, Vernon,' he said over her dying shrieks. He raised his gun again.

'But you promised . . .'

'I lied.' The leader shrugged, pointed his weapon in Vernon's face and pulled the trigger. His team followed suit, opening fire on the two remaining Federation chemists. They were still in their death agonies as the team swept back out of the lab as fast as they'd arrived.

Less than two minutes later the vans stormed out of the gates, their headlights sweeping the empty road. In the front passenger seat of the lead vehicle, the team leader took out a small remote. Without pausing a beat, he hit the detonation button.

The gigantic explosion filled the night sky behind them as they sped away with their cargo.

CHAPTER 34

Crowmoor Hall
3.16 a.m.

The vibrations of the silent ringer reverberated against the dull sheen of the long mahogany table. Stone picked up the phone. He'd been expecting the call, knew who it was from – and it was right on time. He said nothing, waited for the vampire on the other end to speak.

'It's done,' the voice said.

Which was all that needed to be said. Stone hung up and smiled down the length of the table at the seated assembly of his inner circle. Lillith was at his right-hand side. She'd dispensed with red leather in exchange for glistening black. The light of the night's battles and victories still danced in her eyes. She drummed her long, black fingernails impatiently on the polished wood, waiting for him to reveal what the call had been about.

To Gabriel's left was the blonde, Anastasia. Down the table was the hulking shape of Zachary. Anton's beady gaze was fixed on their leader.

'Well, brother?' Lillith finally asked him.

'Our plans progress,' he replied. 'The demise of the Federation is now an inevitability. We control their weapons. The tiger's teeth have been pulled.'

'Then we move on to the next phase,' Anastasia said with a delicious laugh. 'And the real fun begins.'

'All in good time,' Stone replied calmly.

'First I want to massacre the rest of the bastards who did for Petra and Kenji tonight,' Lillith said through bared teeth, fists clenched on the tabletop. 'I'm going to find Alex Bishop. I'll find her. And I *will* make her suffer.'

Stone pursed his lips. 'There are more pressing issues to deal with than mere revenge,' he said. 'Leave such crude impulses to the humans.'

'What issues do you mean, Gabriel?' Anton said, intently watching every flicker of Stone's face. 'The Federation—'

'The Federation are less of a concern,' Stone interrupted him. 'They will be dealt with according to plan. No, I refer to another matter. While you were in London, I was . . . elsewhere.'

Lillith crossed her arms and looked at her brother. Her expression was clear: she knew perfectly well where he'd been that night, and she disapproved of his dalliance with his new plaything. She'd wanted Kate Hawthorne dead that first night. But she said nothing.

'I encountered a human there,' Stone went on.

'An officer of their police. He told me something that disturbs me greatly.' He paused. 'He told me that he was in possession of a certain artefact. I speak of the cross of Ardaich.'

His words caused a sharp silence to fall in the room. Lillith scowled and kept staring at him. 'The cross? The cross of legend?'

'That old story,' Anastasia snorted. 'Vampires don't need to worry about crosses. We all know that.' She looked round and saw their serious expressions. 'Don't we?'

Stone shook his head. 'At a mere eighty years of age, you're far too young to know these things, Anastasia. I can assure you that the legend of what the humans came to call the cross of Ardaich is very real indeed.'

'Then we have to hunt this human down and kill him,' Lillith said. 'The simple ways are the best.'

'And how do you think we can do that?' Zachary rumbled. 'If the motherfucker has the cross, we can't touch him.'

Stone stared at him coldly. He didn't approve of human profanities being used in his presence, unless it was by his own choice.

'Do you really think he has it, Gabriel?' Anton asked.

Stone clicked his tongue. 'He may be bluffing; then again, he may not. But even if he doesn't have possession of the cross, the mere fact that

201

he knows of its existence makes him a grave threat to all of us. We cannot afford to take risks.'

'I agree with Lillith,' Anastasia said. 'If this human is with their police, he should be easy to find. We can make him disappear, along with whatever it is he may know or may have found.'

Stone was silent for a moment, thinking hard. Then he stood up, walked over to the door and tugged twice on a thin cord.

Far away through the twisting passages of the mansion, the bell rang to summon Seymour Finch.

Their assistant arrived in minutes. Lillith eyed Finch with distaste as he grovelled and scraped his way to the table like a beaten dog looking for scraps, his eyes bright with adoration and terror.

'My loyal servant,' Stone said. 'I have another task for you.'

Finch nodded eagerly. 'It will be a pleasure to serve you, Mr Stone. Whatever you wish.'

'A human has become a problem for us. We believe him to be a police officer, and he may be in possession of an item that is very important to us. Your task is to find out who he is, where he lives, what he knows, and with whom he might have shared this knowledge.'

'And then cut his fucking throat,' Lillith purred, drawing her finger abruptly across her neck. Zachary and Anton chuckled.

Stone glowered sternly at her. 'No. No harm must come to him – not until we can be absolutely certain that he's the only one involved.' Turning back to Finch, he went on, 'This is a delicate matter. Depending on how much he knows about us, it may be necessary to isolate him from his colleagues, prevent him from talking. Do you understand?'

Finch nodded. 'Yes, master.'

'Good. I leave it to you. You'll report back to me on my return.'

Lillith looked across at him. 'Your return? From where?'

'I have one more small item of business to attend to. Then I need to make a journey. East,' Stone said. He paused a beat before adding, 'To *them*.'

CHAPTER 35

Greg opened his eyes, ready to spring up to his feet and engage his attacker. But something was different. He wasn't lying on the cold stone floor of the underground chamber beneath the house. He was lying on damp grass.

He blinked and raised his head, trying to make sense of where he was. A cool breeze caressed the wetness on his cheek. He struggled up into a crouch and his head connected with something hard. He reached up to feel it. Solid metal. Running his hand downwards, he felt the steel bars a foot away from his face, cold and slippery with dew.

He was in a cage. Around him, the long grass rustled gently in the breeze. The chorus of the birds in the trees heralded the dawn.

He gripped the bars in his fists and tried to bend them apart, but the steel was thick. They didn't give a millimetre. He fell back on his haunches, beginning to breathe hard.

Then he noticed the object on the other side of the bars. The compact notebook computer whirred away quietly in the grass. Its screen was flipped open to face him, and the fixed black eye of a webcam was trained on the cage.

The screen was dark except for a shadowy face in its centre, watching him intently. It was Stone. Greg stared back at him, and saw the vampire smile.

'Good morning, Greg. Or should I say *good night*? I'm staying up late to watch this. It's well past my bedtime.'

Greg tore his gaze away from the screen. The red glow of dawn was breaking over the treeline. He tried to speak, but no sound came out.

'I believe the word you're looking for is "predicament",' Stone said. His smile widened. 'That's certainly what you're in, my friend. Now, remember I said you were going to deliver a message for me? That's exactly what's going to happen.' He paused, and his hand appeared on the screen holding a slim object that Greg recognised instantly. It was the tube of Solazal tablets they'd taken from him the night before.

'I can see what you're thinking, Greg,' Stone said. 'You're asking yourself, "Did I take my Solazal?"' He shook the tube. 'Dear me. Still a lot of pills left. I do believe you forgot, didn't you? Time will tell. And I think you may be running out.'

Greg was beginning to tremble as he struggled to remember. Alex's warning rang round and round in his head, and his stomach flipped as the truth hit him.

Stone was right.

Greg looked up at the red glow in the sky, just as the first shimmering golden edge of sun broke over the treetops. He flinched away from the light, but not before he felt the terrible pain lance through his eyes. Rays of sun speared between the bars of the cage. One passed across his hand, and the flesh instantly sizzled and blistered. He let out a sharp cry and jerked his hand away.

'Looks like you forgot, all right,' Stone chuckled. 'How wonderfully entertaining this promises to be.'

There was nowhere Greg could crawl to escape the steady rise of the sun. Even curled up in a tight ball with his arms over his face, he could feel its glare on him. He smelled the smoke that was beginning to rise from his clothes and hair, the acrid stench of charring flesh. Saw his hands blackening and curling like singed paper. The first flames licked across his skin.

He was a soldier. If he was going to die, he'd at least die facing his enemy. He turned towards the screen.

'Damn you, Stone,' he yelled.

'I was damned millennia before you were born,' Stone replied. 'But I was smarter.'

Greg screamed as he burst alight. He could feel his flesh shrivelling, turning to ash.

The last thing he saw as he burned was Stone's laughing face.

CHAPTER 36

Lavender Close, Wallingford
The next morning, 8.03 a.m.

'You again,' Gillian Hawthorne snapped as she recognised the Detective Inspector's voice on the other end of the phone.

'I'm sorry to call so early, Mrs Hawthorne.' Joel's voice sounded ragged and weary, as though he hadn't slept all night. 'I was checking on Kate.'

'Kate's fine. She's asleep.'

'Nothing wrong?'

Gillian frowned. 'I told you, she's fine. There's nothing wrong with her at all. Now please go away and stop calling us.' She put the phone down. Bit her lip and chewed on a fingernail.

She wasn't about to let that Solomon man know just how anxious she really was about her daughter. It hadn't taken Gillian a second look at Kate that morning to tell she was very sick. Her sleeping face was drawn and strangely pale. The skin was becoming almost translucent, so that the veins in her temples and her neck were disturbingly visible. Gillian had shuddered. Her daughter looked like a corpse.

Moments after talking to Joel Solomon, Gillian picked the phone back up and dialled Dr Andrews's number.

Bill Andrews had been the Hawthorne family's private physician since Kate had been a baby. The kindly old doctor was almost like an uncle to her, and he sounded deeply concerned when Gillian called him at home and described the symptoms.

'Don't try to bring her to the clinic. Let me come and take a look at her.'

Gillian was watching at the window as his car pulled up in the drive a little while later. She met him at the door.

'Thanks for coming, Bill.'

'How is she?'

'I'm terribly worried.'

At exactly 8.45 a.m., Jeremy Lonsdale's Gulfstream jet left the tarmac of a private airfield in Surrey and climbed steeply into the overcast sky. Its crew of three had received hurried instructions from their employer to set a course for Russia, carrying with them the strange cargo delivered to the airfield by chopper. It appeared to be nothing more than a heavy crate, seven feet long, edged with steel – but whatever was inside was a secret closely guarded by Mr Lonsdale as well as by the two taciturn and intimidating men in dark suits who had clearly been hired to stay glued to its side at all times. The two men had barely spoken to anyone, and when the crew did overhear them

208

conversing quietly between themselves, it was in some Eastern language they didn't understand. But Mr Lonsdale had said no questions, and that was good enough for them.

Lavender Close, Wallingford
8.47 a.m.

'Hello, Kate,' Dr Andrews said as Gillian showed him into her daughter's bedroom.

Kate was burrowed under the covers. At the sound of his voice, she peered suspiciously over the edge of her duvet.

'It's dark in here,' the doctor said, glancing at the drawn curtains.

'She has to have them like that. She can't seem to stand the light.'

'Let's see.' Dr Andrews walked over to the window and opened the curtains a crack. Kate let out a loud moan and retreated quickly back under the duvet as a shaft of sunlight cut across the room and hit her in the face.

Dr Andrews raised his eyebrows at the reaction. He closed the curtain and went over to sit on the edge of Kate's bed.

'May I?' He turned on the bedside lamp. 'Your mother tells me you've been getting bad headaches. Is that right?'

Kate didn't reply.

'That's all right. You don't have to answer.' He gently peeled the duvet off her. 'I'm not going to hurt you, Kate,' he said as she protested feebly. 'I just want to have a quick look at you, so we can make you—'

He stopped mid-sentence when he saw the marks on the girl's neck.

'So we can make you better,' he finished. He gently moved her head so he could study the strange lesions up close. Slipping a thermometer into her mouth, he noticed how pale her lips were and shook his head curiously.

Gillian Hawthorne stood back with her arms crossed as he examined Kate in silence. When he'd finished, Kate huddled back deep under the duvet, making small groaning sounds.

Dr Andrews turned to Gillian. 'Has she been off her food lately?'

'Not until she fell ill. She eats like a horse. It's a wonder she stays thin.'

'No food fads, diets? She hasn't become a vegan or anything?'

'Nothing like that at all. She's a perfectly normal girl.' Gillian shot a look at her daughter. 'Or at least, she *was*.'

The doctor heard the tone of her voice but chose to ignore it. 'She's displaying symptoms of anaemia. Her heartbeat is rapid and a little irregular. Her fingernails show signs of iron deficiency. She's weak and she's getting headaches. Has there been any change in her menstrual cycle?'

'We don't really talk about that. As far as I know, nothing.'

He nodded. 'I'll prescribe iron tablets, and that should get her going. In the meantime you need to get her to eat plenty of red meat, maybe some liver.'

'I'm not taking fucking iron tablets, you old piece of shit,' Kate's voice hissed from under the covers. 'And the only liver I'll eat is yours, you bastard.'

There was a stunned silence in the room. Dr Andrews had seen it all in his years as a medical practitioner, but something in the girl's voice and the way she was peering at him over the bedclothes sent a shiver down the back of his neck. He'd known this child all her life. Knew her as a sweet, charming, happy and warm personality. But now her eyes were hard and cold.

Gillian Hawthorne exploded. She strode over to the bed and started shaking Kate violently. 'You apologise for that! You hear me?'

Dr Andrews took her arm. 'Gillian—'

'I know what's going on. It's that Maddon boy. *He's* the one who's done this to you.'

'Calm down, Gillian. She needs to rest. I think we should leave her.'

The doctor was pensive as he shut Kate's bedroom door and ushered her mother down the stairs. Gillian was flushed and agitated as she made tea in the kitchen. The doctor pulled up a chair at the pine table, frowning to himself. He took a bottle of pills from his pocket and unscrewed the lid.

'What's that?' she asked, handing him a cup of tea.

'Not for her, for me.' He popped two in his mouth and washed them down with his drink.

'Are you all right, Bill?'

He smiled. 'I get a little tired sometimes. My heart. I'm fine, though. Let's talk about Kate. What are those lesions on her neck?'

'I don't know. I took them to be lovebites. God knows what—'

'I'd say that unless she's been getting lovebites from a Rottweiler, we're looking at some other cause. In fact, I'm more than a little concerned about them. Has Kate been seeing anyone?'

Gillian let out a snort. 'You mean boys? Just that worthless degenerate from next door.' She told him what she knew about Dec's arrest, the drugs, the visit from the police the following morning.

'I wish you'd told me these things earlier,' the doctor said. 'Apart from the physical symptoms, Kate's behaviour strongly suggests that she's been severely traumatised. The drugs are a significant concern. We might also have to investigate the possibility of an aggravated date rape. That could explain the injury to her neck. Which means I'll have to do a full examination.'

'She hasn't been raped, Bill.'

'How do you know that?'

'I just know.'

He shook his head. 'I'm sorry, Gillian, but that's not enough. And I'll also have to notify the police.'

'Bill, no, please. I can't have the police involved in this. My family—'

'You may not have a lot of choice, Gillian.'

'Look, please, Bill. Can't we just do whatever tests are necessary first, to find out what's wrong with her before we start—'

'Creating a scandal?'

'I want what's best for Kate,' she said firmly. 'I don't want this out in public until we're absolutely sure.'

Dr Andrews looked at her long and hard. 'Fine. Then I'm going to book her into the clinic as quickly as I can. Then we can start to try to figure this out.'

CHAPTER 37

Alex had been pacing impatiently up and down her living room floor when, a few minutes before nine a.m., the phone had rung. She'd been on it before the first ring was over.

Harry Rumble's voice had sounded terse. 'I need you over here. Right away.'

The sense of worry was palpable as she strode through the VIA headquarters. Rumble was in his office with Garrett and Kelby, one of the admin chiefs. There was a grim silence between them. Rumble was standing bent over his desk with his fists planted on its leather top, looking careworn, his hair ruffled, his tie crooked. In front of him was a plain cardboard box, three feet long, two wide.

'What?' Alex said, frozen in the doorway.

Rumble lifted a fist off the desk and pointed at the box. 'This just arrived by motorcycle courier.'

Alex approached the desk and lifted the lid of the box. A puff of fine grey-white powder wafted out. 'It's ash,' she said, looking up at Rumble with a frown.

'It's more than ash,' Kelby said.

Alex rolled up the sleeve of her black satin blouse and stuck her arm into the box up to the elbow. The ash was still warm. Her fingers felt something inside. Something hard, brittle and rough.

Bits of bone.

And something else. It was warmer than the bone, smoother. She pulled it out and examined it.

'Fuck,' she muttered. She tossed the blackened dog tags down on Rumble's desk with a tinny clatter. The name, rank and serial number stamped into the metal belonged to Lt Greg Shriver USMC.

'Guess we can call off the search,' Garrett said dryly.

Alex fired him a look that made him back up a step. Before Rumble could stop her, she ripped open the box, and its grisly contents spilled out over the desktop. Fine ash rose up like a dust cloud. Garrett sneezed.

Alex reached down and picked up what was left of Greg's charred skull. Flakes of carbon fell away as she took it in her hands. His empty eye sockets stared back at her. Just last night, he'd been there with her. Now he was this.

I'm sorry, Greg.

'We'll get these bastards,' Rumble said. Then, noticing Alex's frown: 'What is it?'

'There's something in his mouth.' She poked her fingers in between the charred teeth, brushing away the bits of soot and ash from inside. Wedged at the back of where his throat had been was a small object, black plastic, two inches long. She rooted it out and held it up to show them.

It was a USB flash drive, and it definitely hadn't been in Greg's mouth when he'd burned up.

'Looks like someone has sent us a message,' Alex said. She put down the skull. There was black soot on her fingers. She wiped it away quickly.

'Kelby, run that,' said Rumble. 'Let's take a look.'

Alex dropped the flash drive in Kelby's palm. He flipped open a laptop on a side table and was about to insert the drive into a port when the office door burst open.

They all looked round to see the pale, startled face and wide eyes of Jen Minto looking at them.

'I'm sorry, sir.' Minto's voice was shaky. 'You have to come and see this.'

'In a minute,' Rumble said irritably. 'We're busy.'

Minto gulped. 'With respect, sir, you *really* need to come and see this. Now.'

They followed her out into the operations room. Every desk was deserted.

'Where did everyone go?' Rumble asked.

Minto pointed at the far end of the room. The entire VIA office staff were crowding around the banks of enormous screens where broadcasts from all over the world played twenty-four/seven. Right now, news channels across Europe were broadcasting the same images to a babble of mixed languages.

'Let me see.' Rumble pushed through to the front. Alex followed, and stood next to him as they stared at the screens.

'That's—'

'Terzi,' Alex said. 'Or was.'

On the centre screen a pretty Sky News reporter in a bright orange jacket was talking to the camera. Her hair was blowing in the wind and wisps of sleet were drifting by. In the background, fire crews were hosing down the scorched, smoking rubble of what used to be the pharmaceutical plant in the Italian Alps.

'. . . speculation about the cause of the blast. Italian police have yet to comment on initial claims that this may not have been a chemical explosion, but a terrorist attack. Sources have revealed tonight that extremist anti-vivisection groups may have made threats against the company in the past, despite assurances that no animal testing takes place . . .'

Rumble had seen enough. He grabbed a remote and muted the sound to the whole bank of screens at once. The room was plunged into shocked silence. Then, after a few moments, everyone began to talk over each other in panic as the full implications of what had happened began to hit home.

Rumble jutted out his jaw and let out a long breath. 'Where's Slade?' he demanded loudly.

'Here, sir.' A squat, porky vampire with straggly hair and a patchy beard pushed through from the back of the crowd. His shirt was hanging out of his bulging waistline. They called him The Slob, but behind the scenes Doug Slade was one of the most important cogs in VIA's operations, responsible for managing and distributing supplies of Nosferol, Solazal and Vambloc for all its agents. And it was through his team that Solazal was rationed out to the thousands of vampires across the Federation's global realm via its network of vampire doctors and pharmacists.

'Doug, what's the state of our stockpiles?'

'Of everything?'

'Of everything.'

Slade shrugged. 'Whoever did this timed it just right, because we were just about to ship a massive order out of there. Stocks are low to desperate. Especially on the Nosferol front.'

'How desperate is desperate?'

'Running on fumes, basically.'

Alex was working hard to remember exactly how much Nosferol she had in her private stock, and how many prepared rounds of ammo were in her armoury. She thrust her hand in her jeans pocket. One tube of Solazal, three-quarters full. Enough for a few days. Two more tubes in her bedside drawer – or was it just one? Like everyone else, she'd been waiting for a delivery.

Kelby said in a stunned voice, 'What, this happened in the middle of the night and we're only getting to hear about it from the human media? How come none of our own people there alerted us?'

'They're destroyed,' Alex told him. 'They're all gone.'

'How long before we can restart production?' Rumble asked Slade.

Slade puffed out his hairy cheeks. 'Well, even if the formulae had been wiped off the mainframe, as long as we still had a drop left we could still analyse the stuff and start over. No emergency there, okay? But it's gonna take weeks before we can get supply flowing again. Maybe months before it's back to normal.'

Rumble exploded. 'Months! I'm going to find out just what happened here!'

'Who would have done such a thing?' Minto said, fear in her eyes.

'The Trads,' Alex said. 'Just like I told you, Harry.'

Everyone turned. Slade goggled at her. 'The who?'

'You can't know that for sure,' Rumble warned her.

'No? Let's see.' Alex was already heading back to his office. She snatched up the USB drive and came running back into the operations room. She inserted the drive into the computer network and tapped a few keys to divert the image to the big wall screens. 'Harry, get the sound back up,' she called over. 'Everyone quiet.'

The panicky buzz died away. The assembled vampires turned back to face the screens. Even Garrett was too preoccupied to frown about the fact that Alex hadn't called Rumble 'sir'. For a few breathless moments, the screens were black – then they suddenly flashed up into life.

From a deep leather chair in a darkened room, a man gazed down at them. Not a man, a vampire – their instincts told them that instantly. His face was half in shadow, but visible enough to show his sleek, aquiline good looks, the thick black hair swept back from his high brow, and the wry, mischievous twinkle in his eye. He seemed to watch them for a moment; a smile crossed his lips as though he were savouring what he was about to say.

'Good morning, VIA.' His voice was smooth and soft. 'None of you know me, but I know you all very well. Chief Harry Rumble. Special Agent Bishop. We have never met. But I'm sure we will – soon. Allow me to introduce myself. I have gone by many names in my time. The one by which I am presently known is Gabriel Stone.'

Rumble snapped his fingers at Kelby, who nodded and ran to a computer terminal.

The face on the screen smiled. 'Rumble, call off your minion. It is pointless to search for me on your database. Your so-called Federation has no record of my existence.'

'Shit, can he *see* us?' Minto gaped.

'He can't see us,' Alex said. 'He's just smart. He knows exactly how we think.'

'You gotta love this guy,' Slade muttered, and Minto jabbed him in the ribs. Around the room, vampires exchanged nervous glances.

'Is he kidding us?'

'Does he look like he's kidding?'

'Quiet, people,' Rumble commanded.

'By now,' Stone continued after a dramatic pause, 'I'm sure you will all have become aware of the tragedy that has befallen the establishment in Italy where you manufacture your obscene poisons. And I am sure you have all been wondering whose hand it was that has struck you this blow. Look no further. It was I. I am now in possession of your loathsome stockpiles of drugs, and, I believe, some hundred thousand rounds of the ammunition that your treacherous Federation authorises you to use against your own kind.' He shook his head in disgust. 'The disgrace that is VIA ends here. Know that I will destroy you. All of you. You are traitors to the vampire race, and your time is over.'

CHAPTER 38

Joel had gone into the office early that morning to run a trace on the registration number of the McLaren F1. After more than an hour's worth of triple and quadruple checking, he'd had to give up. There was no record of the car anywhere.

He was heading out of the door when the phone rang on his desk.

'Joel, it's Sam.' Carter sounded serious. 'Have you heard yet?'

'Heard what?'

'Then you haven't. They found another body this morning, early. Oxford centre, right under the Bridge of Sighs. It was ex . . . it was like the other one.'

'Exsanguinated?'

'Dry as a witch's tit. Poor bugger. Some post-grad maths boffin by the name of Mickey Thompson. First we thought he'd been chucked off the bridge. Broken glass everywhere. But there aren't any lacerations on him, except for where his neck's been ripped open. And if he'd fallen he'd have a few fractures. Just talked to Jack Briar.

Zilch. So maybe the crazy bastard who did this was the one who jumped off the bridge. Must have smashed himself up a bit. Nobody could take a leap like that and not get hurt.'

'Any blood at the scene?'

'Just the victim's. We're checking all the casualty departments now in case this nutter turned up there. Anyway, it's official. We're looking for a serial murderer, and a right maniac to boot. Thought I should fill you in.'

Joel grabbed a squad car and headed out to the JR. Dec Maddon was sitting glumly in the hospital foyer.

'What happened to the sling?' Joel asked, noticing it was gone.

'Junked it.'

'The doctor say that was okay to do?'

'Fuck the doctor,' Dec said. 'I've got the name of the house. I kept thinking about those birds. Crows. That's what made me remember. It's Crow-something house, manor, something like that.'

'Then let's go.'

Joel let Dec sit with his work laptop as they drove. *If Sam Carter could see me*, he thought. Letting a kid on a drugs charge get his hands on the police databases.

'Got it,' Dec said triumphantly, tapping keys. 'Crowmoor Hall. Just a couple of miles out of Henley.'

Joel nodded and put his foot down.

As the countryside flashed by, few words passed between them and there was no mention at all of vampires. But it was the things left unspoken that screamed out, filling the space around them as they drove, bonding them into a tenuous alliance. They were like two co-conspirators, each just as uneasy as the other. Joel focused on his driving, speeding the police car down the country lanes.

'There's where I crashed the VW,' Dec said, pointing at the tight bend up ahead. The verge was ploughed up, a fence flattened, and the trunk of a big sycamore tree badly scarred from the impact. 'We're close. Any minute now we should see the pub I passed. There it is. Everything looks different in the daytime.'

After a few more miles, the road narrowed into a twisty and winding lane, overhung with branches, slippery with decaying leaf matter. The high wall of the stately home seemed to go on forever, before the wrought iron gates eventually came into view.

'There, see?' Dec pointed up at the stone birds perched on the gateposts. Even in daylight, they looked sinister.

Joel was about to park up at the roadside when the gates suddenly whirred open to let them in. They looked at each other.

'They're expecting visitors?' Dec said.

'They're obviously expecting someone.' Joel drove the car through.

Dec was frowning as they headed up the gravel

drive between the trees. 'The vampires have to have someone working for them. They can't come out during the day.' He turned worriedly to Joel. '*Can* they?'

'Let's just take this one step at a time, Dec,' Joel said. He noticed the kid was trembling.

The driveway straightened and widened out into a great circular forecourt. The grand house stood before them, all gothic towers and chimney stacks and angled roofs. The stonework was mossy and stained dark in places; here and there was a broken window, damaged guttering, loose slates. The main entrance was built in classical style, with columns and a broad flight of steps leading up to the grand doorway. Leaves littered the steps, and the sculpted angels framing the entrance were pitted with age.

A tall, gaunt, bald-headed man stood at the top of the steps, watching the car closely as it pulled up and studying them with a curious and thoughtful expression.

'Recognise him?' Joel whispered as they got out.

Dec shook his head. 'He is one scary bastard. Jesus Christ, look at his *hands*. The fucking size of them.'

'Quiet. Leave the talking to me.'

The gaunt man came down the steps to meet them with a raised eyebrow and a ghost of a smile. Up close, he looked almost reptilian. His voice was dry and throaty. 'Officers?'

Joel flashed his police card. 'Detective Inspector Joel Solomon. This is Mr Maddon.'

'My name is Seymour Finch. Personal assistant to Gabriel Stone. May I be of assistance?'

'Yes. I wondered whether you'd be kind enough to help with a few queries regarding a reported incident here at Crowmoor Hall?'

Finch's face cracked into a parched grin. 'Certainly. What incident are you referring to? Have vandals been in the grounds?'

'Could we talk inside?' Joel said.

Finch led them into the marble-floored hall. Dec threw a look at Joel as if to say 'this is *definitely* the place'.

'I would appreciate some explanation, Inspector. I'm a very busy man.'

'See that door there?' Dec blurted out to Joel. 'That leads to the ballroom.'

Joel silenced him with a glare.

'Ballroom?' Finch said.

'Could we take a look?' Joel asked him.

'Why, certainly, officer.' Finch walked slowly across the marble floor, grasped the bronze handles of the double doors and swung them open with a creak.

Inside was a huge conference room with a long, long table flanked by dozens of identical chairs. There was a whiteboard, a screen and projector, and a raised stage with a speaking podium and more chairs facing it in rows.

'They've changed it,' Dec said in response to Joel's searching look. 'It was all different. There was a dance floor there, and the rest of the room

226

was full of old furniture and stuff.' He pointed. 'Those are the same. The paintings. Old portraits. I remember.'

'The oak panels are seventeenth century,' Finch said. 'And the tapestries are very valuable. But I should like to know what this young man is talking about, and why you are taking up my time.'

'Mr Maddon is helping me with an official police enquiry,' Joel said coolly.

'That's the guy there,' Dec said. He pointed up at the largest of the portraits, which took up a whole wall panel between two bay windows. It showed a strikingly handsome, aristocratic-looking man in his late thirties or early forties. 'The one without the mask. Their leader.'

Joel stared hard at the painting, closely scrutinising the face. Was this the same man – if it had been a man – that he'd chased from Lavender Close?

'Inspector. Really.' Finch was becoming impatient now. 'What is this about?'

'Who is that?' Joel asked, motioning at the portrait.

'That is Mr Stone. My employer.'

'And where is Mr Stone at present?'

'He is out of the country.'

'Where did he go?'

'He's in Tuscany,' Finch said curtly. 'Staying at the home of a close friend of his.'

'I'd like to know Mr Stone's whereabouts on Hallowe'en night.'

'Hallowe'en?' Finch frowned, as though unfamiliar with the expression.

'The last night in October,' Joel explained as patiently as he could.

'Forgive me,' Finch said without any trace of apology. 'You may be disappointed to know that Mr Stone was already in Italy at that time.'

'Bollocks, he was here,' Dec blurted out.

Joel silenced him with a sharp look. 'I'll want to verify that. Who is this friend?'

'Jeremy Lonsdale,' Finch said.

'Jeremy Lonsdale the cabinet minister?'

'That is correct. Now, as you appear not to have a warrant to search the premises, before I throw you out I would like an explanation for this harassment.'

'We have a report that a serious incident took place here on the night in question,' Joel said. 'Involving the ritual murder of a teenager.' As soon as the words were out, he regretted saying them. He'd gone out on a limb a few times in his career, but this was climbing to the tip of the branch and then sawing it off behind him.

Finch stared at him for a moment, then burst out laughing. 'Here, in the *ballroom*?'

'Not here, down in the crypt,' Dec interrupted. Joel groaned inwardly. He should have made the kid stay in the car.

'Mr Maddon has a florid imagination,' Finch said dryly. 'As you can see, the house is being extensively renovated while we build the new conference centre. But we are yet to discover anything resembling a crypt. A wine cellar, yes, at the other end of the house, below the kitchens on the east wing. But it is flooded and filled with rubble. Would you like to see it?' he added with mock earnestness.

Dec was undeterred. He pointed at the far end of the room, next to the stage. 'There. Look. See that bit of old carpet on the wall? There was a curtain there. There's a door behind it. That's the way down to the crypt.'

Before Joel could stop him, he was running down the length of the room. He jumped up onto the stage and started tugging at the corner of the tapestry. Finch's eyes were popping out.

'Inspector, I would ask you to keep your puppy on a leash. That "bit of old carpet" happens to be priceless. It's fifteenth century. A Stone family heirloom. And I can assure you there is no doorway behind it.'

Joel ran after Dec and pushed him out of the way. He turned to Finch. For some reason he couldn't fathom, this guy was giving him the creeps. 'You won't mind if I check behind it? I'll be careful.'

'It's your funeral,' Finch replied, standing back with folded arms.

Joel glanced up at the top of the tapestry. It was ancient all right, the kind of thing that probably belonged in a museum. It hung from wooden rings on wall-mounted hooks. As carefully as he could, he lifted its corner and peeked behind. With a flush of annoyance, he noticed that Dec had ripped part of its edge in his enthusiasm.

And worse, when Joel looked behind, there was no doorway to be seen. Just solid wall. He felt for a seam or a crack, a telltale draught. There was nothing.

He turned back round and the dismay must have been visible on his face.

'Satisfied, Inspector Solomon?' Finch said. 'It *was* Solomon, wasn't it?'

'I didn't imagine it,' Dec muttered resolutely. 'There's a passageway behind there.'

There was nothing more for it. Between clenched teeth, Joel thanked Finch for his time, and then virtually dragged Dec back outside.

'Do you still wish to verify Mr Stone's whereabouts?' Finch asked from the steps as they walked back towards the police car.

'That won't be necessary,' Joel said.

Finch nodded stiffly. 'Thank you, officer. Be assured that your superiors will be hearing from us.'

There was a strange light in his eyes as Joel drove off.

They were silent long after they'd driven out of the gates and started making their way back towards the main road.

'I'm fucking telling you I didn't dream it.'

Joel didn't reply.

'So what happens now?' Dec asked.

'I'm taking you home.'

'You don't believe me any more, do you?'

'No, Dec. I don't.'

But Joel knew that was a lie. After a silent drive to the edge of Wallingford, he dropped Dec off at the bottom of Lavender Close a few minutes before noon. He turned the car round. He wasn't heading back towards Oxford.

He was going straight back to Crowmoor Hall.

CHAPTER 39

The VIA office had been in a state of shock all morning following the double bombshell. First the news of the destruction of the Terzi lab, then the video message from the mysterious Gabriel Stone. Many of the VIA staff sat in stunned silence at their desks, barely able to function. Others huddled in groups in corners to jabber and whisper furiously among themselves while gofers scurried by. The frantic scouring of the archives had revealed exactly what Stone had predicted it would: nothing. There was no trace whatsoever of the vampire on any Federation records, no way to track him, not a shred of a clue as to who or where he might be.

While the rest of the building's top floor struggled to come to terms with the situation, Harry Rumble was in his office, on two phones at once and typing emails as he talked. After an hour of helping Slade go back through the drug distribution records in the vain hope of finding a useful lead, Alex walked in Rumble's door to find him slumped and haggard at his desk, tie crooked, hair wild. Xavier Garrett was lurking in the background, filing papers.

'I've just got off the phone with Brussels,' Rumble said wearily to Alex. He was referring to the main headquarters of the Federation Ruling Council, housed in a high-rise building just a few hundred yards from the European Parliament. 'I talked to Gaston Lerouge.' The way he said the name, he might have ended the sentence with an emphatic *'himself'*. Gaston Lerouge was one of the Supremos of the Ruling Council. He held court within the plush FRC offices like a dauphin prince, surrounded by an army of lackeys, and was second in command only to the legendary Olympia Angelopolis, co-founder of the Federation, the Lady of Steel, the one they called The Vampress.

'What an honour,' Alex said. 'The great Lerouge actually condescending to speak with a lowly VIA chief. So what did our illustrious leader and former toy salesman have to say for himself?'

Garrett looked over at her. 'That's enough of that kind of talk, Agent Bishop. A bit of respect would be in order.'

'Turns out that the same moment our friend Stone was delivering his message to us here,' Rumble went on, 'they got an email with the same video clip. The source is untraceable, before you ask.'

'How are they taking it?'

'Official version? Stone is just a minor blip, and we'll have a new pharma lab up and running again before you know it. Nothing to worry about.'

Alex nodded. 'Yeah. Real version?'

'Going apeshit,' Rumble said. 'Or else why would they be calling a general meeting three days from now, in Brussels? Lerouge will be there, along with Achmed Hassan, Cornelius Borowczyk and all the other Supremos. The Vampress will preside, no less. My presence is requested, and I want you there with me.'

'Me?'

Garrett strode over to the desk, pointing a finger at Alex. 'With respect, sir, you can't be seriously thinking of taking her into a meeting with these people. She's insubordinate, a loose cannon. And this is way above her grade.'

For once, Alex wasn't too quick to contradict Garrett. 'Do I really need to be there, Harry? They don't usually have field agents at these kinds of events.'

'You're my top operative,' Rumble insisted. 'And besides, this is no ordinary meeting.' He turned to Garrett, who was trembling with indignation. 'You'll be there too, Xavier.'

Garrett smiled smugly, and relented right away.

As Alex left Rumble's office and headed out of the building, she had other things on her mind than waste-of-time conferences with a bunch of stuffed shirts and bureaucrats. She was thinking back to the young guy Dec Maddon, and his wild story of a big house where a girl had been slaughtered by vampires. As she walked to the Jag, she took out her phone.

'Thames Valley Police,' said the breezy female voice on the other end.

'Is DI Solomon available, please?' Alex asked.

'One moment.' A pause. 'I'm afraid he's not at his desk. May I ask who's calling?'

But Alex was already turning off the phone and getting in the car.

CHAPTER 40

Gillian Hawthorne parked the Rover 75 in the drive before carrying the Sainsbury's shopping bags round the passage to the back door, the way she always did.

'Mrs Hawthorne?'

Gillian turned. She let out a loud huff when she saw Dec Maddon approaching from next door.

'What do *you* want?' she snapped. 'Aren't you supposed to be in prison or something?'

'I want to see Kate,' he said.

'Do you indeed? No chance.'

'Is she all right?'

'That's no concern of yours.' Gillian turned her back on him and continued up the path.

'I've got to see her,' he yelled after her.

She wheeled around. 'You've caused enough trouble as it is. Stay away from my daughter, or I'll have the police down on you again. And don't forget that Kate's father is a solicitor.'

'*Please*, Mrs Hawthorne—'

'Get lost.' Gillian stomped round the back of the house, leaving him standing there looking forlorn. As she turned the key in the back door lock she glanced up at Kate's bedroom window. The curtains were still tightly closed.

Dumping the shopping bags on the kitchen surface, she turned on the grill, opened the pack of sirloin steak and sliced some bread. When the steak sandwich was prepared, she laid the plate on a tray with a glass of milk and carried it up the stairs. Balancing the tray on one hand, she turned the handle of Kate's door and went inside.

Her daughter was still lying in bed, on her side with her back to the door and the duvet pulled up tightly around her neck. It was dark, and the air in the room was stale. Gillian felt like pulling back the curtains and throwing open the window, but thought better of it. She laid the tray down on the bedside table.

'Kate, I brought you something to eat.'

No response.

'Come on, darling. Dr Andrews said you needed to get something down you.'

Kate didn't reply.

'For God's sake, I've just cooked this specially for you. I know you're not feeling yourself, but I'm getting a little tired of this routine.' She reached out to shake Kate's shoulder.

Dr Andrews was the first to get the call.

'I'm sending an ambulance,' he told the hysterical

mother once he'd drawn a breath and collected himself from the shock of the news. 'And I'm on my way.'

And minutes later there were sirens and flashing blue lights all over Lavender Close and Dec Maddon standing there in the middle of it all screaming *what's happened? What's happened?*

CHAPTER 41

Seymour Finch was in the gazebo, staring across Crowmoor Hall's grounds at the river beyond and deep in thought, when he felt the presence and turned to see the young police inspector walking across the lawn towards him.

'What a surprise, Inspector. I didn't think we'd be seeing you again quite so soon. I've just been talking to the valuation people at Sotheby's, by the way. You can expect to receive our invoice for damages shortly.'

'Enough crap, Finch.' Joel strode up the gazebo steps and looked the man in the eye. 'You and I are going to have a talk.'

Finch's gaunt face crinkled into a dry smile. 'Splendid. And what will the topic of our conversation be?'

'You're going to tell me the truth,' Joel said. 'You're going to show me how you open that hidden passage in the ballroom. And then you're going to take me down to the crypt. I know it's there.'

Finch's smile widened to a grin, and then he gave a mirthless laugh, like the sound of sawing wood. 'You do have a vivid imagination, Inspector. I thought the police only concerned themselves with the facts.'

'Start talking.'

Finch shrugged. 'Very well. If that's what you want.' He motioned down the gazebo steps. 'This way, please.'

Joel looked warily at the man for a second or two, then started down the steps.

He hadn't even reached the lawn before the flash of white light filled his head and he felt the wind explode from his lungs. The impact was like being hit by a train. The ground suddenly rushed up to meet his face, and then he felt nothing more.

The first thing Joel registered as the smudged blur of unconsciousness slowly faded back into light was the familiar, concerned face of Sam Carter peering down at him. The second thing he saw was the police officers and paramedics milling about the lawn.

And then he saw Finch.

Joel did a double-take.

Finch was sitting on the steps of the gazebo with a paramedic crouched by him, mopping blood off his face. He looked like he'd been in a serious fist-fight, one eye blackened and puffy, lips split open, his teeth rimmed with red, blood smeared over his bald crown.

'You've really done it this time, haven't you,

Solomon?' Carter muttered out of everyone else's earshot.

'I didn't do anything.'

'Love to say I believed you, Joel, but look at the guy. Have you lost your mind?'

'I didn't touch him.'

'Then how did he get like that?'

'I don't know – someone else did it. Or he did it to himself.'

'He says you attacked him. Says he had to defend himself and got lucky.'

Joel shook his head in protest, wincing at the pain that lanced through his skull. He felt as if he'd gone ten rounds with a heavyweight champ. It seemed impossible that Finch could have done this to him. And that was the whole problem, because there was no way anyone could see Finch as anything but the victim here.

'No. I just came to ask him some more questions.'

Carter sighed. 'You're in deep shit. You know who Finch works for, don't you?'

'Yeah, yeah, I know who he works for.'

Finch looked like a frail old man as the paramedics escorted him into the ambulance. Joel watched as it drove away, and then it was him being escorted to the waiting police car.

CHAPTER 42

London docks
1.15 p.m.

Alex had to retrace her steps three times up and down the quayside before she felt certain of what she was seeing.

She hadn't quite known what she was going to find when she returned to the wharf where the *Anica* was moored: the place swarming with police and forensics teams, maybe, everything sealed off with crime scene tape, dozens of people running around talking on radios. Or maybe the vessel would be much as she'd last seen it the night before – a floating graveyard of dismembered corpses that might, just might, offer up some kind of clue about the vampire attackers who'd ambushed them here, maybe even a lead that could guide her all the way back to the mysterious Gabriel Stone. She knew that might be too much to hope for. Stone seemed like a guy who'd had a lot of practice in covering his tracks.

But she hadn't expected to find this.

An empty space where the *Anica* had been just the previous night. The ship was just gone.

'Who's helping you, Stone?' she asked herself out loud as she gazed at the vacant mooring. 'How are you making all this happen?'

The rathouse pub that was Paulie Lomax's and his cousin Vinnie's watering hole of choice wasn't more than a fifteen-minute walk from the dock. Alex stepped inside the door to be greeted by the surly stares of a bunch of severely nicotine-stained, tattooed, hard-drinking individuals. There were a couple of wolf whistles as she made her way up towards the bar and one of the card players in the corner yelled out something obscene. She wondered whether it would be witty and appropriate just to take out the .44 Smith and blow the top of his head off; maybe, but that wasn't going to help with the business at hand. Without turning round, she gave him the finger instead. She ignored the whooping and cheering, and walked up to the bar.

In a London that was almost completely homogenised by the inexorable rise of the plastic middle class and the sterile health-and-safety culture that seemed to be taking hold everywhere, she almost relished the spit and sawdust, sweat and grime of a place like this. It reminded her of the old days. You just didn't want to be a woman back then.

The guy behind the bar was battered and grizzled

and looked like he'd served his time in the boxing ring and lost just about every fight he'd been in. He grinned wolfishly and leaned on the pitted wood as she approached.

'All right, darling. What can I do you for?'

'I'm looking for Paulie Lomax.'

The grin dropped. 'Paulie Lomax?'

'Guy they call Four-Finger. And his friend Vinnie. You know them?'

'Maybe I do. Maybe I don't. One thing I do know, love, is that I don't know you.'

'Maybe you've heard of Rudi Bertolino?' she said, returning his stare. 'He's a friend of mine.'

The barman shrugged. 'You need to talk to Cheap Eddie. Through there.' He motioned at a door in the corner.

On the other side was a dingy corridor. It was lit by a naked bulb encrusted with last summer's dead bluebottles. There was another door at the end of the passage, and she went through it without knocking. Inside the room, a morbidly obese guy of about sixty was sitting on a worn armchair, reading a rumpled copy of the *Racing Times* with a fat stogie clamped between his teeth. The room stank of stale cigar smoke. He didn't glance up as the door creaked open.

'Can't you fuckin' knock, Terry?'

'No wonder they call you Cheap Eddie,' Alex said as she walked in and shut the door behind her. 'That thing smells like shit. Or is it you?'

A brindled pit bull stalked out from behind the

fat man's armchair, locked eyes on Alex and drew its lips back in a snarl. Alex calmly turned to meet its gaze, and it whimpered and drew away with its tail curled up tight between its legs.

Cheap Eddie stared at the cowering animal, then up at Alex. He plucked the cigar out of his mouth. 'What've you done to my dog?'

'Nothing yet.'

His bloodshot eyes bulged. 'Who the fuck are you?'

'Someone who'll go easy on you if I get the information I want.'

He scowled, then his stubbly face creased up into a laugh. 'Oh yeah? And what information would that be, flowerpot?'

'Like where I can find Four-Finger Paulie Lomax and his mate Vinnie.'

Eddie took a big puff of his cigar and blew a cloud of smoke at her. 'Never heard of them.'

Alex didn't blink at the billow of foul smoke around her face. 'I don't have time for smart guys, Eddie.'

'I'm not sure I like your tone, sweetheart.'

'Better get used to it,' she said. She slipped the .44 out of its holster, took a step towards him. Grabbed him by the throat, yanked him towards her and stuffed the gun muzzle hard under his cheekbone. 'I really hate repeating myself, Eddie.'

He struggled against her grip. Close on thirty stone of muscle and lard, lifted half out of his armchair, one-handed, by a woman a fraction his size, and he couldn't budge her an inch. Beads of sweat formed on his brow.

'Okay, okay. They was here a few nights ago. Haven't seen 'em since.'

'See how well we're getting on now? Who were they with?'

'Bunch of foreigners. They were talking in the corner.'

'That's it?'

'That's all I remember.'

'Sure?' She cocked the gun.

Eddie went a shade paler. 'Wait. Hold on. Later on, after closing time, I was stacking crates in the alley when I saw Paulie hanging about with this big black geezer and this woman.'

'Good-looking woman with black hair?'

Eddie nodded. 'Real corker. Looked like she stepped out of a lads' mag.'

Alex thought hard. So Rudi Bertolino hadn't betrayed her. He'd been used to feed her information that would lead her into a trap. But how had Stone's people known he was her informant?

'Where does Paulie live?' she asked Cheap Eddie.

'Harlesden somewhere.'

'You'll have to do better than that, Eddie.'

'I don't have the address, honest.' He gulped. Sweat poured off his nose and through the white bristles over his upper lip. 'But I can get it.'

Alex let him go, and he slumped back into his armchair, breathing hard. She holstered the revolver and grabbed his wrist and a ballpoint pen from his desk.

'You call me on this number,' she said as she wrote it across the back of his chubby hand. 'I'd better hear from you, Eddie. And I'd better not find out you talked to anyone about our chat. Either way, I'll be back here to finish it.'

CHAPTER 43

Thames Valley Police Headquarters, Kidlington
1.49 p.m.

'I 've just got off the phone,' Chief Super-intendent Page said as Joel was marched into his office by two officers in uniform. 'You want to know who with?'

Joel said nothing. Sam Carter stepped into the room after him and hung about uncomfortably in the background.

Page glared at Joel from across the broad desk. He was a heavyset man in his late fifties, with a downturned mouth like a razor slash. When he was pissed off, which was most of the time, the rash of broken veins across his cheeks glowed scarlet. At this moment they were the wrong side of beetroot.

'Do you know whose employee you beat up? Do you have *any* idea the kind of friends Gabriel Stone has?'

'I didn't beat anyone up,' Joel muttered resignedly. 'But I have the feeling you're going to tell me anyway.'

'Jeremy Lonsdale. Name familiar?'

'Let me think,' Joel said. He could feel Carter's gaze on his back, silently pleading with him to watch his mouth.

'Probably our next Prime Minister. You certainly pick them, Inspector.' Page shook his head in disbelief, and his jowls wobbled. 'What's wrong with you?'

'Nothing.'

'What's *wrong* with you?' Page repeated more loudly. 'Destruction of valuable antique property. Accusations more bizarre and ridiculous than anything I've heard in nearly forty years in the force. Letting some dopehead kid fill your brain with nonsense. Secret passages. Underground crypts. And then beating up an innocent member of the public. Did you know Seymour Finch has a terminal medical condition?'

He punches pretty well for a dying man, Joel wanted to say. But that might have been pushing his luck.

'And that's not all,' Page went on, warming to his anger. 'I had a talk with a solicitor this morning. A certain Jonathan Hawthorne. Ring any bells? Apparently you were round at his home yesterday afternoon, harassing his family and upsetting a sick girl. Tell me this isn't true.'

'I wouldn't call it harassment.'

'So you're not denying this?'

'Something's going on, sir.'

'Damn right something's going on. In your head. Meanwhile, we've got a suspected serial killer

249

going around our county. And this is what I have to deal with? One of my best officers going into a complete fucking meltdown.' Page's voice had risen to a shout, and he was out of his chair with his fists on the desk. His whole body seemed to be quivering with rage. 'You're suspended, Solomon.'

'*What?*'

At the back of the room, Carter rolled his eyes. 'Told you so,' his expression said.

'Six months. That's it. No questions. And consider yourself bloody fortunate that you're dealing with reasonable men. Jeremy Lonsdale has told me that neither Mr Finch nor Mr Stone will be pressing charges. If something like this got into the press . . .' Page puffed out his cheeks. The veins were alarmingly inflamed. 'Doesn't bear thinking about.' He pointed a stubby finger in Joel's face. 'But I'm warning you. I know you. I know you're a determined bastard when you want to be. Go anywhere near the Stone estate – I'm talking within a mile of it – or anywhere near him or any of his employees . . .' He made a face. 'You even *think* about them, and I'll have your bloody head on a plate. Tell me that's as clear as I could possibly make myself.'

'It is very clear, sir.'

'Yes, it is. Now get out. I don't want to see your face or hear your name for six months. I just hope that when you come back you'll have learned some sense.'

★   ★   ★

Joel stormed out of Page's office and slammed the door behind him with a noise like the crack of a rifle shot. He was halfway down the corridor when the door opened again and Carter came running out after him.

'Hey, slow down.'

Joel pointed. 'That stupid bastard has no idea what's going on here.'

'And you do?'

'I think I do, yeah.'

'So tell me. I'm all ears.'

'I'm not sure you'd want to know.'

Carter looked at his watch. 'I have a meeting this afternoon, but I can spare a few minutes. Let's go for a pint.'

Thirty minutes later they were sitting at a quiet corner table in the Wheatsheaf pub in central Oxford, just up the road from the police station. Talking quietly, Joel spilled out what he knew, what he feared, until there was nothing left to say and he was staring numbly into his beer. His head was still bursting with pain from where Finch had hit him.

Across the table, Sam Carter was quiet for a long time. He picked up his beer, was about to take a sip, then put the glass down again.

'Vampires,' he said in a flat tone.

'This is exactly how I told you you'd react.'

'Uh, vampires, Joel. The Undead. Human sacrifices.'

Joel shook his head. 'It's not a sacrifice. They do it to get the—'

'The blood. Yeah, yeah, I get it. I've seen the movies.'

'This is not a movie, Sam. This is real.'

'This is real.'

'Absolutely real. I saw them. And I've seen them before. Years ago.'

'You've seen them before.'

'You just going to keep repeating everything I say, or are you going to tell me what you think?'

Carter stared at him. 'You're completely fucking serious, aren't you? Do you have *any* idea what you're laying on me with this?'

'You've known me a long time. When have I ever bullshitted you?'

'Yeah, but this—'

'Okay, you think it's crazy.'

'No, I wouldn't use that word. Floridly insane, maybe – crazy doesn't quite cover it.'

'Thanks.'

Carter jabbed a finger at him. 'Listen to me like you've never listened to anyone before. Do not – do *not* – breathe a single solitary word of this to anyone else. They won't just put you on suspension. They'll have you fucking committed, mate.'

'You think all this doesn't sound mad to me too?'

'Be straight with me. Are you drinking? Doing drugs? Happens to the best of us. Goes with this shitty job. Christ knows I have moments when I'd like to dive in a bottle of Jack Daniel's and swim around in there the rest of my life, happy as a sandboy. Except I don't, Joel. I bounce back, every fucking time, because that's what you do.'

'I'm not drinking, and I don't do drugs. You know that.'

'Yeah, and I also know Tania walking out hit you a lot harder than you liked to let on.'

Joel sighed. 'That was nearly seven months ago. I'm over it.'

'Good. Then here's my advice. Find yourself a nice young lady. Take a holiday together somewhere that has lots of sun and sand and cocktails. Shag your brains out for a week or two.'

'I hate beaches,' Joel said.

'Right. I forgot you're one of these nutjobs who gets his jollies hanging off a cliff face or diving into some icy lake in the middle of nowhere. Whatever. All I'm saying is, get out of here and forget about the Super, forget about everything. Most of all, do yourself a favour and forget about fucking *vampires*. Jesus Christ, Joel.'

Joel shook his head. 'I can't do that. I have to go on with it, my own way.'

'I was afraid you'd say that.' Carter sighed. 'Fine. You're my friend. If you need me, you know where to find me.' He looked at his watch. 'Shit. Got to run.' He slurped back the last of his beer, got up and clapped Joel on the shoulder. 'You take care, all right?'

'I'll be fine.'

'Seriously?'

'Get out of here. You're going to be late.' Joel watched Carter muscle his way out of the door, then finished his drink and went to get another. For a few minutes he sat drinking and gazing into the middle distance.

Maybe it was true. Maybe he'd just lost his mind.

With all his heart he yearned to be wrong, to have just concocted all this out of a stress-frazzled brain. More than anything, he wished that he could take advantage of his suspension to relax, take it easy and then wake up one morning and realise that these crazy ideas had simply evaporated from his mind.

But he knew that wasn't going to happen. This wasn't just going to go away. Things could only get worse, and he was going to have to face it, alone. Completely alone.

Or maybe not.

Maybe I could have helped you.

As the words came back to him, he reached for his wallet and dug out the business card Alex Bishop had given him in the hospital.

What had she meant by that? There was only one way to find out. And he couldn't pretend to himself that he didn't want to see her again anyway. He dialled her number, but the answering service told him the phone was switched off. He swore.

'I've got to do something,' he muttered to himself.

Then he knew what that something was.
He left his drink unfinished on the table.

By four in the afternoon, he was hard on the throttle of the Hayabusa, battling against a ninety-mile-an-hour wind as he headed north away from the city to a place he hadn't seen for eighteen years and had never wanted to see again.

CHAPTER 44

90 km from Norilsk, Central Siberian Plateau
6.45 p.m. GMT/1.45 a.m. local time

The journey wasn't far from double the distance between London and Moscow, and Gabriel Stone had been dormant in his crate for most of the time that Jeremy Lonsdale's borrowed Gulfstream had been cutting eastwards across Europe.

Many time zones had come and gone, and it was late night by the time the jet reached the small airfield a few kilometres from the remote mining outpost of Norilsk. Stone emerged from the sanctuary of his container into a world utterly different from the one he'd left behind him. The temperature had dropped to minus fifteen centigrade.

One of only three cities worldwide residing in a continuous permafrost zone, Norilsk lay at the heart of the Russian province known as Krasnoyarsk Krai. More than two million square kilometres of sub-arctic tundra, mountains and lakes, it was one of the most inaccessible and inhospitable wildernesses on the planet. For the community of mostly miners that endured the conditions there, it was an icy hell.

For the other creatures who had chosen it as their home, it was perfect.

Stone breathed the still, freezing air, gazed up at the stars twinkling in the vast black sky and, just for an instant, he almost envied a human's capacity to appreciate beautiful things. Almost.

A black Mercedes four-wheel drive equipped with snow chains had been waiting for him and his escort at the airfield. It had driven them far out into the wilderness, a single black speck on an endless expanse of frozen tundra overlooked by the towering Putoran Mountains. No human would have built a road where they were going.

At the outer limit of where a car could travel, they were met by a small procession of snowmobiles and skimmed at speed over the white landscape to a place where no human would willingly venture. Another civilisation dwelled here, far from the eyes of the world.

Stone left the convoy on foot. The wind howled and eddies of ice whipped around him as he walked alone to the base of the gigantic mountain that was his destination. He soon found the cave entrance, almost completely blocked by snow, and made his way downwards through winding icy tunnels carved twenty centuries ago. He was excited about the meeting that was about to take place, but though he would never have admitted it, certainly not to any of his circle and barely even to himself, mingled somewhere within that sense of excitement was an emotion that Gabriel Stone had very seldom experienced in his very long existence.

He was afraid. His Masters had that effect on him.

As he approached the citadel hidden deep inside the mountain, the ice tunnels were draped in red satin and the ornate crystalline sculptures on the mirror-polished ceilings, higher and more grandiose than in any human cathedral, depicted mythological scenes from the Old Times. As he'd done on his previous visits, he made his way to a cavernous ante-chamber on the outer ring of the citadel. The chamber was bare except for a semi-circle of red satin-covered thrones. He sat and waited there, listening to the whistle of the wind around the ice walls and going carefully through the report he was about to make.

Before long, one of the Masters arrived. Stone recognised him as one of the Elders, a creature whose age couldn't easily be counted. The tall, thin figure was draped from head to foot in a hooded robe. Stone got to his feet and bowed formally as he entered the chamber. The robe's sleeve fell away from a long, bony hand as the Master gestured for him to stay seated. The clawed fingers reached up and slowly peeled back the hem of the hood.

The pale, translucent, blue-hued skin of the Master's bald skull was lined with veins and wrinkles. The ears were long and pointed. When the Master sat on the throne beside his and turned that dark gaze on him, Stone was reminded of how tiny he'd always felt in the presence of such deep, terrible wisdom. He had spent a great deal of time learning from them but, even so, their magnificence was humbling to him. A human would simply, instantly, die of terror in such a place. For Stone, it was a religious experience.

They exchanged the traditional greetings in the guttural, harsh tones of the Old Language.

'My heart sings to see you again, *Krajzok*,' the Master said, using an expression that translated roughly as 'Young One'.

'You honour me,' Stone replied graciously.

'Later we will feed. First, Young One, tell me. How does your task progress?'

'I hope you will be pleased to hear that the plans are well underway.' Stone carefully ran through the account of the destruction of the Terzi plant, the acquisition of the pharmaceutical stockpiles, and the slaying of many enemy agents. Use of the heretical term 'Federation' was something to be avoided when referring to the opposition, knowing that even its mention would invoke fury. The fury of the Masters was not something Stone wanted to witness.

'Now the traitors are weak,' he said in summation. 'Before long, we will strike against them using their own weapons, and finish them.'

259

The Master reflected a while. 'I am not alone, Young One, in finding your use of these abominable technologies deeply discomforting. Is there no other way?'

Stone was very careful in his reply. 'I share your sense of unease, Master. Yet I find the irony somehow appropriate. Let the filth perish by the same means they employed against their own, more worthy, kin. Once the task is fully accomplished, you may rest assured that these evil creations will be consigned to history along with their creators.'

The Master nodded slowly. 'You are not unwise, Young One. You have repaid our trust in you. Thanks to your noble efforts, our nation will soon reclaim its rightful place.'

'Ever your servant,' Stone replied, bowing his head.

The Master peered deep into his eyes. It was as though a searchlight were scanning his mind.

'I sense you have more to tell us,' the Master said with a thin smile. 'Something important.'

All throughout the long journey to Russia, as he'd lain there in his box, Stone had been debating furiously with himself as to whether he should mention the possible discovery by a human of the cross of Ardaich. To do so would entail explanations that he preferred to avoid. He'd allowed the human to escape him, and that was a sign of weakness he couldn't afford to display.

'Well?' the Master said, waiting.

'I have told you all there is to tell,' Stone lied, using all his mental powers to conceal his true thoughts. Inwardly, he was cringing. The Master was a powerful mind-reader and his wrath would be beyond imagining if he discovered he was being deceived.

'You are sure?'

'I am sure.'

The Master seemed satisfied. He laid his clawed hand on Stone's shoulder.

'Come. You have a long journey back. Feed with us a while before you leave, and let us discuss our plans further.'

CHAPTER 45

It was dark outside Bill Andrews's office window at the private Rothwell Clinic outside Wallingford. In front of him on his desk were Kate Hawthorne's case notes. He'd been staring at them long enough for the words to start to float before his eyes. He took off his glasses and rubbed his face. Fatigue was making his head spin and his brow prickled with cold sweat. He reached for the little bottle of pills in the breast pocket of his white coat, gulped one down.

It had been a ghastly afternoon. Most of it had been spent on the impossible task of trying to console the Hawthorne family. He'd had to listen to Gillian weeping uncontrollably, while struggling to come up with a semi-plausible explanation as to how their lovely, healthy daughter could have just faded away for no apparent reason, in just a matter of days.

The fact was, he was completely stumped.

'Start from the beginning, Bill,' he muttered. He flicked back to the first page and began scrutinising the case notes for the thousandth time, determined to make sense of them.

But how could you make sense of something that seemed scientifically impossible? She was healthy. Normal. All the tests were negative. Technically, there was nothing wrong with Kate Hawthorne – other than the fact that she was lying dead on a steel tray in the main building across the way from his office.

Even more perplexing were the lesions on the girl's neck. When Gillian had first called him out to the house, they'd been livid and ugly, the flesh around them mottled and purple. When he'd caught a glimpse of Kate's dead body under the sheet this afternoon, the marks seemed to have virtually gone.

He frowned. Not even a healthy patient could have healed so fast. How could someone who was dying? It just didn't make sense.

Could he have imagined it? A trick of the light? Too distracted by the chaos and the scenes of grief going on around him?

'Damn it,' he said out loud. 'Let's take another look.' He got up from his desk, left the office and walked through the neon-lit corridor that led to the main building. The mortuary was located in the basement of the east wing. Dr Andrews descended the stairs and pushed through the fire doors into his least favourite part of the hospital.

In what the staff called 'the Cooler' was a wall of stainless steel panels. Behind each panel was a retractable compartment seven feet long and three feet wide, running on rails. They were like the drawers of a huge filing cabinet, each labelled with a name and a number. This was only a small private facility, and the Cooler was never anywhere near capacity. At most, they had four or five cadavers in at a time. He quickly found the compartment with Kate Hawthorne's name and admission number. Taking a deep breath, he gripped the cold steel handle and pulled.

The compartment slid open smoothly on its rails.

He looked inside.

Blinked. Then looked again.

It was empty.

Dr Andrews took a step back. Was this some kind of administrative error? He was about to open another compartment when he heard a voice behind him.

'Hello, Doctor. Looking for me?'

He swung round.

Kate Hawthorne was standing behind him, naked. He gaped, speechless. A rapid drum rhythm started up inside his ribcage.

She smiled.

Holy Lord, those teeth.

The drum began to roll faster, louder, building to a crescendo . . . then . . .

Bang.

'My heart—' Dr Andrews clutched at his chest and cried out in pain as the cardiac attack ripped through him. His knees buckled. He pitched forward, felt his head crack open on the tiled floor.

His eyes rolled up, and through the rising mist he saw Kate Hawthorne beaming bright-eyed down at him, her fangs white against her red lips. Then his vision dimmed, and he saw no more.

Crowmoor Hall
8.12 p.m.

Lillith skidded her bright yellow Lotus Elise to a halt on the gravel, threw open the door and grabbed the bundle from the passenger seat. It wriggled feebly in her arms as she carried it into the dark house. She was sated from her evening feed, but who said you had to be hungry to eat? Something for dessert.

With that thought in mind she made her way through the gloomy passages to the tower in the east wing where her private quarters were situated. The creaking of a door made her turn, and she saw Finch standing there.

'What happened to your face?' she asked him, noticing the bruises. In a grave, solemn tone he told her about that day's incident with Solomon, the police officer.

'Interesting,' Lillith purred. 'So now we know all about our little cross-bearing friend.'

As she spoke, her vampire's mind was turning over at high speed. So much for the human having found the cross of Ardaich, she thought. If his claim had been anything more than a desperate bluff, he could have destroyed them

all. Gabriel would have returned home to a graveyard.

Lillith felt anger rise up inside her at the thought
of her brother. He'd been a warrior once, like her.
No vampire had been bolder, wilder, more wonderfully cruel and impetuous. But he'd changed of
late. She was tired of his cautious diplomat's ways,
frustrated by his endless politicising.

'Did I do well, ma'am?' Finch's voice was
cracked with anxiety. 'I obeyed Mr Stone's wishes
as best I could.'

'You did brilliantly, Seymour. Gabriel will be
very pleased. As am I.'

Finch bowed his head in relief. 'Thank you,
ma'am.'

'Now for the next part of your task,' she said.
'Now that we know who the human is, you are
to pay him a visit. Retrieve whatever evidence he
has to do with the cross, and then slaughter him.'

'Ma'am? I thought Mr Stone said not to kill—'

'I was talking to Gabriel just minutes ago,' she
lied. 'There's been a change of plan. We want the
human dead. You understand me?'

Finch nodded. 'I understand perfectly.'

'Your loyalty will be repaid,' she said.

'If I m-may be so bold as to mention it,' Finch
stammered. 'I have long hoped—'

'That you would be inducted into our circle?
Become one of us?'

'It is my deepest, most heartfelt wish,' Finch said
with a quaver.

Lillith knew that Gabriel would never consider such a thing. Finch was far too useful to them as a ghoul. Not quite a vampire, but not quite a human either. Ghouls dwelt in a shadow world somewhere in between.

'Do this thing for us,' she said, 'and I'm sure my brother will express his gratitude. In the meantime, Seymour, a token of our appreciation.' She passed him the bundle that she'd been holding in her arms. Finch took it from her, and examined it with glittering eyes as it stirred and mewled in his grip.

'Its owner left it unattended,' she said.

Finch looked up at her, melting with gratitude. 'For me?'

'Enjoy,' she smiled.

'Inspector Joel Solomon is a dead man,' Finch said.

CHAPTER 46

Dec lay curled up in a foetal position in his bed with the covers pulled up over his head. He wondered whether he could suffocate like this.

He hoped so.

It was impossible to stop the replay looping through his mind as he relived the scenes he'd witnessed earlier that day. The ambulance crew wheeling the gurney out into Lavender Close. Kate's still body covered by a white sheet. Her mother howling with grief. The whole fucking street out gawping, half of them already prodding their mobiles to text their family members at work about the latest gossip that would keep them morbidly entertained for days and weeks to come. He'd wanted to punch them, ram their phones down their fucking throats.

He'd watched as the gurney was loaded into the back of the ambulance.

Still she hadn't stirred.

Then they'd closed the doors and driven away. With tears streaming down his face he'd sprinted back into the house, crashed into his room and hurled himself into bed. Never to come out. This was it. The end of everything.

It was all his fault. If he hadn't tried to play the smart guy, the man of the world, with those cursed ecstasy pills. If he'd just been himself, ordinary old Dec Maddon. Then Kate would still be alive.

He'd lain here in bed all through the day, rocking from side to side and sobbing on his pillow, only a few snatches of fitful sleep offering any respite from the torture.

Through his pain he'd heard the sounds of the street outside, cars coming and going, voices. The familiar engine note of his ma's Renault Clio pulling up on the driveway after five o'clock when she got back from work. Mrs Jackson from number twenty calling across to her, 'Have you heard?' His ma's cry of horror as she was told the news, and then a lot of talking in low voices that he hadn't been able to make out. He'd sunk back into his torpor, not responding when his mum had come to his room five minutes later to see how he was.

For once she didn't scream at him for lying in bed with his shoes on. He heard the door shut and her soft steps walk away. Some time later the diesel clatter of the Transit told him his da and brother Cormac were home. More raised voices downstairs, followed by an unnatural hush all through the house.

Now it was dark in the room. A lot of time had passed and with its passage Dec's emotions were changing. Instead of a crippling, paralysing depression, he could feel a white hot tide of rage building up inside. Instead of losing the will to live, now he was suddenly tingling with energy, his mind tightening into focus until he could think of only one thing.

He leapt out of bed and burst out of his room. Raced past Cormac's door and up to the end of the hall, where the door to his parents' room was open. He stepped in, already feeling bad about what he was going to do. Hanging over the head of his folks' bed was a heavy brass crucifix. He strode up to it, reached up his hand to it, then drew back with a pang of guilt.

I'm just borrowing it, he thought. *And they're not even that religious anyway.*

He grabbed it off the wall and weighed it in his hand. It felt good. Like a weapon. His mind filled with visions of himself confronting those monsters. Grabbing one and plunging the blunt end of the metal into its heart. He imagined how it would scream and shrivel up and fall around his feet like crisps of burnt paper. Then he'd kick it into a cloud of ash and move on to the next bastard vampire in the line. Send them all to hell, where they belonged.

He thrust the crucifix like a dagger into his belt, feeling suddenly invulnerable. Gripped with wild fury, he charged down the stairs three at a time and almost crashed into his ma, who was coming up with a mug of tea and a plate of biscuits.

'Thought you might be wanting—' she began.

'I'm going out. Need to borrow the Clio. Okay?'

Her startled gaze landed on the crucifix in his belt. 'What are you doing with that thing?'

'Off to kill some vampires.'

'What?'

'See you, Ma.' He bounded down the rest of the stairs. Through the living room doorway he could see his da and Cormac slumped in front of the TV. Their long faces told him right away that they knew about Kate. Cormac was muttering something and shaking his head as he cracked open a can of lager and foam spat over his jeans. They both looked up as Dec went dashing past, making for the front door.

'You all right, son?' his da called out, voice full of worry. Dec barely heard him as he snatched his mother's car keys off the hook by the door.

Mrs Maddon came thudding down the stairs after her son. 'You listen to me, now . . .'

'Bye, Ma.'

'Liam, talk to him!' she yelled at her husband. 'Cormac!'

But Dec was already out the door. He leapt in the Clio, reversed down the drive with a squeal of tyres and sped away down Lavender Close.

He knew exactly where he was going.

CHAPTER 47

Alex could almost smell Cheap Eddie's cigar from the other end of the line when he called her back.

'You took your time,' she said. 'I've been waiting hours.' She checked her watch as she spoke. 9.42 p.m.

'Yeah, well, I had to ask around, didn't I?'

He gave her the address. Before he'd even finished saying it, she had turned the car around, pointing north towards Harlesden. The sat-nav gave her a thirty-five-minute ETA – but it didn't know who was driving. She got to Harlesden a shade before ten, and five minutes after that she was parking the Jag in the dingy road where Paulie Lomax lived. Some street kids were loitering nearby and eyeing up the car, but shrank away disconcerted when she caught their eye and smiled sweetly at them.

The concrete stairway leading up to Paulie's flat reeked of piss and lager vomit, and the graffiti that covered the block walls was an exercise in nihilism. *Fuck you. Fuck this. Fuck everything.*

Someone had fucked with the lock on Paulie's

door, too. The whole cylinder had been punched through the wood from the outside and was lying among the splinters on the peeled linoleum of the entrance hall.

'Surprise, surprise,' Alex muttered to herself as the stink reached her nostrils over the smell of stale sweat and booze. To a vampire, the scent of live human blood was the most enticing thing in the universe but the stench of dead blood was the most repellent, and they could smell it a long way off. It was coming from behind a door, and she knew what she was going to find even before she kicked it open.

All that remained remotely recognisable of Paulie Lomax's human form was the four-fingered right hand that lay curled on the floor. It had been roughly severed at the wrist. It looked like a maimed spider that had died trying to drag itself away to safety.

The rest of him was smeared up the wall, across the bed, over the threadbare carpet. Some unidentifiable chunk had found its way up to the ceiling and snagged on the lightshade. Other than the muted thump of rap music coming from an adjoining flat, the only sound in the place was the soft *plop . . . plop . . . plop* as congealing blood dripped down onto the floor.

'Keeping busy, Stone,' Alex said out loud as she walked back out to the street.

⋆ ⋆ ⋆

The clouds had parted and the full moon was sparkling on the early autumnal frost that covered the lawns of the stately home. Dec tiptoed through the grounds, glancing furtively around him as he went. The brass crucifix from his parents' bedroom, thrust through his belt like a short sword on his left hip, was all that held back the rising tide of panic as the adrenalin-fuelled lust for revenge that had sustained him on the drive from Wallingford to Henley quickly ebbed away. The tremble in his hands was getting worse. He was beginning to think he'd been too hasty. He was a fool – should have called Joel Solomon before venturing out here alone like this.

The bare, crooked fingers of the trees seemed to claw at him as he made his way through the grounds. Things that had no place in this world would be awake now. Perhaps watching him at this very moment from the shadows of the trees and the dark windows of the old house.

Too late. You're here now.

Shivers seized him from head to toe as he heard the rustle of something moving towards him through the foliage. Unable to help himself, he broke into a run through the fallen leaves and crackling twigs. Something snagged his foot and he fell with a grunt and twisted in terror to look back – and saw the badger ambling away through the bushes.

Dec picked himself up, feeling stupid and shaken, and resumed his creeping progress towards the manor house. A breathless dash across the open stretch of lawn and he'd made it to the wall. With his back pressed tight against the pitted stonework and his heart in his mouth, he edged down its length, keeping his mind resolutely closed to the horrors inside.

Then, without warning, a side door burst open just a few yards ahead, and Dec almost collapsed in terror as a gaunt, bald-headed figure stepped out. This was it. He was caught. Out in the open, with nowhere to hide and nowhere to run. They must have been watching his approach from behind the darkened windows. His heart began to race out of control, his chest so tight it felt like his ribs would crack.

But nothing happened. Finch paused, looking out across the gardens, and Dec realised the man was quite unaware of his presence. Finch quietly shut the side door behind him and began to walk away from the house.

Dec swallowed hard, fighting to control the quaking in his knees. He peeled himself away from the wall and followed Finch across the grass, creeping stealthily from bush to bush. His hand moved to his belt and his fingers closed on the cold, reassuringly solid metal of the crucifix. As the moonlight shone off the back of Finch's bald head, Dec imagined swinging the cross with all his might and splitting it open.

Kill the lackey first. Then move on to the rest of the bastards.

For Kate.

Finch walked on, following a winding path away from the lawns and through the trees, towards a dark, lopsided structure that looked like an old shed or gardener's hut. Finch opened the door with a creak, and stepped inside. For a few moments, Dec lost sight of him in the darkness and squinted to see. Then a soft glow of light filled the hut as Finch reappeared in the doorway holding a paraffin lantern.

Dec crouched behind a shrub and watched through the open door as Finch placed the lantern on a table before squatting down on the floor to pick something out of a cardboard box. It was some kind of package, wrapped up in paper like a bag of fish and chips. Dec watched breathlessly as the man carefully unwrapped it, dipped a hand inside and then brought his hand up to his mouth. Sure enough, he'd gone into the hut to eat.

Perfect, Dec thought. While the fucker was distracted, he'd sneak up on him and knock his brains out.

Dec moved closer.

Finch didn't see him.

He moved a little closer.

Finch continued to eat, making little smacking sounds.

A few more steps. Dec raised the crucifix like

an axe. His heart was thumping like crazy, and he had to fight to control his breathing.

Then he stopped.

And stared at the food in Finch's hand, realising with a shock what it was that the man was munching on.

It wasn't a piece of fish. It was a baby's arm. Blue, mottled, severed above its dimpled little elbow. Finch was gnawing on the bone, sucking and slurping and groaning to himself in pleasure.

Dec didn't even feel the crucifix slip from his fingers. The next thing he knew, he was running like hell away from the hut, sprinting across the grass. *Which way was the wall? Which way?* Twigs cracked and snapped underfoot and the leafless branches whipped his face as he stumbled along.

The sound of a voice stopped him dead in his tracks.

'Hello, Declan.'

Very slowly, he turned.

He knew that voice.

She moved sinuously towards him. She was wearing a long white dress; it looked like a shroud in the darkness.

'I knew you'd come,' she said softly.

'Kate?' he gasped in astonishment. It was her . . . and it wasn't.

He'd never seen her look this way before. The thin white material clung to every curve of her body as she stepped out into the patch of moonlight between the trees. He could see she was naked underneath.

'But you're dead.'

'I didn't die,' she whispered to him. 'My mother made it up, to keep us apart.'

She was beautiful. He couldn't stop staring at her.

'Kiss me, Declan,' she said, and her lips parted.

CHAPTER 48

Ten miles from Dornoch, the Highlands of Scotland
10.41 p.m.

The Hayabusa's trip meter read four hundred and thirty-five miles as Joel rode up the bumpy path through the trees. A fox darted away as his headlight cut through the overgrowth of thistles and brambles. Rounding the bend in the path, the semi-derelict cottage came into view up ahead. He fought the urge to turn the bike right around and ride back down the whole length of the country.

Joel parked the bike in what had once been the front yard, turned off the engine and peeled himself painfully out of the saddle, stiff and aching and frozen to the core from the long ride. But the chills running through his body weren't only the effects of the cold. Just being here again had filled him with dread.

He lifted off his helmet and looked around. The last time he'd seen the cottage, it had stood in its own clearing. Now, after nearly twenty years of neglect, the woods had encroached on the

279

building. The naked branches raked the roof and scraped against the walls to the sway of the cold wind. The whitewashed walls were thick with moss, and the ivy had grown over most of the windows. He stared for a long time at the front door, still splintered in half from where the vampire had smashed his way in all those years ago.

And as he stood there, memories flooding back to him, Joel thought about the strange, wonderful man who had been his grandfather.

The mystery of why Nicholas Solomon had suddenly, sometime during the mid-1970s, abandoned his respectable middle-class existence, left his wife for no apparent reason and disappeared virtually overnight to lead a reclusive life up here in the middle of nowhere had always been a contentious issue in the Solomon family. Joel's parents had brought him up to believe that his grandfather was selfish, obsessive, mad as a bag of snakes, someone for whom 'eccentric' was way too kind a word. 'Crazy Nick' was what they'd called him.

For years after his unexplained disappearance, the family had refused to have anything to do with him. Joel had been about five years old when his father had, for reasons that had never been discussed, decided to make contact with Crazy Nick again. One of his early memories was of his father talking on the phone to a private detective he'd hired to track the old man down. Soon after that the family had tentatively made contact with him and paid their first visit to his Highland hideaway.

It hadn't been a welcome one. Nicholas Solomon had seemed deeply unhappy about their presence, nervous and on edge and impatient for them to leave. His father had said the old man resented them – but young Joel had never believed that. It had seemed to him that he was the only one who could see the sadness in his grandfather's eyes as they said their goodbyes. As the years passed and the visits to the isolated cottage became more frequent, Joel had always felt that the growing bond between him and his grandfather was the only thing holding the family together. He'd loved the old man dearly. Always would.

Technically, the abandoned cottage was Joel's own property. The uncle and aunt who'd taken him in after the tragedy hadn't wanted to know about the place, and it had passed to him when he'd turned eighteen. He hadn't wanted to think about it, let alone renovate it for sale. Let it rot.

The broken door groaned loudly as he pushed it open and stepped inside, shining his torch into the entrance hall. Weeds had invaded the gaps between the stone tiles. The place smelled strongly of damp earth and rats and decay.

It smelled like a grave.

He walked into the mouldering shell that had been the living room, gazed for a few moments at the spot where his parents had lain dead. And the place he'd seen in a thousand nightmares . . . where he'd killed his grandfather. His right hand twitched. Even all these years later, he could still feel the impact of the blade up his arm as it sliced through flesh and bone.

He tore himself away from that spot, beginning to shiver badly now. Remembering the flask of chicken soup he'd brought with him, he unslung his backpack. The soup was still warm, and he gulped two cups of it down gratefully.

He hated the thought of having to stay the night here, but the wind was building into a storm outside and he couldn't face another single mile on the Suzuki. He screwed the half-empty Thermos shut and dug in his backpack for the firelighters, candles and matches he'd picked up in the eight-till-late shop near his house. By candlelight he dug the damp ash out of the fireplace and lit a couple of solid fuel firelighter cubes. After checking that the smoke was drawing up the chimney properly, he smashed a chair and used the wood to get a blaze going. When the warmth finally began to permeate the room, he stripped off his clammy leathers and changed into jeans and a thick jumper. He sat by the fire to finish the rest of the chicken soup, trying to shut out the memories that kept returning.

When the flask was empty, it was time to explore the house. He reluctantly got to his feet.

The white circle of torchlight bobbed ahead of him as he climbed the stairs. There were just two doors leading off the cottage's poky landing. One lay ajar. Joel remembered it as the bedroom in which he and his parents had slept on their visits here. He didn't look inside. He turned the handle of the other door and pushed.

His grandfather had called it his '*sanctus sanctorum*', the hallowed space where he spent hours deeply immersed in his 'work'. Joel's father had never let him venture in there. Maybe because, for all the scornful remarks that he made about Crazy Nick's bizarre obsession with the supernatural, he'd respected his wish not to be disturbed. Or maybe just because he didn't want his son's head to be filled with any more of that nonsense than it already was.

The young Joel had formed a vivid image in his mind of what the mysterious room must look like: his grandfather bent over his desk, surrounded by piles of ancient books, poring over abstruse manuscripts, written in ancient, forgotten languages, lost in his quest to discover the secrets of vampires. His child's imagination had pictured every detail, down to the pipe rack on the desk, the pot full of rich-smelling tobacco from some exotic land, the inkwell and quill pen. Maybe a rumpled bunk in the corner where his grandfather would retire, exhausted, after his hours of study.

Joel opened the door, shone the torch inside, and saw for the first time that the room was nothing like he'd imagined. It was a plain, simple bedroom, nothing more. A single bed, a wooden

283

chair, a dressing table and a big solid antique wardrobe that took up most of the opposite wall. No books, no desk, no rolled-up manuscripts, no vampire-killing paraphernalia to be seen.

So what had his grandfather been doing up here all those hours? Napping?

On the dressing table sat a picture frame. The photograph inside was mildewed and discoloured with age and damp. Joel picked it up and wiped away the cobwebs from the dusty glass. He swallowed as he gazed at the photo. He could remember the day it had been taken, with the self-timer on his father's old camera. It showed the four of them sitting on the stone wall outside the cottage. Joel's grandfather was smiling and had his arm around his grandson's shoulder, squeezing him to his side.

Everyone looked so happy. Just a few hours later, three of the four would be dead.

Joel set the picture down and yanked open a drawer of the dressing table. There wasn't much inside. A dusty pair of spectacles. An old mechanical day/date wristwatch that had stopped just before four o'clock on March 13. A tortoiseshell comb with a few white hairs snagged in its teeth. Joel touched them, feeling a wave of sadness rise up inside him.

He didn't even know exactly what it was he was looking for. It seemed impossible that his grandfather hadn't kept some record of his dark, mysterious 'work'. There had to be something here about vampires. Something about the cross of Ardaich that he'd talked about so often.

Joel heard his voice again in his mind.

'It must be a very special cross, Grandfather.'

'Oh it is, my boy. Very, very special, and quite unique. The ancients spoke of its incredible powers against the forces of evil. It is like no other cross.'

'What does it do to a vampire?'

'Even just to go near the cross would mean the most horrible end for them, Joel.'

'It kills them?'

'You can't kill something that's already dead. No, it destroys them. Completely and utterly, so they can never, ever come back.'

'Where is it now?'

'It was lost, Joel. Many, many years ago. Some people have thought it was just a myth, but I know it exists. The world will be a much safer place once it's been rediscovered, believe me.'

Joel closed the dressing table drawer and went over to the wardrobe. Its door creaked on rusty hinges as he opened it to shine the light inside. Again, there was nothing, just a few old clothes. A cardigan he remembered his grandfather wearing, now thick with dust and mould. He shut the door and kept searching – but he was fast running out of places to look.

His heart jumped when he found two cardboard boxes under the bed. Kneeling in the dust, he dragged them out and started rooting through them. He found yellowed receipts, a warranty for a fridge-freezer, a rail ticket dated 1977, a tin full of old coins, a maintenance manual for a Series II Land Rover, a yellowed photo of his grandfather in naval uniform, standing in a leafy park with his arm around a pretty brunette Joel barely recognised as the grandmother he'd only ever known as a white-haired old woman.

Just then, a sound from behind him made his heart squirm with fear. He dropped the torch and the room went black.

CHAPTER 49

Dec's world was a swirling tunnel of disconnected thoughts, colours and sounds. He saw a child, running, laughing, and realised it was himself. Then his mother's face appeared in his mind, distorted like a reflection in a warped mirror. Her voice was muffled and faraway. *What are you doing with that thing,* he heard her say before her image dissolved and he was drifting away on a soft current. Just drifting through the darkness. A fuzzy white blur began to take shape, coming closer. He didn't know what it was but he felt himself drawn towards it. Then he smiled as the shape enveloped him in its warmth. The touch of her lips. The sharp sting that made him wince, pain mingled with pleasure. Her soothing voice in his ear.

'*Hello, Declan.*'

'Kate,' he muttered. 'Kate. I love you. Ka—'

Tap. Tap.

Dec stirred. Where was he? His eyelids fluttered open and he could suddenly feel the seat pressing against his back.

He was in the car. It was dark. Shafts of light

287

from outside, diffused by the condensation that misted the windscreen. Cars passing. Someone was tapping on the window next to where his head was slumped against the door. He turned groggily and narrowed his eyes at the face that was peering at him through the glass.

'Oi, Dec. Roll your window down, you dozy bugger.'

Dec rubbed his eyes. He groped for the window button and felt the cold, damp wind on his face as the glass whirred down.

'What're you doing in your mum's car?' the voice said.

Dec stared, trying to place the face of the young, blond, tousle-haired guy who was grinning in at him. 'Who are you?'

'Jesus, mate, you're right out of it. Sat stalled in the middle of fucking Wallingford. You're just asking for the cops to find you here. In enough trouble already, don't you think?'

Dec nodded slowly. 'Matt,' he mumbled.

'Yeah, yeah. Remember me? Only the guy you work with. Christ, what a state.'

Matt from the garage. He remembered now.

'I'm not pissed,' he slurred.

'Could have fooled me, mate. Come on. Get out of the car. You can't stay here.'

Dec fumbled for the door catch, and the next thing he knew he was sprawled on the wet ground.

'I'm going to be sick.'

He felt Matt's hands gripping his arm, helping him stagger to his feet. He leaned against the side of the Clio, breathing hard, almost overwhelmed by nausea.

'I'm taking you home to sober up,' Matt said.

'I told you—' Dec managed to say, then had to clamp his mouth shut and swallow back the rising bile.

'You'd better not chuck up in my Subaru,' Matt warned him. Dec could barely keep his eyes open as his workmate led him over to the blue car parked behind the Clio and helped him into the passenger seat. He rested his head against the dash as Matt locked up the Renault, pocketed the keys and came trotting back over. 'Your old lady's gonna fucking murder you for this,' he said cheerily as he got in next to Dec. 'That should be fun to watch.' He grinned. 'While yours truly is the hero who saved you from the police. Should be good for a beer or two.'

'Dontwannagohome,' Dec moaned.

'Why not?'

'Please.'

'Family tiff, huh?' Matt looked at him, then shrugged. 'Fine. I know how that goes. You can crash over at my place. All the same to me.'

Dec closed his eyes. The next thing he knew he was lying on a couch and Matt was nudging him awake and giving him a mug of steaming black coffee.

'Get this down you, mate. Sober you up.'

Dec was too weak and dizzy to protest. He slurped at the coffee.

'I'm going to call your folks to say what's happened and where your mum can pick up her car.'

'Don't tell them I'm here,' Dec said. Or thought he said. He might have just imagined it, but he was getting so disorientated he couldn't even tell. The nausea was getting steadily worse. The strong black coffee hadn't helped at all.

'Listen.' Matt's voice echoed from somewhere a million miles away. 'You're probably too out of it to remember, but me and a couple of mates're off to Mexico tonight. I'm leaving in half an hour.'

Dec must have mumbled something in response, because Matt went on: '. . . the wedding I was telling you about? Back in a week. Try not to burn the place down while I'm . . .'

Dec heard nothing more. He was already gone and drifting far away.

CHAPTER 50

Joel heard the sound again.

It was coming from the wardrobe. A strange scuffling, scratching noise.

He fought back the terror and groped for the torch. He tried the switch and to his relief the beam cut through the darkness. He aimed it at the wardrobe. The sound had stopped. Heart thudding, he stepped over and pulled open the wardrobe door.

A sudden movement from inside startled him. A large rat clawed its way out from among the clothing and dropped down to the floor with a soft thump. Joel followed it with the torch beam as it scuttled away to escape under the bed.

Where had the animal come from? The wardrobe had been empty just moments ago.

Joel shone the light back inside the wardrobe and saw the small hole in the back panel. The rat must have come from there.

But that didn't make sense. There should have been solid wall on the other side. He put his fingers to the hole and felt a draught coming from somewhere.

Joel stepped inside the wardrobe and pushed gently against the back panel. It didn't budge at first, but with a little more pressure it gave with a crack and hinged away from him like a door. He brushed away the thick matting of cobwebs and stepped through the hidden doorway.

And now he knew where his grandfather had spent all those private hours.

The secret study was cramped and windowless. The torchlight picked out a desk and chair, piles of old books, scattered heaps of notes. Joel ran his hand excitedly over the desktop and opened the middle drawer.

The first thing he saw in the drawer, lying on its side among the dust and mouse droppings, was a revolver. He hesitated for an instant, then picked it up. It was heavy in his hand, an old-fashioned lump of steel, its blued finish pocked with corrosion. He recognised the antiquated design as a 1940s service Webley .455, the type of gun that had flooded post-war Britain and found its way into a lot of illegal arms caches. Obviously one had managed to fall into his grandfather's hands, too. Joel broke open the action and saw that there was just one tarnished brass cartridge in the cylinder. The rest of the chambers were empty.

Joel wondered about the gun. It didn't make sense for his grandfather to have kept one as defence against vampires – especially not one with only a single bullet in it.

There was only one answer. It was simple and

brutal, and when it hit him it filled him with sadness. The gun hadn't been meant for defence against vampires at all. The old man had intended to use it on himself, if they ever caught up with him. One shot to the head, to save himself from a fate worse than death. Only, when that day had finally come, the gun had been out of reach. Joel stared at the weapon in his hand and his vision was clouded by sudden tears. He blinked them away.

The only other item in the drawer was an old notebook. He laid down the revolver and flicked through it. It was badly damaged with damp, half chewed by mice, but he recognised his grandfather's handwriting on the mouldy pages. He quickly slipped it into his back pocket, then scooped up an armful of books and papers. He was halfway to the door when an afterthought made him go back to pick up the old gun. He stuck it in the back of his jeans.

His own time might come. At least he'd know what to do.

Downstairs, the fire was nearly dead. Joel smashed up another chair and revived the blaze with the splintered pieces. Then he settled on the rug by the hearth and spent the next hour going through the things he'd found.

The books were mainly about old European folklore – witchcraft, Druidism, pagan ritual, early Christianity. His grandfather had made underlinings and notes here and there in the margins. Then there was a Romanian grammar and vocabulary book dating back to 1807, and a tatty volume on ancient Slavic languages. Nothing much there to go on.

Joel turned to the diary, and his heart sank when he realised he'd underestimated the extent of the damage that the ravages of time could inflict. Half the pages were stuck together and as fragile as moth wings, falling to bits when he tried to part them. The rest either had been nibbled away by rodents or were so heavily stained with mildew that large patches of his grandfather's writing were virtually unreadable.

But there was enough to make his heart beat and his hands tremble with the knowledge that he'd found something important.

He'd had no idea just how deeply his grandfather had been into this stuff, or how much of his life he'd devoted to it. This was thirty years' worth of his research, dating from after the war to the time when he'd become a recluse up here in the Highlands. Half diary, half notes, the pages were scrawled in a hand that would have been hard to read even if the paper hadn't been virtually ruined. It charted travels that Joel had never known the old man had undertaken, long before he'd been born. Visits to libraries in Bucharest, Prague, Moscow, Jerusalem, Delhi, as well as other destinations that Joel couldn't make out.

Several pages of the diary were devoted to a series of detailed sketches in pencil and ink, some of them faded away almost to nothing. Their subject was the same every time. It was a rugged stone cross.

'The cross of Ardaich,' Joel muttered to himself. So this was it.

A number of the drawings seemed to depict the artefact as being made of plain stone. In others it featured strange carvings, like runes, or the letters of some ancient alphabet. But what they all had in common was the Celtic design, the head of the cross intersecting with a circle, like the reticule of a rifle sight. One of the drawings depicted it alongside a human hand for scale. It wasn't big, maybe fourteen inches long.

Joel's fingers fluttered as he turned another page. Under a heading that he could just about make out as 'Origin of the cross', his grandfather seemed to have been piecing together the history of the strange artefact from the many sources he'd studied over the decades.

Joel grabbed his backpack and took out his map and a biro. He used the back of the map to copy down the bits of the text that he could make out.

ORIGIN OF THE CROSS

. . .

5th century . . . Ringan (N??) travels to Scotland on orders of . . . On his long journey he meets a holy . . .

. . . gives Ringan a heavy sack. In the sack is a lump of rock, just larger than a man's

head. He tells Ringan it is a talisman that will protect against the Dearg-dhu.

. . .

In Scotland, Ringan builds his church. Is going to build the strange rock into the wall when he receives a visit . . .

. . .

. . . local village is being preyed on by a creature they call the Baobhan sith. He uses the rock to . . .

When he witnesses its power . . . master stonemason . . . sculpt it into a . . .

. . . known as the CROSS OF ARDAICH . . .

. . . resurfaces two centuries lat . . .

. . . disappeared from view . . .

There were many gaps – too damn many. And even the bits that Joel could read made maddeningly little sense. Who was this man called Ringan, and what was the significance of the bracketed letter N after his name? What were the *Dearg-dhu* and the *Baobhan sith*? The language looked like Gaelic. He spent a few minutes rooting through his grandfather's books on ancient folklore, but could find nothing to explain the words. He returned to the diary. Nothing more was readable until the following page, where he could just about make out a few fragments of sentences.

. . . 963 A.D. cross believed sighted in . . .
. . . observed strange powers . . .
. . . blessed ability to ward off revenants and . . .

That was about it. Joel struggled on, but the lower he went down the page, the more unreadable the writing was. In some places his grandfather just seemed to have been jotting down random notes in a hurry, as if he'd been taking them from a book. A column of words stood out:

Vetalas
Moroi
Lamashtu

After a few more ruined pages was another diary entry. The date was 1975, the year the old man had moved to Scotland.

April 1975. Am travelling to Venice . . .
Looking forw . . . at last . . . staying at the hot . . .
. . . the location of the cr . . .
legend tells it was concealed . . .
church of . . .
. . . 1631 the city was caught in the grip of the Black Death
. . . ANCHI . . .
. . . 666

. . .
Salvation lies at the feet of the Virgin

That final line, the last piece of legible writing before the page ended in a ragged black stain, was striking. What was 'salvation'? Joel quickly gave up on it and went on studying the rest. 'Anchi' was obviously half a word, written in capitals, its first letters obliterated by mould. When Joel tried to scrape it away, the paper just came apart. He gave up, and chewed his pen as he stared at the number underneath.

666. The biblical Number of the Beast. His skin crawled as he read it over and over.

But not as much as when he read the words overleaf.

15th April 1975.
I have destroyed one of THEM, but there are more.
   . . . narrow escape. Who will believe what I've seen?
Now THEY will come looking for me. I must hide.
   . . . my loved ones . . . not safe for them
   God protect me.

Joel was stunned by the realisation as he read the entry over and over again, willing the faded writing to reveal more.

But it was enough. Now he knew why Crazy

Nick had walked out on his family and tried to hide himself away as best he could all those years ago. He hadn't been crazy at all. He'd been trying to protect them all from the horror he'd encountered back in Italy.

Knowing that one day the vampires might catch up with him again.

CHAPTER 51

Joel had left his grandfather's cottage at dawn, vowing for the second time in his life that he'd never return. His eyes were burning with fatigue as he parked the bike outside the Georgian house in Walton Well Road and wearily climbed the steps to the glass-panelled front door. Too tired to even strip off his bike leathers, he trudged up the passage towards the kitchen to brew himself a badly needed coffee. By the time he'd reached the kitchen door, he'd already unzipped his backpack and was flipping through his grandfather's notebook like a man possessed. He walked into the kitchen on auto-pilot, his eyes glued to the faded writing. And almost fell over as his foot caught on something lying on the floor.

He looked down. The ceramic tiles were covered with debris. Drawers ripped out and upturned, shelves torn down, containers of utensils hurled across the room. Glancing through the open-plan archway into the living room beyond, he saw it had been taken apart too. His bookcase was collapsed on its face across the wreckage of his coffee table. The carpet was slashed to ribbons and half the floorboards had been prised up. The place looked as though a Panzer Division had gone through it.

Joel sensed a rapid movement out of the corner of his eye, then something silvery flashed down in front of his face. He realised it was a garrotte wire just in time to get his hands up to protect his throat. The wire closed in tight across his wrists, pulling back with maniacal force. Only the thick cuffs of Joel's leather jacket saved his hands from being sliced clean off. He lashed out with a backwards headbutt and felt his skull connect with something solid. Out of the corner of his eye he could see the bald crown glistening under the kitchen light and the wizened face contorted in effort.

It was Seymour Finch, and this time he meant to kill.

As he struggled desperately to get free, Joel could feel the wire biting through the leather. Any second, it would be through – and then death would be an instant away. He kicked out with his right foot, found the edge of the kitchen worktop with his toe and pushed hard against it, hurling his weight backwards. They toppled over together and crashed to the floor, and he felt the impact of his weight drive the wind out of Finch's lungs. For the shortest instant, the man's grip on the garrotte went slack, and Joel was able to wrench the wire away from his neck and twist out from under it. He went to kick Finch in the ribs, but the man was already up on his feet. Joel saw the blur coming for his face too late to react. The heavy fist caught him on the jaw and sent him sprawling to the floor.

Lying there with the taste of blood filling his mouth and his vision flashing with white spots, Joel saw Finch spot the fallen notebook and snatch it up. He ripped through the pages and his eyes lit up in animal triumph.

Joel staggered to his feet, glanced around him for a weapon. The knife block was across the other side of the kitchen – he'd have to go through Finch to get to it. A cast-iron saucepan lay on the floor. Edge-on, it was as good as an axe. Joel was about to grab it when he remembered the uncomfortable lump of steel that was still shoved down the back of his jeans. He'd ridden so many miles with the old Webley in his belt that he'd no longer registered what it was.

He ripped it out and aimed it at Finch in the two-handed stance he'd been taught in his police firearms training. Lined the rusty sights up centre-of-mass on his target, thumbed back the hammer and yelled, 'Down on your knees. Or I'll kill you.'

Finch's eyes widened in surprise, but he recovered quickly from the shock. Then he charged with a wild scream.

Joel didn't have time to pray that the ancient

weapon would still fire. Finch was just a yard away when he squeezed the trigger. The room filled with the huge noise of the gunshot, and the revolver kicked back against his palm.

Finch flew backwards as if he'd been jerked off his feet by an invisible cable. He hit the floor and slid across the tiles, thrashing and roaring, blood pumping from the hole in his chest. Then, incredibly, he sprang back up on his feet and made a mad dash for the hallway, still clutching the notebook. He burst through the front door with a crash of breaking glass and out into the street.

Stunned, Joel stood there for a moment, with the smoking revolver in his hand. Coming to his senses, he threw the empty weapon down and gave chase.

By the time he'd run out of his front gate, Finch was already twenty yards away, sprinting like a wild man down Walton Well Road and leaving a trail of bright blood splashes in his wake. Joel went after him, racing down the hill past the rows of red-brick houses. He was certain he could catch the man. He'd come first in every police athletics and running competition he'd ever entered, even done some weekend training in the Welsh hills with the boys from the Territorial SAS and not entirely disgraced himself. But after just a few yards he realised with a shock that this maniac, even with a large-calibre bullet in his chest, was outpacing him. He willed himself to run faster.

It quickly became clear where Finch was

heading. At the bottom of Walton Well Road was an old stone hump bridge, and beyond it was Port Meadow, a vast expanse of open country protected from the developers by ancient common land laws, where the snaking river Thames became the Isis.

Finch reached the bridge and dropped out of sight. By the time Joel had got there, Finch was already sprinting across the grass, aiming for the river. Joel pressed on, forcing all the power he could muster from his legs. His racing feet ripped through the long grass as they neared the water.

Finch was nearly fifty yards ahead of him now. Joel saw him slither down the reedy bank and disappear – a moment later, he saw him again. Finch had boarded a small wooden boat. His muscular fists gripped the oars and his arms moved like pistons. He was covered in blood, more like some kind of fiendish machine than a man. Water foamed white as the boat surged forward. Joel caught a fleeting glimpse of the notebook lying in the bottom between Finch's boots. He saw the twisted smile on the man's lips.

He's getting away.

But there was one chance. Thirty yards down-river, an iron footbridge spanned the water. Finch had almost reached it.

Joel threw himself into a fast sprint through the long grass. He reached the footbridge and propelled himself up the clanking metal steps four at a time. Raced across until he was right over the water, and looked down over the rail just in time to see the prow of the rowing boat emerge from under the bridge, and the top of Finch's bald skull gleaming with exertion. Joel clambered over the rail. It was a ten-foot drop. If he delayed half a second too long, he'd hit the water in the boat's wake and there would be no hope of catching Finch as he rowed frenetically away.

Joel launched himself into space.

The boat and its occupant rushed up to meet him with frightening speed. Joel had timed it right. He landed squarely on top of Finch with an impact that almost knocked the wind out of him. But the man was too powerful an adversary to give him even a split second's chance to recover from the shock. Joel pummelled his face and head with blows. Felt his knuckles smashing in the cartilage of his nose. Blood sprayed. Finch lashed out with his fist and caught Joel above the eye. Joel fell back in the boat. Finch roared up onto his feet and came at him with a stamping kick that would have crushed his ribs if it had landed. Joel twisted out of the way just in time, and Finch's boot almost crashed through the bottom of the boat. The ferocity of his kick rocked the little vessel violently. Finch lost his footing and fell with a splash into the water.

Joel dived straight in after him, gasping at the shock of the cold water. He resurfaced to see Finch just two feet away, white foam boiling around him and turning rapidly pink as he struggled back towards the boat. Joel grabbed the bald man brutally by the ears and headbutted him. And again. Finch's eyes blazed in a mask of blood.

Joel was too terrified to hesitate even for a moment. He punched him three, four, five times in the face, numb to the blows the bald man was landing on him in return. Pain was something to worry about later. He dug his fingers into Finch's collar, plunged his head under the water and held him there. Finch's strong hands thrashed underwater, lashed punches at his stomach, grasped for his wrists. Joel gritted his teeth and used every ounce of his strength to keep him under. The man's head twisted from side to side and Joel could see his bared teeth as he tried to tear into him like an animal.

Ten seconds. Twenty. Bubbles erupted to the surface as Finch flailed wildly for air. Joel hit him again and kept him down. The water was clouded pink around them.

It was a full minute before Finch's struggles had diminished to nothing. Joel let him go and watched the inert body bobbing on the swell.

The rowing boat had drifted in towards the bank. Joel kicked out towards it, reached up over the side and felt in the bottom. It was half full of water, and, to his horror, his raking fingers found the notebook almost completely submerged. He splashed away from the boat, holding his grandfather's work clear of the surface, and hauled himself up the bank by fistfuls of reeds. He collapsed on his knees on dry land, spluttering and coughing and feverishly checking the pages of the notebook. It was soaked and bloody.

He heard voices.

Two young women were approaching down the towpath on the opposite side of the river, accompanied by a little girl who was playing on a portable computer game as she walked. Joel pressed himself flat among the rushes and waited breathlessly for them to pass by. They had only to glance to their right, and they'd see Finch's corpse drifting face-down, spreadeagled in the water, turning a slow horizontal cartwheel as the current eased him away downstream. It was just pure luck that the women were too deep in conversation, and the child too engrossed with her electronic gizmo, for them to spot him floating past.

When they were at a safe distance, Joel let out a long wheezing sigh of relief and shakily got to his feet. Only then did he begin to realise the kind of shit he was in. It wasn't enough that he was suspended from duty for harassing and assaulting an innocent man. Now he'd shot that same man in his own home with an illegal handgun, then killed him in broad daylight with his bare hands.

He made it back to his flat without meeting anyone in the street. Safely inside, he carefully laid the soaking wet notebook over the bathroom radiator to dry as he stripped off his dripping, mud-smeared clothes and blasted away the filth and blood under a hot shower.

He knew he couldn't stay here. Once the sun had gone down and Finch's vampire master realised his servant wasn't coming back, Joel would be vulnerable to a far worse visitor than any mortal man. He couldn't fight them. He was going to have to run and hide, and figure out his next move.

'You see, Joel, of all the things a vampire fears, this one cross is what they dread most. And the person who wields it – well, that person is the most powerful enemy those monsters have in all the world.'

He could only hope that the old man hadn't just been clinging to some old myth.

But where to start searching for this mythical cross of Ardaich? Such clues as the notebook offered gave him precious little to go on.

He couldn't do this on his own.

Someone had said they could help him. Now it was time to call her.

CHAPTER 52

'Remember me?' he'd said on the phone earlier that afternoon.

'The belligerent police inspector,' she'd replied. 'Funny, I was just thinking about you.'

'Can we meet? I need to talk to you.'

'Can you come to London?'

'I'm kind of at a loose end for a while. I can go anywhere.'

'I live in Canary Wharf. Take down this address.'

That was how, just after three in the afternoon, Joel came to be standing inside the luxurious glass lift in his motorcycle leathers, heading for the top floor of the expensive apartment building over-looking the river.

What kind of journalist must this Alex Bishop be, he wondered to himself. You'd have to be rolling in money to live in a place like this. His own meagre police salary wouldn't buy him a broom cupboard here.

The lift doors glided open and he stepped out into an airy landing filled with exotic plants and the scent of flowers. In one hand he was carrying his crash helmet, in the other the holdall that he'd hurriedly packed full of clothes before escaping from his place in Jericho. He had no idea when he'd be able to return there.

The sweeping view across London was breathtaking. He paused for a moment, gazing out through the tall windows. Rays of late autumn sunlight shone brightly through the glass roof.

'Hello again,' said her voice behind him. He turned to see her leaning casually in her doorway. She was wearing faded jeans and a chunky roll-neck kimono-style woollen jumper. Her auburn hair caught the sunlight.

A few seconds went by before he realised he was staring at her.

'What's the holdall for?' she asked with a smile, noticing the bag at his feet. 'Going somewhere?'

'Right now, I have no idea where I'm going,' he said. 'A lot of it depends on you.'

She raised an eyebrow. 'Really?'

'You said you could help me. Here I am.'

'Then you'd better come in.'

The penthouse apartment was even bigger than he'd imagined. Joel's place could have fitted inside it four or five times over. He felt self-conscious as he trudged across her plush carpet in his heavy bike boots, worried about setting down the holdall in case it had road dirt on it after being strapped to the back of the bike. But she didn't seem to mind. While she disappeared into the kitchen to get them drinks, he settled nervously in a creamy leather armchair and looked around him at the pictures on the walls. Taste and style were commodities that Alex Bishop seemed to have in abundance, alongside the money to enjoy them.

She returned with a tray, laid two heavy cups filled with foamy cappuccino on a glass-topped table, and curled up in the armchair facing him.

Joel took a sip of the coffee. It was the best he'd ever tasted.

'I'm glad to see you again, Inspector,' she said.

'It's Joel. And I wasn't kidding. I really do need your help.'

'This has something to do with the boy in the hospital?'

He nodded.

'I thought so. How is he?'

'He's fine. But there's more. A lot more.'

'Are we talking about vampires, Joel?'

He hesitated before saying, 'Yes, we are.'

'There's something I have to tell you, Joel. Before we go any further. I haven't been completely honest with you.'

'Meaning what?'

'Meaning there are things about me I've been hiding from you. I'm not really a journalist.'

'I didn't think so, seeing this place.'

'I'm kind of an investigator,' she went on.

'Private detective?'

She laughed. 'Put it this way. It's not humans I investigate. My interest is in the paranormal.'

'Ghosts and spirits?'

'Vampires, Joel.'

'You believe in them.'

'I ought to. Let me tell you a story. Eight years ago, my elder sister fell very ill. The doctors were baffled. Pernicious anaemia, they thought. She had all the tests, but they couldn't find anything. But I noticed something strange. Something nobody seemed to take seriously.'

'The bite marks?'

She nodded. 'I knew what was happening. I hid in my sister's room one night. I saw him visit her. Drinking her blood. I couldn't do anything to stop him. The next day, I told my family. They thought I was crazy.'

'I know the feeling,' Joel said. 'What happened to your sister?'

'She died.'

'I'm sorry.'

'And then she came back. As one of them.' Alex paused, and sorrow misted her eyes for a moment before she continued. 'I finished her. Ever since that day, I've dedicated myself to researching everything I could find out about these creatures.'

Joel didn't speak. Couldn't say a word. Sitting there in this luxurious environment, he was suddenly transported back to that dark place.

She was watching him keenly. 'You've had a similar experience,' she said. 'I can tell from the look in your eyes. That's why you were so quick to believe the boy's story.'

Joel met her steady gaze. 'It's all true,' he said. 'Dec Maddon saw vampires. And I know where they are. When I find what I'm looking for, I'm going to go back there and destroy them all. That's where you come in. I think I need your help to find it.'

Alex sipped her coffee. 'What is it you're looking for?'

Joel didn't reply right away. He stood up, went over to his holdall, unzipped a side pocket and took out his grandfather's notebook.

'The thing I'm looking for is described in here. It's called the cross of Ardaich.'

With a sudden crash, the coffee cup fell from Alex's fingers and landed on the table in front of her.

The glass top shattered with the impact. Jagged shards and spattering coffee rained down onto the carpet. Alex's eyes had opened wide and she was suddenly pale; then she quickly regained her composure. 'Shit, look what I've done.' She dropped down to her knees and started picking up the pieces of glass.

'Let me help,' Joel said. He quickly stuffed the notebook in his pocket and crouched down beside her.

'I have a dustpan and brush in the kitchen,' Alex said. She hurried away to fetch them while Joel carried on gathering up the bits of glass, fishing out the long, pointed shards first before moving on to the small slivers that glistened everywhere on the carpet.

As Alex returned from the kitchen, he glanced

up at her. For a moment he found himself thinking how good she looked – and that moment's lapse of concentration was enough for him to gash his finger on a razor edge of broken glass. He drew his hand away. The blood was oozing out rapidly. 'Damn. I'm dripping on your carpet. Where's the bathroom?'

She didn't reply for a moment, and he noticed the way she was gazing fixedly at his bleeding finger, a peculiar look in her eyes. Maybe she was squeamish, he thought.

'Oh . . . yes, sorry,' she said, collecting herself. 'Through there. Are you okay?'

'It's just a nick,' he replied as he walked to the bathroom door, cupping his other hand under the cut finger to avoid leaving a trail of red splashes across the floor.

He cursed himself for his stupidity as he washed away the blood at the washbasin in her plush bathroom. As he wrapped his finger up with his handkerchief, he couldn't resist glancing round the room. In his experience, women's bathrooms, however big, always seemed to be cluttered with an extensive and mysterious arsenal of beauty products, soaps and gels, shampoos and hair accessories, and to reek of perfumes and lotions. But Alex Bishop's bathroom looked as though it had never been used. He shrugged. In a place this size, she probably had her own en suite.

When he rejoined her in the living room, she'd

finished gathering up the glass and was mopping up the coffee stains from the carpet.

'I'm sorry,' she said. 'I don't know how I managed to do that. The cup just slipped.'

He wagged his bandaged finger. 'We're both clumsy, then.' His grandfather's notebook was lying on the armchair he'd been sitting on. He picked it up and slipped it in his pocket.

'Let's go outside. I fancy a breath of air, don't you?' She led him through the sliding door that led out onto the balcony, where a table and two chairs overlooked the view of the river.

'Anyway, about the cross . . .' he said tentatively.

Alex's face tensed a little at the mention of it. 'How did you hear about that?'

'Is it true? It really exists?'

She nodded solemnly. 'But it was supposed to have been lost, a long time ago.'

'That's what my grandfather said, too.'

'Your grandfather?'

'Let me start at the beginning,' he said.

CHAPTER 53

As they sat there in the pale afternoon sunlight and Alex listened intently with her eyes fixed on his, her hair blowing in the breeze, her chin cupped in her hand, Joel told her everything . . .

. . . Except for one detail. He couldn't bring himself to confess what he'd done to the beloved old man.

Nor did he mention the fact that, just a few hours ago, he'd killed a man with his bare hands.

'I know they're after me,' he finished. 'It's not safe for me to go back home, until I find that cross. That is, *if* I find it, and *if* it really has the powers that it's supposed to have. Personally, I find that kind of thing very hard to believe. But it's all I've got.'

'There are a lot of things people don't readily believe,' she said, 'but which are true. Let's have a look at this notebook of yours.'

He took it out of his pocket and handed it to her.

'It's old,' he said. 'Not in great condition.'

'So I see.' As she carefully turned the pages, the

torn-off, folded-up back cover of the map slipped out.

'That's where I copied out the bits I could read,' Joel explained. 'Which isn't much to go on, is it?'

'Your grandfather was obviously a very clever man,' she said. She'd already reached the final page.

'You've read it all? So fast? It took me ages.'

'I'm a speed reader.'

'Does any of it make sense to you?'

'Let's go through it. You see this list of words here?'

'I couldn't figure those out at all.'

'You wouldn't, unless you'd studied ancient languages. This one, *Vetalas*? Sanscrit, meaning vampire. *Moroi* is an old Slavic word for the same thing. Your grandfather probably jotted these down to remind him of what to look for in the ancient texts he found in all these libraries.'

'*Lamashtu*?'

'A goddess worshipped by the Babylonians. She was said to have drunk human blood. As you see, vampire mythology goes back a lot further than most people know.'

Joel clicked his tongue impatiently. 'Okay, this is all very educational. But what about the cross?' He reached out to take the notebook from her hand. 'It's cold out here. Do you want to go inside?'

'I'm fine.'

Joel opened the notebook at the page that

described the origins of the cross and the travels of the enigmatic Ringan. 'Who was Ringan?'

'I don't have the answer to that,' she replied. 'And I think your grandfather might have been wondering about it himself. See how he put an N in brackets after the name, with a question mark? Who was "N"? Good question.' She fished in the pocket of her jeans, and came out with a BlackBerry smartphone.

Joel couldn't help but smile to himself as he watched her dial up a Google search and type the name 'Ringan' on the tiny keys. He liked the intensity of this woman. She was already hooked. He could feel it, and was glad he'd come to her. She was someone who'd been through the same things he had. Someone he could trust.

She shook her head. 'Ringan comes up all over the place. But not the Ringan we're looking for, unless he was some pop star's kid or some kind of Indian recipe.'

'How about keying in "Ringan Scotland"?'

'I'll try.' She tapped the keys, scrolled down. 'Nothing.'

'Shit.'

'Wait. Here's something. From the Royal Commission of Ancient and Historical Monuments of Scotland. St Ringan's Chapel, in Stirlingshire.' She read out loud. '"An old chapel called St Ringan's, where those who died of the plague in 1645 were buried. The chapel was in existence by 1497 although no trace of it survives."'

'No good to us,' Joel said. 'We're looking for something much older than that. My grandfather said fifth century.'

She grimaced. 'You're right. Hold on. Take a look at this.'

Joel shifted towards the edge of his seat. 'What've you found?'

'The alternative name of St Ringan's Chapel is St Ninian's Chapel.'

He looked at her. 'Ninian. The N in brackets.'

'Let me dig a little deeper here.' Alex stroked a few more keys on the BlackBerry, then smiled. 'Here. "In Scotland, Ninian is also known as Ringan." Same guy. Good old Wikipedia. Now—'

Joel was tense as he watched her retracing the research footsteps of his grandfather decades earlier.

'Okay,' she said with a flourish. 'We can start filling in the gaps. According to three history sites I've just checked out, legend has it that long before he was ever beatified, Ninian was sent to Scotland during the fifth century on the orders of St Martin, who ordered him to bring Christian teachings to the Pictish people who later became the Scots. St Martin sent a contingent of stonemasons along with him to build his church there.'

Joel checked the scribbles on the back of the map. 'So on his travels, Ninian meets this holy man—'

'—Who entrusts him with the rock he tells

Ninian has magic powers. I don't know if Ninian believed him at the time, but seemingly he got the chance to find out for himself when locals approached him for help with their *Baobhan sith* problems.' She pronounced it 'baa-van-shee'.

'Sounds like you know what a *Baobhan sith* is, then,' he said.

'Guess.'

'A vampire?'

'Yup. They were also called "The White Women of the Highlands". They took the form of beautiful young women who seduced men by inviting them to dance, lured them somewhere quiet and then drank their blood.' Alex smiled.

'What's funny?' he asked.

'Nothing. I was just thinking about something.'

Joel couldn't read the look in her eye. He glanced back at the notebook. 'So this lump of rock supposedly had powers against these vampire creatures. And then, according to what my grandfather wrote, after he saw what it could do, he had one of the stonemasons sculpt it into a cross.' He paused. 'Which means, I guess, that whatever powers the cross apparently possesses don't have anything to do with the power of God, forces of good warding off evil spirits and all that kind of thing. There's some other reason why it can do what it does. But being a good Christian, Ninian felt he had to rework it into a religious icon. I suppose that was the only way they could understand it.' He frowned at Alex. 'Just what are we dealing with here?'

'I really don't know,' she replied. Joel thought there was a slight nervous tone to her voice, but he was too taken up with the mystery to dwell on it. He traced his finger along one of his grandfather's sketches of the ancient artefact. 'If the stone was only just a bit larger than a man's head, the cross can't be that big. Fifteen inches tall, maybe. Question is, where did it go after that?'

'April 1975. Your grandfather travelled to Venice,' Alex said. 'Looks like he tracked it that far. But did he find it?'

'He got close,' Joel said. 'But he never found it. Maybe he was planning to go and look for it again one day. I don't know.' He sighed. 'I just wish he'd told me more about his work. I was just a kid, and my father didn't like it when the old man used to try to talk to me about these things. They used to argue endlessly about it. And then . . . then it happened, and it was too late.'

Alex leaned back in her seat. The afternoon was wearing on, and the sun was dipping slowly over the London skyline. A cold wind was blowing in from the river, streaming her hair across her face. She brushed it away pensively.

'I'm sorry they suspended you from your job,' she said. 'But, like you said, now you have some time on your hands.'

'And not a lot else,' he said.

'You're serious about finding this cross, aren't you?'

'I've no choice in the matter.'

'Then how do you feel about a trip to Venice?'

CHAPTER 54

Darkness was beginning to fall by the time Alex skidded the Jag into the Schuessler & Schuessler parking lot and made her way up to the top floor. Rumble was in his office talking to Xavier Garrett when she barged in without knocking. Both vampires turned as she marched up to Rumble's desk.

She jerked her thumb at the door. 'Take a hike, Garrett. I have some news to tell Harry.'

Garrett looked at Rumble. Rumble nodded quietly. Garrett scowled ferociously at Alex as he left the room.

'I'm listening,' Rumble said, and Alex spent the next five minutes telling him about her meeting with Joel Solomon.

'The Federation rules expressly forbid fraternisation with a human,' Rumble warned her. 'You know the penalty.'

'Then it's time to start making exceptions to the rules. Without him, we wouldn't know that Stone is hiding out at a stately home near Henley-on-Thames. It's called Crowmoor Hall.'

Rumble stared. 'How does this Solomon know that?'

'Remember the Hallowe'en party? The kid who thought he saw vampires? He didn't imagine it.' She perched herself on the edge of Rumble's desk. 'This is our chance, Harry. We can take them.'

'And how do you propose to do that? Storm the place? Maybe you've forgotten that these are the same guys who just relieved us of enough Nosferol to destroy every vampire on the planet. They have it all, and we have just about none. I'd say the balance of power has shifted a little in their favour. And you want to go in there like Rambo.'

'I didn't mean now,' she said impatiently. 'I meant when I get back from Venice.'

'Now you've totally lost me. Why would you go to Venice?'

'Because that's where Joel Solomon believes he's going to find the cross of Ardaich.'

There was a long silence. Rumble pushed his glasses up his nose and stared at her hard.

'I don't have time to explain it all right now, Harry. When I get back, you'll know everything. What I need you to do now is authorise an expense account for me. No limits.'

'What about the FRC conference in Brussels? I'd have liked you there with me.'

'What about it? Don't you think this is more important?'

'I don't know.'

'Listen to me, Harry. This is the only chance we have. Just as you said, the balance of power has tipped away from us. Stone has all the guns. But what if we could find the cross? And what if the legends are true?'

'Yeah, what if?'

'But suppose they are. We can take Stone and all his followers out, just like that.' She snapped her fingers. 'It would stop this insurrection in its tracks.'

'There's a problem with your logic. You're a vampire, Alex. And vampires can't even go near the cross of Ardaich. That thing even gets pointed at you, you'll wish Stone had shot you with one of your own Nosferol bullets.'

'I can't be the cross bearer,' Alex said. 'But Joel Solomon can. And he wants this more than anything. He hates vampires. He told me so.'

'Where is the human now?'

'He's at my place.'

'Alex, if anyone at FRC got wind that you were harbouring a human in your own home—'

'But they won't. Will they, Harry?'

'You're making me an accomplice, for crying out loud.'

'It wouldn't be the first time you've covered for me.'

'This is different.'

'Well, apparently this is war,' she said.

Rumble paused, thinking hard, then let out a long sigh. 'Say this cross really is in Venice. Which

324

is improbable. And say you and he are able to find it. Which is highly unlikely. You'd be putting yourself at enormous risk.'

Alex shrugged. 'You know me, Harry. I've taken risks before.'

'And by allowing you to recover it, I'd be endangering all of us. What if this Solomon finds out who you really are, and about VIA?'

'He won't.'

'You're sure about that? Have you thought about how you're going to explain to him that you can't go near the damn thing? Won't he find that just a teeny bit odd?'

'I'll think of something, Harry. I always do, don't I?'

Rumble mulled it over for a while, then pulled a face. 'I don't like it. Not one little bit.'

'But you don't have any better ideas. Do you?'

CHAPTER 55

Not long returned from his journey, Gabriel Stone was still fresh with the memory of his meeting with his Masters as he paced his subterranean study.

All seemed to be going well. All, that was, but for one thing that continued to plague his mind: the cross, and the accursed human who claimed he'd found it. Finch was supposed to have been giving him a report. Where was he? There was no sign of him, and that made Stone uneasy.

That question was still burning in his mind when the phone rang. He hesitated to pick it up. He was expecting no calls. That meant that to answer the phone could mean having to converse with a human, something he only did for one of two reasons: either because that human was useful to him in some way; or because that human's blood was shortly to become a meal. The rest was trivial and distasteful to him. Such things were Finch's duties.

He hesitated a moment longer, then picked up the phone. 'You may speak,' he said stiffly. The human protocol was alien to him, and he had no time for it.

There was a second's surprised silence on the end of the line, followed by a voice that told him they were calling from Thames Valley Police.

'What seems to be the problem?' Stone asked cautiously.

'I'm afraid I may have some bad news, sir. You have an assistant called Seymour Finch?'

'I have.'

'The body of a man has been recovered from the Isis River earlier this afternoon. He had no papers on him and so far we've been unable to make a formal identification, but one of our officers called out to a previous incident at your home thought he recognised the deceased as Mr Finch.'

'I see,' Stone replied slowly. 'Tell me, officer, what was the cause of death?'

'I'm afraid we are treating it as suspicious, sir. A firearm was involved in his death. I'm very sorry.'

'As am I,' Stone said, without a trace of emotion.

'We've been unable to locate any next of kin for Mr Finch. I'm afraid that means I have to ask you, as his employer, to identify the body here at the police morgue before we launch a full criminal investigation. We can send a car to collect you if necessary.'

Stone turned to read the antique clock on the mantelpiece. A few minutes after five. 'Is it dark yet?'

'Beg your pardon, sir?'

'I said, has night fallen?'

'Ah, I understand,' the stupid human said. 'We appreciate how busy you are, sir. No, the facility will be open until late. We can send the car for you any time.'

'I will telephone you back,' Stone said.

But he wouldn't be doing it on that particular phone, because he slammed the receiver down so hard that it shattered into a thousand pieces. He raised his face to the ceiling and his scream of rage filled the flickering shadows and reverberated off the stone walls. He paced furiously up and down, grabbing anything that lay in his path and dashing it violently against the wall. He seized a priceless Ming vase from a pedestal and hurled it like a missile through the centre of the gilt-framed Florentine mirror that hung over the fireplace. A shower of broken glass rained down, snuffing out the flames of the silver candlesticks. He screamed again.

Lillith came rushing into the room, hearing the noise.

'Gabriel—' She stopped and looked at him. 'He's dead, isn't he? Our servant?' There was a tremor in her voice, and she was watching him with round eyes. He'd never lost his temper in her presence, not in all the centuries they'd roamed the earth together.

He stopped smashing things and turned to glare at her, reading her expression. There was more than just fear and outrage in her eyes. There was a tinge of guilt there, too, that she was trying hard but failing to hide. He stepped towards her, and the way she backed off told him he was right.

'What have you done?' he demanded.

'Nothing.'

'What have you done, Lillith? Lie to me, and I'll destroy you. I will *end* you.'

'Don't hurt me,' she pleaded, cowering. 'I only did it to help us.'

'Explain yourself.'

'Seymour found out who the policeman was. His name's Solomon, Joel Solomon. He's an inspector. And he was bluffing you. He doesn't have the cross.' As she spoke, the fear in her eyes was changing shade to a spark of defiance. 'You could have taken him that night, Gabriel, but you were too afraid.'

'You're telling me that this Solomon has murdered our most trusted of servants, because you ignored my specific commands? You sent Finch there to kill him, didn't you?'

'How was I to know the human would get the better of him?'

Stone drew back his hand to slap her. He could tear her head off with a single blow. But before he could deliver it, the door burst open and he spun round to see Zachary entering the dark study. He glared at him in fury at the interruption.

Zachary was clutching a small silver mobile phone in his giant fist. Through his rage, Gabriel recognised it as the one they used to communicate with their main contact within VIA.

'A text message has arrived,' Zachary said urgently. 'The Federation leaders have called an emergency conference in Belgium. We have all the details. Venue, date, time, and who'll be there. All of them in one place.'

'Perfect,' Gabriel said. His rage suddenly subsided. This was exactly what he'd hoped for.

'There's more,' Zachary said. 'And you won't like it.' He coughed nervously, glanced down at his boots. Not even a huge and powerful vampire wanted to be the bearer of bad tidings to someone like Gabriel Stone.

'*What?*'

Zachary swallowed hard and came out with it. 'Our informant says that the Federation agent Alex Bishop and a policeman called Joel Solomon are travelling to Venice to find the cross.'

Solomon and VIA working together. It was humiliating enough to have been duped by the human but to hear that he was conspiring with the hated enemy was unendurable. The enormity of it made Gabriel grind his teeth.

He ordered Zachary harshly out of the room, and began pacing again. His mind was working hard on a counter-strategy. With Finch gone, he would need a whole new plan.

Lillith came up to him and clasped his hands. 'Let me go after them. I'll destroy the VIA scum before she finds anything. I'll tear the human apart and feast on him and bring you back his head on a platter.'

'No, sister. It is my *wish* that they find the cross.'

She frowned. 'You would allow this to be brought on us? Our kind has long wanted the cross to be suppressed. It's too dangerous. This is madness.'

'It's precisely because the cross is dangerous that we cannot afford to ignore it,' he told her. 'The time has come to unearth it, so that it can be properly dealt with.'

'But who can we rely on to take care of it, now that—' Lillith stalled in mid-sentence, not wanting to say Finch's name.

'You've trusted me for many years,' Gabriel replied softly as he stroked her hair. He ran his hand down the contour of her neck, down her shoulder. His touch lingered on the curve of her breast. She half-closed her eyes, let out a small gasp.

'Trust me now,' he said.

CHAPTER 56

The Private Members' Library, Houses of Parliament, London 9.03 p.m.

Jeremy Lonsdale was so completely absorbed in the speech notes he was putting the finishing touches to that he hadn't realised until now that he was the only one left working late in the library that night. He'd nearly finished his amendments; it would soon be time to go back to the luxury Kensington townhouse where he spent the two days a week that he wasn't in Italy or at his country pile in Surrey.

He didn't entirely relish the prospect of going home to an empty house. His work was now all that allowed him to take his mind off his troubles, and since his return from Tuscany he'd thrown himself back into it with renewed vigour. Home was where the terrifying reality of his predicament was never far enough from his thoughts.

He picked up his pencil and made another small annotation to the wording on one of the printed sheets under the light of the banker's desk lamp.

He reread it, and nodded with approval; it sounded much more sincere that way. Satisfied, he pushed the sheet of paper away from him, out of the glow of the lamp, and picked up another. Then an afterthought occurred to him, and he reached again for the first sheet.

His fingers groped on the bare desktop. The sheet was gone. He angled the lamp, but all he saw was an empty expanse of dull green leather. Maybe it had fluttered down the other side and was lying on the floor? He scraped back his chair and began to rise to his feet.

The voice in the empty room stopped him short.

'Fine speech, Jeremy.'

It was Stone. He was standing just beyond the light of the desk lamp, perfectly still and merged into the darkness. As he stepped towards the desk, his cape-like black leather coat glistened. In his hands was the missing sheet of paper.

'I am sure this piece of masterly hypocrisy will earn you the faith of the gullible,' Stone said.

Lonsdale glanced nervously around him. 'How the hell did you get past security?' he blustered.

Stone chuckled. 'Do you not know me yet, Jeremy?'

'What do you want?'

'Simply to speak to you, Jeremy. And to charge you with a task.'

'A task?'

'One of vital importance to all of us. Two of my enemies are on their way to Venice, on a mission to find and bring back a certain historic artefact. One of these enemies is a member of your own lowly species; the other, to my shame, belongs to my own kind. Once they find the artefact, I want you to take possession of it. The vampire is to be slain – I will supply you with the necessary.' Gabriel paused. 'As for the human, my wish is that he be taken alive. I'll deal with him in my own way. A personal matter.'

Lonsdale glared indignantly. 'I'm a politician, not an assassin and a kidnapper. You're not going to send me here, there and everywhere to commit crimes for you.'

'You make me laugh, Jeremy. Please, spare me this display of moral indignation. You and your kind have been ordering the death and incarceration of your fellow men since time began. In any case, whether you carry out this task with your own hand is of no concern to me. Such services can be bought. I'm sure you have the appropriate contacts – if not, now is the time to make some.'

'What is this historic artefact that's so important to you?' Lonsdale asked.

'A simple cross, of Celtic design.'

'But you told me your people had no fear of crosses—'

'This is a cross like no other. I couldn't possibly expect a human to understand, nor do I have the patience to share my knowledge with you. Suffice to say that it's highly dangerous to us – though not, as fate would have it, to your despicable race. That's why you shall act as my courier. You will deliver the cross to an agreed destination, where I may witness its destruction from a safe distance.'

'Then this cross really is a threat to you,' Lonsdale said.

Stone arched an eyebrow. 'I know precisely what's in your mind, Jeremy. You're thinking that an object of such power offers a most convenient way to rid yourself of my presence in your life. You would use it to destroy me.'

Lonsdale held up his hands. 'No, no. I swear, the thought never—'

'Quiet. Don't insult me with lies.' Gabriel smiled. 'If you weren't a devious and treacherous little vermin, I wouldn't have enlisted you in the first place. But you would do well to remember my superior intelligence. You can't outwit me, and you will certainly never destroy me.' He paused. 'Have you paid a visit to your son recently?' he said nonchalantly.

Lonsdale looked blank. 'I don't know what you're talking about.'

'Your son Toby. A fine boy. Doing well at that expensive boarding school you sent him to.' Gabriel slipped a photo from the breast pocket of his long leather coat and dropped it onto the desk. It had been taken with a long lens, and showed a boy of about ten, frozen in mid-stride, his face lit up with innocent joy as he dashed across a muddy field clutching a rugby ball.

Lonsdale stared at it aghast. 'How did you find out about Toby?'

'Another little secret your potential voters can't know about. The bastard spawn of your fling with your former secretary.'

'I love that boy,' Lonsdale said. 'More than anything. He's just an innocent child. You can do what you want with me – but please, don't harm him.'

'I'm fully aware of your affection for the child,' Stone replied. 'And, were I to share your frail human tendency towards emotional attachments, I'm sure I might even find it quite touching. Rest assured that nothing untoward will befall young Toby, as long as you do as I ask. But the merest transgression, and what happened to the hapless female at your initiation ceremony will seem like a kindness in comparison to what your son will suffer.'

Lonsdale screwed his eyes shut. 'I'll take care of it. I won't fail you.'

When he looked again, the vampire had slipped away into the dark.

CHAPTER 57

The Metropole Hotel, Venice
10.08 p.m. local time

'I can't afford this place,' Joel said under his breath as they walked through the luxurious hotel lobby. 'You're looking at a guy on half pay for the next six months.'

'Who says you're paying?' Alex replied.

'I can't let you—'

'Relax. My family's rich. Money isn't an issue.' She smiled to herself, thinking about the expense account she'd persuaded Harry Rumble to set up for the trip to Venice. If they were going to be here for a while, searching for an ancient cross that might not even exist, they might as well do it in style. She led the way to the desk and tried to book two double rooms next to one another. The hotel manager shook his head and said all they had available was a suite with two separate bedrooms. He named an astronomical price for the night, and she booked it without hesitation.

They'd brought little luggage with them. A uniformed porter grabbed Joel's holdall in his left hand. He was fairly well built and lifted it effort-lessly but when he went to pick up the leather travelling bag Alex had been carrying just moments before, he could barely get it off the floor. He shot a look of amazement at her, heaved it up with a grunt and led the way towards the lift.

'What have you got in that thing?' Joel asked, watching the porter struggle and sweat.

'We girls like to carry a lot of stuff around with us,' she replied casually.

'Tell me about it.'

The suite was lavish and seemed to ramble across at least half a floor of the hotel. Their sepa-rate bedrooms were on a palatial scale, a blue satin-draped four-poster in hers and a gold satin one in his, each with its own balcony looking out over the canal. Joel walked out onto his and leaned on the stone balustrade, transfixed by the view. The moon was full and bright on the rippling water. The city lights twinkled like stars. Feeling her presence, he turned suddenly and saw her standing close behind him.

'Did I startle you?' she smiled. 'Sorry.'

'I was miles away. Just looking.'

'First time here?'

'First time just about anywhere,' he replied. 'Unless you count rock climbing trips in the Lake District and weekends in Blackpool with my aunt and uncle. Sausage and chips on the pier. Not quite the same, is it?'

She walked up close to him and ran her eye along his shape as he leaned on the balcony. He was lithe but strong. She could smell his skin and his hair. It felt strange to want to touch him.

'It's amazing,' he said, taking in the view. 'I don't suppose this city has changed much in centuries.'

'No,' she sighed. 'It hasn't.'

They stood in silence for a while, him watching the water and the dark silhouettes of distant steeples and towers against the sky, her watching him. For all the troubles and sadness she could see in his eyes, it was clear to her that he was drinking in the serenity of the tranquil old city with real pleasure. With a jolt of alarm, she realised how natural and relaxed she felt in this human's presence.

Be careful, Alex.

'Feel like a bite?' he said suddenly, turning to face her.

'What?'

'You must be hungry. You want to see if we can grab a bite somewhere?'

'I might pick at something,' she said. 'I don't eat that much.'

Joel had barely eaten in the last thirty-six hours, and his stomach was telling him so. 'Maybe we could hang about here, order something up to the room.'

The selection of cold meats, salads, olives and cheese was delivered to the suite together with two bottles of expensive red wine, all courtesy of

VIA. Joel attacked the food like a man who'd just been rescued from a desert island, piling a plate with cold chicken, smoked ham, a mound of olives and a huge wedge of cheese. Alex daintily helped herself to a couple of tiny morsels, and they settled in two comfortable armchairs facing each other in the suite's vast living room. Joel didn't seem to notice her lack of appetite. As he munched and drank he had his grandfather's notebook spread open beside him on the arm of the chair, and the conversation quickly focused on the clues they needed to crack.

'Salvation lies at the feet of the Virgin,' Joel said, reading from the page and knocking back another glass of wine. He was outdrinking her three to one and getting progressively more bright-eyed as the level in the first bottle dropped rapidly.

Alex sipped from her glass. 'Was your grandfather Catholic?'

'He was raised C of E, as far as I know. I don't recall him ever having talked about going to church, though.'

'Because what if he wasn't just talking metaphysics here? What if he was talking about his own literal salvation? As in, the only thing that he believed could save him?'

'You're saying he was referring to the location of the cross?'

She nodded. 'X marks the spot.'

'At the feet of the Virgin. How many Virgin Marys must there be here in Venice?'

'A few thousand,' she said. 'Maybe more than a few. The Mother of Christ isn't exactly a rarity in these parts.'

'That's a lot of possible Xs marking a lot of possible spots.'

They talked on, throwing ideas back and forth, getting nowhere fast. Joel shoved his empty plate to one side and concentrated harder on the wine. The first bottle was empty now, and he was making inroads into the second, slumping gradually down into his armchair and slurring his words a little.

'What about this "Anchi 666"?' he complained. 'It's driving me crazy. The Antichrist? Damien?'

'My Bible knowledge is a little rusty,' Alex said, 'but what I think the Book of Revelation says is that the number six hundred threescore and six is "the number of a man" who's also the biblical Beast – the Devil's envoy, his representative on Earth. Does it mean vampires?' She shrugged. 'I can't say for sure. In ancient times, a lot of people thought vampires were an incarnation of Satanic evil.'

'Evil is the right word,' Joel muttered, and slipped a little further down in his chair.

Alex didn't reply.

'But where does this get us?' he groaned. He was really slurring now, and having trouble keeping his eyes open. Alex moved over to his chair and put her hand to his lips.

'Shh. Tomorrow. You're tired.'

He nodded sleepily, and closed his eyes. She kneeled by his chair and studied his face as he fell asleep.

Within minutes he'd drifted far away. It was as though she'd been left alone in the room. A strange emptiness came over her, and an impulse made her reach out suddenly and stroke his cheek.

'William,' she murmured softly.

He stirred and his eyelids gave a flicker, then he went still again. She ran her fingers through his hair. She wanted to kiss him . . . She didn't know what she wanted. It felt strange and confusing to be here with this man.

After a few minutes, she stood up. Putting an arm gently under his shoulders and the other under his legs, she scooped him up out of the armchair without waking him and carried him easily through the door of his bedroom. She laid him down on the four-poster and covered him gently with a blanket.

She should have left him then, but instead she stayed with him, sitting on the edge of the bed as he slept. From time to time his brows twitched and he shook his head from side to side and muttered softly to himself as troubled dreams played in his mind. She stroked his hair and whispered soothingly to him, and the frown would melt away from his face so that he looked almost like a child.

What it was that made it so hard to leave his side, she didn't understand. Time passed and in her own thoughts she was seeing herself as she'd been a long, long time ago. Happy, carefree, in love. She remembered the good times.

Then the bad memories returned, the way they always did. Cradling her dying lover in her arms as his blood soaked into her clothes and the life ebbed out of him drop by drop. Knowing there was nothing to be done but to hold him tight and count the precious moments that were going to be their last together.

'Don't go,' she'd pleaded through her tears. He'd seemed to focus for a moment, and whispered his last promise to her.

'I'll come back to you, my love.' Then the light in his eyes had faded to a glassy stare. And that was it. He was gone.

Sitting here now in this dark room after so many years had gone by and so very much had happened, Alex wanted to cry. But to cry was one thing she could not do.

Joel's eyes opened in the darkness. 'What time is it?' he murmured, half unconscious.

'It's late,' she whispered. 'Go back to sleep.'

'I was dreaming.'

'I know.'

'I dreamed you carried me in here.'

She chuckled. 'That's crazy.'

'It felt so real.'

'Just dreams,' she said. A strand of hair fell across his eye. She brushed it away.

'How long have you been sitting here?' he asked softly, with a smile.

'I'll go now.'

He put out his hand to catch her arm as she got up to leave. 'Stay,' he said. She could so easily have broken his grip, but didn't.

What are you doing, Alex?

She let him pull her down towards him, slowly closer until she could feel his warm breath on her lips. His eyes were shining in the moonlight from the window. Then, when the kiss came, there was no going back from it, for either of them.

CHAPTER 58

The Dorchester Bar, London
10.17 p.m.

Slumped on a stool at the end of the curved bar, Kirsty Fletcher drained the last of her gin and tonic and ordered another. She glanced at her watch. More than three-quarters of an hour since her boyfriend Steve had been due to turn up. He was making a habit of that. And just under six hours since she'd walked out of her audition feeling utterly deflated and demoralised. The feeling hadn't gone away. Steve had suggested the Dorchester as a treat, to help drown her sorrows together.

Cheers, Steve, she thought bitterly as she took the first gulp of her second G and T. She followed that up with a bigger one, and before she knew it the ice was clinking against an empty glass. At about twenty quid a sip, she couldn't hang about here all night. There was a bottle of cheap wine in the fridge back home in her little Hammersmith flat; she'd take it to bed, turn on a movie and put the rest of the day out of its misery. Sounded like a good plan.

It was the ripple of whispers from the group of women sitting at the table behind her that made her look round at the entrance.

'Who's he?' the skinny blonde said *sotto voce* behind her hand to the brunette next to her. Kirsty followed their gaze towards the man who had just walked into the bar. He was tall and almost impossibly elegant, but without a hint of affectation. Maybe in his early forties, he was built like a tennis champion and walked with the easy grace of an athlete. His hair was thick and dark, and the eyes beneath the sleek brows were the most vivid blue she'd ever seen. She swallowed.

Ohmygod . . . he's coming this way.

He walked the length of the bar, pulled up a stool two seats away from where she was sitting, and peeled off the long leather coat he was wearing to reveal a beautifully tailored suit. When he ordered a glass of champagne, his voice seemed to trickle like warm liquid over her.

Suddenly she was thinking about hanging around. Just a little longer. She fingered her empty glass. That was when the man turned and gave her a smile that sent a frisson through her whole body.

'I've always hated drinking alone,' he said. His tone was gentle and warm. Kirsty could feel the envious looks of the women at the table.

She nodded.

'Care to join me?' he asked.

She said that she would. He ordered a bottle of

champagne, introduced himself as Gabriel. When he asked her what she did, she blushed and said she was an actress.

'Not a very successful one,' she added, and told him about the few bit roles she'd had, mainly TV, and her failed audition that afternoon. 'That's why I'm here,' she explained. 'Feeling rather sorry for myself.'

He gave her that shattering smile again. 'I believe in synchronicity, Kirsty.' He took out his card and slipped it into her hand.

'Topaz Productions?' She looked up at him, blinking.

'I'm an executive producer,' he said. 'And the funny thing is, we're just about to go into production with a film project I've been developing, and the lead actress just dropped out.' He told her the name. It was a famous one. 'But I must tell you, I never considered her quite right for the part. I was looking for someone like you.'

The champagne just seemed to be slipping down. Kirsty was getting heady. It didn't seem to affect Gabriel. He ordered another bottle. 'It's exquisite, is it not?'

'I like the way you talk,' she said. 'You're not like other men.'

'Maybe I'm old fashioned,' he said.

'I like it. Where are you from? I can't place your accent.'

He smiled. 'All over.'

'Tell me more about the film.'

'Do you have a little time?'

She thought about Steve. Screw him. 'Plenty,' she said.

He paid the bill, leaving the half-empty bottle without a second glance, and she followed him out of the Dorchester. The night was cool and fresh, and the moon was full over London. He walked her towards a car that was lower and sleeker than any sports car she'd ever seen before.

'Wow. What kind of car is this?'

'It's the fastest car in the world,' he told her as he opened the gull-wing door for her. The driver's seat was in the middle, like a racing car. Kirsty climbed a little uncertainly into the passenger seat positioned just behind and to the side. The car felt very low down. Gabriel settled in behind the wheel, flashed another brilliant smile and started up the engine with a rasping roar.

In what seemed like no time at all, they were hurtling down the motorway heading out of the city.

'Henley?' she said when he told her where he lived. 'That's in Oxfordshire.'

'It won't take us long in this,' he said. As the car accelerated and Kirsty felt herself pressed back in her seat, she watched the surreal climb of the speedometer. 150 . . . 180 . . . 190. She blinked, laughed, dizzy from the champagne.

'Do you know how fast you're going?'

'I can go faster, if you wish.'

'Aren't you worried about the police?'

He turned. 'Should I be?'

'What if they stop us?'

'Then I shall simply kill them,' he shrugged casually.

She laughed again. 'You're such a joker, Gabriel.' He obviously had enough money to bribe his way out of any kind of trouble, she thought.

'I never joke,' he replied.

As he'd promised, it wasn't long before they were speeding through the country lanes of south Oxfordshire. He pulled up at the high gates of what looked to Kirsty like a huge estate. The gates opened automatically, and the car rumbled on through them and up a long, winding driveway.

She was babbling with excitement as they pulled up outside the house. 'This is where you *live*?'

'Not all of the time. I have homes in several places.' He killed the engine, climbed out and opened her door for her, taking her hand to lead her across the gravel.

'I've had too much to drink,' she giggled. As he led her inside the grand hallway, she asked him, 'Do you live here alone?'

'Some of my family also reside here. My sister Lillith is here at the moment. You may meet her.'

Kirsty's head was spinning with more than champagne as he ushered her through the house.

'This is the library,' he said. She looked around her at the enormous oak-panelled room, the ornate coved ceiling, the towering bookcases filled with antique leather-bound volumes, the gleaming grand piano in the corner. A fire was crackling brightly in a marble fireplace.

'Would you care for another drink?' he asked.

'Why not?' *What the hell.* She thought about Steve again, and smiled to herself. Sweet revenge.

Gabriel graciously excused himself. Alone in the library, she went over to one of the bookcases and ran her fingers across the polished wood. She opened one of the glass doors and selected a book at random. Carefully flipping open the cover, she saw it was Milton's *Paradise Lost*. She wondered how old it was.

'Very old indeed,' said Gabriel's voice, making her jump.

'You startled me.'

He smiled. 'It was unintentional. I apologise.' He was carrying a heavy silver tray with a bottle of Krug and two slim flutes.

'This is more champagne than I've ever had before,' she said. She sipped her drink as Gabriel walked over to the piano. His hands descended delicately on the keys, and he began to play.

'That's beautiful,' she murmured.

'Composed by someone I once knew. His name was Frederick. Frederick Chopin.'

Kirsty frowned. 'Isn't he, like, dead? As in, dead a long time?'

Gabriel made no reply. He went on playing, and the powerful, melancholic music filled the room. As she listened, Kirsty wandered back over to the bookcase and found one by someone she recognised, Jane Austen. She opened it carefully and saw it was signed by the author.

'This is an amazing collection of books, Gabriel,' she said. 'Some of these must be terribly rare.'

He abruptly stopped playing and stood up. Picked his glass off the piano and sipped it as he walked over to her. 'Just little things I've acquired on my travels,' he said. He reached past her and slipped a book off a shelf. 'Like this one. Turgenev. First edition. It's extremely valuable.' He weighed the book in his hand, then flung it in the fire. It burst open and curled and blackened as the flames devoured it.

She stared at him.

'Just words,' he said. 'The truth is, Kirsty, I have little love for human culture. It amuses me for a while, but ultimately I find it vacuous and oafish.' He stepped closer to her and touched the skin of her shoulder. 'So soft,' he said. 'I could have a coat made out of you.'

'You're crazy,' she giggled. He leaned in slowly to kiss her. She felt the cool press of his lips on hers, and responded. She was breathless by the time he broke the embrace.

'Do you have a husband, a boyfriend?'

'Never mind him,' she breathed.

'So fickle. Frailty, thy name is woman.'

She went to kiss him again, but he stopped her. 'I'd like to see you in costume,' he said.

'Costume?'

'For the role you're going to play. Lillith will take you up to the dressing room. Here she is.'

Kirsty turned in surprise to see a woman slinking her way across the library towards them. She was extremely beautiful. Jet black curls tumbled down over her shoulders and the glistening black leather outfit that hugged her lithe figure. Her skin was like ivory in the soft light. Her eyes glittered black as she approached.

'You called me, Gabriel,' she said without taking her gaze off Kirsty. Her voice was dark, smoky.

'I didn't notice,' Kirsty laughed nervously.

'My sister and I are very close,' Gabriel said. 'You might say almost telepathic.' He tenderly stroked Lillith's shoulder. 'Would you take Kirsty upstairs now? I've left out the costume for her.'

The champagne mist parted as if it had been cleft by a blade. Kirsty frowned. 'You left it . . . But how—'

'That's right,' Gabriel smiled. 'I picked it out for you before I left the house.'

'My brother always prepares things in advance,' Lillith purred.

Kirsty suddenly felt edgy. She looked at her watch. 'Maybe you should take me back to London. We can talk about the film another time.'

'Come with me, Kirsty. You're going to love it.' Lillith took her arm. Her grip was soft but firm. Kirsty wanted to protest, but something in the woman's eyes made it impossible to resist. She allowed herself to be led away. Lillith spoke gently, sweetly, as they walked together out of the library and up a winding red velvet staircase. Gilt-framed

352

portraits seemed to leer at Kirsty out of the shadows as Lillith escorted her down a long corridor. Then they were in a room filled with clothes, like the biggest walk-in wardrobe she'd ever seen. Draped over an ornate chaise longue was a beautiful long white silk dress.

Lillith smiled warmly. 'Go on. Put it on.'

Kirsty picked it up hesitantly. 'It's a little low-cut, don't you think?'

'You're going to look gorgeous in it.'

Kirsty took the dress behind a screen and began stepping out of her clothes. It was as if she was someone else, no longer in control of her own actions. Everything felt hazy and distant. As she emerged from behind the screen wearing the white dress, Lillith drew a breath.

'There. Didn't I tell you? My brother has an eye for beauty.' She came up close. 'Let me zip you up.' She ran her hands over Kirsty's naked shoulders. 'So warm and soft,' she murmured. 'Like velvet.'

Kirsty tried to move away from her. The closeness of another woman was strange, and Lillith's fingers moved on her skin like a lover's.

'Come and look at yourself.' Lillith guided her to the tall mirror and stood behind her, still touching her shoulders. 'See how beautiful you look.'

Kirsty gazed into the mirror. She looked herself up and down, thinking she looked like the bride in someone's fantasy. Then she looked at Lillith's reflection behind her.

Lillith was smiling as she ran her fingers through Kirsty's hair. 'You ought to wear it up, like this. Don't you think?' Her lips were full and red. Then they parted. Kirsty stared at the white canine teeth that were suddenly grown hideously long and curved and sharp. The fangs bore down on her exposed neck.

Kirsty screamed. Twisted away and burst out of the dressing room. She was screaming wildly as she ran all the way back down the corridor. The portraits watched her and seemed to sneer.

Gabriel was standing at the end of the corridor. Kirsty flew into his arms, and he gripped her tightly. She screamed again as she saw Lillith moving fast towards them, her teeth bared in a vulpine grin.

'Get her away from me!' she shrieked.

He pointed at Lillith. 'Stay back,' he hissed at her.

Then Kirsty looked up at Gabriel. There was a look in his eyes she hadn't seen before. Not in anyone's eyes, not ever. She froze. His mouth opened and he leaned towards her. This time, not for a kiss.

'The first bite is mine,' he said.

And the blood spattered down across the white silk of Kirsty's dress.

CHAPTER 59

The Metropole Hotel, Venice
3.02 a.m. local time

Alex and Joel had made love for hours in the pool of moonlight that flooded across the satin sheets.

'You're incredible,' he'd gasped afterwards, as he held her tight. 'You're going to kill me.' She could have gone on and on, but he was completely spent and worn out, and soon fell back into a deep sleep with his arm draped across her naked body. She lay there beside him in the rumpled bed, caressing his cooling skin, listening to the rise and fall of his breathing, her senses bright and alert.

She was sailing into uncharted waters now and she knew it. If VIA ever had the slightest inkling of what she'd just done, it was all over for her. Not her service record, not even Harry Rumble's intervention, could save her from the punishment that was carved in stone on the Federation's sacred list of commandments. They had the power, and they'd use it. She'd be arrested and taken straight to the execution chamber. Strapped in a chair, hardened steel loops around her wrists and her neck. She'd be forced to watch as the vampire executioner filled a syringe from a vial of Nosferol. Then the needle would come closer, and closer. The jab of pain as it stabbed into her arm. The agony as the poison ravaged her body, twenty seconds of horrific screaming torment that lasted longer than a century of walking the earth. There was no pain like it. The horrors that humans had inflicted on their own kind, the witches and martyrs and torture victims through the ages, didn't even come close.

She shuddered. Joel stirred beside her, muttered her name and rolled over, still fast asleep. She carefully disentangled herself from his arms and stepped naked into the moonlight. She picked up the trail of clothes that lay strewn across the rug and dressed quickly and quietly.

The familiar old tingle was coming over her. She needed to feed, and soon. Glancing back over at Joel's still form under the sheets, for a few intoxicating moments she could sense nothing but the blood pumping through his veins as he slept. Its rich tang filled her nostrils, and she could almost taste the warmth of it on her tongue, running down her throat. Her heart began to quicken as a force that was stronger than her threatened to impel her towards the bed. Not to love him this time, but to bite him. Her fangs began to elongate in her mouth.

This was the dangerous time, when nothing that lived and walked and bled was safe.

Get out of here, Alex. Now. You can't do this to him. Not him.

She tore herself away. Out on the balcony, she glanced down to the narrow street that separated the hotel from the banks of the canal. She looked left, then right. There was nobody around. But there would be, somewhere out there, walking the street. And they were hers.

She flipped herself over the edge of the stone balustrade, dropped the twenty feet to the ground and landed without a sound.

Now it was time to hunt.

Wallingford
2.06 a.m.

Dec was lying sprawled out on the couch at Matt's place. On the table next to him were the remnants of a microwave meal he'd managed to stagger into the kitchen to prepare earlier that evening, but hadn't had the stomach to eat. He had no idea how long he'd been staring unfocused at the television. The images on the screen made no sense to him. Some kind of movie with lots of car chases, but he kept drifting in and out and couldn't follow it. Feverish extremes of hot and cold kept washing over him, leaving him sweltering one minute and racked with shivering the next.

He had only the vaguest notion of what he was doing here. His memories were all confused and mixed up. It was impossible to get comfortable on the couch; he could hardly move without getting nauseous and every twist of his body brought a sharp pain in his neck. He touched the sore spot with his fingers, then withdrew them with a wince as he felt the raised puncture marks, crusted in dried blood. What had he done to himself?

He became aware of a strange sensation in his groin, like a pulsing tingling feeling – then realised it was his phone vibrating in his pocket. He took it out groggily and pressed it to his ear.

His brother's voice. 'Where are you? Me ma's going mad with worry and me da's about to have a fookin' heart attack. Why have you not come home?'

'Hi, Cormac,' Dec slurred into the phone.

'What's wrong with you, bro?'

'I'm okay,' Dec lied.

'Speak up. I can hardly hear you.'

'Tell them I'm fine. I just want to be alone for a bit.'

'Where are you?' Cormac said again.

'Promise not to tell,' Dec muttered.

'You know I won't clipe.'

'I'm at Matt's place,' Dec said. Then there was sudden silence on the phone. He squinted at the screen and saw that the battery had gone dead. He swore weakly and let the phone tumble out of his hand. He closed his eyes.

He didn't know how long he'd been out of it when a sound woke him.

It was the sound of something scraping against the window. With an effort, he propped himself up on his elbows and peered across the room.

The curtains were open. On the other side of the glass, standing on the window ledge, was Kate. She ran her nails down the pane and looked at him imploringly.

'Let me in, Dec. Please.'

Dec fell off the couch and started crawling across the floor towards her. Halfway to the window, he stopped. He put one hand up to the wounds on his neck.

This isn't Kate. Kate's dead.

'It's so cold out here, Dec,' she mewled. 'Don't you love me any more?'

He hesitated.

'Let me in,' she pleaded. 'I want to be with you. I've *always* wanted to be with you.'

She looked so sad and pathetic and vulnerable out there. His heart went out to her. He managed to grab the backrest of a chair and haul himself unsteadily to his feet. Staggered the rest of the way to the window. Reached out and grasped the window catch.

CHAPTER 60

The Metropole Hotel, Venice
6.23 a.m. local time

'Where did you go?' Joel mumbled sleepily from under the covers.

Alex froze where she stood on the balcony. Behind her, the light of dawn was breaking over the Venetian skyline. For a second she thought Joel had seen her climb over the balustrade from the street below, and her mind raced to find an explanation for the unorthodox entrance.

'I didn't hear the door,' he said, rubbing his eyes and sitting up in bed, and she could breathe again.

'I sometimes don't sleep well at night,' she explained nonchalantly. 'A walk helps. Didn't want to wake you.'

Joel kicked his legs out from under the rumpled sheets. 'You should have woken me. I'd have come with you.'

She smiled. 'A girl likes to be alone sometimes.'

'What about now?'

'Now I want to be with you.' She walked over

360

to the bed and rested her hands on his shoulders.

'I can't believe you were just out in the cold. Your hands are toasty.'

'I have good circulation,' she said. Especially when her veins were filled with someone else's fresh blood. The recent memory of last night's two victims replayed in a flash through her mind. The first had been a young guy on his way home from a late-night bar. She'd stalked him in silence for a few hundred yards before jumping him in an alleyway.

The second had been something of an indulgence. She'd been making her way back to the hotel, crossing a bridge when a solitary gondolier had appeared like a vision through the pre-dawn mist and drifted up the canal beneath her. Too much to resist. By the time he'd realised he had an uninvited passenger, his blood was being sucked from his neck.

She'd only just had enough Vambloc left for the second one. Running out was a big worry.

But now, at least, Joel was safe with her. And that mattered a great deal.

'Look what we did to this bed last night,' he said, smiling as he started unbuttoning her coat. 'It's wrecked.'

'Impetuous,' she murmured. The coat slipped from her shoulders, and then his fingers were running up under her blouse. She pushed him down on the bed and clambered astride him.

After making love for the second time in a few hours, they called room service. During breakfast in bed, he kept looking at her and wanting to clasp her hand. 'This feels so weird to me,' he said. 'We've only just met, but it's like I've known you all my life.'

'Maybe you have,' she replied.

It was bright, crisp and cold as they wandered the streets and squares of Venice. Hours of discussion, of studying the notebook and racking their brains still hadn't led them anywhere, and the day was beginning to pass them by with nothing to show for it.

By the time noon had come and gone, they were walking almost aimlessly through the old city. On their left, row after row of moored boats and gondolas drifted on the sparkling waters of the Grand Canal as they passed the Doge's Palace and the Archaeological Museum. During high season the place would have been swarming with thousands of people, but today only a thin smattering of tourists were ambling around the spectacular sights, snapping cameras here and there as their guides pointed out sites of interest and rambled through the history of the different buildings.

'What are you looking at?' Alex smiled, catching Joel's eye as they walked under the pale sun.

'I was admiring the view,' he said, not taking his eyes off her.

'You've got to keep your mind on what we're looking for.' She tried to sound reprimanding, but the grin on his face was infectious, and she couldn't stop her smile from widening. 'Be serious.'

'I am serious. I want to find this thing and go home. You know, that looks heavy,' he added, pointing at the colourful backpack she was wearing. Whatever she was carrying inside, the straps were strained tight over her shoulders. 'Want me to take it for a while?'

'I can manage, thanks.'

'Let me guess,' he said. 'More girl stuff.'

'You said it. Plus I brought along my mallet and stakes, in case we run into any vampires.'

'Now who isn't being serious?'

She was about to reply when she sensed something behind them. She glanced over her shoulder at the crowds of people, scanning the faces of the tourists. They all seemed to be either gazing around them at the Venetian scenery, or perusing their guidebooks, or fiddling with the settings on their cameras.

All except two pairs of eyes. Both hidden behind sunglasses, both angled towards them. The pair of men were hanging back a hundred yards or so as Alex and Joel turned inland and emerged into the huge open space of St Mark's Square.

'What?' he said, noticing the sudden look of tension on her face.

'Don't look now,' she said, 'but apparently someone

else is less than interested in the architecture too. Back near the wall over there. Five o'clock. There are two of them.'

Joel pretended to stumble over an uneven paving stone. 'Got them. You think they're following us?'

'I don't think they've mistaken us for Brad and Angelina, do you?'

Up ahead, a slender young female guide was pointing up at St Mark's Basilica, the huge cathedral that dominated one end of the square and the huddled streets and buildings beyond, for the benefit of the small crowd of Americans who were tagging slowly along in her wake. She looked like she was having to work hard to maintain their attention. As they caught up with the group, Alex and Joel caught snatches of her talking about its five Byzantine domes. A few zoom lenses whirred and shutters clicked. The tourists all gazed dully at the magnificence of the ornate sculptures and dazzling mosaics, the glittering pyramidal spire of the enormous bell tower next to the basilica. Alex also gazed casually up at the buildings, but only so she could throw a discreet glance back towards the two men – and saw that they'd melted into the crowd. But she hadn't imagined them.

'How does anybody know we're here?' Joel said tensely.

'Interesting question. I was wondering the same thing myself.'

'At least they can't be . . . you know. Not if

they're walking about in daylight.' Joel thought of Seymour Finch and quickly realised that was small consolation.

'No,' Alex said after a moment's pause. 'No, they can't.'

Pressing deeper inside the crowd, they used its cover to scan the square far and wide for any trace of the two men. Alex could see nothing but she was certain they were still being watched from a distance.

The tour group had drifted closer to St Mark's Basilica, and the guide pointed out the large bronze horses that overlooked the square from the cathedral's facade.

'They were said to have been part of the treasure sacked from Constantinople during the Fourth Crusade,' she told the disinterested crowd. 'Napoleon Bonaparte removed them to Paris in 1797, but they were restored to Venice eighteen years later. Sadly, the horses you see here are only replicas, but I'm pleased to tell you that the real ones are inside, if you'll follow me—'

One of the families of tourists had with them a chubby little girl of about seven. Where her face wasn't smeared with chocolate, it was mottled red with bored dissatisfaction. She twisted grumpily to her mother and complained loudly, 'Mommy, I wanna see the *vampires*!'

Alex snapped her head round to stare at her through the crowd. The child caught her eye and her face turned pale – but then everyone started laughing at her comment, and the tension of the moment was diffused. The guide smiled.

'I believe our learned little friend is referring to the gruesome discovery, made just last year right here in Venice, of skulls that some have claimed once belonged to *real-life vampires.*'

A mutter ran through the crowd as they momentarily forgot all about Napoleon and the Fourth Crusade.

'That's right,' the guide went on, obviously pleased that she'd got their attention at last. 'Vampires. They were the skulls of women, and they had had bricks or stone wedges hammered into their mouths to stop them from biting more victims. Then, just like in the story of *Dracula*, they would have been staked through the heart.' She paused, and pulled a face. 'But the terrible truth is that these women, far from being blood-sucking monsters, are likely to have been the hapless victims of a superstition that was still very prevalent during the time that the Black Death struck the city during the sixteenth and seventeenth centuries, killing 150,000 people, a whole third of Venice's population.'

Another fascinated murmur from the crowd. The guide was on a roll now.

'The plague was actually believed by many to be a form of vampiric possession, because of the way the victims' mouths would ooze blood as they succumbed to the disease. In fact, the succession of plagues that struck Europe during the centuries was responsible for encouraging a mass belief in vampirism. Thankfully, we now know that Count Dracula and his brides are *not* stalking the streets of Venice.'

Everybody laughed, except Alex and Joel.

'For those of you who may be interested,' the guide went on, 'the terrible ravages of the Black Death in Venice are depicted in artwork by painters such as Tintoretto and Zanchi, whose works are displayed in the Scuola Grande di San Rocco.' She smiled. 'But now, returning to the famous basilica here in front of us . . .'

Alex didn't hear any more. She glanced at Joel, and could see that he'd had the same idea.

'Did you get that?' she asked.

He looked stunned by the realisation. 'Zanchi.'

'Right. Take away the Z and you've got—'

'Anchi. The bit we couldn't figure out.'

She nodded. 'We were reading it wrongly. The guy was a painter. And what do you always see depicted in Italian artwork from that time? The Virgin Mary.'

'Salvation lies at the feet of the Virgin,' Joel said.

'Which means we need to go to the Grand School of San Rocco.'

They broke off from the tour group and hurried away across the square, back towards the Grand Canal. Out of the corner of her eye, Alex spotted the two men reappear from a doorway and start following them at a fast trot.

As they approached the edge of the canal, a

waterbus was pulling into the side to let off passengers. Alex glanced back as they boarded and saw the two men exchange looks of frustration. She gave them a little wave.

'Bye, bye, assholes.' She smiled to herself as the waterbus burbled away.

CHAPTER 61

After the morning's sunshine, the afternoon was turning quickly chilly as a thick mist rolled in like smoke from the water. Alex's hair was beginning to drip with moisture as they eventually found the baroque facade of the red and cream building that was the Grand School of San Rocco.

Inside, the place was virtually deserted. As they walked from room to room and gallery to gallery, gazing around them at the displays of Venetian art, Joel leafed carefully through the guide leaflet he'd grabbed from a tourist information stand in the foyer.

'Hey!' he said as Alex plucked it from his fingers and started skimming through it at high speed.

'Got it,' she said. 'We need to go this way.' She pointed towards a broad upward flight of white marble steps, and tugged his arm.

'What's that way?'

'This,' she said, and pointed at the enormous painting that adorned the wall to the right of the staircase. The gleaming mural depicted in intricate detail a crowd of miserable-looking people in various poses, pointing upwards with looks of reverent astonishment as a heavenly apparition descended on a cloud to meet them.

'I'm not exactly an art expert,' Joel said, walking up to it.

'You think I am?' Alex waved the leaflet at him. 'Check it out. *The Virgin Appears to the Plague Victims*, by Antonio Zanchi, born 1631.'

'You and your speed reading.'

'And he painted it when he was thirty-five years of age,' she added meaningfully.

Joel frowned. 'And that's relevant because—'

'Because it means you can forget Damien and the Antichrist. 666 was just a date, with the number one chewed away.'

'1666,' he muttered. 'Damn.'

Alex climbed two more steps so that she could get a closer look at the divine host that the artist had depicted floating down from the sky, surrounded by a retinue of angels.

'Here's our Virgin Mary,' she said, pointing. 'Appearing from heaven to offer solace to the miserable plague victims.'

Joel peered at the canvas, looking for the salvation that was supposed to lie at the Virgin's feet. 'I don't see anything there. Certainly not a cross.'

'Nor do I.' Alex paused a few moments, then let out a sigh. 'I don't think it's here, Joel. I was hoping for more. Shit.'

Joel looked at her. 'You're sure about that?'

'Quite sure. There are just so many gaps in your

grandfather's notes. We obviously missed something important.'

'Wonderful. We're in the wrong place.'

'Yeah,' she replied thoughtfully, gazing down the broad expanse of marble staircase into the middle distance. Then a smile spread over her face.

'You're taking it awfully well, considering that was our only real clue and we're now going to have to scour the city with nothing more to go on.'

She turned to him. 'San Rocco. A saint. Must have been a fairly important guy, no? Lots of people wanting to celebrate his name?'

'I'd imagine so. What are you trying to say?'

She zipped through the leaflet again and stopped almost instantly at a page. 'There. Just as I thought. San Rocco didn't only give his name to the school,' she said. 'Where do you go looking for a Virgin in Venice? A church.'

'So?'

'So how about the Church of San Rocco, right next door?'

They ran back outside. The mist was thickening as dusk approached, and droplets of moisture hovered on the golden light from the doorway of the nearby church. A sign on the entrance told them they had only a few minutes before the place closed for the evening.

'We'd better be quick,' Joel said as he glanced hurriedly around at the beautiful displays of frescoes on the domed ceiling, the intricate gilding and gleaming marble, the paintings hung around the walls.

'We won't be long,' Alex said in a low voice.

From the instant she'd stepped inside the building, she knew. The sensation in her head, in every cell of her body, was one she'd never experienced before. It wasn't pain. It was something more profound, and far more terrible.

'The foot of the Virgin,' Joel said, pointing at a magnificent onyx statue of Mary near the altar.

'No.' Alex was staring at another statue, one tucked away inside an alcove in the wall. She could easily have missed it if the strange feeling hadn't guided her there. It was small and plain, simple alabaster, pitted with age. She took a step towards it, and a sudden surge of intense discomfort made her draw a breath and move quickly back. The weight of her backpack suddenly felt enormous, driving her into the floor.

'It's this one,' she gasped.

Joel was too intent on the statue to notice her reaction. 'How can you be so sure? Like you said, there must be thousands of statues of the Virgin Mary in this city.'

'Trust me, I'm sure.'

He frowned and peered at her. 'You don't look so good all of a sudden. What's wrong?'

'I feel a little queasy, that's all.'

'You want some water or something?' he asked tenderly, moving close to her and running his hand down her shoulder and arm.

'It'll pass,' she said, clutching her head as she gazed down at the ornate stone floor. 'What's more important is what's under there.'

'Under us? Sewers? Catacombs?'

'There are no tunnel systems under Venice. The city is built at sea level. No, the cross is under us, but we're going to have to dive for it.'

'You're not being serious, are you? How can you know this?'

'Joel,' she said earnestly. 'You came to me, remember? You said you wanted my help.' She had to make an effort to speak clearly. The terrible sensation inside her felt like it could rip her apart. In fact, she knew exactly what it was capable of doing to her, and it wasn't a pleasant thought.

Joel didn't argue. Outside, dark canal water slapping at the church foundations gave off a faint smell of human waste, and he remembered what she'd said about the city's lack of a sewerage system. He didn't want to think about what he might be swallowing if he took a swim in there.

Alex looked pale and weak. She didn't step near the water's edge, but shrugged off her backpack and laid it on the ground while she backed away to steady herself against a stone pillar.

'I'm staying up here,' she said. 'I'm not feeling so great.'

'We need to get you to a doctor or something,' he protested. 'You're obviously not well. We can come back here tomorrow.'

'Please, Joel. Let's get it done.' She took a torch from her backpack and tossed it over to him.

He sighed, stepped to the edge and looked down at the brackish water slurping against the algae-streaked brickwork three feet below him. He kicked off his shoes, filled his lungs, and jumped.

CHAPTER 62

The shock of the icy water was stunning. The pressure roared in his ears. He could see the church's craggy foundations through the swirling murk. He was too worried about getting poisoned or hypothermic to be angry that he was probably getting soaked for nothing.

All the stonework was crumbling. He'd once read that Venice was a sinking city, disappearing a few more inches into the sea every year. By the time he was an old man, many of its walkways and buildings would be under water forever. That was, if he ever got to become an old man . . .

The decaying foundations disappeared downwards out of sight in the gloom. Kicking with his legs, he shone the torch and ran his free hand along the slippery stone. He could see nothing that could give him access under the church. He'd been down for more than twenty seconds already. He was on the verge of giving up when, through the murk, he spotted a fissure in the stone. It was almost completely covered with algae. He kicked his legs and dived a little deeper to examine it.

Scraping away the slime, he found that it was big enough for a man to slip inside. Forty seconds under. He could still make it. He squeezed his body through the gap, shining the torch ahead of him. All he could see were the floating particles of dirt he'd dislodged as he forced his way in. He kicked out to press deeper into the fissure. It widened a little, and now he was a long way in. He kicked again.

But his foot wouldn't move. It was trapped. He was stuck here, deep inside the crack in the church's foundations. Horror lanced through him, and a stream of bubbles involuntarily burst from his mouth. He struggled to release himself, losing more precious air with the effort. He kicked with all his might, almost dropping the torch in the process – and suddenly he was free again.

But now he had only seconds before his lungs reached bursting point. He wasn't sure whether he had enough air to get back to the surface. Thrashing wildly about in panic, he lost his bearings. He didn't know which way was up and which was down any more. His fingers raked the slimy stone. His heart was pounding.

Then his head was bursting clear of the surface and a long gasp exploded from his lungs. But when he blinked the filthy water from his eyes and shone the torch beam around him, he saw that the surface he'd found wasn't the one he'd just dived into. He was inside an underwater cave, a craggy ceiling of wet stone just a few inches above his head. By his reckoning, he must be right beneath the church. At one time there might have been room in here for a man to clamber almost clear of the water, but with the progressive sinking of the city there was only enough space for his head and shoulders.

Something was sticking out of a crack in the cave wall. An old bit of sacking, rotted with age. Bracing his legs for support, he reached out and grasped it, and found that the decayed cloth was wrapped around something hard and cold that had been wedged into the crumbling foundations. He gave it a tug and a wiggle, and it came out with a shower of stones. With his heart in his mouth he tore the layers of sacking away.

He let out a whoop when the gleaming Celtic cross fell into his hand.

It was about fifteen inches long, with rune-like markings and strange designs sculpted into the outer ring that connected the crosspiece to the shaft. It was made of some type of stone that he'd never seen before – quartz-like, denser than granite, creamy white in colour with flecks of black and vivid green. He clutched it to his chest and closed his eyes. He'd found it.

He couldn't wait to show Alex. He stuck the precious relic in his belt, took a deep breath of the cave's stale air, and swam his way back out of the cave. Seconds later he broke the surface and clambered up onto dry land, too excited to feel the numbing cold.

'Alex! Look!'

No reply. She was nowhere to be seen. Glancing around, he saw that she'd unzipped her backpack while he'd been underwater. It lay empty on the pavement near the water's edge, and beside it was the mysterious object she'd been toting around with her. He crouched down to examine it. An oblong steel case, the kind photographers used to protect their fragile equipment. The latches were undone and the lid was open, showing the foam padding inside. As well as something unusual. The case was thickly lined with a dark material that he realised with bemusement was lead. That explained the weight of the thing. But why had she brought this with her?

'Alex?' he called again.

'I'm here,' she replied. She was twenty yards away, hanging warily back behind another pillar.

'What're you doing hiding behind there?' he asked, puzzled. His extremities were beginning to tremble with cold now. 'I found the cross, Alex. I found it!'

'Put it in the case,' she called over to him. Her voice sounded terribly weak, as if she was having to make an extreme effort to push the words out.

'What's wrong with you?'

'I'm not well, Joel. Put the cross in the case, okay? It's radioactive,' she added desperately in a rasping croak. 'I was going to tell you. It's not safe to handle.'

He frowned. 'Why the hell would it be radioactive?

It's only a bit of old stone.' He took a step towards her, waving the cross in the air. 'Look.'

'Don't come near me!' she screamed. The exertion caused her to collapse to her knees, clutching her sides with a moan. Under the glow of a streetlamp, he could see from the pallor of her face and the dark rings that had suddenly appeared around her eyes that there really was something terribly, shockingly wrong with her.

He was about to say something when the wind was knocked out of him by a heavy impact that came out of nowhere. It sent him tumbling to the ground, still clutching the cross. He twisted up to see a big guy in a black bomber jacket and beanie hat moving in to stamp on his ribs. Joel rolled out of the way of the kick, but suddenly another man came running out of the shadows and booted him in the stomach. Joel doubled up in pain. He lashed out with the cross, felt it connect with bone, and heard a yell of pain. He staggered to his feet, only to be sent crashing back down on the hard ground by a punch to the face.

CHAPTER 63

Joel's attackers circled him. Four of them, all dressed in similar black clothes and wearing the cold, impassive expressions of hired thugs. The one who'd kicked him held something in his hand. Even before the long tongue of steel flicked out, Joel knew it was a switchblade. And something told him this was no ordinary mugging.

'You're coming with us,' one of them said. 'Someone wants to talk to you.'

'Think again. I'm not going anywhere.'

'Fine. Then we'll do it the hard way,' the guy said. The circle closed in towards Joel. Four to one.

'Put it in the case!' Alex screamed from behind the column. Her voice broke up into a racking cough.

Joel ignored her. He swung the cross at his attackers. It was all he had to defend himself with, and he wasn't about to toss it away.

But the four guys weren't that easily put off. They all rushed him at once. He clubbed one of them, aiming for the side of the head, but the blow was deflected. One grabbed his wrist, another caught him with a hard punch to the jaw. Stars exploded in his eyes. He felt the cross fly from his hand. It turned a somersault in mid-air and landed in the steel case. The force of its landing caused the lid to slam shut.

By then Joel was down on the ground and curled up in a ball to protect himself from the kicks and punches raining down on him. He was too preoccupied with trying to escape being beaten to death to notice Alex get to her feet in the background. The pallor in her face had vanished abruptly and the sharpness in her eye was back as she came striding fast towards Joel's attackers. Two broke away from the fight when they saw her coming, leaving their friends to take care of Joel while they dealt with this crazy woman who seemed to think she could take them on. They had their orders, in any case. She wasn't supposed to leave here alive.

'Leave him alone,' she said as she walked up to them. 'One warning is all you get. Then you die.'

One of the men laughed. 'Listen to her. She's fucking nuts.' His friend reached inside his jacket and his hand came out with a .45 automatic.

The first man stopped laughing. 'Thought we were meant to use the 9-mils they gave us.'

'Fuck that,' said the guy with the gun. 'What for? You know me. I'm a big-bore kind of guy.' He aimed the pistol at Alex and squeezed the trigger . . . Twice, three times, four times. The heavy-calibre slugs took Alex in the chest and she went straight down on her back and lay still. The sound of the gunshots reverberated across the canal.

'There. Who needs poxy 9-mils anyway?' the guy said, putting away his smoking pistol.

Joel's cry of rage when he saw Alex go down was cut short by another kick to his stomach. In his fury he grabbed his attacker's leg and sent the guy tumbling backwards. He leapt to his feet in horror.

Just in time to see Alex get up again.

Faster than the eye could follow, her hand shot out and her fist closed on the wrist of the guy who'd shot her. One wrench, and his arm was broken. Compound fracture, the bone jutting out of the ripped flesh and tearing through his jacket sleeve. Another wrench, and she'd ripped his arm away completely at the shoulder, like a large joint of meat in her fist. His empty sleeve dangled at his side as his knees buckled and he collapsed in instant shock.

Alex swung the severed arm like a club at the one who'd laughed. The wet end caught him in the side of the head with a showering spatter of blood and battered him to the ground. She stepped over to him and drove her heel through his face, before turning back to his friend, who was gibbering and shaking violently in a pool of his own blood. Alex bent calmly over him, seized his head between her hands and twisted it until there was a splintering crack like a branch snapping.

Straightening up, she shunted the body into the canal with her foot. Where the four shots had punched through her coat, the edges of the bullet holes were still smoking.

Joel saw it all, but the remaining two thugs had their backs to Alex and were too intent on him to have noticed anything. She walked swiftly up behind them and, before they had time to react, she reached out her arms, jerked them off their feet and cracked their heads together with bone-shattering power. They hit the ground, dead.

And there was silence. Carnage littered the canal-side. The pools of blood quickly spread to the edge and began trickling into the water.

Joel stood, swaying on his feet, blood running down his face, gaping down at the two corpses lying in front of him with their skulls virtually fused together. In that instant he was transported back eighteen years. He was a child again, cowering behind the banisters of his grandfather's cottage, just a few feet from the bodies of his parents who had been murdered in just the same way.

Her strength. The speed. No human could move that way, kill with that kind of ease. Especially not after taking four bullets to the chest.

Alex finally broke the silence. 'We need to get away from here.' She stepped over the dead men and grasped Joel's arm. He jerked away from her, still winded from the punches and kicks he'd taken. But it wasn't the beating he'd taken that was making it hard to stay on his feet.

He knew now. He understood.

The way she'd dropped her cup that time at his mention of the cross. The way she'd seemed transfixed by his bleeding hand when he'd gashed himself on the broken table. This woman he'd trusted. This woman that he'd made love with.

'You're one . . . one of them. You're a vampire.'

'Listen to me, Joel. It's not what you think. Not exactly.'

He raised his hands to his face, pinched the flesh of his cheeks. *Wake up, Joel.* 'Tell me this isn't happening,' he muttered. 'Tell me it isn't true.'

'Joel—'

'Don't come near me!' He backed away from her. She took a step towards him, reaching out her hand towards him, and they circled one another on the bloody pavement.

'Please,' she said. 'There are things you need to understand.'

'Like how you manage to walk in daylight? Pass yourself off as a human?'

'Things aren't the way they used to be.'

'I don't care. You bite people and suck their blood.'

'I don't kill to do it. It's different now.'

'Vampires are the good guys now, is that it?'

'Not all. Just my side.'

'You're a curse.'

'I'm not your enemy, Joel. Gabriel Stone is. Yours, and mine. And he's the worst enemy you can imagine. If you'd let me explain what's happening—'

Joel felt his foot nudge something solid. He took his eyes off her just long enough to see that it was the lead-lined steel case. He made a lunge for it, grabbed it with both hands and wrenched it off the ground. He saw her pupils dilate as he clutched it to his chest.

'What does it do to you?'

'Joel—'

'Answer me or I'll open this lid and find out for myself.'

She sighed. 'Your grandfather was right. The cross has the power to destroy us.'

'Why this one? Why just this one cross?'

'I can't say. Nobody knows.'

'You lied to me. All that bullshit about your sister. You *used* me. Then what – once I'd helped you to find the cross, were you going to kill me, too? Was that the plan, Alex?'

'No, Joel.'

'There's something you don't know about me. I told you I believed in vampires – but I didn't tell you that I'd killed one once. It was a long time ago, but I can do it again. And believe me, if I could kill my own grandfather, I'm pretty sure I can kill you.'

'One hour,' she said. 'That's all the time I need to explain it all to you. Then you'll understand why we need you, why it's important that you work together with us.'

He frowned. 'Us? You mean vampires?'

'There's a whole world you don't know about, that no human knows about. I work for the Vampire Federation, and we're under attack from an uprising led by Gabriel Stone and his people.'

'Do you think I care about your politics? You're a *vampire*, Alex.'

'You will care, because it's bad news for humans if Stone succeeds. You and I need to get this case back to London, and we'll destroy Stone together.'

Joel shook his head violently. 'Go,' he yelled. 'Get out of here. This is your one chance to get away from me. If I see you again, Alex, you're just another vampire. God help me, I'll finish you along with the rest.'

'Give me the case, Joel. Don't mess about.'

'Come a step closer, I open the lid. I swear.'

'You'd do that to me?' she said softly. 'After what happened between us?'

'What happened between us was an obscenity,' he heard himself say.

Police sirens cut through the night air, still far off but growing steadily louder. Joel glanced across the canal and saw lights flashing in the mist. The bow wave of the approaching police launch was white against the dark water.

He turned back to Alex. She was gone.

He clutched the case tightly to his chest and began to run.

CHAPTER 64

If there were any vampires on the evening flight home from Venice, they had no idea what the quiet passenger in the damp, rumpled clothes sitting alone near the back of the plane was carrying in the small metal case that seemed to be his only luggage.

Gazing numbly out of the window at the dark sky, Joel could see his own pale, bruised, haunted-looking reflection staring back at him. He was oblivious of the other passengers and ignored the small girl who kept pointing at him and asking her mother what had happened to that man's face. He barely acknowledged the cheerful stewardess who came by offering food and drink. Didn't even feel the pain from the split in his lip or the purple swelling around his left cheekbone. Anyone watching him would have been unable to detect the smallest flicker of expression on his face as he sat there immobile, almost catatonic. But inside he was screaming in turmoil as he contemplated the task that faced him now. Peaks and troughs of conflicting emotion flooded over him like the temperature extremes of a violent fever – elated and thrilling to the drumbeat of war one instant, crippled by terror the next and wanting to run and run and keep running and never look back.

But he knew it was no longer his decision to make. He was the bearer of the cross, and there was only one road he could travel. Come what may, he was far beyond recall.

The shakes didn't begin for real until after landing, when he tried to insert the key of his rental Ford Mondeo into the ignition and found his hand trembling so badly it took him three attempts to start the engine. He leaned back against the head restraint. Closed his eyes and took three deep breaths.

All right, Solomon. Here we go. This is it.

The night was starless and oppressive as he drove. He stopped at a motorway services to buy a plastic torch and a bar of chocolate that he didn't have the stomach to eat. All through his journey, he tried to force his mind to stay blank. And failed.

Then, on the stroke of eleven p.m., his head-lights swept across the tall iron gates of Crowmoor Hall. He put the car in neutral, letting it idle as he reached over to his left and rested his trembling hand on the metal box on the passenger seat next to him. He flipped the catches and opened the lid. The cross gleamed dully under the soft glow of the instrument lights. He lifted it carefully out from the foam padding and held it tight in both fists.

This is the end for you bastards, he thought. And

it wouldn't stop here. He was going to dedicate himself, the way his grandfather had: as long as it took, to take down as many of these monsters as he could. The politician, Jeremy Lonsdale – was he also one of them? Then his time was coming, too.

And then there was Alex.

He sat staring at the cross, visualising her face. Dangerous thoughts drifted through his mind. He shook them away. He needed to be strong, and stay strong.

The wind was rising, coming in gusts that shook the car and plastered falling leaves onto the windscreen. Crowmoor Hall's gates lay open in the darkness. He swallowed hard. Throwing open the car door, he stepped out into the chilly night with the cross in his right hand and his new torch in his left. He muttered the first prayer he'd said in many years, and set out up the crunching gravel drive. Every step that he took towards that place sapped his courage a little more and made him grip the cross more tightly.

As he approached, he could see that the house was completely in darkness. The front door was swinging in the wind and flurries of dead leaves were blowing across the mosaic floor of the entrance hall. Joel walked into the house and shone the trembling torch beam around him.

'Stone!' he yelled, but it came out as a dry croak. He wet his lips and called out again, and his voice echoed.

He stood and listened a long time to the sounds of the house. A branch was tapping against a window somewhere. The wind whistled around his feet, leaves scraped across the floor. Sounds of emptiness.

Across the hall was a door. It was the same one through which Seymour Finch had led him and Dec to show them the 'ballroom' that had turned out to be a conference room. Joel turned the handle and the door creaked open. He shone the torch inside. The room was just as he remembered it, except for the bare space on the wall where the portrait of Gabriel Stone had hung previously. At the far end of the room, the tapestry still covered what Dec had claimed was the hidden doorway leading down to the crypt.

Joel walked the length of the room and tentatively switched on a side lamp. With some reluctance he laid down the cross and the torch, then grabbed one corner of the tapestry with both hands and gave it a violent tug. Something ripped. Wooden rings clattered to the floor, and the tapestry crumpled from its mountings and fell in a dusty heap at his feet. He kicked it aside.

Just as he'd done the last time, he examined the wall. Up close in the light of the lamp, he thought he could make out a hairline crack extending all the way from the floor to above his head. He used the Mondeo's ignition key to pick a hole in the rich, velvety fleur-de-lys wallpaper. After a few minutes of frantic scraping, he'd uncovered the clear outline of a doorway in the plasterwork behind.

He shoved, hard, and then shoved again. Nothing moved. Nearby stood an elegant antique table on brass castors. He yanked it towards him, put his weight behind it and rammed against the wall with all his strength. The crashing thud seemed to echo all through the house. He froze, listening intently, but heard only the soft moan of the wind.

Dec had been right. About this and about everything else. There was something behind this wall and Joel was damned if he wasn't going to find out what. This could be where the vampires were hiding, for all he knew cowering in fear, sensing the presence of the cross nearby, weak and vulnerable. This could be his moment to strike.

But it was going to take more than a flimsy table to ram through the solid wall. It had barely left a mark. Joel snatched up the cross and ran back the way he'd come, out into the windy night. There had to be a tool shed somewhere in a place like this. Maybe there'd be a sledge or lump hammer, a wrecking bar. He'd dig his way through with a damn screwdriver if he had to.

His heart was fluttering wildly as he ran through the grounds. Every rustling bush signalled a sudden attack; every creaking branch was a clawed hand reaching out to grip hold of him; and in every shadow lurked a waiting vampire.

At the rear of the house he found a range of

outbuildings. A well equipped tool shed contained everything he could have wished for – but next to that was something even better. Yellow paintwork glittered in his torch beam. He peered inside the cab of the JCB and saw with a rush of triumph that the key was in the ignition. The first and last time he'd driven one of these things had been years ago, helping Sam Carter prepare the groundwork for the extension on his house. But a mechanical digger had all kinds of other uses too.

Joel leapt into the operator's seat, fired up the engine and the headlights. With the cross clamped between his thighs, he drove the machine out across the yard. Its caterpillar tracks ground and crunched on the gravel as he rounded the corner of the house. He took a long sweeping turn at the front entrance, so he could approach head on. Ten yards from the doorway, he gunned the throttle and the diesel roared as the machine scuttled up the steps and smashed into the ornate stonework. Bricks and plaster and chunks of rendering rained on the roof of the cab. With a terrible scraping screech of rending metal, Joel forced the JCB into the entrance hall. He didn't slow down for the conference room door either. The machine lumbered through like a tank, wrecking everything in its path. The engine was on peak revs by the time it reached the far wall. Joel held it steady on a collision course with the hidden doorway. A second before impact, he leapt out of the cab, hit the rug and rolled clear.

The digger rammed into the wall with a crash that shook the house and brought a large section of decorative coving and ceiling down on top of it. Joel sprang to his feet and ran over to the half-buried machine. He shone the torch through the clouds of masonry dust and saw the battered front of the digger embedded in a great jagged hole. Attached to the remnants of the hidden doorway was a smashed hydraulic arm and an electronic control unit that must have been activated by a remote or a switch somewhere in the house. Beyond it, Joel's torch beam swept into pure darkness.

It was a secret corridor.

His terror as powerfully intensified as his resolve, Joel clambered over the dusty caterpillar tracks and started making his way through the passage, holding the cross out in front of him as he went.

He found himself in a maze of corridors and stairways that seemed to go on for miles. Just when he thought he was lost, the torch picked out something on the floor. A drop of dried blood. Then another. He followed the trail down and down.

All the way down to the crypt.

CHAPTER 65

'Where are you?' said Rumble's voice on the phone.

'Still in Italy,' Alex said. 'I'm on a train heading for Bologna. Flying back to London from there.'

Her carriage was empty apart from her, a couple of backpackers and a businessman who'd fallen asleep behind his laptop. Quarter to one in the morning, and the train was speeding through the night, chattering softly on its rails. In the distance were the scattered lights of a village.

'*Bologna?*'

'It's a long story, Harry.' Since she'd boarded the train in Venice earlier that night, afraid to return to the hotel or fly straight back to London in case she bumped into Joel or found herself on the same plane as him, Alex had been putting a lot of thought into how she was going to explain herself to Rumble. It was hard to think straight with her head full of what had happened between her and Joel. She cursed herself for her weakness.

'Save it for when I see you,' Rumble said. 'Is Solomon with you? Can you talk?'

She bit her lip. 'I'm alone right now.'

'You wouldn't be coming back unless you'd found the cross,' Rumble said. 'Am I right?' He sounded excited. That wasn't going to last long, Alex thought.

'Yeah, we found it. It was hidden under an old church. It had been there for centuries.'

'The legends – they're true?'

'You wouldn't want to get too close, if that's what you mean.'

'But the case – the lead lining – it worked? The way you thought it would?'

'It worked fine.'

'This is great. Congratulations, Alex. When you land, I want you to bring it straight here to VIA. Then we'll figure out the next step.'

Alex gritted her teeth. She'd given him the good news. Now for the bit she was dreading.

'I'm afraid it's not that simple, Harry. The truth is, I don't have it any longer.'

Rumble paused a beat, his excitement fading fast. 'What the hell do you mean, you don't have it?'

'We were attacked.'

'Stone's people?'

'Maybe, maybe not. All I know is that they were humans. Nothing I could do, Harry. They took it.'

Rumble was silent for a beat as the news sank in. 'You let a bunch of humans take the cross from you? How can that be?'

'You had to be there, Harry. It just happened

that way.' Alex knew she was landing herself in a whole storm of trouble saying it, but it was a better option than telling Rumble the truth. If VIA got wind of the fact that Joel Solomon had the cross and meant to use it – not just against the Federation's enemies but indiscriminately, against any vampire he could find – his death sentence was as good as written. And she knew all too well that she'd be the field agent chosen to hunt him down and kill him.

She'd bought some time with the lie. Now she had to find a way to find Joel and take the cross back from him. How to do that without either hurting him, or getting herself destroyed in the process, was something she'd have to figure out as she went along. All she knew was that the clock was ticking for her. If he started zapping vampires all over the place and the news got back to the Feds, she had a date with the termination chamber.

'This is serious, Agent Bishop,' Rumble said.

It was a bad sign when he called her that. 'Tell me about it,' she replied.

'Here's what we're going to do. You're not flying back to London tonight. I want you to get your arse over to Brussels for the FRC conference tomorrow afternoon, two thirty sharp.' He paused. 'And . . . Agent Bishop?'

She knew what was coming from the change in his tone.

'You'd better start thinking about how you're

going to explain to the Ruling Council how, with all the other shit that's hitting the fan, you allowed a weapon that's been safely hidden away for centuries to fall into the hands of the enemy.'

CHAPTER 66

Crowmoor Hall
Midnight

Joel walked on through the dark passage, down and down, deep underneath the mansion. With every step he tensed a little more and the struggle against his instinct to run away became more difficult.

Nobody attacked him. No vampire was lying in wait for him in the many shadows that he desperately swung the torch into, left, right, and left again. The light beam flashed against bare grey stone and thick matted cobwebs.

But something *was* here. As he walked on in dread, he was aware of a worsening smell. It quickly grew to an overpowering rancid stench that made it hard to breathe and his stomach flip. Then, shining the torch beam upwards, he let out an involuntary cry.

The corpse of what had once been a young woman dangled like a side of meat from a butcher's hook in the vaulted ceiling. The white silk bridal dress she'd been wearing when she died hung from her in tatters and was caked in dried blood. Her neck had been slashed open to the bone and her chest was ripped apart to expose shattered ribs and internal organs. She'd died with a look of the worst terror Joel had ever seen on a victim's face.

She hadn't been hanging here long enough to smell like this. There was something else down here, too, and it couldn't be far away. He swallowed back the rising nausea and played the light around him. A few feet away was a raised stone block circle in the floor, a yard or so in diameter, that looked like a well. Its mouth was covered with a thick round slab. As Joel shone the beam on it, he noticed finger marks in the dust around its edge. Someone had moved it recently.

Laying down the cross for a moment and gripping the torch under his arm, he grabbed hold of the edge of the slab and tried to move it. It was incredibly heavy. Joel thought of Finch and the uncanny strength that the man had seemed to possess.

On the third attempt, the slab shifted a couple of inches with a grinding of stone on stone. Joel recoiled and almost fell back at the stench that burst out from the dark hole. He used his sleeve to cover his nose and mouth, and kicked wildly at the slab's edge until he'd moved it far enough to shine the torch down there.

The hole might have been ten feet deep, or it might have been fifty. There was no way to tell how far down the pile of human remains went. In the snatched glimpse Joel caught before he staggered away to empty his guts out all over the floor, he saw dozens of grey, mottled dead faces peering up at him. Homeless people, runaways, illegal immigrants, people lost in the system or whom nobody would report missing. Whoever they'd been, it would be a hard and terrible job identifying them. Among the dead, severed body parts lay scattered, flesh gnawed from bone.

As Joel stood there bent double, dry-retching and coughing now that his stomach was emptied, he already knew what was going to be the sight most indelibly seared into his memory, destined to haunt his dreams for the rest of his life. It was the shattered and limbless baby skeleton lying on the top of the grisly pile. The bones had been picked clean.

Tears of rage stung his eyes as he kicked the slab back into place over the hole. He grabbed the cross and moved on.

At the end of a long, winding tunnel leading off the crypt he found a room that he immediately knew was Gabriel Stone's private study. Clearly a vampire of taste and style, Joel thought as he looked around him at the sumptuous furnishings. But a vampire nonetheless, and this wouldn't be over until he was sent back to hell where he belonged.

Still seething with anger and disgust and holding the cross of Ardaich out in front of him like a beacon as he stormed room after room, Joel systematically flushed out the rest of the mansion. His fear had completely dispersed. All he wanted was to find these bastards and watch them die. But with every new door he kicked in, half-expecting to see his torch beam land on a huddled cluster of terrified vampires inside, his hope diminished. It took a long time before he could admit it to himself, but in the end he had to face the truth. The unlocked gate, the open front door, the missing portrait, the empty rooms: it all added up to the conclusion that Crowmoor Hall's occupants had abandoned the place.

How had they known? Could they have sensed the cross coming? Or had one of their contacts somehow tipped them off? Whatever the answer, they were gone. All that remained of them was the gruesome evidence left behind in the crypt.

Back down in Stone's study, Joel ripped through the enormous antique desk for any possible clue as to where the vampires might have fled. There was nothing. Unless they returned, he'd lost them – and he had a strong feeling that they weren't coming back, at least not for a long time.

It was raining as he trudged back up the gravel driveway with a heavy heart and the cross dangling limp at his side. So much effort had gone into finding the vampires' nest, and now they'd simply upped and moved on somewhere else. Dec Maddon's discovery had ultimately come to nothing.

Joel stopped. *Dec Maddon.* The kid had been right about everything so far: the spider tattoo on the dead girl's neck; the sculpted birds on the gateposts; the hidden door to the crypt. Without him, he'd never have come this far. Was there anything else the teenager might have seen or overheard? Even just a tiny clue that could help track Stone and his entourage to their new lair? That thought drove Joel into a run. He leapt into the Mondeo, laid the cross back in its case and skidded away from Crowmoor Hall forever.

As he drove, he dialled Dec's mobile but got no reply. He looked at his watch, only now realising how late it was. But he couldn't waste precious hours waiting until morning to make a polite visit to the Maddon home.

On his way to Wallingford he stopped at a village and made an anonymous call to Thames Valley Police to alert them to the stash of dead bodies and human remains at the former residence of Gabriel Stone. Let Carter and the boys sort that out, he thought as he walked back to the car in the rain. He had more pressing business to take care of.

CHAPTER 67

The Ridings, near Guildford, Surrey
Two hours earlier

Jeremy Lonsdale had been nursing a crystal tumbler brimming with malt whisky in the top-floor study of his country home and fretting over his predicament when he'd heard the two Great Danes start up a chorus of frenzied barking and baying down below. He cursed loudly, smacked his tumbler down on the table and threw open the window.

'Castor! Pollux! Shut your fucking holes!' he roared out into the cold night air. The dogs fell silent, as if shocked by their master's uncharacteristic outburst. Lonsdale slammed the window shut and went back to his brooding contemplation.

A minute later, as he was refilling his glass from the near-empty bottle of Highland Park, the dogs started again. Lonsdale ripped through the door of the study and went thundering down the stairs, ready to kick the hell out of the two animals for interrupting his thoughts. It was a large house, and he was puffing and red by the time he neared the bottom of the last flight of steps.

Then he halted mid-stride and almost stopped breathing when he saw the five people standing in his hallway.

No, not *people*. It was Gabriel Stone and his entourage. Behind Stone stood the hulking black giant and Anton, the sardonic-looking weaselly one. To his left was the blonde called Anastasia. And to his right, the raven-haired beauty Lillith. Lonsdale hadn't seen the four since the night of the initiation ceremony. He felt the colour drain from his face all the way down to his shoes. The tumbler slipped out of his fingers, bounced on the stair carpet and shattered on the hallway tiles with an amber spatter of whisky.

'Surprised to see us, Jeremy?'

Lonsdale opened and closed his mouth soundlessly as he searched for something to say.

'Are you not going to invite us into your fine home?' Stone asked.

'O-of course,' Lonsdale stammered. 'Please, forgive my rudeness.' He ushered them into a drawing room.

'Hello, Jeremy,' Lillith said with a seductive smile, gently raking his arm with a fingernail as she walked by.

Lonsdale cleared his throat and tried to smile. The congenial host. 'Would you, um, like a drink?'

'That depends on what you're offering,' Anastasia said, eyeing his throat.

Stone gestured at an armchair as if he were in his own place. 'Please, take a seat, Jeremy. As you may have gathered, this is not a mere social call. We're here to discuss business.'

Lonsdale sat nervously, glancing from one vampire to another. They stood around him in a semicircle. Big Zachary folded his muscular arms across his chest. Anton wore a deep frown. Anastasia had one eyebrow raised in amusement and Lillith toyed distractedly with the hilt of her sabre. Stone stood in the middle, his eyes narrowed. Lonsdale couldn't read his expression, and that worried him more than anything.

'What business would that be, Gabriel?' he asked, trying to sound nonchalant.

'Don't play the innocent with me, Jeremy. You know what this is about.'

Lonsdale swallowed. 'Venice?' It came out as a squeak.

'Venice. Precisely. Did you not receive my package, containing the equipment and full instructions?'

Lonsdale tried to swallow again, but his throat was dry. He wished he had another drink. 'Yes,' he managed.

'And you instructed the men you hired to follow those instructions to the absolute letter?'

'Use the special bullets to kill the woman, take the man alive, bring back the item and hand it over to me. Exactly as you said. I was very clear.'

'Then where's my cross?'

Lonsdale frowned. 'I can only assume it hasn't been found yet. I'd have heard something—'

'Lamentably underinformed, Jeremy. As usual, several steps behind the rest of us. Must I do everything myself?'

'What are you talking about?'

'You have your little contacts, I have mine. And imagine my surprise to hear about a recent minor incident in Venice. It involves four highly incompetent and thoroughly dead thugs, a great deal of spilled blood, and one missing cross that is now in the hands of a human whom I hadn't ideally wished to possess it.' Stone sighed, shook his head in disgust. 'Your continuing failure makes me angry, Jeremy.'

Lonsdale flushed. 'Hold on. I saw to it that the special ammunition – Norbenol or whatever you call it – was passed on to the men. What more was I supposed to do, load the guns for them myself?'

'Nosferol,' Stone replied in a silky voice. 'And I strongly advise you not to lose your temper with us.'

But Lonsdale was on a roll. 'How could I have known they wouldn't use the stuff? I couldn't exactly tell them what it was for, could I? "Oh, by the way, you're going to Venice to shoot a bloody vampire." These men are common thugs, not Abraham Van fucking Helsing.'

'*Were* common thugs, Jeremy. And you, my friend,' Stone added, pointing, 'are an imbecile.'

Lonsdale shut up. There was silence in the room as Stone paced up and down the floor.

'I've been lenient with you so far, Jeremy. This time, I'm afraid I must punish you.'

Lonsdale's jaw dropped. 'No. Not Toby. Please. I'll do anything.'

Lillith chuckled. Zachary and Anton exchanged grins. Anastasia was staring at the politician with undisguised contempt. 'Let me have him, Gabriel. I'll make him sorry, believe me.'

'No. I have other plans for him,' Stone told her. Turning back to Lonsdale, he said, 'With Solomon in possession of the cross thanks to your cretinous mistake, we are forced to abandon the country temporarily until our agents are able to catch him. And, just as you helped us get in, you're now going to get us out. I want to be in the air within the hour.'

'But—'

'A freight vehicle will be arriving at the airfield containing all our personal effects. You will ensure these are stowed safely on board.'

'That isn't possible,' Lonsdale protested. 'I can't get the crew together that fast. You can't just take off in a jet whenever you feel like it.'

'You *will* make it possible, Jeremy. Or must I involve young Toby in this?'

Lonsdale cracked. He slipped off the chair, collapsed to his knees and started crying and wringing his hands forlornly.

Lillith looked at her brother. 'So this is his

punishment, Gabriel? Making him lend us his flying machine? Have you gone soft?'

'They call them aeroplanes,' Zachary reminded her, and she growled at him.

'I haven't finished,' Stone said, not taking his eyes off the cowering, weeping politician. 'Lillith, your sword, please.'

Lillith drew out the long, glittering blade and handed the weapon over to him. Stone held out his left palm. With a deft motion he slashed the sharp edge across his hand, cutting deep into the flesh without a flicker of expression. A trickle of dark blood oozed out of the gash, flowed down his wrist. He tossed the sword back to Lillith, then nodded to Zachary. The big vampire stepped forward, grabbed Lonsdale off the floor and stopped him from struggling as Stone raised his bleeding hand to the politician's mouth and forced him to drink. Blood dripped down his chin and spattered across his shirt. He swallowed, gasped for air, swallowed some more.

'Good. Zachary, release him.'

Lonsdale fell back down to his knees, choking and spluttering gobs of blood onto the carpet. 'Oh, God. What have you *done* to me?' he wheezed, clutching his throat.

Stone dabbed at his wound with a silk handkerchief. 'Congratulations, Jeremy. You've just taken your first step into a whole new world. I hereby nominate you as my replacement servant, bonded to me henceforth. From now on, until the day of your death or such time as I release you from my service, whichever comes first, you will act as our personal assistant. Living with us, travelling with us, organising our external affairs and acting as our human liaison officer.'

'That's a fancy name for a ghoul,' Anastasia explained helpfully.

Lonsdale choked out an unintelligible reply.

'Needless to say,' Stone added, 'we'll have open access to all your bank accounts, all your resources and your homes here in Surrey, in London and in Tuscany. I think that's reasonable.'

'But . . . the twenty million you t— I gave you,' Lonsdale gibbered.

'It's a grand vision we are working to realise,' Stone replied. 'An expensive business. I'm afraid we need all the support we can get. You're not objecting, are you, Jeremy?'

'No way this one could ever take Seymour Finch's place,' Anton spat. 'I mean, just look at him. How can this pathetic piece of shit ever make the grade? He's let us down already.'

'True,' Stone said, smiling down at Lonsdale. 'But he's a politician, and that fascinates me. Never before have I come across a human so delightfully corrupt, so utterly devoid of moral fibre. He has but one scruple, his love of his bastard offspring – but that will pass soon enough.

I believe that, in time, he will make a very fine ghoul indeed.'

Lonsdale was wild with shock, his hair sticking out at all angles and his face shiny with tears and blood.

'M-my career,' he stammered in a high-pitched squeal. 'I could have made Prime Minister. I could have been European President one day.' He clasped his hands together. 'Just think how useful I could be to you, with so much power.'

They all laughed.

'You just retired, motherfucker,' Zachary said.

'You'll adore living with us, *dear* Jeremy,' Anastasia purred.

'He seemed to enjoy his stay at the castle last time,' Anton muttered, shooting a sly look at Lillith. Zachary stifled a giggle.

'You get to eat our leftovers,' Lillith said. 'After a while, you'll come to love them as much as Seymour did.'

'And maybe he can get Toby to come and stay with us, too,' Anastasia added, warming to the idea. 'I so much like the younglings.' She licked her lips. 'Tender and sweet. Hmmmm.'

Stone grabbed Lonsdale by the hair and hauled him to his feet. 'Enough of your self-pitying bawling, ghoul. Call your air crew.'

Lillith wrapped her arms around her brother and kissed him tenderly on the mouth. 'And so, we move on to Stage Two,' she whispered.

He nodded, smiling. 'We'll drop you and Zachary off en route as planned.'

'This is the part I've been looking forward to the most,' she said.

CHAPTER 68

Joel skidded the Ford to a halt outside the Maddon house, went running up the drive and hammered on the front door. The street was in near silence, just the light patter of the rain on the slick pavements. After a few moments he saw an upstairs light come on behind blue curtains. Seconds later, the downstairs hall lit up and a shape appeared behind the frosted glass of the door.

'Who is it?' said a rasping voice.

'Police,' Joel replied. 'Open the door, please.'

The door opened slowly. Behind it stood a man who looked like a heavier, hairier and balder version of Dec. He was wrapped in a tartan dressing gown and didn't look too happy to be disturbed.

'Mr Maddon?'

Dec's father ran his eye up and down Joel. 'You don't look much like a policeman to me, so you don't,' he said gruffly. 'Let's see some ID then.'

'Mr Maddon, I came to see Dec.'

'Right. Where's the ID?'

'My name's Joel Solomon.'

'I don't care what you call yourself. Show me your warrant card or get the fuck off me doorstep. It's almost one in the friggin' morning. People are trying to get some sleep here. We work for a living.'

A middle-aged woman Joel took to be Mrs Maddon appeared in the hallway with her arms folded. She was about two feet shorter than her husband but looked twice as hard.

'Who is it, Liam?'

'Some joker says he's a cop,' Liam Maddon said, still staring at Joel. Mrs Maddon's brow creased.

'Is this about our Dec? Has something happened?'

'Isn't he here?' Joel asked her.

'We're telling you nothing, mister, until we see some proper identification. This bastard could be anybody, Beth.' He turned back to Joel. 'Understand? Now fuck off.' And he slammed the door in Joel's face.

Joel stood on the doorstep for a moment, then sighed and started heading back to the car, wondering what to do next.

As he was about to get into the Mondeo and drive off, he heard footsteps behind him and a voice said, '*Psst!* Officer?'

Joel looked round to see another version of Dec Maddon sneaking down the drive towards him. He looked about five, maybe six years older than his brother, dark and unshaven and was built like he did a lot of weights.

'I'm Cormac,' he whispered.

'Joel.'

'I know who you are. Dec's talked about you. I'm sorry me da sent you away. He can be a right wanker sometimes, so he can.'

'Where is Dec? I need to talk to him.'

'That's what I came out here to tell you. Dec's gone funny.'

Joel glanced up at the house. The upstairs light had gone off again and the house had fallen into darkness, but someone could still be watching from the window.

'Let's talk in the car.' He slung the metal case into the back seat as Cormac climbed into the passenger side.

'Cameras, is it?' Cormac asked, pointing at the case.

'Yeah,' Joel said, shutting his door. 'Now, I think you'd better explain. How has Dec gone funny?'

'Ever since the wee girl next door died.'

Joel stared at him. 'Kate Hawthorne? Dead? When?'

Cormac shrugged. 'Couple of days ago. Terrible, isn't it? She just faded away, like. Family's in a right state. I never liked them much. Bunch o' snobs, especially that Gillian. But you have to feel sorry for them.'

'Where's Dec now?'

'Gone to stay at a mate's. Won't come back to the house. He's just acting weird, like.'

'Have you seen him?'

'Just talked on the phone a couple of times. He sounded ill. I went round there but he wouldn't let me in.' Cormac frowned. 'He may be a wee shit, but he's me brother. I'm worried about him.'

'Tell me where this mate's place is.'

'I'll show you the way as we drive.'

Joel glanced at the case on the seat behind them. 'I think it's best if you stay here, Cormac.'

CHAPTER 69

Cormac had been reluctant to stay behind, but his directions were good and it didn't take Joel long to find the block of concrete flats in Brewer's Lane on the other side of Wallingford. Joel left the car in the shadows a few yards down the lane and walked the rest of the way, clutching the metal case tightly under one arm and wondering what he was going to find at this Matt's place. Metal steps wound up and round onto each terraced balcony. He climbed two flights, checking door numbers until he came to the one he was looking for.

The pale blue door to Flat 22 was open an inch. Joel listened to his instincts and didn't knock. He pressed his hand against the worn wood, praying the hinges weren't creaky, and slipped silently inside. He found himself in a narrow passage that was dimly lit by a lamp shining through from the open door at the far end. Through the gap he could see garish floral carpet, the corner of a peeling James Bond poster tacked to the wall, and the end of an old couch that had someone's hand resting on it.

Someone was talking inside the room. Joel tensed, listening hard. The voice was little more than a whisper, but he recognised it as Dec's. Who was he talking to?

The answer came a second later when Joel heard a low giggle.

A girl's voice.

Joel's blood turned ice cold. Scarcely breathing and terrified to make a sound, he slowly unclipped one of the catches of the metal case. Then the other. And opened the lid just a fraction.

That was enough to tell him all he needed to know. The quiet room exploded into uproar. A piercing, wailing shriek of agony and terror. Dec's voice yelled, 'What's wrong, Kate? What's wrong?'

Joel slammed the lid shut, sealing the cross back inside its lead lining. He burst into the room to see Kate Hawthorne scrabbling desperately across the carpet, frantic to escape. She made a dive for the window, but he quickly stepped across and blocked her exit. Her eyes were fixed on the case. She backed away like a cornered leopard – frightened but dangerous. She rolled back her red lips and Joel quaked at the sight of the long curved fangs. There was a smear of blood on her chin, and her fingertips were red with it. Her hair was tousled, feral. She was naked underneath the translucent white dress she was wearing.

'You!' she hissed at him. 'Policeman.'

Dec stood frozen next to the couch, watching the scene in horror. His eyes were sunken, his cheeks hollow and colourless. The wounds on his neck looked as if they'd crusted over and been reopened several times. Fresh trickles of blood were running down to his shoulder, soaking into the material of the grimy T-shirt that clung to his emaciated torso. He staggered towards Joel.

'What are you doing to her? Leave her alone!'

Joel shoved him lightly in the chest, and he fell back on the couch. 'This isn't Kate, Dec. Kate's gone.'

'He's lying,' Kate spat. 'Don't listen to him.'

'How long has this thing been feeding on you?' Joel demanded, pointing at her. At that moment, she tried to make another break for it, and he opened the box a crack. A huge ripple of pain seemed to shudder through her body and she collapsed to the floor, thrashing and writhing. Joel smelled burning, saw the smoke rising from her bare flesh. He shut the lid.

'That's just a small dose of what's in here,' he told her. 'You know what it is, don't you? You know what it can do to you.'

'Stop it!' Dec shouted at him from the couch. 'What are you doing? You're hurting her.'

'She's a vampire, Dec. Forget about her.'

The kid turned to gaze at Kate with tears of longing in his eyes. 'We love each other. We're going to be together forever.'

'She's been living here with you, hasn't she?'

Dec nodded. He pointed at a cupboard. 'She sleeps there during the day. I take care of her.

That's how it's going to be. Nothing you can do about it, get it?'

'This has to end,' Joel said. 'If she keeps feeding on you like this, you know what you'll become. One of them.'

Tears flooded down Dec's cheeks. 'I don't fucking care any more. I love her, man.'

Coiled in the corner, Kate was slowly recovering from the blast of the cross's energy. She raised herself up weakly on her elbows. 'He loves me, you fuck. Leave us alone.'

Joel shook his head. 'I'm sorry for what's about to happen,' he murmured. Shaking with anticipation, he moved his hand to open the box and take out the cross. Now he would see exactly what happened when a vampire was exposed to the full force of its power. Kate saw what he was doing and screamed.

But then a thought came to him and he stopped. 'How did she know where to find you, Dec? Did you tell her where you were?'

Dec just looked at him. Joel grabbed him by the collar of his bloody T-shirt and hauled him off the couch and shook him violently. It was shocking to feel how little the kid weighed.

'How did she find you?' he repeated.

'She just did,' Dec muttered. 'I don't know how. I was here, and she turned up. Don't hurt her, Joel. For fuck's sake, don't hurt her.'

Joel let Dec slump down again, thinking hard. The idea that was forming in his mind seemed crazy – but in a reality that had already been turned upside-down, even a crazy idea made perfect sense.

He was thinking about the potentially infinite relationship of vampire to victim. One created another, then on it went down the line, one new vampire after another being endlessly hatched out of the wreckage of its human host. Stone had created the Kate Hawthorne who lay before him now. She was his progeny, eternally bonded to him; and, left to her own devices, the fledgling vampire girl had been about to turn Dec into the next link in the chain. The same connection must exist between every single vampire and each of their victims.

Stone had turned Kate at Crowmoor Hall – that much was clear – and yet he'd been able to find her home in Wallingford. Just as Kate had, in turn, managed to find Dec here.

What was guiding them? Some kind of extra-sensory homing ability? Clairvoyance? The same nebulous psychic connection that seemed to enable human twins to sense one another's emotions, even their whereabouts, over distances that defied rational explanation?

Joel took a step towards her. 'Where's Gabriel Stone?' he demanded.

Kate glowered up at him. 'Fuck you.'

'Not the answer I was looking for,' Joel said. He took another step. 'You want me to open this case?'

Kate flinched violently, slumped back down to the floor and let out a tortured moan.

'Where is he, Kate? Tell me.'

'He's gone,' she blurted out. 'Far away from here.'

Against the wall to Joel's right was a home assembly bookcase bulging with well-thumbed issues of car books, motoring magazines, repair manuals, a few tatty sci-fi and thriller paperbacks. Stuffed in between a Subaru maintenance manual and *Classic Supercars* was a big hardback world atlas. It looked immaculate and out of place in Matt's book collection, like an unwanted gift that was only on the shelf out of obligation. Still clutching the case, Joel grabbed the atlas on an impulse and cracked it open, flipped a few pages and laid it flat on the floor showing a double-page spread of the world map. He thrust the book across the carpet under Kate's nose. 'You show me where he went. And I promise I'll free you.'

'Show him, Kate,' Dec groaned faintly from the couch.

'Never!' she spat out.

'You think he cares for you?' Joel shouted at her. 'He's gone. He was just playing with you. You've nothing to be loyal to.'

Kate went quiet, defeated. She looked warily at Joel. Her fangs had receded and, apart from her wild hair and the blood on her chin and hands, she seemed just like any other normal girl again. Joel thought of Alex, and his throat tightened so badly he wanted to scream.

'Can you do it?' he asked her.

'You'll set me free?'

'I promised.'

Slowly, reluctantly, Kate sat up and closed her eyes. Her chin sank towards her chest. She began to sway gently backwards and forwards, as if falling into some kind of trance.

Dead silence in the room. Joel could hear the beating of his own heart.

Kate reached a hand out across the open map. Extended her bloodstained index finger. It hovered uncertainly over the pages, wavered back and forth, and for a moment Joel was certain his idea really had been crazy. But then something in the girl's expression seemed to focus, and her finger landed right on the small shape that was England, leaving a red print on the paper.

'He travels,' she murmured. Joel could see rapid darting movement behind the pale skin of her closed eyelids. Then, slowly, like the upturned glass moving of its own accord across an Ouija board in a séance, her finger began to move across the map. It traced a jagged red line of blood from west to east. Joel watched in morbid fascination as the line skimmed the southern tip of the Netherlands, moved across into Germany, then the Czech Republic and on into Hungary. It moved a little more, then came to a trembling halt. Kate's hand went limp and she slumped back down to the carpet, mumbling something indistinct.

Joel snatched the atlas from her and stared at the spot where the line of drying blood ended.

She'd traced a path southeast across most of Europe, all the way to the northern reaches of Romania. The line broke off somewhere in the middle of the Carpathian Mountains.

'You said something just then. A word. What was it? Kate?' Forgetting himself, he was about to reach across to shake the girl's shoulder – then drew his hand away quickly and laid it on the lid of the case so he could yank it open if she went for him. He was too close to this vampire to get complacent.

Her eyes fluttered open and she mumbled it again, more clearly this time.

'*Vâlcanul.*'

The accent she used to pronounce the word sent a tingle down Joel's back. That wasn't something she'd learned in school. It seemed to come from some other place, as if the word was being channelled through her. He knew he'd been right. Backing away from her, he shut the atlas and tossed it on a chair.

'You promised you'd free her,' Dec croaked from the couch.

'And I meant what I said,' Joel replied.

He stared down at the girl on the floor, and she gazed up at him with pleading in her eyes. He was suddenly looking at a normal seventeen-year-old, a pretty girl with red hair and intelligent blue eyes and her whole life ahead of her.

Except he wasn't.

He opened the lid of the case. Her wild cry filled

the room as he reached inside and his fist closed on the cold cross. He drew it out with a shaking hand.

'*Nooo!*' Dec screamed, twisting up off the couch and making a desperate lunge at Joel. Joel side-stepped him, and the kid crashed to the floor with a wail.

Before the cross was even out of the case, Kate's shriek was dying on her lips. Joel felt a sudden surge of heat in his fist as the cross seemed to pulse with invisible, ferocious power. Faster than he could register, the invisible force of it hit her. Blew her apart. Obliterated every shred of her being. Like something out of a nightmare, she disintegrated before his eyes.

Then it was over. Her final cry seemed to echo in the crashing silence. Joel looked grimly down at the mess on the floor that had once been a beautiful, happy young girl, and for the second time that night he tasted the harsh sting of vomit rising up in his throat.

Dec was struggling to his feet, ashen-faced and trembling. 'You killed her.'

'You can't kill what's already dead,' Joel said quietly. 'I did what I promised. I freed her.'

Dec nodded slowly, swallowed hard and gingerly touched the wound on his neck. He looked at Joel. 'I'm going to become one of them, aren't I?'

Joel glanced at the cross in his hand. He held it out. 'Touch it,' he said.

Dec tentatively reached out and brushed its surface with his fingertips.

'Take it,' Joel said softly, and Dec grasped it in his palm.

Nothing happened.

'I think you're going to be okay,' Joel said.

Dec stared at the cross in his hand, blinking in confusion. 'She bit me. She drank from me.'

'I don't know exactly how this works, Dec. She'd only just been turned herself. Maybe her powers weren't strong enough. Maybe if she'd come back to you a few more times, drank a bit more . . .' He shrugged. 'You've been lucky.' Already Joel thought he could see a change coming over Dec's face. Almost as though he'd been freed too, from some kind of hypnotic power that had held him like a fly in a web. Joel laid a hand on his shoulder. 'I'm very sorry for your loss. You've been brave, Dec. I'm proud of you.'

Dec rubbed the tears from his face with his sleeve. His face twisted in sudden disgust.

'I've been weak,' he sniffed. 'I shouldn't have tried to stop you. I should never have let her in here.' He handed the cross back to Joel. 'What *is* that thing?'

'Just a little something I picked up on my travels,' Joel said.

'Where are you going now?'

'To take you home to your family. They're worried about you. After that, I'm going to finish this once and for all.'

'Let me go with you. I want to be there too. I want to see the fucker who did this to my Kate go down.'

Joel shook his head. 'This is something I've been waiting eighteen years for. I need to do it alone.'

CHAPTER 70

It was a dull early afternoon and clouds were scudding low over the airport terminal as Alex stepped out into the damp Brussels air. She popped a Solazal. Three left in the tube.

She'd been expecting to see Harry Rumble waiting for her in the lobby, but no sign. Then she spotted the gleaming black Mercedes SUV with mirrored windows across the tarmac. The back doors opened simultaneously and two figures she knew instantly were VIA agents stepped out across the car park to meet her. One was tall with thin white hair, the other dark and ruddy. Both were wearing long black coats over grey suits, like bad imitations of police detectives. They weren't smiling.

'Where's Rumble?' she asked them.

They didn't reply. She shrugged and followed them to the car. The driver had the engine running and didn't glance back at them in his mirror as they got in. Alex sat sandwiched between the two sullen agents.

'So I suppose this is meant to intimidate me,' she said. 'The whole silent act. What do I call you guys?'

The two agents stared fixedly ahead and said nothing.

'Have it your way. I'll call you Chico and Harpo. How about that?'

'He's Agent Bates,' the tall, white-haired one muttered out of the corner of his mouth. 'I'm Agent Verspoor.'

'It's a pleasure to meet you boys,' Alex said. She wasn't expecting a reply, and spent the next few minutes staring out at the drab scenery as the Mercedes sped around the outskirts of Brussels. Belgium. Land of chocolate and chips, and not much else.

The Hotel Grand Châteauneuf sat secluded in twenty acres of its own wooded grounds a few kilometres from Brussels. The high level of luxury and even higher security made it perfect for the big-shot conferences and summits that were regularly held there. Bilderbergers, global business cartels, now vampires. The Mercedes was halted at the barred gates and the driver showed his paperwork to the armed private security guard that stepped up to meet them. A nod and a wave, and they glided on through the gates and into the rolling grounds. The hotel appeared through the trees as they came closer, all steel and glass and concrete. To Alex's eye it looked slab-like and postmodern, but she guessed the brutal architecture appealed to the powermonger types. The main building could have been a grounded space station, with a giant glass dome in its centre that caught the dull sunlight.

429

Up ahead, a procession of other vehicles was filing up towards the car park as vampires arrived from all over the world. Their driver slotted into a parking space and Bates and Verspoor escorted Alex from the car. As they followed the crowd funnelling towards the entrance of the main building, she could see the limos of the top Ruling Council dignitaries parked in a cordoned area. More agents were milling about, some of them conspicuously armed and glancing about nervously. Whatever stocks remained of Nosferol were sure to have been diligently reserved for VIP protection, Alex thought.

Her two goons shadowed her every step of the way as she walked into the hotel lobby and glanced around for Harry Rumble. She spotted him through the crowds, standing in conversation with Xavier Garrett. Rumble didn't seem his usual self-possessed self as she approached him.

'I like the way you sent this double act to pick me up,' she said. 'Am I under close arrest or what?'

Garrett smirked. Rumble shifted nervously and looked down at his feet. 'I wouldn't put it that way exactly.'

'Then exactly how would you put it, Harry?'

'We can talk about it later,' he said. 'It's just about time for us to go in.' The crowd was beginning to break up and drift towards the stairs leading to the main conference room. As they walked, Alex noticed the grim look on Rumble's face.

'What's the matter, Harry? It can't just be because of Solomon, can it?'

He shook his head. 'There have been more incidents. While you were in Italy the field stations in Bombay, New York and Tokyo were hit. Nosferol grenade attack. No survivors. Late last night there was another attempt, Paris this time. If the grenade hadn't failed to go off, every one of our agents there would have bought it, too.'

'Stone,' she said. 'He's tightening the screw.'

'And we don't know what we can damn well do about it. The bastard has us by the balls.'

They entered the conference hall and Alex glanced up at the high glass-domed ceiling she'd seen from the car. The banked rows of plush red velvet seats could seat up to five hundred, and they were filling up quickly. A host of ushers with Federation insignia on their smart red uniforms were running back and forth, attending to the delegates, smiling and shaking hands, offering glasses of blood. The elegant classical music piping into the room from hidden speakers was all but drowned out by the buzz of conversation. Rumble was whisked off to join a contingent of VIA section chiefs seated in the front row among other Federation leaders, while Bates and Verspoor steered Alex up the sloping side aisle towards a seat in the row second from the back, looking down from on high at the broad stage below. She got the distinct feeling she was being sidelined. They pointedly sat behind her, spaced two places apart as though that seemed more intimidating.

There was nothing she could do except sit back and watch the conference hall fill up. She could feel the sense of anticipation building in the room as the event ticked steadily closer, but the overall atmosphere was downbeat. Many faces were frowning. Some of the conversations taking place among the rows of seats and in the aisles were more like arguments. Whether the Federation leaders liked to admit it or not, Gabriel Stone's uprising had everyone deeply rattled.

The buzz halted abruptly with the first signs of movement down below and, one by one, to a thunderous applause, the dignitaries hosting the conference filed out from behind the curtain and made their way to the long, curved podium. Alex had never seen them in the flesh before but, like every other vampire in the place, she could put names to the faces that appeared on the big screens flanking the stage. Hassan. Borowczyk. Korentayer. Goldmund. Mushkavanhu. Behind them followed the rotund figure of the FRC Number Two, Gaston Lerouge. The Supremos took their places, three to a side. The seventh, central, seat remained empty; and then the applause intensified and there were shouts as Olympia Angelopolis burst out from behind the curtain. She swept across the stage, dressed in a flowing white gown that shimmered under the lights, mirroring the silver of her hair. The imperious, unsmiling features of the Vampress filled the screens over the stage. She paused graciously to acknowledge her reception and raised a hand. The applause died away.

Then the great Olympia Angelopolis spoke.

CHAPTER 71

'On behalf of my fellow Supremos of the Ruling Council, I thank you all for gathering here today. Let us begin with a minute's silence to mourn the lamented passing of Supremo Teshigahara, Councillor Sen and the other victims of the recent atrocities committed against our great Federation.'

There was a soft murmur of assent among the audience, and a reverential hush hung over the auditorium. Olympia and the other Supremos solemnly lowered their heads. Up on the big screens, Gaston Lerouge was seen to wipe away a tear, even though everyone in the room knew that vampires couldn't cry. After exactly fifty-nine seconds, Olympia abruptly raised her head and ended the silence. 'Thank you. Now, let us begin.'

Why am I here, Alex thought as the talking began. She could have been out there trying to find Joel instead of wasting time listening to this. She slumped deeper in her seat, put her feet up on the backrest of the row in front of her and folded her arms. She could feel the eyes of

Verspoor and Bates right behind her, boring into her.

Right from the start, the main thrust of the meeting was exactly the party line she'd been expecting. Gaston Lerouge took the floor and spent most of the first hour stirring the audience's shared outrage with an impassioned account of the recent acts of sabotage, murder and robbery committed against the Federation by the new rebellion, the instigators of which he described as terrorists and insurgents. Having whipped up the sentiments in the room to a pitch, Lerouge masterfully changed gear and talked at length about the Federation's long history: the struggle to establish order in the early days, the first successes and failures, the heroic efforts of esteemed colleagues such as The Lady of Steel herself to bring peace and harmony to what had been an embattled, divided, grievously endangered race. Were the sacrifices of the Founders to have been in vain? *No,* the audience roared. Was this towering monument to democracy, this paragon of justice and good, to be brought down by a rabble? *No!*

Visibly moved, Lerouge handed the floor to his colleagues. The next hour was spent reassuring the audience that in no way was the Federation under any significant threat from the uprising. Thanks to the worthy efforts of VIA and its global network of agents, the situation would be fully in hand within six months at the latest; the Federation would continue to march undeterred onwards and upwards. Ramming home their message of a bright and optimistic future, the screens overhead displayed a slideshow of the plans for the construction of the new Federation pharmaceutical plant in Andorra. The audience duly nodded and marvelled.

Olympia Angelopolis thanked her colleagues and took up the baton once more.

'In the light of the recent crisis, however, and as a result of protracted debate, the Federation Ruling Council has reluctantly elected to implement a range of new measures. From now on, every registered Federation member will be required to report twice yearly to their local VIA office so that we may keep updated records of their movements and activities.' She paused to let the audience absorb this, which they did with only a very few shrugs and raised eyebrows, then went on: 'Second, as a result of diminished supplies, and to enable us to get production back to normal, we propose the introduction of a new levy on prescriptions of Solazal and Vambloc for all registered members. Federation personnel and VIA agents are, of course, exempt.' The Supremo smiled at this display of her organisation's generosity.

In the moment of silence before Olympia continued, Alex raised her hand.

'Excuse me, ma'am?'

Many faces turned to look at Alex. The Supremo had not invited questions.

Olympia scanned the crowd; on the big screen her face had darkened a shade. 'And you are—?'

'Alex Bishop, VIA Special Agent, London.'

'Ah, yes,' Olympia said knowingly after a brief exchange of glances with Lerouge. 'And your question, my dear?'

'Given your confidence that the current crisis can be resolved within the next six months anyway, I wondered what the reasoning was behind the tightening of controls on registered members? The Federation's enemies aren't registered. Isn't that the whole point?'

In the front row, Rumble's shoulders seemed to sag a little. Garrett twisted round in his seat to sneer at Alex, and then whispered something behind a cupped hand in his boss's ear.

Olympia flinched a little. 'We feel that under the present circumst—'

'Ma'am? Excuse me, I hadn't finished. And are we to take it that the new tax on Vambloc and Solazal will be lifted once production returns to normal?'

The crowd seemed to hold its breath while Olympia Angelopolis paused for a long moment. Her eyebrow twitched. 'These are highly pertinent points,' she finally said in a measured tone, 'which will be fully discussed at a later time. Thank you for your questions. Now, moving on . . .'

Alex slumped back down in her seat and smiled to herself as the talking resumed. The Supremos skirted around the issue of the remaining new measures and went on to discuss their plans for major organisational improvements within FRC admin departments. All typical politico talk, Alex thought, designed to distract and cajole when all they wanted was to tighten their grip on everyone.

Time passed, and Alex eventually tuned out and turned to thinking about what the Ruling Council had in store for her later. There was going to be some kind of private disciplinary hearing, for sure. What might come of it? No VIA operative had ever been terminated for neglect of duty, but they could easily revoke her Special Agent status. She'd do her best to fight her corner. Whether Harry Rumble would stand up for her remained to be seen.

Sidelights automatically lit up in the aisles as the conference droned on and the window of sky in the glass dome above the conference hall grew steadily darker. Every so often from her vantage point at the height of the auditorium, Alex spotted a delegate shoot a furtive glance her way and whisper to the vampire sitting next to them. She ignored them. She'd become more interested in watching Xavier Garrett in the front row.

For some time now, he'd been looking more and more restless, shifting constantly in his seat, looking at his watch frequently and looking over at the exits. He was acting the way a human would if they urgently needed to go to the bathroom. Something was plainly eating him.

On stage, the Supremos moved with funereal pace from one point of the agenda to the next. Alex hardly heard a word of it. With each passing minute, she was becoming more focused on Garrett. He was virtually jumping up and down in his seat, bursting with impatience about something.

Then, as Olympia and Lerouge paused between items and the audience broke into applause, Alex noticed a commotion down at the auditorium entrance. A messenger had slipped into the hall looking agitated, and was talking to the security guards. As the audience went on applauding, the security guys began talking on their radios.

Something was happening. As Alex watched, the messenger was allowed through to speak to Olympia and Lerouge. A lot of frowning and discussion, and then, to a general mutter of surprise, all seven Supremos suddenly left the stage and filed out of the room under security escort. An announcer came on stage and announced that the conference was being temporarily suspended; the talks would resume in just a few moments, and would everyone please remain seated while the ushers came round with refreshments?

As the announcer hooked up his mike, Garrett suddenly jumped out of his seat, hurried past the front row without a glance at Rumble, who was deep in conversation with another VIA chief, and slipped away through a side exit.

'Acting a little strangely, Xavier,' Alex murmured to herself. She had to know more.

'Hey. Where do you think you're going?' Verspoor said as she stood up.

'To catch the new Baxter Burnett movie,' she told him innocently. 'It's playing at the UGC multiplex in town. Can't miss it.'

'You sit back down right now,' Bates ordered, pointing at her seat.

'Sorry, guys,' Alex said with a smile, and punched them both simultaneously in the head. The blows would have killed humans. Verspoor and Bates flopped unconscious in their seats. 'You were pretty boring company anyway,' she muttered. Nobody in the rows ahead of her had noticed anything. She hurried out between the seats, trotted down the sloping aisle and made it to the side exit unseen.

Just in time to see Xavier Garrett disappearing around a bend in the plush corridor. He was talking on a mobile, glancing at his watch again, hunched over with a secretive air.

'Go,' he was saying into the phone. 'Go!' He was flushed, quivering with excitement.

'Hey, Garrett,' Alex called after him, running to catch up. 'What're you so worked up about?'

Garrett turned to stare at her. He flipped his phone shut. 'You're not supposed to be out here.'

440

'Who was that on the phone?' Alex asked him. She could hear a noise in the distance. A steady, rapid-fire *thump-thump-thump*. Building fast, doubling in volume every second.

'Nobody,' Garrett said.

'You were calling someone.'

The sound was rising like a violent storm coming up out of nowhere, getting ready to tear apart everything in its path. It was the unmistakable rapid beat and turbine roar of helicopter rotors, hovering over the building. The windows began to rattle in their frames.

'I was calling my wife,' Garrett whined.

Alex shoved him. 'Bullshit.'

'Don't you touch me.'

The noise was getting even louder.

'It was you who tipped Stone off about Venice, wasn't it, Xavier? Nobody knew except me and Harry. Listening at the door's a very nasty habit. And it's my guess you're the one who told them Rudi was my informant.'

He backed off a step. 'You're way out of line, Agent Bishop.'

'What's Stone paying you?' She had to shout to be heard over the noise.

'More than *you* can imagine,' Garrett yelled. He stumbled away from her, pulling a 9mm Beretta from his jacket. Aimed the heavy automatic in her face. 'It doesn't matter anyway. It's all over for you now.'

Alex stared into the pistol's muzzle. Just four

inches down that little black hole was the nose of the copper-jacketed bullet, hollowed out and filled with the Nosferol that she now was sure Xavier Garrett had helped the Trads steal from the Terzi plant. One flick of his finger, and the bullet would cross the space between them in a tiny fraction of a second and bury itself in her brain. That would only be the start of her troubles.

A trained agent would have shot her without a flicker of expression. Alex knew that, because she was one of them, and had trained many of them herself. Xavier Garrett was not one of those. From the white of his knuckles on the grip of the Beretta and the crazed look in his eyes, she could tell he'd never pointed a pistol at anyone in his life before. And someone who'd never fired a shot always flinched first.

He flinched.

She moved.

The gun boomed in his hand and hot gases burned past Alex's face as the bullet screamed by her ear. Before Garrett could even think about getting off another shot, she'd swiped the weapon from his hand. He stumbled away from her, his face full of terror.

Alex aimed the Beretta at him, debating whether or not just to gun him down. She glanced at the ceiling. Everything was shaking from the tremendous noise of the helicopter.

'What's happening?' she yelled at Garrett.

Then, suddenly, from the corridor leading to the conference hall, came the deafening blast of automatic gunfire and the sound of screams.

CHAPTER 72

'It's over!' Garrett brayed at her in triumph.

Or he would have done, if Alex had let him complete the sentence. He still had a syllable left to go when the 9mm Nosferol round made a third eye in his forehead.

No need to hang around to see the result. She turned and sprinted towards the conference room. Burst through the exit door she'd come from. And saw the lights of the helicopter gunship hovering over the glass dome. The glass was shattered. Twin 30mm cannons slung beneath the aircraft's nose were raking and strafing the inside of the conference room, churning up everything in sight. Vampires were cowering, running, stumbling, falling, being blown into meat, convulsing and shrieking in their final agonies. Grotesquely mutilated corpses and burst-open body parts littered the remains of the auditorium like the floor of a slaughterhouse. The sharp acid stink of Nosferol in the air made Alex recoil.

Without even thinking about what she was doing, she ducked between the shattered seats and punched the Beretta upwards, firing at the chopper, again and again, the pistol bucking in her hands. Her bullets pinged harmlessly off its armour. Then the floor was erupting into pieces as a snaking line of gunfire raced towards her almost faster than she could move out of the way. She dived for cover and planking and bits of chair were blasted into pieces that rained down on her.

'Alex!' The scream came from just yards away. Harry Rumble's voice. He was crawling on his hands and knees under the shattered remnants of a catering table. She made a dash towards him, slid to her knees on the broken glass and sprawled under the table next to him. Its flimsy surface offered as much protection from heavy machine-gun fire as a sheet of baking paper. But the chopper had acquired a new target and was distracted as a couple of vampires who had bolted for the main exit were sliced in half and their dark blood sprayed upwards in an arc. The machine guns pummelled their bodies into jelly where they lay.

'This conference is over,' Alex said. She grabbed Rumble's wrist, dragged him out from under the table. Together they dashed for the side exit. The chopper turned its nose towards them like a predator. The walls exploded into plaster dust and wood chips as they dived through the door and out into the corridor. 'Run!' she yelled in his ear, still gripping his wrist. She led him at a sprint the way she'd followed Garrett.

Rumble let out a cry as he saw the body. 'Xavier?'

'He sold us out to Stone, Harry. Who do you think is doing this? Now keep moving. There's got to be a way out of here.' She checked her pistol. One round left. She'd always enjoyed challenging odds.

They raced through the hotel, running blind. A door led into an empty kitchen, and she led Harry between the rows of steel worktops to an exit at the far end. Another narrow passage, another fire door that crunched off its hinges as she kicked it open. The luxury lobby of the Grand Châteauneuf was now just yards away. She could see the dark sky through the entrance doors, and the flash of the gunship's lights on the trees.

Alex smashed the last door open.

'We're going to make it!' Rumble gasped.

'Not quite,' said a voice.

Alex turned to shoot, but a blow out of nowhere knocked her hard off her feet and sent the Beretta tumbling from her hand. She looked up as a group of vampires in black tactical clothing swarmed into the lobby around them. They were armed with short, curved sabres. Two grabbed Harry Rumble and forced him to his knees.

'Nice try,' said the heavily-built male vampire who'd knocked the gun away from Alex. He walked casually over and picked up the fallen weapon, ejected the last round and tossed the gun away in disgust. 'We've no use for these things any more. It's back to the proper old ways from now on.'

The thud of chopper blades above the building was fading. The gunship had done its work and was now flying away. Through the glass doors of the lobby, its long bulky fuselage lit up by the floodlights illuminating the hotel grounds, a Chinook transport helicopter sat on the front lawn, its twin props rotating at idle speed.

Alex slowly picked herself up. There was little use fighting. She counted a dozen, maybe fifteen, vampires circling her and Rumble. Behind them, the seven Supremos had been rounded up and cuffed together. There were blades pressed against their throats from all sides. Olympia Angelopolis was whimpering in terror.

Not all the prisoners were Federation top brass. Four other vampires were dragged into the lobby and thrown to the floor. Rough hands searched them. Alex watched as her last remaining Solazal tablets were confiscated and tossed into a Ziploc pouch.

'Do 'em all here?' said one of the attack squad to his leader, pointing at Alex, Rumble and the other non-VIP prisoners.

'Good a place as any,' the leader replied casually.

The Supremos were kept at a distance as, one by one, the rest of the captives were made to kneel. Vampires in black held on to their arms while the biggest of the squad gripped his sabre, brought the blade back and then whooshed it sideways with a hum of air and a ripping squelch as it sliced

447

through the victim's neck. One by one, all four of the other struggling prisoners were decapitated while Alex and Rumble watched. Their headless bodies were dumped in a pile, and the heads kicked like footballs into a corner.

'Bastards,' Rumble muttered.

'You all had it coming a long time ago, you Federation fuckers,' the leader said.

The executioner walked over to them, grinning. His dripping sabre left a trail of blood spots across the lobby carpet as he approached. He pointed a black-gloved finger at Alex.

'Eeny.'

Then at Rumble. 'Meeny.'

At Alex. 'Miny.'

Back to Rumble. 'Mo.'

'Fuck this, we'll be here all day,' said the leader. 'Stop messing around and do the bitch first.'

'Fine, fine.' Strong hands seized Alex's arms and held her powerless. The executioner took a good grip on the slippery hilt of his sabre. 'Sorry, sweetie. Nothing personal.'

She spat in his eye.

'Nice. That makes it easier.' He drew back the blade.

Alex closed her eyes and prepared herself. She thought about William. And about Joel Solomon. Maybe he was right. Maybe she deserved what was about to happen to her.

But the blow never came. A harsh female voice cut through the lobby.

'No!'

And Alex opened her eyes again.

It was Lillith. Halogen spotlights gleamed off the red leather of her tight jumpsuit as she came swaggering across the lobby and the assault team vampires parted to let her through.

'Agent Bishop,' she laughed. 'Told you I'd catch up with you sometime, didn't I?' Towering behind her was the massive shape of the powerful black vampire Alex had last seen in the battle at the London Eye. He'd swapped his tactical combat gear for a black shirt and a tangerine suit that shimmered like silk. His eyes were hidden behind shades and his grin was broad and dazzling.

The executioner stepped back in disappointment and lowered his sabre. Lillith reached across her body and drew her own blade from its scabbard with a rattle of steel. She walked up to where Alex was still being held on her knees and swished the sabre through the air a couple of times, relishing the moment.

Alex looked down, refusing to make eye contact with her. Then she felt the cold steel of the weapon's tip touch her face.

'Look at me, Agent Bishop.'

The point of the blade ran down Alex's cheek, stroked her lips, then Lillith pressed up hard under her chin and forced her head up.

'I said, *look* at me, bitch.'

Alex glowered at her. Lillith smiled. 'I wonder how your head would look on a silver platter. We could have delivered it to your Federation bosses. That is, if you still had any. Shame – me and Zachary here would have loved to slice that pretty little neck of yours.'

Zachary gave a low chuckle.

'Don't miss your chance,' Alex said. 'You might not get another.'

'My brother's looking forward to meeting you,' Lillith said. 'He's got plans for you.' She whipped the sabre away from Alex's chin and slid it back into its scabbard. Turning to the assault team vampires, she said, 'Okay, load her up with the others.'

The assault leader pointed at Harry Rumble. 'What about that one?'

Lillith surveyed Rumble with disdain. 'Who is he?'

'Just the VIA head in London.'

'Really? How interesting. And you were about to give him the chop?' She strolled casually over to Rumble, swaying her hips. He flinched away as she ran her fingers down his cheek. 'Nice little bonus. Gabriel will be pleased. Fine, bring him along too.'

Alex and Rumble were hauled to their feet and dragged over to join the Supremos. The vampires in black prodded them with the swords towards the exit and marched them outside towards the Chinook. Its enormous rotors began to turn faster and the whine of its turbines rose to a roar as the pilot readied for lift-off.

'Whatever you're being paid to do this, I can triple it,' Olympia Angelopolis pleaded with Lillith as she was bundled into the rear hatch of the helicopter.

'I know you and your cronies have stashed away plenty during the last few years,' Lillith said. 'But we're not interested in your money.'

'I could rip her tongue out if you want,' Zachary offered.

Lillith shook her head. 'She's going to need one for the little show we're putting on.'

Alex and Rumble exchanged quizzical glances. Neither of them spoke. The vampires in black shoved the rest of the prisoners on board. Lillith gave them a mocking wave as the hatch was closing.

'Bon voyage, Federation scumbags. Pretty soon you're all going to wish you'd never been turned.'

The hatch clanged shut, the cargo hold went black. Moments later Alex felt a rising sensation as the big Chinook took off into the night.

CHAPTER 73

Hours passed. Voices in the dark, vibrating space of the cargo hold.

'Where are they taking us?' Lerouge sounded agitated and fearful.

'They must surely let us go,' said Borowczyk.

'It is an outrage.' Goldmund's voice. 'An outrage, pure and simple.'

'The question is, what do we do about it?' Alex said. 'We can't just sit here.'

'The field agent.' Olympia Angelopolis's voice muttered scornfully from the darkness. 'And what exactly is it you propose to do? As you seem to have so many wonderful ideas as to how we should run our affairs.'

'For a start, I wouldn't waste my time trying to bribe these guys,' Alex answered. 'You can't buy your way out of this one so easily.'

'Then what, Alex?' Rumble's voice. He sounded subdued.

'We have to fight.'

'With what? They have swords. They might still have Nosferol bullets, too.'

Alex gave a snort. 'Maybe Gabriel Stone's right

about us, Harry. Seems to me that with all this Federation bullshit, we've forgotten who we are. We're vampires. Vampires fight. They don't plead and beg.'

Rumble drew a breath. 'Alex—'

'You will please to remember whom you are addressing,' Hassan said indignantly in his thick accent. 'You are in the presence of Supremo Angelopolis.'

'I know exactly whose presence I'm in,' Alex said, and the conversation settled into a brooding silence. She could feel Harry Rumble frowning at her in the darkness.

The Chinook flew on and on. The night ticked slowly by. There was a landing that Alex guessed was for fuel, and then the chopper took off again. None of the prisoners spoke. Alex began counting the hours since she'd taken her last Solazal. Just before two in the afternoon, she remembered, which meant that the effect would start to wear off sometime in the early hours of the morning. She'd have bet that none of the others had taken any much later than that. None of them would survive the sunrise.

Gabriel Stone was forcing them to remember what it was like to live as real vampires. The thought almost made Alex smile.

As the hours ticked by, she knew that Harry Rumble and the Supremos had the dawn on their mind, too. Gaston Lerouge seemed especially nervous. Then, with still time to spare before the first rays of the sun began to lighten the sky, they felt the chopper begin another descent and then settle on solid ground. The rotors slowed and the hatchway opened abruptly. The same black-clad vampire guards who'd loaded them on board hauled them out one by one into the cold night air.

Alex looked around her. Moonlight shone on distant mountains and the high stone walls around them.

'We're in a *castle*,' she whispered to Rumble.

They didn't have much chance to talk as the guards grabbed them and separated them. Alex was shoved at swordpoint through a barred doorway and down a narrow arched passage to a cell.

She breathed a sigh of relief. No windows. At least Stone hadn't devised a little barbecue session when the sun came up in a few hours' time. He clearly had other plans. The cell walls were about four feet thick, solid rock, and the steel door was too tough even for a vampire to get through. There was little else to do except hang around to find out what Stone's plans might be.

Alex curled up in the corner of the cell, and the long wait began.

CHAPTER 74

Bucharest, Romania
1.32 p.m. local time

The freezing rain was turning to sleet and the pavements outside the airport were gleaming and slippery. Joel's spirits were sagging as he waited in a huddled queue for a taxicab. A rattling, grime-streaked Peugeot lurched up and he loaded his rucksack and the metal case in the back seat. The dashboard was littered with junk and the smell of the sickly air blasting through the vents didn't help Joel's stomach much. He'd almost been sick twice on the plane, but he'd eaten so little in the last twenty-four hours that he had nothing to throw up.

The driver jerked his head back at him and said something in Romanian. Joel pronounced 'Gara de Nord', the name of the city's railway station, as best he could; the guy nodded and sped out of the airport to join the heavy traffic heading into Bucharest. They fell into a stumbling conversation, but Joel's Romanian was even more rudimentary than the driver's English. After a few minutes of pointless grouching about the shitty weather, the guy concentrated on swearing at other drivers and Joel slouched back and numbly watched the beat of the wipers. His hand rested on the case on the seat beside him.

He couldn't believe he was doing this.

It was a wild ride through the city. Romanian drivers seemed to consider the rules of the road as only suggestions, and the taxi had several near misses as it hammered over the potholes and ruts on the way to the railway station. Bucharest must have been pretty once, but the architectural legacies of Ceauşescu's harsh Communist regime stood like squatting concrete toads among the classical buildings and baroque facades. Stray dogs seemed to be everywhere, sauntering casually across the path of the speeding, honking traffic, in no hurry to get to the other side. Joel was glad when the taxi pulled up with a screech outside the columned entrance of the Gara de Nord Bucureşti.

He checked the train timetables – he had half an hour to wait. He found a quiet café inside the station and took a table in a corner. The coffee was stale, but at least the place was warm and dry and he could sit a while and think before he set out on the next leg of his journey. He unzipped the document pouch on the front of the rucksack and took out the page he'd torn from Dec's friend's atlas. He slid his coffee cup to one side to unfold it across the table.

The sick feeling in his stomach came rushing back worse than ever as he gazed at the ragged line of dried blood that ran across the paper. The fingerprints had turned crusty and brown. Some bits had flaked off and fallen onto the table when he'd unfolded it; the sudden thought that they were crumbs of congealed vampire blood made him swipe them away with a frisson of horror.

He took another slurp of coffee and tried to focus his thoughts. The fact was, he still didn't know exactly where he was going. Avoiding Kate Hawthorne's blood, he traced his finger across the map for the hundredth time since yesterday, staring at names like Brasov, Târgu Frumos, Râmnicu. They meant nothing to him. As for the name he'd managed to force out of the doomed girl, there was no mention of it anywhere – not here on the atlas, not in his guidebook, not on any map he'd found online during his rushed research before leaving Britain. But it had to be here somewhere, among the horrible fingerprints that clustered around a zone of the Transylvanian Alps about a hundred and eighty miles to the northwest of Bucharest.

Had to be. He'd come too far to let himself be shaken by doubts. And so his best plan – right now his only plan – was to travel blind into the rough area marked in blood on the atlas page. When he got there, he could start asking questions and hope they led him somewhere.

Through the café window he could see his train

now winding its way into the station. He checked his watch, stuffed the page back into his rucksack, grabbed his stuff and went to catch his train.

The rolling hills, dramatic mountainscapes and sweeping pine forests weren't enough to keep Joel awake as the train lurched and ground its way steadily northeastwards during the next few hours. When he awoke from his dark dreams it was nearly three in the afternoon and the train was slowing for its approach into the medieval town of Sighişoara. In the street outside the railway station he passed hot food vendors selling grilled meat and pastries, but still couldn't bring himself to eat anything. The sky was pale grey and the rising wind had a cold, hard bite. He pulled up the collar of his jacket, shouldered his rucksack and clutched the precious metal case tightly under his arm as he wandered the town.

The old part of Sighişoara was a fortified medieval stronghold perched on a hill. The streets were cobbled and the towers and steeples of Orthodox churches dominated the skyline. He knew from his guidebook that at the height of the season the streets would be full of tourists eager to visit the ancient seat of Transylvanian royalty, former home of Vlad Dracul, father of the legendary Impaler. He passed a sign for a museum of torture, and then the abode of Vlad himself, now converted into a restaurant. Even here, as far as the modern world was concerned, things had moved on; legends that had once struck terror were now just tourism marketing gimmicks. It made him feel all the more foolish as he loitered uncomfortably about the half-empty street, eyeing each passerby as someone he could potentially collar and ask about the whereabouts of this 'Vâlcanul'. How would he appear to them, this damp-sodden, wild-eyed guy who'd travelled all this way searching for vampires to kill? Like some kind of nut, most likely. He was beginning to think it himself.

Four times he was on the brink of approaching someone – and four times he shrank back at the last moment. In the end, hating and cursing himself for his stupidity, he gave up and walked away.

On the edge of the town was a minor road that snaked away and upwards through the pine forests. He walked desultorily for a mile, kicking stones and feeling the sleet work cold, damp fingers into his clothing. The sky was getting darker and the momentum that had driven him here was fading with the light. He was starting to descend rapidly into a state of gloomy despondency. His situation now struck him as completely absurd – coming to this place had been a terrible mistake.

He was still feeling that way when the pickup truck splashed by him on the road. Its one working brake light flared through the sleet, and it pulled over on the verge. The driver was alone, a bearded, chubby guy Joel instantly warmed to. The lived-in cab of the truck smelled of coffee and cigarettes and there was lively Romanian folk music zinging over the radio. A lift to nowhere seemed like an attractive proposition, and he climbed in.

CHAPTER 75

Joel's saviour's name was Gheorghe. He seemed a man of easy ways, smiling and laughing constantly, and it was obviously of no concern to him at all that neither of them could understand anything the other was saying. The truck bounced and rattled its way up the winding mountain passes. Every so often the walls of the pine forest would drop away and Joel caught a glimpse of the dusky mountain landscape behind. The warmth of the heater blasted away the chill from his hands and feet, and he felt his resolve beginning to return like a spreading whisky glow inside him. After a while he even relaxed enough to tell a joke, some daft thing Sam Carter had had the office in an uproar with a while back. Gheorghe plainly didn't understand a word but nonetheless found it so amusing he had to wipe tears from his ruddy cheeks. Then, in the chuckling pause that followed, Joel threw away his caution and tentatively asked about Vâlcanul.

And he knew right away he was on to something, because that was when Gheorghe suddenly clammed up tighter than if he'd been slapped.

461

There was no more laughter, no more joking, and a deep silence fell over them. Any other time, Joel might have regretted killing the atmosphere of camaraderie they'd struck up – but his heart was racing and his hands trembling with excitement. He had no idea what road he was on, but he knew now that it was the right one.

It wasn't long afterwards that the truck's headlights picked out the mossy roof of a log house through the trees, then another, then the steeple of an old wooden church. Gheorghe seemed keen to continue alone, and the small village looked to Joel like a place where he could carry on his investigation. They parted amicably, almost apologetically, and Gheorghe took off up the road looking relieved.

Joel sighed and made his way into the heart of the tiny hamlet. The temperature had dropped a couple of degrees while he'd been with Gheorghe, and he dug his hands deep in his pockets as he walked. Light from the rambling rows of log houses spilled out onto the unpaved road; he could smell the woodsmoke drifting from their chimneys. As he walked on, he heard the sound of hooves from out of the gloom, and moments later a horse-drawn carriage passed by in the opposite direction, carrying a load of firewood. Just a few miles from the tourist trade of Sighişoara, and a few hours from the modern city bustle of Bucharest, he was in a whole other world. The place was a time capsule.

Light and music drew him towards what seemed to be the village's only bar. A few drinkers turned to stare at him and eyed his rucksack and case as he walked in, ducking to avoid the low beams. He didn't feel up to beer, and paid a few lei for a coffee. While he sipped it, sitting on a stool at the bar, he caught the eye of the barman and dared to mention the name Vâlcanul again. All he got were a lot of strange looks, but that didn't deter him. Feeling braver now, he left the bar and stopped the first people he met in the street outside, a pair of tiny elderly women who looked like sisters. In the faltering mixture of sign language and pidgin English he was developing, he asked them the same question. 'Can you tell me where I can find a place called Vâlcanul?'

The women shot glances at one another and scurried on past him. Joel wasn't sure whether they'd understood his attempt at communication and was heading further down the street to find someone else to ask when he was halted by a shout from behind him. He turned to see an old man hobbling with a stick towards him. The two ladies watched from a distance.

The old man had a shaggy mane of pure white hair, skin like tanned leather and no teeth. He spoke even less English than Gheorghe, but the wary glint in his eye gave a clear message. *Why are you looking for Vâlcanul?*

Then it really did exist. Joel was trying to formulate his next question when the old man grasped his arm with a bony hand of surprising power, waving his cane at one of the houses. He seemed to want him to come back there with him. Joel followed, wondering where this was leading.

A woman emerged from the finely crafted wooden door of the house, framed in the light from the hallway. She was in her fifties and bore a strong resemblance to the old man, but with black hair and a full set of strong white teeth – she was clearly his daughter. Her father spent a couple of moments jabbering at her in quick-fire Romanian, and she looked at Joel with concern.

'You are American?' she asked in English. Noticing his surprise, she added, 'I am a teacher.'

'I'm from Britain,' Joel said. 'I'm looking for—'

'I know what you are looking for,' the woman interrupted him. 'Why do you wish to find this place?'

'Can you tell me where it is?'

'This is not a place you should go.' She seemed unwilling to mention its name. 'Nobody goes there. Nobody lives there any more.'

'You're sure?'

'Stay away from that place.' She pointed at the case. 'You are photographer, yes? Many beautiful pictures you can take here. No need to go to . . . to there.'

'I'm not a photographer,' Joel said. In the background, the old man was jabbing a gnarled finger up at the sky and muttering the same words over and over. 'What's he saying?' Joel asked the woman.

'The snows are coming early this year, and it will soon be night. My father is saying that it is not safe to travel up the mountain.'

Joel felt his eyes light up. 'Then this Vâlcanul is further up the mountain?' He turned to scan the dark horizon beyond the trees. 'Which way?'

'You must stay down here,' the woman insisted. 'Tomorrow the *autobuz* comes and will take you back to where you came from. You stay with us the night. We have a room and a bed.' She smiled. 'I make polenta with sheep's cheese and sausage.'

'It sounds delicious,' he said, meaning it. 'And I'm very grateful to you for your offer. But I really need to get to Vâlcanul.'

'Then you will not come back,' she said with a pained expression.

Joel thanked her as best he could, and she very reluctantly told him which road to follow out of the village and through the forest. Then, hardly able to keep from breaking into a run, he hefted his rucksack and started walking back down the street. There had to be someone around who could rent him a small truck or a cheap four-wheel drive.

A few minutes' walk from the middle of the village, he came across a small garage. Light was shining from the main building, which was little more than a corrugated iron shack surrounded by a stained concrete forecourt. There were two solitary fuel pumps that looked like relics from the forties. As he walked nearer, he saw a scraggy Alsatian dog that might just as well have been a wolf lying on the ground between heaps of scrap car parts and old tyres. The animal appeared relaxed but its amber eyes were watching his every move. Joel was fifteen yards from the shack when its ears pricked up and it gave a low growl. It was only when he saw the chain that tethered the dog to a railing that he beat down the urge to turn round and walk quickly back the way he'd come.

He walked up to the shack and peered in through the gap in the doors. A rusty collection of cars and a couple of trucks were lined up against the back wall. Tools were littered all over the place. An engine stood partly dismantled on a workbench.

'Hello? Anyone there?' At the sound of Joel's voice, the dog jumped to its feet and rushed at him, barking and snapping and baring its fangs, but was jerked short on the end of the chain. Joel repeated 'Hello?' There didn't seem to be anyone around. Joel wondered where the mechanic was. Probably in the bar he'd just come from.

He slipped inside and looked at the vehicles. It was a desperate collection. The only one that still had all its wheels was a corroded old Matra-Simca. Joel lifted the bonnet and found himself looking at an empty hole where the engine used to be.

Outside, the dog was still going crazy on the end

of its chain, but the noise didn't seem to be attracting anyone. This wasn't helping him. Time was passing too quickly.

That was when he spotted the tarpaulin-draped shape in the corner and walked over to investigate. Under the dusty cover he found a motorcycle. It was a Russian Dnepr mounted to a sidecar, an old Communist-era replica of a wartime Wehrmacht BMW. It was rugged and battered, with tyres that wouldn't have looked out of place on a tractor. The machine was a far cry from the slick 200mph superbike he'd left behind him, but something like this would be a lot better suited to the kind of harsh terrain he expected to find where he was going. He gave the handlebar a waggle, heard the hollow slosh of fuel in the tank. The key was in the ignition. On the sidecar's single seat was a scuffed open-face helmet, with a pair of antiquated leather gauntlets stuffed inside, and glass goggles on an elasticated strap.

Joel glanced furtively around him. The dog had finally stopped its noise. No footsteps on the fore-court outside. He twisted the key, clambered on board the machine and tried the kickstart. The old flat-twin 650cc engine rumbled into life. Everything seemed to work. It was crude, but it was perfect.

After five more frustrating minutes, still nobody had turned up. Opening up his wallet, Joel plucked out a thick wad of the banknotes he'd drawn out back in Britain. He counted out four hundred euros, left them in a curling pile on the bonnet of the old Simca, then chucked his rucksack and the case into the sidecar.

CHAPTER 76

I t had been an interminable, numbing wait for
something to happen before the sound of footsteps echoed in the passage outside. Suddenly
alert, Alex jumped to her feet as a key grated in
the lock and her cell door creaked open.

'Haven't I seen you somewhere before?' she said
to the man who walked in the low arched doorway.
He looked somewhat dishevelled in a rumpled suit
and his face was pale, a nervous twitch making
one eyebrow jump. In his arms was an oblong
box, which he laid on the floor of the cell. Two
guards stood behind him, swords at their sides,
eyes fixed on Alex.

'The Master requests the pleasure of your
company for dinner in the great hall,' the familiar-
looking man said.

Alex stared at him. 'I *do* know you. You're Jeremy
Lonsdale, the politician.'

The man flushed, said nothing, and motioned
at the box. Alex shrugged and opened it.

Gabriel Stone was seated luxuriantly in an enormous chair in front of a roaring fire when Alex

was ushered into the great hall. The place was something out of a medieval fantasy. Settings for two were laid out intimately close together on the gigantic oak dining table in the middle of the room.

'So here I am in the hall of the mountain king,' she said as she walked in. 'And you must be the great Stone. I remember you from your little presentation.'

'In the flesh.' He rose from his chair and gave a stiff, formal bow. 'The pleasure is all mine, Agent Bishop. And you must call me Gabriel.'

'What's the idea of sending this for me to wear?' she asked, tossing him the long, white dress that had been in the box.

'I thought you would look fetching in it,' he said with a twinkle.

'It's ridiculous.'

'A little dated, perhaps. It once belonged to Marie Antoinette. But very elegant, wouldn't you say? Then again, I imagine when one is compelled to live cheek by jowl with the seething mass of humanity, one must get used to abiding by their strange fashions.' Stone laid the dress on the back of his chair, walked up to the table and picked up a crystal decanter. 'Drink?'

'Some hospitality,' she said. 'At last.'

'You must forgive my having kept you waiting so long.'

'Only a whole night and most of the next day.'

'My most humble apologies. I had some things

to arrange for later tonight.' He smiled. 'All will become clear. I trust the accommodation was to your taste?'

'Delightful.'

Stone gave a charming smile and poured out two goblets of fresh, sparkling blood from the decanter.

'Please, have a seat.' He handed her her drink. 'Not what you would call ethically procured, I'm afraid. What's that expression the humans use now? Fairtrade?' He chuckled. 'We don't deal in that up here.'

Alex toyed with the stem of her goblet, then pushed it away from her.

'Whatever have they done to you?' he said with a shake of the head. Reaching in the pocket of his silk jacket, he took out the half-empty tube of Solazal tablets that she recognised as the one the guards had taken from her in Brussels. 'Look at this,' he sighed, dropping the tube disdainfully down on the table. 'Vampires on drugs. Really.'

'I didn't say I liked taking the stuff. It's how I was able to do my job, that's all.'

'Ah yes – your job. The muscle behind the evil minds of your ruling self-appointed elite. Enforcing the arbitrary rules of tyrants, worming the Federation's insidious influence ever deeper into the daily lives of your fellow vampires. The incident with the actor is a prime example of just how petty and paranoid these despots are.'

Alex raised her eyebrows in surprise. 'Baxter

471

Burnett? Wow. Xavier Garrett really has been keeping you informed, hasn't he?'

'As if the youthful appearance of a Hollywood star could bring down the whole edifice of your Federation. Absurd.' Stone gave a contemptuous wave. 'Merely an exercise in control for its own sake, as anyone can see. And you. Are you not ashamed of what you've become? Passing yourself off as a human being? Mimicking the lifestyle of an inferior species? How far can a vampire fall, Agent Bishop?'

'Some humans are better than others,' she said.

'You're thinking of Solomon,' he replied, watching her face very closely. 'There is some special liaison between you, I see. More than a mere collaboration.'

She shrugged. 'We used him, that's all.'

'You're too used to dealing with rank and file vampires. I have the power to see deeper, and I can tell from the look in your eyes that your feelings are strong for this human.' He paused. '*Alex* Bishop. Short for Alexandra, I presume? You won't mind if I call you Alexandra?'

She looked down at her hands. It had been a long time since anyone had called her that.

'You're thinking about the past,' he said. 'How long has it been?'

'A little over a century,' she said after a beat. 'A hundred and thirteen years, if you have to know.'

'A mere fledgling. Little more than an infant. Yet you were one of us long before the dark days of the Federation. You must surely remember the way it was before this grubby little hive of bandits introduced their era of tyranny.' Stone leaned back in his chair, sipped his goblet. The flickering fire cast a glow over his handsome features, and there was a light in his eye as he talked. 'To cheat the sun, embrace the night. Living dangerously, living free. To hunt, to feed like a real vampire, honouring our sacred heritage and a culture that had reached its pinnacle when human beings were still dragging their knuckles in the dust and grunting like apes. How far have they really come, I wonder?' Stone smiled. 'They call us Undead – but it's the finest, most worthy existence there can be. And *this*—' His eyes suddenly burned with rage as he snatched up the tube of Solazal, waved it in the air and then tossed it into the fire. 'This is how your slavemasters repay countless millennia of hallowed tradition.'

'I'm no slave of theirs,' Alex said.

'I can see that. Yet it astounds me that someone of your obviously high intelligence could have fallen for their shameless propaganda. Even today's human dictatorships, for all their transparent crudeness, are more sophisticated. They at least make the effort to dress up their so-called democracies as something fair and egalitarian. Your rulers, by contrast, don't even try to conceal their corruption.'

'I see you've been studying human dictatorships up close,' Alex replied. 'Wasn't that the politician

Jeremy Lonsdale who brought that rag to my cell earlier?'

Stone laughed. 'Currently pursuing a new career direction. His predecessor sadly passed away at the hands of your friend Solomon. You're observant, Alexandra. A quality I admire in you, as well as your loyalty. I, too, serve a master.' Her expression of surprise made him smile. 'You didn't know that, of course.'

'I thought you were the leader of this revolt against the Federation.'

'Merely its general. I take my commands from beings superior even to myself.'

Alex frowned in puzzlement. 'I don't understand.'

'The original forebears of our race. The purest blood, the most ancient and hallowed line. The Übervampyr.'

Alex was stunned. It took a few moments before the steady look in Stone's eye convinced her that he was serious.

'The Über race is ancient history. Part of legend. Isn't it?'

'Rather like the cross of Ardaich. It would be unwise to confuse legend with myth.'

'They exist? Still, to this day?'

'Yes, they are here still,' Stone replied. 'Compared to them, I – we – are nothing. And I am proud to serve them and help bring about their long-dormant plans for this planet.'

'Destroying the Federation was just the beginning,' Alex said, understanding.

'The very first step, of a very great many. But the first step is often the most important. With vampires freed from the shackles of oppression, they will begin to rediscover the taste of freedom. Just a tiny taste, in comparison to the exquisite liberty we will all enjoy once the Masters' plans are brought to fruition.'

'What are you talking about? A vampire takeover? Of the whole planet?' Alex almost laughed.

Stone nodded earnestly. 'Invasion, enslavement, complete control. That kind of thing.'

'Killing humans indiscriminately?'

'No worse than what they do to one another. In any case, their numbers are grossly excessive. Look what this parasitic race has done to its home planet in the mere blink of an eye since it achieved so-called civilisation. Tell me, Alexandra, what other of God's creatures so wilfully and wantonly ravages its own habitat to the extent that, left unchecked, it must ultimately destroy itself?'

'*You* talk of God?'

'I am, after all, a vampire of philosophic joys.'

'And an ecologist, too.'

He chuckled warmly. 'I only want the best, Alexandra. And humans are simply not worthy to remain the stewards of this planet. They have lost their paradise. Yes, there will be some culling. Kill some, turn some, in the time-honoured way. The rest, we will farm, like the beasts of burden they are.' He smiled. 'You look shocked. Why be so

475

coy? You're a vampire. Take pride in yourself. Embrace it to the full.'

Alex shifted uncomfortably.

'You haven't touched your drink.'

'I'm all right, thanks.'

'Drink it. You know you want to.'

She reached out for the goblet. Drew her hand back hesitantly.

'You see? You can't fight what you are.'

'Where are they? The Übervampyr?'

'I'm afraid that's one detail I cannot reveal to you. Unless of course,' Stone twiddled the stem of his goblet '– and this was very much my purpose in wanting to spend this evening in your beautiful company – I'm able to persuade you to come and work for me.'

'You've got to be kidding.'

'Not in the least. I will soon be disposing of your Federation colleagues. They are worthless to me. You, on the other hand, have amply displayed a range of talents that are far too valuable simply to snuff out.'

'That's just about the nicest threat I've ever heard.'

'I hope you consider it carefully. It would be highly regrettable, criminal even, to have to send you to the same fate as awaits your loathsome former colleagues. I would be quite devastated.'

'Do I detect a whiff of moral scruple, Gabriel?'

He moved a little closer to her. 'I'm not the monster you take me for. In fact, I would surprise you, should you get to know me better. I think you and I would rub along very well.' He paused. 'What do you say, Alexandra? You and I, together. You at my side, helping me bring about the grandest plan in the long history of the vampire culture?'

'What about Lillith? I have a feeling she wouldn't be too pleased.'

'Oh, Lillith.' Stone waved his hand. 'Never mind her.' His eyes lit up. 'Does that mean you'll accept my proposal?'

'I didn't say that.'

Stone nodded thoughtfully, then rose from his chair. 'I must leave you now. There are some matters I must see to before tonight's proceedings can be completed. Please don't think about trying to escape. You have exactly two hours to decide.'

CHAPTER 77

As he rode, Joel refused to regret having turned down the offer of a hot plate of food and a bed for the night back at the village – though that wasn't easy as the bumping, rutted road towards Vâlcanul worsened with every mile. He was grateful for a third wheel on the rugged terrain, but the thick leather gauntlets weren't doing much to keep out the cold wind and his fingers were becoming numb on the bars. The old man had been right about the snow, too. The horizontal sleet that stung Joel's face as he rode was turning to thickening flurries of white. He had to keep wiping the flakes from the glass of his goggles, and the rocky road was slowly disappearing in the feeble glow of the Dnepr's headlamp as it merged with the snowy verge.

After another arduous hour, and just as his hands and feet were beginning to feel like lifeless lumps of meat, Joel caught a glimpse of stone buildings a few hundred yards ahead.

Vâlcanul. From the directions he'd managed to prise out of the teacher woman, he knew this had to be the place.

Not a single light was shining. Not a soul around, no vehicles anywhere to be seen apart from his own. The village was even smaller than the one he'd come from, and it seemed to be completely deserted. From the rotted doors and glassless windows, the collapsed roofs, the weeds growing through the paving stones, it was as if nobody had lived here for a hundred years.

Joel braked the bike to a slithering halt in the middle of the snowy street and dead silence filled his ears when he turned off the engine and climbed down from the saddle. The clouds had parted. Pale moonlight shone down through the wisping snowflakes. Joel removed his goggles, unstrapped his helmet and gazed around him at the scene of desolation.

Could this be the right place? It was hard to imagine Gabriel Stone abandoning his manor house in England for a remote ruined mountain village. Joel reached into the sidecar, opened the case and took out the cross, remembering the way it had seemed to thrum with its own life when he'd been near Kate Hawthorne. He gripped it tightly in his fist. It felt cold and inanimate.

There was nothing here.

Joel couldn't do anything to repress the weight of bitterness that settled over him. He'd come all this way for nothing. And now he was going to have to stay the night in this dismal place. But where? Most of the houses were nothing more than roofless shells.

Then he noticed the old church. It overlooked the houses from the end of the street, standing at the top of a gently sloping rise. Sections of roof were still in decent order, enough to provide a bit of shelter. Joel left the bike where it stood – he didn't think anyone was going to steal it.

There wasn't much left inside the church except for its bare stone walls. Joel found a spot away from the icy wind that whistled through the broken stained glass windows, laid down the case and grimly started rooting around in his rucksack for his little Primus stove, a box of matches and a can of soup. As he struck a match with trembling fingers, he glanced out of the smashed window. From this slightly higher ground, he had a better view of the craggy mountain peaks rising out of the pine forests, like rows of jagged white teeth stretching from horizon to horizon under the pale moon.

Then he stopped, did a double take and stared. The match burned back and singed his fingers; he dropped it without taking his eyes off what he'd just seen.

Perched on the summit of a nearby mountain, bathed in a shaft of moonlight, was a castle.

CHAPTER 78

The craggy battlements loomed high against the night sky. As Joel got closer, every rise of the Dnepr's engine note as it lurched over the bumps made him cringe in case the noise reached listening ears. He didn't dare use the headlight, and only the deep moon-shadows sloping away down the steep rocky banks either side of the road kept him from riding off course and tumbling a thousand feet down to the black depths of the valley below.

Fear had its icy fingers around Joel's guts and was wringing them tight. A kind of madness was rising up inside him that almost made him want to laugh with terror. All that prevented his mind from cracking completely was the thought of the cross of Ardaich, nestling on the sidecar seat just a few inches from his right knee. He'd left the case behind in Vâlcanul. He no longer had any use for it. He was riding into war now – and whatever fate was lying in wait for him up there, there wasn't a force on the planet that could have persuaded him to turn back.

Up ahead, the snowy road snaked all the way up to the castle gates. If he'd had any notions of storming right up to them like a conquering knight on his charger, they melted quickly away at the memory of the attack in Venice. Stone had humans working for him as well as vampires, and until the fangs came out, the only way to tell one enemy from another was to get close to them with the cross. One would shrivel up and die, but the other might easily just put a bullet in his head. He needed to approach by stealth.

He was still a quarter of a mile from the castle walls when he decided that the bike's engine noise was too big a risk, and turned off the ignition. The machine coasted a few yards, and he jumped out of the saddle and used its momentum to roll it off the road and hide it behind a large rock on the verge.

Here we go, Solomon. This is it.

By the light of the moon he studied the lie of the land. The castle had been built to withstand sieges and wars, and its architects had known what they were doing. Except for where the raised roadway wound up to the gates, the base of the massive walls dropped away down a sheer cliff face. No ancient army could have scaled it successfully, weighed down as they would have been by shields and armour and weapons. Even if a few had made it to the top, archers in the battlements would have mown them down in the open killing field between the cliff edge and the foot of the wall.

But a single, skilled climber, armed with just a small stone cross, had a chance to get up there unseen. It had been a while since he'd done any rock climbing but, tracing his eye up the cliff face, Joel reckoned he could make it. It was a hell of a challenge, and he was mad even to think of attempting it, on his own, in the dark, without ropes or crampons or any kind of proper equipment.

But then, he reflected, he *was* mad. Had to be, to be here at all.

He zipped open his rucksack and shook all the contents – spare clothes, his stove and food supply, documents and passport, anything that was surplus weight – out into the footwell of the sidecar. He put the cross inside in their place and carefully closed the zippers and Velcro fastenings, before taking off his jacket and looping the rucksack straps around his shoulders and waist over the sweatshirt underneath. It cheered him immensely to think he was a walking anti-vampire weapon now, lethal just by his presence. The adrenalin was rushing through his veins so fast, he didn't even feel the cold any more as he went scrambling down the snowy bank and traced a zigzagging path through the trees to the base of the cliff.

CHAPTER 79

Exactly two hours after Gabriel Stone had left her alone to wander about the great hall, Alex was summoned again and Lonsdale escorted her through the winding passageways of the castle, the vampire guards close behind.

She could see the heaviness in Lonsdale's step, the dullness in his eyes and the way his head hung low as he walked. The ancient practice of enslaving humans as ghouls had been one of the first things the Federation had abolished when it had seized power, and Alex had been there at the reading of the proclamation. Trust Gabriel Stone to have flouted the law with such audacity. Lonsdale gave off an air of complete pathos – she couldn't help but feel just a little sorry for him.

The pale ghoul showed her through a tall doorway into a brightly lit room filled with state-of-the-art equipment. A large and expensive-looking digital film camera was mounted on a tripod, pointing at an empty carved oak throne.

A rack-mounted DVD recorder was connected to a large screen.

Stone looked breezy and relaxed in an open-necked white shirt and silk necktie. Lillith had draped herself over a divan in the corner, while Zachary and the other two of his inner circle were watching over the prisoners. Rumble and the seven Federation Supremos were huddled together, surrounded by the sword-wielding guards. Olympia Angelopolis had completely lost her famous composure, but she still managed to look proud next to Gaston Lerouge. Hassan, Goldmund, Korentayer, Mushkavanhu and Borowczyk stood gazing down at their feet, refusing to make eye contact with anyone.

'Alexandra,' Stone called with a bright smile, looking genuinely pleased to see her. Alex noticed the hot glower that Lillith shot at his back as he walked across to greet her. 'Thank you, Jeremy,' he said to Lonsdale. 'That will be all for now. You may return to your hole until I call for you again.' He took Alex's elbow. 'Let me show you what your friends and I have been up to for the last couple of hours,' he said warmly. 'I must say it's all been going marvellously.' He turned to Olympia. 'We've been having rather a lot of fun down here, have we not?'

The Vampress let out a humiliated sob.

'Perhaps I really should go into film-making after all,' Stone went on. 'Let's take a look at the fruit of our labours.' He aimed a remote control at the

DVD player. The screen lit up and, framed there in high definition, sitting slumped and defeated on the oak throne under the bright lights, was Olympia.

'In her final and most spectacular public appearance,' Stone smiled.

On screen, the Supremo confessed openly to a host of injustices, and pleaded guilty to charges of corruption and the murder of innocent vampires whose only crime was to honour their ancient heritage. The creation of Solazal and Vambloc had not, she admitted, been done with the interests of vampires at heart, but right from the very beginning had been conceived as a deliberate scheme to enrich her and her colleagues at the expense of their fellows. She told the camera that the burden of her sins had become too heavy to bear, and she now planned to go into seclusion and hide her face away from the vampire community in everlasting shame.

Stone turned off the DVD. 'That just about sums it up. It's taken us a little while to get everyone's confessions down on film, but I must say I'm very pleased with the results.'

'They made me say it,' Olympia protested.

'Of course we did,' Stone said. 'Everyone had their own script.'

'Written by me and Lillith,' Anastasia cut in proudly.

'The finest hour of the Federation,' Stone went

on. 'This is how they will be remembered. Confessing their sins, laying bare their consciences, asking forgiveness of the citizens as they release them from the yoke of oppression. Magnificent.' He beamed. 'And now, thanks to our friend Xavier Garrett, who kindly provided us with access to the Federation register, word will be sent out to each and every vampire in the database, summoning them to gather en masse at prearranged venues across the world, where these confessions will be screened. The Federation will be officially disbanded. The beginning of a new era is upon us.' He turned to Alex with a flourish. 'Which brings me neatly back to you, Alexandra. Have you decided to accept my offer?'

Lillith's eyes narrowed into slits and she uncoiled herself from the divan. 'Your offer, Gabriel? You said you were going to film her with the others. You never mentioned anything to me about an *offer*.'

Stone ignored her and went on smiling at Alex. 'Well? What is it to be? Will you join us? Or do you choose to be executed along with your illustrious Vampress and her acolytes?'

A mutter of horror rippled through the little crowd of prisoners. '*Executed?*' Lerouge burst out, his eyes darting wildly from side to side. 'But you told us we'd just be sent into exile—'

Stone made an apologetic gesture. 'A slight deception on my part, I concede. But how else

487

could I have drawn such wonderful performances from you all?'

Lerouge started struggling and screaming. 'You'll never get away with this!'

Stone gestured to one of the guards. A quick stroke of a sword, and Lerouge's head was swiped clean off his shoulders. The head bounced into the fireplace and lay there sizzling. The remaining Supremos cringed and sobbed. Harry Rumble stared hard at Stone but remained silent.

'Now, what was I saying? Oh yes. My offer, Alexandra. I'm waiting. Don't disappoint me.'

'Here's my answer, Gabriel,' Alex said, glancing at Olympia. 'You were right. I've been working for tyrants. There isn't a decent vampire on the Ruling Council. As an agent for VIA, I've been the instrument of their corruption. I suspected it all along. There were things I noticed, but chose to keep quiet about. Now I see differently.'

Stone walked up to Alex and laid a hand on her shoulder. 'You make me very happy.'

'You can't be fucking serious, Gabriel,' Lillith said.

'You didn't let me finish, *Gabriel*,' Alex went on. 'I may have seen through them, but that doesn't make me want to come over to your side. Not after the things you told me. Yes, I'm a vampire – but I could never be like you.' She sucked in a breath. 'So my answer is no. I still believe in what the Federation could have been. What it could be. What it will be one day.'

There was a silence in the room. A smile had

spread over Lillith's face. Stone raised his eyebrows and let out a regretful sigh.

'Then on your own head be it,' he said. 'Let the executions begin.'

CHAPTER 80

The mountain wind stripped Joel like a knife as he struggled up the cliff. His hands were raw, every muscle in his body screaming at him to stop. But there was nowhere *to* stop when you were clinging to a steep rock face with only a few narrow ledges and the occasional clump of protruding vegetation between you and the valley floor a thousand feet below. Risking a glance downwards, he could see how far he'd come. A few more minutes, and he'd reach the base of the wall.

He climbed on, glued like a spider to the sheer slope, relying more on feel than the dim moonlight as he worked his painstaking way from handhold to handhold, foothold to foothold. Climbing was a game of strategy. Beating the mountain was all about planning your route; pick the wrong one, and the mountain beat you.

So far, Joel was winning. But then a small ledge of rock that had looked like a good left foothold suddenly gave way with a crack. The sudden weight transfer tore Joel's left hand from its grip, and he felt himself going. Faster and faster, scrabbling desperately for a hold. He didn't scream or cry out – everything happened too fast in that moment of eerie silence, as surprise gave way to denial and then to shock. By then it was too late and the long drop was inevitable. Joel felt himself spinning downwards.

Something raked the side of his face. With a terrible splintering and crackling, his fall was arrested. A lancing pain in his right shoulder, and he felt the flesh rip. Then the waist girth of his rucksack was yanked brutally against his lower ribs, squeezing the air out of his chest. His legs kicked in open air as he hung helplessly from whatever it was that had broken his descent. The pine-studded valley was a very long way down below him.

He twisted his head painfully upwards and saw that a protruding dead tree, growing out of an overhang that he'd avoided on the way up, had speared through the right strap of his rucksack, tearing away some of his shoulder with it. Blood was already spreading through his sweatshirt. He was caught like a fish on a hook.

He tried swinging his legs to move his body so that he could regain a hold on the rock face. The dead tree gave an ominous crack and he felt himself lurch half an inch.

Bad idea, he thought as he dangled there in space. The tree cracked again, then a long creaking groan became a ripping, splintering crackle.

And a second later, it gave. This time Joel had

time to cry out '*Shiiiit!*' as he felt himself going. Falling, he closed his eyes.

He hit the rocks face down with a grunt of pain.

Slowly, he dared to open his eyes again. He wasn't spread out in a quivering pool of spattered flesh and burst entrails over the valley floor. He was still remarkably alive, and a reassuringly long way up with the mountain wind still whistling over him. Even more reassuring was the solid slab of rock he was lying on. Wincing at the pain in his torn shoulder, he scrabbled to his feet and whacked his head painfully against something hard above him.

At that moment, he understood what had happened. When the dead tree had broken, it hadn't snapped clean off but had lowered him into what seemed to be a cave entrance that he'd missed in the darkness. He rubbed his bruised head and felt his way around inside the mouth of the cave. There must be some way to clamber back out to the rock face and continue his climb.

Something crunched underfoot. He reached down and felt brittle fragments – then his groping fingers found the rest of the skull and he fell backwards.

He sat there panting against the wall of the cave. The empty eye sockets of the human skull seemed to watch him. They weren't alone. As his vision adjusted to the darkness he could see dozens of other skulls heaped in piles. No, not dozens, hundreds.

And he realised fully where he was. At one time this must have been an escape tunnel leading out of the castle – or maybe an invasion tunnel leading in. Whatever steps or bridge had been built there had long since eroded or rotted away. In the centuries since, the tunnel had been used for another purpose.

He was standing in the dump where the vampires threw away the remains of their victims.

It wasn't hundreds of skulls that Joel passed on his stumbling way through the dark passage. It was thousands. After a while he stopped trying to even count. The tunnel led sharply upwards, with crude steps cut into the rock. He followed them up and up to the sound of the steady drip of water and the rasping echo of his own breathing. The steps kept spiralling upwards until his legs felt ready to collapse under him. More skulls littered the ground, and ribcages and scattered limbs. He soon became as numb to them as he was to the pain in his shoulder and the blood still seeping through his shirt.

And then he came to the manhole cover. It was two feet above his head, a concreted circular hole with iron rungs for access in and out. He hesitated, then gripped the rusted handles of the lid, mustered his strength and scraped the cast-iron plate a few inches sideways. Powdery snow showered down onto his face. Very slowly, he eased the cover all the way aside and poked his head up through the hole.

He was inside the castle courtyard.

The snow had intensified while he'd been in the tunnel, covering up the cobblestones and drifting against the inner sides of the walls. Rapid flurries of snowflakes swirled and spun through the strong beams of the floodlights that illuminated the castle grounds. A layer of white had settled on the two battered four-wheel-drive vehicles parked up just inside the gates. Joel knew Gabriel Stone liked cars, but these didn't seem quite the vampire's style. They had to belong to the men he paid to guard and carry out tasks for him.

Joel squeezed up out of the manhole. Moving fast, he shrugged off the rucksack, took out the cross and shoved it diagonally into his belt. He dumped the empty rucksack back in the hole and then, as quietly as he could, grated the iron cover back into place.

A few yards off was a narrow archway, beyond it a passage with doorways either side. There wasn't much he could do about his footprints in the snow as he sneaked away towards the passage. He had to hope they'd be covered over before anyone spotted them.

With one hand on the shaft of the cross, ready to draw it from his belt like a dagger, he moved furtively through the castle. From outside, the place had looked enormous and imposing; inside, it was like a fortified town, a maze of streets and winding lanes and squares. Many of its buildings still bore signs of their original purpose: an old smithy still had its forge and anvil, disused for centuries, and there were remnants of ancient straw on the cobbled floor of the stable block. Pitted stone staircases spiralled up to the sentry watchtowers along the battlements, and he passed a long barracks where two hundred or more troops might have been stationed. A thousand years ago, the self-contained castle community would have been a hive of bustle and industry.

Before the vampires had come to claim it.

Looking up, Joel could see the upper sections of the castle dominating the town. Like the bridge of an old sailing ship where only the captain and senior officers were allowed to stand, he guessed the grand towers and lofty halls would have been the exclusive domain of the castle's lords and masters. That was where he would find Gabriel Stone.

Joel heard voices and shrank back against a wall as a group of shadowy figures appeared under an archway, heading towards him. He ducked into a building and watched through a craggy porthole, straining to see the figures more clearly. They were thirty yards away; then twenty-five. As they came closer, Joel gripped the cross and tried to calculate how close Alex had been to it in Venice before she'd started showing signs of distress. But nothing happened. The cross remained cold and lifeless in his hand.

The figures passed through the light of one of the floodlamps. They were wearing heavy greatcoats and fur hats, cradling rifles and talking to each other in a language that could have been Romanian, or some kind of dialect version of it. From their swarthy features Joel guessed they must be rustic locals, maybe gypsies. They were completely oblivious of the cross's presence and that worried him as much as the rifles they were carrying. Against these guys, he was completely unarmed.

Joel watched the men walk by and wondered whether they had even an inkling of who their employer really was. Did they know they were protecting a vampire? Did Gabriel Stone pay such men in money, or did he have other ways of holding their allegiance?

He waited until the patrol had passed by, then stepped out of his hiding place and started to move tentatively away. Ducking through the arch the men had come through, he glanced back over his shoulder to check nobody had spotted him.

And froze to the sharp *snick-snack* of a rifle bolt.

CHAPTER 81

Stone and his group led the Federation prisoners out into the night. The wind was howling and the snow lashed down as Alex, Harry Rumble and the remaining six Supremos were shoved down a flight of steps leading from the great hall and surrounding buildings to the upper courtyard that overlooked the castle grounds. Through the curtain of swirling snowflakes, Alex could see the maze of lanes and streets down below, the tiny trucks parked up inside the gates in the distance.

At a gesture from Stone, the guards halted the prisoners. A few yards away, standing in the middle of the wide cobbled courtyard, was a tall oblong shape, some eight feet high, covered with a canvas sheet that crackled in the wind and was weighed down at the corners with bricks. Big Zachary stepped over, kicked away the bricks and pulled back the sheet to reveal the thing underneath.

It was a guillotine. Simple, but deadly – a rectangular vertical wooden frame with a heavy chopping blade suspended at the top by a crude pulley mechanism. Two steps led up to the horizontal platform on which the victim would be strapped to a plank and their neck secured between wooden stocks. A side lever released the blade, and a wicker basket was positioned underneath to catch the victim's severed head as it fell.

'Last used in the Place de la Révolution, Paris, 1793,' Stone said proudly, running his hand down the side of the grim device. 'I had to go to some trouble to obtain it after the mob had finished giving the chop to the French aristocracy. I always knew it would come in useful one day.'

Lillith pointed at Alex. 'Let's get this started. I want her to be first.'

Stone shook his head. 'No, Lillith. This has to be done properly. The men first, in order of seniority.' He scanned the five male Supremos. 'You,' he said, pointing at Hassan.

'You animals,' Olympia shouted. 'You can't do this!'

Stone arched an eyebrow. 'Really? You would have preferred a Nosferol termination?'

The guards took Hassan's arms and marched him to the guillotine. He was shaking badly and protesting as they tied his wrists behind his back and strapped his body tightly to the plank. Then it was slid into place and the wooden chocks positioned around his neck to stop his head thrashing about.

'Something's missing,' Anastasia said. 'We should have got a drummer.'

The blade was in position. Zachary pulled the retaining pin from the activation lever and looked to Stone.

Stone gave a nod.

And Zachary yanked the lever. The blade came whooshing down in the frame. Its diagonal chopping edge impacted against Hassan's neck with a sound like a knife hacking through a cabbage. His legs jerked against the restraining straps, then his body flopped and lay still as his head bounced into the wicker basket.

'Quite clinical, isn't it?' Stone said. 'Far quicker than, say, being left out to burn in the morning sunrise – which is what will happen to any of you who resist.'

Lillith gave a hoot of triumph, went striding over to the basket and snatched Hassan's head up by a fistful of hair. His face was frozen into an expression of terror. She spat in his sightless eye. 'Here's one Federation tyrant who won't be bothering us any more.'

The guards busied themselves unstrapping the decapitated body and carrying it away to the side. Dark vampire blood was already soaking into the plank. Stone pointed at Goldmund, who began to bluster and panic.

'Next.'

CHAPTER 82

The fourth guard must have been lagging behind his companions to light the cigarette that was glowing red in the darkness. Joel had almost run right into him. Moonlight glittered off the barrel of the rifle as the guard stepped out of the shadows. Joel backed off, raising his hands, and he saw that it was just a young guy, maybe eighteen or nineteen, smooth-featured and missing the heavy moustache of the older men. There was as much fear as aggression in his eyes.

'Wait,' Joel said. 'Hold on. There are worse things than me in this place. Let's talk about this.'

The young guy narrowed his eyes, seemed to hesitate for a second, and then opened his mouth to call the others.

Joel moved faster than he'd ever moved in his life. Twisting out of the line of fire, he grabbed the end of the rifle barrel, yanked it hard towards him and then shoved it back towards the guard with all his strength. The gun was an obsolete military rifle, an old Lee Enfield .303. Joel had shot one, once, on the thousand-metre firing range at

Bisley while there to compete in a police pistol competition. Even more than the harsh recoil of the weapon, he remembered the solid steel butt plate that had left a painful weal on his shoulder for hours afterwards. It was that same metal plate that he rammed into the young guy's face now. It caught him across the bridge of his nose and silenced the shout that had been on his lips. Blood hit the snow.

Joel didn't want to hurt him any more. 'Listen to me,' he pleaded, letting the rifle drop to the ground. 'Try to understand.'

The young guy was bent over, whimpering in pain from his broken nose. His hand flashed down to his boot and, before Joel could register what was happening, the knife was punching out towards him in the dark. There was nothing he could do to stop the blade from sinking deep into his stomach.

But the cross in his belt saved him from a fatal wound. The point of the knife glanced off the hard stone and Joel felt the cold steel slice into the soft flesh of his side, above the left hip.

The young guy started yelling loudly for the others. His head bursting with pain, Joel hit him hard in the face and he went sprawling in the snow.

Joel staggered back a step with the knife still lodged in his side. He gritted his teeth, took hold of the slim wooden hilt and cried out in agony as he drew it out of the bloody wound. The young guy was trying to get to his feet. Joel knocked him back down with a kick to the face. He threw away the red-smeared knife, spotted the fallen Lee Enfield lying in the snow and snatched it up. Footsteps and voices were approaching fast from around the corner. The rest of the guards had been alerted.

Joel ran like crazy, slipping in the snow and trying to fight the pain in his side. He willed himself to go on. He *had* to get to the upper levels of the castle.

Goldmund's headless body was thrown on top of Hassan's as Lillith drop-kicked the head over the edge of the battlements with a whoop. Next up was Korentayer, who showed much less grit than his two predecessors and had to be dragged on his knees to the guillotine.

As Alex watched the unfolding horror, her mind was racing through a thousand ways she could get out of this.

None of them were possible.

Korentayer's head became the next addition to the basket, then Borowczyk's. Lillith was bored with disposing of the heads by now, and let the guards take it away to be added to the pile along with his body. Zachary hauled on the rope and the bloody blade climbed back up to the top of the frame. Last to go of the male Supremos was Mushkavanhu. He shook off the guards' hands and walked with dignity to the guillotine. The final look he shot at Gabriel Stone before they strapped him down would have shaken any mortal man and most vampires to the core – but Stone only smiled. Zachary pulled the lever.

Chop.

'Now that one,' Stone said, pointing at Harry Rumble. The guards were well into the routine now, and had grabbed Rumble's arms almost before their master had given the order.

Rumble turned towards Stone as they led him to the blood-soaked machine. 'You may think you've won, Stone. You're wrong.'

'You should study history, my friend. You'd know that the finest speeches are often the most misguided. Take his head off.'

Zachary brought the blade back up as Rumble was secured to the plank. Alex was frantically trying to think of a way she could stop this, but there were just too many of them – and she knew that if she tried something and was caught, Stone's threat of exposure to the dawn sun hadn't been a joke. She thought of poor Greg, and her heart pounded.

Anastasia was standing a few yards away, watching with a smile. Just at that moment, her knees seemed to buckle and she gave a violent shudder.

Stone looked at her sharply. 'Anastasia? What is it?'

She staggered forward a step, clutching her head

between her hands. 'I . . . *felt* something. It's . . . Gabriel, something's wrong. I don't feel well.'

'Me neither,' Zachary muttered, swaying on his feet beside the guillotine.

Suddenly, moans and cries were erupting from the whole assembly of vampires. Alex could feel it too, and it was a sensation she remembered experiencing not so long ago.

Then the sound of gunshots cracked out from nearby.

CHAPTER 83

Joel was running as fast as he could, but the knife wound in his side was slowing him badly. Just a few dozen yards to go and he'd have made it to the upper courtyard. He was sure he could see figures up there, silhouetted against the light from the buildings beyond, and a strange rectangular object that he couldn't make out properly in the gloom. Something was happening.

He glanced behind him and swore. He was leaving a blood trail over the snow that a blind man could follow. His trousers were slick with it, and the nausea was making him light-headed. But he could tell from the shouts and running footsteps behind him that his pursuers weren't far behind. He had to keep moving.

A splintering explosion as a bullet smashed into the masonry a foot from his head; a millisecond later, the crash of a rifle shot reverberated over the castle grounds and the boom echoed around the mountains. He ducked down and ran harder into the blinding snow, grinding his teeth, limping badly. There was a bend up ahead, and just below it was a ruined low wall. He dived under cover, threw the rifle out over the craggy stonework and pressed his cheek to the stock. An instant later the racing figures of the three guards he'd seen earlier appeared around the corner and ran right into the Lee Enfield's sights. He squeezed the trigger. The massive detonation filled his ears and the rifle kicked back viciously against his injured shoulder. He saw one of the men clutch his chest and go down with a cry.

Joel worked the bolt, fired again, and saw a second gypsy pitch sideways into the snow, dropping his weapon. The third man had fallen into a crouch behind a pile of rocks. The gun in his hands was shorter and stubbier than the big bolt-action rifles, with a long stick magazine. In the quarter-second it took for Joel to duck down behind the wall, a roaring blast of submachine-gun fire raked the masonry and showered him with dust and stone fragments. Keeping him pinned down with steady bursts, the guard got to his feet, leapt over the bodies of his comrades and came running at the low wall. In two seconds he'd have jumped up onto it and his bullets would be raking the ground where Joel lay huddled under cover.

Joel rolled out from behind the wall, frantically working the bolt of the Lee Enfield. Lying on his back, he thrust the rifle up into the air at the same instant that the gypsy appeared on top of the wall. Their gun muzzles were just three feet apart.

In the same split second that Joel felt the Lee

Enfield recoil in his hands, the gypsy's submachine gun spat flame. The .303 tapered round from the rifle caught the man under the chin and he fell soundlessly back over the wall with most of his head blown away.

Joel dropped the rifle. He knew he'd been hit, and badly. His hands went to his thigh and he almost fainted when he felt the ripped material of his trouser leg and the tattered flesh and the hot blood welling up through his fingers.

'We're under attack!' Lillith yelled. 'It's the cross!'

Stone's face was pale. 'Solomon is here.'

There was chaos in the upper courtyard as the vampires scattered and fled ahead of the approaching danger. In their panic, Stone's group seemed to forget all about the remaining prisoners. Olympia Angelopolis managed to scurry away unseen and disappeared among the shadows while the guards stood about in horror-stricken confusion.

Alex finally had her chance. Fighting the terrible sensation that was welling up inside her, just the way it had in Venice, she sprinted over to the guillotine and started ripping apart the straps holding Harry Rumble to the blood-soaked plank. He stumbled free.

'What the hell's happening?'

'Joel's here,' she gasped. 'He's coming. We need to get away.' She took hold of his wrist, and they ran. Her only priority in that moment was to get away from the deadly energy of the cross. They could worry later about details like how they were going to escape from the castle. 'This way, Harry,' she shouted as they flitted through the darkness.

Stone was dragging Lillith away up the steps towards the great hall and yelling frantically at the vampire guards to go and intercept the human when she twisted away from him.

'Let me go down there. I can take Solomon.'

'You can't, Lillith.'

'I've got a gun,' Zachary said, pointing urgently up at the window of his quarters in the tower above the great hall.

'Get it now. We have to stop this human at all cost.'

Zachary went lumbering as fast as he could towards the buildings.

Anton stood rooted, his face twisted in hatred. 'I don't need a gun,' he spat. 'I haven't lived for four hundred years to be brought down by some *human*. This isn't going to happen to us.'

Anastasia tried to stop him. 'No, Anton, you'll be destroyed.' But he pushed her out of the way and staggered off in the direction of the shots. The guards saw him and followed his lead, their agony visibly increasing with every step.

'Come back, Anton!' Anastasia screamed, going after him.

'Let them go,' Lillith said. 'They'll hold Solomon back while Zachary gets the gun.'

But it was too late. Anastasia took off at a sprint.

'Fools,' Stone muttered. 'Come on, sister.'

CHAPTER 84

Joel could feel his strength draining away along with his fast-spilling blood as he dragged himself up towards the huge flight of steps leading to the upper courtyard. Sweat was pouring into his eyes despite the bitter cold. He'd dumped his empty rifle now. All he had was the cross, and he held it out in front of him like a beacon.

Dark shapes appeared at the top of the steps. A dozen or more figures in black, with drawn swords glinting and wild screaming faces. Their leader opened his mouth, and the last thing Joel saw of him were his bared fangs.

Then the cross obliterated them. It was like mowing down an infantry charge with a heavy machine gun, except the only sound was the frenzied screaming as their bodies were smashed down and blown into tatters by the sweeping power emanating from his hand. The last figure to appear on the steps, staggering in the wake of the others, was a woman. Her blond hair billowed in the wind as she hurtled down towards him, mouth agape. She shrieked as her companions were destroyed in front of her, but was running too fast to stop herself. Fifteen yards from where Joel stood with the cross, her body hit the energy field and blew apart like burnt paper.

Joel raised the cross higher and dragged himself onwards.

Alex and Rumble had ducked out of sight of their captors and were running through the castle. Darting through an arched doorway, they found themselves in an armoury room filled with ancient cannons and suits of armour. Swords, battle shields, halberds and spears decorated the walls. Alex spotted a side door lying ajar, beyond it a long, dark passage. 'I think this could be somewhere to hide, Harry.'

Rumble made no reply.

'Harry?' She turned around.

Just in time to see Rumble falling to his knees. His severed head blinked up at her in surprise before it rolled away across the floor; then his decapitated body slumped down on its belly.

Lillith stepped over him with a wild fire dancing in her eyes.

'This is all your doing, bitch.' As she spat out the words, she swung her bloody sabre hard and fast, and Alex only just managed to twist out of the way of the hissing blade. She somersaulted backwards and landed on her feet. An array of glittering weapons were mounted across a crimson shield on the wall just a few feet away. Leaping up, her fingers closed on the basket hilt of a long, curved sword.

Lillith's teeth were bared as she took another vicious swing that would have lifted Alex's head clean from her shoulders if she hadn't parried the blow with her own blade. The high armoury room filled with the zinging clash of steel on steel as Lillith struck and slashed with ferocious energy. Alex desperately blocked every stroke.

'You can't beat me,' Lillith sneered. Alex was backed up almost to the wall now, with nowhere to go. The sabre came whooshing at her sideways. She brought her own sword up to deflect it, but the angle was awkward and the crashing impact of the blades loosened her grip on her hilt. Her weapon clattered to the flagstones.

'Ha! What did I tell you?' Lillith backed off a step, grinning. She raised her sabre for the killing blow and was just about to strike, when she faltered and a cry of pain burst out of her lips.

As Lillith toppled over to the floor, Alex caught a glimpse of Joel Solomon framed in the archway on the far side of the armoury room. He was barely able to stand, covered in blood. Then she, too, felt the pain and began to scramble away in fear. Lillith crawled like a maimed insect towards the far exit. As Joel came on a step, dripping blood, Alex waited for the final surge of the cross's power to destroy her. Their eyes met.

'Go on, then,' she shouted at him. 'Finish me.'

A few steps, and the force of the cross would tear her apart. He seemed about to come running at her – then he stopped and leaned weakly against the archway.

'I can't,' he mumbled. He screwed his eyes shut and for a moment he seemed about to faint. 'I can't.'

'It's what you want, isn't it? You told me that next time you saw me, you'd destroy me. What are you waiting for?'

Tears ran through the blood on his tortured face. 'Why you? Why did you have to be one?'

'Finish it!' she yelled. 'Don't draw it out. Get it done.'

He shook his head. Wearily raised his empty hand and pointed towards the side door and the winding, dark passage Alex had spotted earlier.

'Get out of here. Don't let me see you again.' Then he stepped back, and kept moving away from her, lowering the cross.

Alex climbed shakily to her feet and stumbled through the arch into the echoing corridor. Her footsteps quickened, and she ran and ran until she was lost deep inside the castle's hidden passages. As she stumbled onwards in the dark, a strange sound came from her throat. One she hadn't heard herself make for over a hundred years.

She was crying.

CHAPTER 85

Gabriel Stone stormed through his castle, cursing Lillith for having left his side. He shouted for his ghoul. Lonsdale appeared from behind some drapes.

'What are you hiding there for?' Stone yelled at him in fury. 'You're supposed to protect me, not go skulking off like a rat. Get back there and kill the human.'

Lonsdale swallowed and looked blank. 'How?'

'Zachary has a gun,' Stone snapped. 'Even you can work a gun, can't you?'

They rushed into a hallway to find Zachary thundering down the grand staircase towards them, clutching the gun he'd been keeping in his quarters. The shiny, long-barrelled .357 magnum revolver was dwarfed in his fist. Stone grabbed it from him.

That was when Lillith appeared in the doorway behind them. Her eyes were ringed with black and she was unsteady on her feet. Her chest heaved with the effort to breathe.

'He's coming. He's right behind me.'

Zachary's eyes opened wide with horror, and

he ran over to a window overlooking the outer wall.

'I'm outta here,' he rasped. He drew back his massive fist and smashed it through the glass, piled himself through the jagged hole and disappeared into the night.

Stone and Lillith were about to follow, when they both simultaneously felt the crippling power of the cross wash over them once more. Lillith fell back from the window, clutching herself and crying out in fear. Stone whirled round to see the human Joel Solomon limping towards them. Seizing Lillith's arm, Stone took off at a staggering run, knocking over a table and shattering a vase in his haste to get away.

'Help me, ghoul!' he roared, tossing the gun to Lonsdale. But Lonsdale stared in terror at Joel, and fled in his master's wake. The vampires crashed through a doorway and emerged on the castle's upper battlement. A narrow walkway ran along the rim of the wall, leading to a round turret that had once been used to spot approaching enemy armies. Beyond the battlement wall, the sheer cliff face dropped away into the night.

Lillith screamed. The human had appeared on the battlement behind them.

Joel didn't know how much longer he could go on. A black mist was rising up to cloud his vision, but he could still see the vampires frantically trying to escape along the battlement wall. Only one of them seemed unaffected, the haggard, wild-eyed man whom Gabriel Stone was clutching tightly behind him like a shield. His face looked familiar, but through the fog of his pain and nausea Joel couldn't place it. He barely even registered the large, heavy handgun in the man's fist.

As he staggered out onto the battlement after them, the biting wind almost knocked him off his feet. He steadied himself and took another step towards them. They were backing away towards the tall round turret, and he had them cornered.

'You're finished, Stone!' he shouted through the roar of the wind, blinking the driving snowflakes out of his eyes. 'It's over!'

He took two more steps forward and heard the leather-clad woman vampire let out another tortured wail as she pressed herself desperately against the far wall of the turret.

Gabriel Stone seemed to have shrivelled with terror. He shoved his servant roughly onto the battlement.

'Kill him! Shoot him! Don't just stand there, Lonsdale!'

Lonsdale moved cautiously along the wall. Raised the pistol and took an unsteady aim at Joel.

'Kill him!' Stone roared.

Alex had lost all sense of where she was when she suddenly smelled the night air. She ran out of the winding passage to find herself standing on the high outer castle wall. The howling gale ripped at her hair.

Fifty yards away through the blizzard she could see Gabriel Stone and Lillith. They were cowering, cringing in terror and fury at the top of a tower at the very far corner of the opposite battlement wall. Running her eye along, she spotted Joel's ragged, bloody figure, dragging himself along the walkway with the cross in his fist. She was out of its range, but Stone and Lillith were dangerously close to it and had nowhere left to run. A few more steps, and it was over for them.

Standing halfway between Joel and the two vampires was Stone's ghoul, Lonsdale. In his hand was a big revolver. Alex watched helplessly as Lonsdale aimed it at Joel. Stone's screaming commands to shoot were being snatched away by the wind.

Joel must have seen the gun, but he was behaving as if he no longer cared. He took another limping step and raised the cross higher.

There was nothing Alex could do to stop what was about to happen.

Lonsdale seemed to hesitate, then, half-turning his face away, he squeezed the trigger. The revolver recoiled up in his hand, a halo of white flame bursting from its muzzle.

Joel kept coming. Lonsdale fired again, and this time his bullet found its mark. Blood spattered on the snowy battlements. Joel flailed with his arms and went down on his back, still clutching the cross.

'Joel!' Alex screamed. But she was powerless to

do anything – as long as he held the cross she couldn't go near him. His body lay slumped on the battlement. Snowflakes were settling rapidly over him, turning red as they melted in his blood. He wasn't moving.

CHAPTER 86

Jeremy Lonsdale lowered the heavy pistol. He stared at the fallen man he'd just shot. Turned to look at Gabriel Stone in the tower behind him. The vampire was gesticulating wildly at him through the blizzard.

'Pick up the cross, you cretin. Get it away from us! Throw it over the cliff!' Stone's voice was cracked with pain. Lillith was on her hands and knees beside him in the tower, her black hair plastered over her face as she clutched her head and her body shook violently.

Lonsdale nodded. He understood what he had to do. Still holding the gun, he walked slowly over to the body in the snow and bent down to pick up the cross from the limp fingers of his victim. Blood was seeping across the battlement, dripping down the wall; red on white under the black sky.

Lonsdale turned away, the cross still in his grasp. It seemed to thrum in his hand, and was warm to the touch. He looked out over the craggy castle wall, at the swirling snow and the distant mountains. The wind whipped at his clothes. He raised his arm to hurl it far over the battlement, where it would go spinning and tumbling a thousand feet before it smashed into a million pieces against the rocks below. His master would be saved. The war would be won – thanks to him, Jeremy Lonsdale. The power was his.

He grunted with effort as he hurled the heavy object in his fist. It sailed high up in an arc over the battlements and then dropped away into the night. Then, slowly, he turned to face Gabriel Stone.

Still holding the cross. It was the big revolver that he'd thrown away. He had no further need for it. But the cross . . .

He looked down at it. Its thrumming warmth spread up his arm.

'No,' he said softly. And took a step towards the two vampires.

'Throw it, ghoul!' Stone's scream of desperation cut through the howling wind.

'No,' Lonsdale repeated, loudly this time, and took another step. 'You've come into my life and poisoned everything. You've taken everything from me, taken away the one person I loved. Look at what I've become. And now you've made me a murderer for you.'

'Jeremy, stay away from us. I'm commanding you—'

'I've taken enough of your orders, vampire.' Lonsdale stood straighter. There was a glow in his eyes and his face was contorted as he slowly approached the turret. His knuckles were white on the shaft of the cross. 'I don't give a damn what happens to me any more,' he shouted. 'But by God I'm going to destroy you!'

Stone was frantically trying to shield Lillith with his body, absorbing the energy blast in a bid to save her. But the power of the cross, now just a few yards away, was too much for him. As Lonsdale came closer, Stone collapsed inside the turret beside Lillith. He cried out. Smoking blisters burst out across his skin. Lillith was writhing and shrieking. In one last desperate surge of energy she raised herself to her knees, drew out her sabre and hurled it with all the strength she had left.

The blade whirled hissing through the blizzard. Lonsdale flinched as he saw it flying towards him, but too late. Its point drove hard into his chest and went right through him, piercing his heart and sticking out of his back. He staggered, gasping, blood sputtering from his lips, and for a moment he seemed about to go tumbling down over the battlement, taking the cross with him.

But still he kept on coming, coughing blood, staggering towards them in a jerky dying gait, the hilt of the sabre protruding grotesquely from his chest. His bloody lips were spread into a lunatic grin.

The vampires screamed their fury. There was nowhere to run.

Unless . . .

Lillith grasped her brother's arm. They looked at one another, and understanding flashed between them. Staggering to their feet in the last instant before the cross destroyed them utterly and forever, they linked hands and threw themselves off the turret.

Alex watched from a distance as their bodies went spinning down. After the first hundred feet their linked hands broke apart and they fell separately, turning over and over like tiny dolls. Then the shadows engulfed them and they vanished into the deep, dark valley.

Lonsdale had made it to the turret. Moving like a zombie now as he virtually died on his feet, he clambered up its steps and lurched to the spot where Stone and Lillith had jumped. With his dying breath, he threw the cross over the turret wall and it went tumbling down after them. Then he slumped face down. The weight of his body pushed the sabre through his chest up to the hilt so that the blade stuck up out of his back like a bloody flagpole. He didn't move again.

Joel hadn't moved either.

CHAPTER 87

With a cry of despair, Alex leapt down from the opposite battlement and sprinted across the snowy courtyard to scramble up the wall and get to Joel. She shouted his name over and over as he lay there immobile. The snow was stained red all around him, but the sight of his blood meant nothing to her now – only that he was dying.

She turned him over. His eyes were shut. She said his name again, ran her fingers through his hair.

His eyes fluttered open. 'Alex . . .' he whispered.

'You did it, Joel. Stone's gone. It's over.'

He smiled weakly, then closed his eyes again. His breathing was shallow. Alex knew he wouldn't last long.

She picked him up in her arms and carried him down from the battlements. He had to be taken to a hospital. Her mind worked fast. Even out here, in this remote wilderness, there surely had to be human settlements. If she couldn't find a town, just a humble village doctor could help save Joel's life and radio for an air ambulance.

The vehicles. The vehicles she'd spotted down by the gates, in the lower courtyard. That was the answer. Holding his unconscious body tight in her arms, Alex ran like crazy. Just when she thought she was hopelessly lost in the maze of passages, she picked up the blood trail that Joel had left on his way up, now half-obscured with snow. She didn't glance twice at the bodies of the gypsies. Bursting out of an archway, she found herself in the lower courtyard, a few dozen yards from the main gates.

'Hang on, Joel.'

In moments she'd reached the parked vehicles. Two big off-road trucks, fat knobbly tyres, rows of lamps mounted on heavy bull bars across their grilles. She laid Joel gently down in the snow as she punched out the window of the first vehicle, looking for a key in the ignition. If neither truck had them, it would mean having to search the bodies of the guards in the hope of finding them.

The first vehicle had no keys in it. She swore and held her breath as she ran round to the other, smashing the glass as if it had been eggshell. Her heart jumped. A ring of keys dangled from the ignition.

'You're going to make it, Joel. Hold on.' She scooped him up and laid him down in the back of the truck, hastily covering him with an old blanket before throwing herself into the cab. Two twists of the key, and the engine roared. The courtyard lit up in a blaze of light from the truck's powerful lamps. She cleared the snow from the screen, gunned the throttle and the tyres bit hard into the snow as she floored the pedal and aimed the truck at the gate. With a screech of ripping wood she went crashing right through.

Now all she had to do was get Joel to a doctor. There was no telling how long he had left. It could be a few hours, or a matter of minutes.

The mountain pass snaked away for miles ahead. The blizzard was driving even harder now, and the wipers were barely able to bat the snow away fast enough for her to see where she was going as the truck bounced and slithered down the narrow track. Passing a big rock on her left, she saw an abandoned motorcycle and sidecar, almost completely buried under a drift of white.

Alex hadn't driven far before the grim realisation began to sink in that she wasn't going to find a village, let alone a town with proper hospital facilities, in time to save Joel. Even with her sharp vampire eyes she couldn't make out a single light, a solitary speck of civilisation anywhere on the vast horizon.

Despite her superior senses, it was hard to tell the difference between the road and the deep snowdrifts that the wind had piled up across it and either side. She felt the vehicle lurch violently. A grinding crunch and a squeal of metal against rock. The truck came to a juddering halt at a crazy angle, and with a groan it rolled over onto its passenger side. From the back, Joel let out a moan of pain as he was thrown sideways hard against the window. Alex twisted in the driver's seat and kicked upwards so hard that she tore the door off its hinges. It went tumbling into the snow. She climbed out, grabbed the edge of the overturned truck's roof, and used every ounce of her strength to heave it back onto its wheels.

Then she saw the black stain of the oil seeping out of the ruptured sump, melting into the snow. The impact against the hidden rocks had ripped it open.

Tough shit. She'd keep driving till the engine seized.

She jumped back inside the cab and tried to restart the stalled motor.

Dead. She tried again. Nothing. She wanted to scream with rage.

Joel was stirring behind. Hearing him murmur her name, she jumped down from the cab and went running round to rip open the rear door. Blood trickled out of the back of the truck and began to pool on the snow. She reached out for him, lifted him gently out of the vehicle and set him down on the ground.

His eyes struggled for focus. His lips opened

and closed, and a trickle of blood ran down his chin.

'Don't try to speak,' she whispered, cradling him in her arms.

One century, one decade and three long years since the last time she'd done this.

She was going to lose him. Just as she'd lost her William.

'Alex . . .' he croaked faintly. 'I'm scared.' He coughed. More blood bubbled up from his lips.

'Me too,' she said.

He was slipping away now.

And she lowered her face to his, looked into his eyes as the light in them began to fade away to nothing. She felt his muscles tense in resistance as death wrapped its arms around him, then start to slacken.

And as he breathed his long, last sighing breath, she opened her mouth and bit deep into his neck.

She drank and drank from him. Tasted his blood as it mingled with her vampire saliva and the tears running down her face. Felt his dying energy draining into her veins – and her own powers flowing into him.

When she raised her head and looked down at his face again, his eyes were closed. He looked peaceful, as though he was sleeping.

'What have I done to you?' she murmured.

Something she knew he could never forgive her for.

Because, the next time he opened his eyes – and there would be a next time – it would no longer be as a man. Joel Solomon would have become a vampire.

Alex looked up at the sky. There were still enough hours of darkness to find shelter before the dawn came.

And the snow kept falling.

IN CONVERSATION WITH SCOTT MARIANI

What was the inspiration for the Vampire Federation books?

The original inspiration probably dates back to my childhood. I was vampire crazy as a kid, and always wanting to see old Dracula movies. Then about seven years ago, it came to me that it would be great to write a modern vampire story drawing on some of the classic gothic elements in Bram Stoker's seminal novel *Dracula*: the spooky ship sailing in from Romania, the half-mad ghoul enslaved to his master, the wicked vampire brides, the end battle in the castle guarded by gypsies – it's all right out of Stoker. But at the same time I wanted to combine that with all the hallmarks of a modern thriller – upbeat pacing, fast-talking dialogue, and plenty of explosive action.

Are you still as vampire crazy now as you were as a child?

I suppose I must be! I can't seem to survive long without watching a good vampire movie, whether an oldie like *Nosferatu*, or something more modern and hip like *Blade*. My DVD collection has every-thing from *30 Days of Night* to Eddie Murphy's *Vampire of Brooklyn*!

What is it about vampires that makes them so appealing to people?

Firstly, vampires are scary, and we all love to be scared. But I also think that vampires symbolise qualities many of us secretly yearn to have ourselves. Vampires are incredibly free – at least, when they're not subject to Federation laws. They're unbelievably powerful, can have tremen-dous sex appeal and glamour; and of course there's the immortality factor. That's the allure that seduces Jeremy Lonsdale, the politician in *Uprising* who falls into the clutches of arch-villain Gabriel Stone. Lonsdale had everything a mortal man could desire, and yet he craved the kind of power that only becoming a vampire could offer. Of course, it didn't quite work out for him that way . . .

Do your characters ever surprise you?

Sometimes a character will grow in the telling, or even deviate completely from the original plan. In *Uprising*, Dec Maddon was initially destined to be a minor character, something of a lowlife whose only function in the story was to witness the ritual murder at Crowmoor Hall, and then tell his story to the hero Joel Solomon. He was then going to be turned into a vampire before being viciously destroyed by Gabriel Stone. In short, he was expendable! But as I began writing him, I became sympathetic towards him and his role changed. It was as though there was another layer of him underneath, waiting to be discovered. I realised that Dec should have more of his own journey in the story. And he will have a big role in the next book, which is something I would never have imagined at the outset.

Some of the vampires in Uprising, for instance the villain Gabriel Stone, are much more frightening than many of the recent crop of vampires in books and films . . .
From the start, my vampires had to have fangs! I consciously wanted my character Gabriel Stone to hark back to the Stoker tradition that portrays the vampire as a lethal predator without a single shred of morality. It's a great white shark in human form. Even friendlier characters like Alex Bishop, with whom I wanted the reader to empathise strongly, have something of an edge to them when you realise that you and I are really nothing more to them than a food source! So you're rooting for the heroine, but some part of you is afraid of her, too . . .

If you were a vampire, would you support the Federation?
Good question! I think the Federation was born from a genuine need for vampires to protect

themselves from detection in the modern age, in order to be able to carry on. But what may have started out in a spirit of well-meaning idealism may have been open to abuse and ultimately led to a degree of corruption. I would not entirely blame certain vampires for finding the Federation oppressive and dictatorial; then again, who would want evil predators like Gabriel Stone and his sister Lillith in charge?

A fun setting in the book is the vampire-themed bar/restaurant run by vampires for vampires, right in the middle of London. What made you think of it?
Movie fans may spot lots of film references in my books, especially this one! The idea for the 'Last Bite bar and grill' was inspired by Jack Rabbit Slim's diner in *Pulp Fiction*, where the walls are lined with stills from classic movies and your waitress for the night is Jayne Mansfield or Marilyn Monroe. I loved the idea of doing the same thing with vampires, so it was always in my mind. Then one night I happened to wander into this very loud, very packed, upmarket bar in St James's Street in London, and I thought that it was exactly the kind of place where vampires would hang out – as well as wannabe vampires and people who just want to seem a bit dark and dangerous. So I modelled it on that, and cheekily placed it in the same location. I think the Last Bite would be a great success in real life, actually!

What can readers expect from the next Vampire Federation book?

Lots of surprises, some new characters, some new developments with the existing ones. Dec Maddon will continue his evolution and become a fully-fledged vampire hunter. Joel Solomon will have to try to come to terms with what he's now become. He and Alex will somehow have to confront what's happened between them. The secrets of the cross of Ardaich will be explained, plus we'll be seeing more of those nasty, mysterious creatures living in the Siberian ice caves. And will Gabriel Stone be back? You'll just have to wait and see!